THE MIDDLE-AGED VIRGIN

OLIVIA SPRING

HARTLEY PUBLISHING

Dedicated to A.A

PROLOGUE

'It's over.'
I did it.
I said it.
Fuck.

I'd rehearsed those two words approximately ten million times in my head—whilst I was in the shower, in front of the mirror, on my way to and from work...probably even in my sleep. But saying them out loud was far more difficult than I'd imagined.

'What the fuck, Sophia?' snapped Rich, nostrils flaring. 'What do you mean, it's over?'

As I stared into his hazel eyes, I started to ask myself the same question.

How could I be ending the fifteen-year relationship with the guy I'd always considered to be *the one*?

I felt the beads of sweat forming on my powdered forehead and warm, salty tears trickling down my rouged cheeks, which now felt like they were on fire. This was serious. *This* was actually happening.

Shit. I said I'd be strong.

'Earth to Sophia!' screamed Rich, stomping his feet.

I snapped out of my thoughts. Now would probably be a good time to start explaining myself. Not least because the veins currently throbbing on Rich's forehead appeared to indicate that he was on the verge of spontaneous combustion. Easier said than done, though, as with every second that passed, I realised the enormity of what I was doing.

The man standing in front of me wasn't just a guy that came in pretty packaging. Rich was kind, intelligent, successful, financially secure, and faithful. He was a great listener and had been there for me through thick and thin. Qualities that, after numerous failed Tinder dates, my single friends had repeatedly vented, appeared to be rare in men these days.

Most women would have given their right and probably their left arm too for a man like him. So why the hell was I suddenly about to throw it all away?

CHAPTER ONE

'Aahhhhhh,' I said as I sank my head back into the pillow. 'This feels *so* good!'

Nothing beats the sensation of climbing onto fresh sheets and snuggling up under a warm duvet on a cold January evening. Well, taking your bra off at the end of a long day comes a close second, as does devouring a slab of sticky toffee pudding with creamy M&S custard. But right now, this was utter bliss.

'Another busy day at the office?' asked Rich as he scrolled through some floor plans on his iPad.

'Definitely,' I sighed, sitting up and turning to face him. 'It was non-stop.'

'Go on, then,' said Rich, gazing into my dark brown eyes. 'I can tell you're dying to tell me all about it.'

I chuckled. 'You know me so well.' I took a deep breath, ready to rattle off a lengthy list of today's activities. 'So, this morning I had a breakfast meeting with the beauty director of *Vogue* and lined up some great features for our clients. Then I went back to the office to finish going over the launch activity proposal for the new limited-edition lipsticks MIKA Cosmetics are bringing out with two massive influencers this summer—'

'Remind me of their names again?' asked Rich, putting his iPad on the duvet beside him to give me his attention.

'Céline, the beauty director of *Aspire* magazine, and then Amelia, the mega blogger I was telling you about before, who has 5.5 million Instagram followers. Ringing any bells?' I asked, scanning his crumpled face.

'Um, not really,' he replied, 'but carry on...'

'So then I had to rush over to Mayfair to Daniel's new flagship salon—'

'Who's Daniel again?' interrupted Rich.

'Daniel!' I huffed. 'You know? The celebrity hairdresser who just opened his salon on Mount Street? We organised the massive launch party in November?' His face still remained blanker than a fresh sheet of paper. 'He does all the A-listers and models? Adele? Kate Moss? Jourdan Dunn? Charges five hundred pounds for a haircut?'

Good God. Rich *must* be tired if the penny hadn't dropped by now. We'd spent *months* working on that launch, and literally every newspaper, magazine and website had covered it.

'Ah yes!' he replied finally. 'Bloody hell! He really charges five hundred pounds for a haircut? Does he use solid gold scissors and sprinkle your hair with diamonds afterwards?' He laughed, clearly amused at his own joke.

'Ha-ha. Very funny. Daniel is legendary. He's styled the hair of every superstar you could imagine, has a career spanning over four decades and is *still* at the top of his game...' I saw Rich's eyes beginning to glaze over.

'Carry on,' he said. 'I'm still listening.'

'After that, I had dinner at The Shard with the CEO of an Australian beauty company. Then, when I got in, as you might have heard, I was on the phone to Viktor, the president of Purity Skincare in Canada, as we had to discuss some amendments for Ava's contract...' Yep, I'd lost him again...

As a partner in a top architecture firm and bona fide 'man's man', Rich had about as much interest in celebrities and popular culture as an arachnophobe has in cosying up with a giant tarantula. But despite this, as part of our evening routine, he always tried to listen to the updates of my day at the office, even if, as tonight proved, what I told him often went in one ear and out the other.

'Ava is the hot new star who's tipped to win Best Supporting Actress at the Oscars and is into green, clean living,' I clarified as I reached for my brush and started running it through my glossy black shoulder-length hair. Nope. His expression still remained empty. 'Well, Ava is becoming the new face of the brand, which is *really* exciting.'

'I'll have to take your word for that,' replied Rich. 'And exhaustion is a small price to pay when you're running London's most successful beauty PR agency.'

'Yeah, you're right.' I reflected on what we'd achieved. Last year had been our most successful yet, and even though the new year had just begun, I was confident that we would do even better in the next twelve months. 'I love what I do—there's no way I'd work all these long hours otherwise. But after a fifteen-hour day, having the chance to relax in bed is like heaven.'

'I bet it is,' said Rich.

'After my meeting with Daniel, I *did*, however, make a quick pitstop to buy this,' I said, putting my brush down and peeling the duvet back slowly to reveal my new black silk nightdress, which clung suggestively around my toned size eight figure. 'What do you think?'

'Oh…erm,' stuttered Rich as he quickly grabbed his iPad and fixed his gaze firmly on the screen. 'It's nice… but I…I better get back to these plans and then go straight to bed,' he said, stretching his arms out towards the ceiling and feigning a loud yawn. 'Early start in the morning and all that.'

Well, that went down like a lead balloon. Not really a surprise, as I was used to the excuses by now, but it was worth a try. Maybe it was for the best anyway, considering how tired I was.

I pulled the covers up to my chin and turned around. Then, just as I was about to attempt to go to sleep, the phone rang. WTF? It was 11.30 p.m., which was already a good half an hour past my scheduled bedtime.

'Aren't you going to answer that?' Rich barked, clearly irritated about me taking another late-night international call in bed.

I picked up my iPhone from my mirrored bedside table. As Henri's name flashed across the screen, I realised it wasn't a client call after all. My stomach tightened.

'*Salut, Sophia. Ça va?*' he asked.

'I'm fine, Henri,' I said apprehensively as I repositioned my pillow and sat up straight to help me focus. 'Is everything okay? It's not like you to call so late.'

There was a long pause. It seemed like Henri was trying to compose himself before he could speak. And it wasn't because he was thinking of how to translate his thoughts, as his English was flawless. No. Something was wrong.

'I'm afraid I—I have some bad news,' Henri stuttered. 'Albert has had a stroke.'

The room started to spin. I struggled to keep a firm grasp of the phone, and my body began to shake. A wave of questions flooded into my brain.

'What?' I snapped. 'When? Is he going to be all right? How—'

'I'm afraid he didn't survive. The doctors tried, but there was nothing more that could be done. He's gone, Soph. He's dead.'

This couldn't be happening.

'I…I…I can't believe it.' I paused, desperately trying to think of the right words. 'I'm so sorry, Henri.'

'Thanks, Sophia,' he said. 'The funeral will be next Thursday in Châteaumerveille. We'll start making the arrangements tomorrow.'

Already? Goodness. This was so much to take in.

'Well, of course I'll be there,' I replied.

'That means a lot. I'll send you the details when I have them. Let me know what time you'll arrive, and I'll come and collect you from the station.'

How was he so strong, when I felt like my whole body was about to shatter into a million pieces?

'Will do. Henri, I am so, so sorry. Please pass on my condolences to Marie and Geraldine too. If there's anything I can do or anything you need, please call me.'

Henri thanked me, his voice wavering. I couldn't even begin to imagine the pain he was feeling.

It was difficult to put into words how I felt about Albert. He was like a second father to me. Eighteen years earlier, when I was a twenty-year-old student teaching English as part of my French degree in a small town called Châteaumerveille in France, I'd bumped into him one day in the street and struck up a conversation.

As soon as he'd heard I was from London, he'd excitedly invited me to join him and his wife, Marie, who I later learned was the town's most popular doctor, on a trip to the South of France that weekend along with his two young children, Henri, who was just five at the time, and Geraldine, then seven. But when my mum had freaked out about me going away with strangers, I'd agreed to accept the invitation to dinner at their home the following Sunday instead, which then became one of our rituals. And for the nine months that I lived there, it was always the highlight of my week.

Even when I'd returned to London, our friendship had continued. We'd still see each other every year, either in London, Paris or Châteaumerveille, and we spoke at length at least once a month. Whether it was offering his relationship and career advice or recommending a good bottle of red to impress clients, Albert had always been there for me.

Rich tried his best to console me, but I needed to be alone. I retreated to the living room to lie down on the sofa. After what felt like hours of staring at the bright white ceiling in total shock and wondering why, despite my sorrow, I couldn't seem to bring myself to cry, I went into autopilot. I picked up my iPad and booked my Eurostar ticket to Paris and then the two-hour train journey to Châteaumerveille.

Next, I clicked on iCal to log the dates on my phone. Damn. I'd forgotten. I had a full day of meetings next

Thursday, including one with a big potential new client flying over from New York to meet with me.

Fuck it. There was no way I was going to miss saying a final farewell to my dearest Albert. For once, securing another big beauty account would just have to wait.

IT WAS TOUGH, but somehow I got through Albert's funeral.

He had a good send-off. Over five hundred people attended the service. A huge turnout by any standard, but particularly for such a small town. He had been clearly loved, and had touched many people's lives.

Albert was gone. I still couldn't take it all in. How was it possible for him to be ripped away from us at just sixty? That was no age at all.

This wonderful man had had a massive impact on my life. He was the one I could always count on for honest, non-judgemental advice. I confided in him more than my best friends and certainly my parents. But what now? Where would I be without his guidance and love?

With Albert, I always felt like I could be me. I was just Sophia. Not 'Sophia, the cool and in-control boss', 'Sophia, the reliable long-term partner', 'Sophia, the successful daughter' or 'Sophia, the strong friend'. And that meant so much, because each of those 'titles' came with a list of expectations.

Generally, life was great, but sometimes I found it hard to admit to my parents, Rich or my friends that I struggled. It might seem like I had everything under control at work, and that was mostly true, through trial and error and doing my job for so long. But I also had moments where I didn't know which way to turn and didn't want to shatter the illusion they all had about me always having my shit together, so I'd put on a brave face and soldier on. But with Albert, somehow I never had to worry about that.

No subject was off limits. No emotions were too deep or raw to express. I could tell him if ever I was nervous about pitching for a big account, or I had concerns about my relationships. He would listen intently, then, once he was sure I had finished pouring my heart out, he'd share his words of wisdom. He was like some sort of life magician. I don't know how, but he seemed to know the right way to resolve a problem or a challenge.

He wouldn't always tell me what to do explicitly. Sometimes he'd wanted me to learn a lesson. Not in a bad way. More a case of him recognising that I would grow if he sowed a seed in my brain to help me figure out the answers for myself.

Sometimes I'd sit at my desk in the evenings and we'd Facetime for hours. He would read my face instantly and know whether I was happy or sad. I couldn't hide anything from him. And I didn't ever want to. Our bond was special.

Albert was a father figure. My mentor, confidant, dearest friend and life guru all rolled into one. His smile— it was infectious and would instantly wipe away any sadness I was feeling. He was the kindest, must jovial, loving person I'd ever known. And now I had absolutely no idea what I was going to do without him.

As I stood on the freezing cold platform, waiting for the train to arrive, my thoughts turned to our last conversation on New Year's Day, just a few weeks before I'd received the fateful call from Henri. He'd wished me health and success for the year ahead and then got a bit serious:

'*Ma chère Sophia*,' he'd said solemnly. 'Remember, life is short. You only live once. You must enjoy. If you are not happy, you must do something to change it. And this *métro, boulot, dodo*—this 'train, work, sleep'—it is not good.'

I thought he'd finished, but then he continued, still with an uncharacteristic sombreness in his voice: 'I am proud that *ma petite Sophia* has become big and successful Sophia. But *rappelle-toi* that it is happiness and *amour*, not work, that are most important.'

I took a moment to consider his comments. I understood his concern. Yes, I *did* work a lot. Every time we spoke, whether it was morning, afternoon or evening, weekday or weekend, I was either working, just finished work, or going to work. But life in a fast-paced city like London is *totally* different to a tiny town like Châteaumerveille. Especially for someone ambitious like me. I was making my mark in the PR world. Carving out a successful career. Building an empire. I couldn't do that without putting in the hours. The only place success comes before work is in the dictionary. That was the motto I lived by, and that was how I'd gotten to where I was today.

And who said I wasn't happy? Hadn't I *sounded* happy when we'd last spoken on the phone? Yes, I had my moments like everyone else. He knew that better than anyone. But ultimately I'd created an amazing business and could afford to buy almost anything I wanted, so why *wouldn't* I be happy?

As for love, I had Rich. We'd known each other since

we were sixteen, and after several years of being just friends, we'd become a couple and had been together ever since. We had our ups and downs, but didn't every couple? Besides, he ticked all the boxes. Smart, supportive and handsome. What *wasn't* to love?

I hadn't thought much about Albert's comments at the time. When he'd called, although it was a bank holiday, I was in the middle of trying to send an urgent email to a client. If I'd known that would be the last time I'd speak to him, then of course I would have been more focused. I wasn't proud of that—it was something I was likely to regret for the rest of my life.

But now his comments were troubling me. What exactly had he been saying? That I was an unhappy workaholic who needed to find love? Usually he was perceptive and his analysis of a situation was spot-on. However, this time I disagreed. *Of course*, I knew *normally* it wasn't good to work too much, but it was different for me. I loved my career. Work made me happy. It fulfilled me. Rich was a great guy. Solid. And I was in love.

I am.

Aren't I?

The two-hour journey back to Paris flew by. The first-class carriage was almost empty. Peace and quiet was just what I needed. I checked emails, scrolled through our social media feeds and did some campaign brainstorming. But Albert's comments still raced through my mind. It was like he was there beside me, repeating those words over and over again.

I jumped in a taxi to Gare du Nord, took out my phone, plugged in my headphones, selected my 'mellow' Spotify playlist and clicked on 'shuffle'. *This will calm me.* It didn't.

It was as if I'd put the 'Albert's last words' playlist on as his voice was still ringing in my ears.

I boarded the Business Premier carriage of the Eurostar. After travelling back and forth from London to Paris in the Standard seats with my huge rucksack when I was a student, I'd always vowed to sit in the posher carriage when I became a real grown-up with a proper job. And now that the business was doing well, I was able to do exactly that.

I found my single window seat, then lifted my case up to the luggage rack above. I did a quick scan of the seat. *Hmm, what's that?* I took a fresh tissue out of my handbag and brushed it off. *Good. Just some crumbs. No stains. Should be fine. Headrest check? No stray hairs or dirt. Seems clean enough. I'll be okay here.*

I settled back into the seat, unzipped my boots and unbuttoned my coat. The Eurostar attendant approached with the complimentary drinks trolley. It had been an emotional few days. I could certainly do with a glass of wine.

'A bottle of red, please,' I said. She set the mini bottle and a glass on the faux wooden table in front of me. 'Thank you.'

I picked up the glass and examined it from every angle. Shit. There were some marks along the rim. *I can't do it.*

'Excuse me,' I said, calling her back. 'Could I have another glass, please?' The attendant, a French brunette, frowned before remembering that wasn't a very customer-focused reaction.

'Certainly, madame,' she said, flashing me a fake smile whilst gently placing another glass on my table.

I scrutinised the new glass. *Thank God. That's much better.*

'Thank you,' I said, indicating that all was right in my OCD world again.

I have a thing about glasses. Well, cleanliness in general. Glasses have to be clean. No water marks. No smudges. Otherwise I can't drink from them. I know it's not logical or sensible. If anyone else saw the glass, they'd say it's fine. And I'm sure it is. It's just something that I've always had. Just a touch of OCD. Nothing major. Not life-crippling or anything.

I've heard that Jennifer Aniston and Cameron Diaz also had a thing about germs and cleanliness. Lots of people have it. And a lot worse than me too. I'd work on it. See someone and get it sorted. Just as soon as I found the time. Difficult, as there was always so much to do.

I unscrewed the lid of the bottle, poured the wine into the glass and took a large gulp. *That's better. I can relax now. Or attempt to...*

Did I *really* work too much?

Okay, Albert. I get it. This is one of your classic 'sewing the thinking seed' moments. You're obviously trying to tell me something and are not going to get out of my head until I give this some proper thought, so all right. Let's do this. Let's start with talking about work.

Since I'd launched my agency, BeCome, fourteen years earlier, I'd worked at least twelve hours a day, pretty much seven days a week. But come on, Albert! Look at what I got in return. I got to promote some of the best brands in the beauty business. I'd won dozens of awards and achieved more than I could ever have imagined.

Yes, it had come with huge sacrifices, and it did mean I had zero personal life. The only downtime I got was watching *Game of Thrones* with Rich maybe once a week (whilst simultaneously scrolling through Instagram, Snapchat and Twitter to keep on top of the latest influencers). I tried to see my friends and family maybe once a month, although it wasn't unusual for me to cancel if something urgent came up at work…

But just look at the rewards. I had a beautiful three-storey, four-bedroom townhouse in Clapham, complete with a state-of-the-art home office, plus a dream dressing room filled with all the designer clothes, shoes and handbags any woman could ask for. I'll admit, the house had become more like a place to sleep and eat in between going to and from work, whereas when I'd bought it, I had hoped to do more exciting things there, like throw dinner parties and have my friends stay over. But, no one's life is perfect.

I *definitely* was happy though. *I* controlled my destiny. I could do what I wanted and go away whenever I liked. I mean, it had been a while since I'd *actually* been on holiday, but technically, if I wanted to, I *could*. Well, preferably around the Easter, May, August and Christmas bank holidays, though, to minimise time out of the office…

And I *did* enjoy myself. I had a *great* time with my family at Christmas. Remember I told you all about it? I might have made my excuses and gone up to my old bedroom with my laptop straight after dinner, to get a head start on brainstorming the new fragrance account we'd just won, rather than relax with everyone in the living room, but I wanted to get my ideas down whilst they were still fresh.

So maybe I needed to work on the having fun/happiness bit, but *love*? I had *that* point covered. I *loved* Rich. I knew him *so* well. He was kind and a wonderful friend. Yes, definitely a great companion. I mean, we'd had those wobbles in the past, which I told you all about, and we didn't have sex, kiss or do anything physical anymore, but that was normal in a long-term relationship, right? And there was always so much to do at work, and I was always tired and busy and...

Shit.

He's right.

Albert's words rang like sirens in my ears.

'Life is short. You only live once. You must enjoy. If you are not happy, you must do something to change it...rappelle-toi *that it is happiness and* amour*, not work, that are the most important.'*

How did I not realise it before? It seemed so obvious. I'd been on a treadmill—so focused on the business, being the best and carving out this amazing career that I'd lost sight of everything else. I'd constantly put work before my family, friends, my relationship, my well-being. In fact, my whole fucking life.

Was I actually *in* love or did I just love the stability of having Rich around? If I was honest with myself, we became more like brother and sister or flatmates every day.

There was no passion. Despite sleeping in the same bed every night, I could barely remember the last time Rich and I had even shared a peck on the lips, never mind anything else.

It had been so long since I'd had sex, I was pretty sure

my virginal status had been automatically restored. I was thirty-eight, not ninety-eight. Surely I wasn't ready to say goodbye to having fun in the bedroom already?

Rich was comfortable, safe and predictable. And up until I received the call from Henri last week, that had all been okay. But now, thinking about Albert's last words, I was beginning to feel like I couldn't live like this anymore.

Albert had been right all along. I wasn't living. I was existing.

I wasn't working to live and enjoy life. I was living to work.

If I kept going on like this, it could be *me* who found myself in an early grave. And what would I have done with my life? Yes, I would have built a successful business, but was that enough? Was that what I really wanted? What about fun and true happiness? And kids? I'd always said I'd like to have at least one. But had I left it too late?

Fuck. This was a big wake-up call. Far from being idyllic like everyone always assumed, in fact my life was a mess. But at least I'm still alive.

As Albert warned me, life is short, so I couldn't waste any more time. I needed to make some big decisions. Yes. Things had to change drastically. And fast.

CHAPTER TWO

I reached into my handbag, pulled out my yellow personalised notebook and thumbed my way through to find a fresh page.

There was no point just saying things would change. For this to work, I needed to take action. Commit to a formal plan. A specific list.

It needs a name. What should I call it? *Life Plan*? No. *Master Plan*? That didn't work either. Sounded like something from a James Bond film, where the evil baddie hatches a *Master Plan* to destroy the world.

No. It needed to be something positive. *Let me think...*

This was all about the changes I was going to make to improve my life: to show Albert I was putting my time on this earth to good use. So...

Yes.

In big, bold capital letters at the top of the page I wrote:

M.A.P.

An acronym for: Make Albert Proud. *It's perfect.*

Now I had the title, I'd write this down and make it happen.

Okay, what would I like to change about my life? Well, I definitely had to start with this:

1) Stop being a workaholic/have a better work-life balance

It might sound cool running your own business, and in many ways it is. You get to choose when you work and how much you get paid. You call the shots. But the bit they *don't* warn you about is the long hours (kiss goodbye to weekends, evenings and holidays), the stress of being responsible not just for big client budgets (and even bigger expectations), but also for the livelihoods of your team. If the money isn't there to pay them at the end of the month, they won't be able to cover their mortgage/credit card bills/buy food etc. It's lot of pressure.

Don't get me wrong—I *love* what I do. But as Albert said, all work and no play is bad, so I can't let that passion cause my personal life to go to shit. I need to see my family and friends more. Make time for our monthly catchups at the very least and not be an arsehole by cancelling or turning up late because I feel the need to be available to clients 24/7.

I need to not work late every night and at weekends. What's the point of spending years building a talented team who are always asking for more responsibility, which will help lighten my workload, if I'm going to continue micromanaging?

Time to set boundaries and not be all about the work.

2) End my relationship

So this is huge. I've been with Rich since I was twenty-four and soon it will also be our fifteenth anniversary. How did *that* happen? Whilst it might seem like a big milestone, we haven't really had fun or a proper relationship for ages and I know we're growing apart. I love Rich dearly, but we're not *in* love. Well, at least I'm not, anyway. I realise that now.

I think we've both known for ages that it's over. We stay together because it's easy, but that's not a way to live. We've stagnated for years, and the longer we remain in this relationship, the more of our lives we'll be wasting.

This is a massive decision. Just thinking about it does kind of scare the shit out of me. Not only the part where I'll have to break the news and hurt Rich, but also the prospect of being single at my age after being coupled up for so long. I'm definitely *not* looking forward to going through all that dating stuff again.

Fuck. It's going to be beyond tough, but if something isn't working, no matter how hard it is you've got to grow some balls, be brave, speak up, end it and move on.

Who am I kidding? If only it was that simple. It's easy to *sound* strong and say those words in theory, but I'm pretty sure that actually putting it into practice is going to be significantly harder…

Tough titty. As difficult as it will be, I can't be a wuss. It has to be done. No turning back.

3) Experience passion

I feel a bit cheeky writing this one, but what the hell. I'm doing it anyway. Now that I've had time to think about it, my work addiction and relationship rut has made me forget one fundamental thing: I'm still a fully functioning *woman*. And women have *needs*!

Like I said, there's no hope of rekindling that side of things with Rich now. It's too far gone. Not just the physical side—there are other factors too. But on the subject of being intimate, as many people in a relationship will understand, if you leave it long enough, it's easy to quickly forget about how amazing it feels to have great sex. Well, it's been an eternity, so I can't *quite* remember the specifics, but I *think* I used to enjoy it.

Even if the memory of my sexual experiences has faded, my imagination is still firmly intact, so I do have the ability to at least fantasize about it.

I mean, I'm not asking for the earth (well, not initially, anyway). Right now I would *love* to have a long passionate snog. Oh, and what I wouldn't give for some hot guy to gaze longingly into my eyes like I was the sexiest goddess who ever graced the universe, rip my clothes off in the throes of passion and kiss me all over.

Just thinking about it gives me the tingles…I'd be prepared to give up chocolate for a month for one night of passion…

Actually, let's be realistic. Maybe a week. I *really* like chocolate…

Yes. Some passion would be pretty amazing. Not sure how likely this is though, as the guys my age are probably all chasing twenty-one-year-olds with legs up to their armpits and breasts the size of two helium balloons.

Nope, don't care. I want it, so it's staying on the list.

Okay, what's next?

4) Go on an educational holiday

Oh yes, this one is one hundred percent needed too. I'm lucky enough to travel to Paris, Milan, LA and New York a fair bit for work to see clients or for press launches, but outside of this, apart from going to France to visit Albert and Marie (around the Easter or May bank holidays, of course), one of the only times I do go somewhere for pleasure is for my birthday. The thing is, though, these past few years, everything has become so monotonous:

Go to a posh country hotel (typically in the UK). Have a fancy dinner. Return to room. Both feign tiredness to avoid the awkwardness of not having sex in the huge four-poster bed. Wake up. Have breakfast, then maybe have a couple of spa treatments. Meet Rich at reception, drive home marvelling all the way at how *wonderful* it is to get away from London. How *refreshed* we both feel and gush about the fact that we *really should do this more often*. Zzzzzzz…

Yes, yes, I know. *Poor me*. I should hire the the the Royal Philharmonic Orchestra to play millions of violins in sympathy. Talk about first world problems.

The thing is, though, as amazing as it is and as fortunate as I know I am (and trust me, having worked non-stop for the past fourteen years to earn this lifestyle, I really *do* appreciate it), after a while, whether it costs five or five hundred pounds, when you've done something year in, year out, even the nicest treats can feel dull. That's why a lot of rich people are often miserable.

Last year I was so bored that I vowed that this year I would stimulate my brain and do something different. Maybe visit a place I haven't been to before (preferably somewhere warm, though) on a photography course, or learn to paint? I'm not quite sure what or where yet, but I'm determined to do this for my birthday in April.

On the subject of birthdays, I'd also like to…

5) Throw a party

I had one for my thirtieth but was so stressed about making everything perfect, as if I was organising a client event, that I forgot to actually enjoy myself. If I did it again and could manage to switch off the perfection button, that would be fantastic. I could invite my friends and family and show them I haven't completely forgotten how to have a good time.

Looking forward to it already.

6) Look into adoption

Now I'm approaching thirty-nine at lightning speed, as the newspapers keep telling me (and have been since I was thirty-five), I have a better chance of winning the EuroMillions jackpot (around 1 in 116,531,800), than having my own child naturally.

Of course my family (notably my mum) has been banging on about my ticking biological clock for donkey's years. At the time I thought I still had ages to worry about all that. As far as I was concerned, I had the perfect partner, so it was just a question of *when* rather than *if.* But then we won one big account after another, one year rolled into the next, and before I knew it I was thirty-eight and sounding like the stereotypical, much maligned 'career woman' who had put work ahead of starting a family. Except it wasn't that cut and dried.

A few months ago, I'd even contemplated discussing it again with Rich, but he too was wrapped up in his work, which had become increasingly demanding. If I wasn't mistaken, having a baby meant that we had to actually *do the deed*, and lately that's been as likely to happen as Kit Harrington ringing my doorbell at 1 a.m., asking if I'd be up for a booty call.

Plus, the more I started to question our relationship and realise that Rich and I no longer had a romantic connection, the more it seemed wrong to consider having a child together.

But I won't sit around waiting to find a man to try and fertilise eggs that the media tell me may be past their 'best-before' date. I'll take things into my own hands, go and see a specialist and look at my options as a (soon-to-be) single woman. Maybe I could still look into the IVF route using a sperm donor? Or perhaps a surrogate? I need to get the facts and find out what is both feasible and right for me. Either way, I'll start looking into things. Yep, that's going on the list.

7) Have fun/live life to the full

Last and by no means least, whatever I do, wherever I go, whoever I meet, I'm always going to try to make the most of the situation. To embrace it and live life to the full. I know it's a bit of a catch-all point, but I'm self-aware enough to admit that I can be a bit uptight and rigid at times. So I recognise that I need to relax a tad, try not to overanalyse everything and go with the flow more.

Within reason, of course, though, as planning helps me feel *so* much better. The mere thought of disorganisation makes me want to break out in a cold sweat. You know, like when paper and pens aren't lined up straight on a desk, or when the cushions aren't equally spaced on the sofa (don't you just hate that?). But I *can* do this. I *will* do this!

Yes. I will make 'living life to the full' the mantra I follow at all times.

I proudly set the pen aside on the table, took another sip of my wine, then flicked backwards through the pages until I reached the beginning of my notes. I read over the seven points again. How amazing it would be if I could achieve everything in the next twelve months, so that by the first anniversary of Albert's passing, I could show him that I'd taken his comments on board and really started living my life?

Exhaling deeply, I felt a rush of satisfaction, followed by excitement and then a twinge of fear as the reality of the challenges that lay ahead, hit me.

All this in one year?

Abso-fucking-lutely! No more hiding. No more existing. This wasn't going to be easy. Particularly for a creature of habit like me. But in honour of my dearest Albert, I was determined to tick off every single one of those goals and make him proud.

And if I was going to really begin living, now I'd made these big decisions, I had to tackle the most difficult ones straight away.

First (and possibly the hardest) to address? Point number 2: End my relationship with Rich.

CHAPTER THREE

Today was the day. It *had* to be. I couldn't procrastinate any longer.

We were now in February and I'd been back from France almost a week, yet I still hadn't done it. I knew I had to end my relationship with Rich, but it just never seemed to be the right time.

If I did it in the morning, then I could ruin his entire day. And what if he got upset, jumped in the car, drove to work and had an accident? I couldn't live with myself.

I considered having the talk on Tuesday, but he had that pitch to redesign a new library in North London. I knew how much work went into the pitching process, so doing it then, when he really needed to focus, would be just plain evil.

I'd thought about Wednesday night too, but then I'd got back late from a client dinner. Plus, my mum always said never to go to bed on an argument, and surely we'd argue about it somehow. Or perhaps I'd say I wanted to end it and he'd say: *'Brilliant! You took the words right out of my mouth—I'm sooo relieved you feel the same way!'* No. I doubted that would happen.

That was the other thing. The *words*. How to say it. I hadn't had much practice at ending relationships. Well, personal ones anyway.

Whilst I was a high achiever academically and professionally, I hadn't had a huge amount of experience with men. And less so with ending relationships, hence my apprehension.

Much like how I was all about work now, before Rich, I was all about the studying. Getting straight A's for my GCSEs, then for my A-levels and going on to secure a first-class French degree at UCL didn't just happen. I had to put in the hours. Which hadn't left much time for men.

I had a few boyfriends at college. Nothing that lasted more than a couple of months, though. Then a three-year relationship with Kevin when I was about eighteen, which had ended when I'd got back from living in France and he dumped me.

So it had been a while since I'd had to go through ending a personal relationship. And even then, I think I only ever dumped one guy. Carl Curtis when I was seventeen, who I'd been going out with for all of six weeks, when his insensitive housemate told me on the bus one afternoon whilst I was travelling back from my Saturday job working in Boots that they'd been sleeping together. When I'd confronted him later that evening, screaming 'Why didn't you tell me you were fucking Debbie?' he'd casually replied, 'Because you didn't ask.' Bastard! It hadn't been difficult to end things with him.

Rich was a different kettle of fish altogether. I'd known him half of my life. We'd been partners for fifteen years.

As much as I knew it was the right thing to do, because in truth, our relationship had been broken for years, it was hard not to be sentimental.

He'd been so supportive. And he'd put up with a lot of crap from me. It wasn't all his fault that our relationship had gone down the toilet. I had to take at least fifty percent of the blame—perhaps more. I was always working, or busy or exhausted, so would often push him away when he tried to make advances. And then I suppose after a while, he got tired of trying. So when I did instigate things again, I got why he might not have been so enthusiastic. He was busy with his work too. Plus he's very much a creature of habit. Probably happy to do the same thing, eat the same food and follow the same routine for the rest of his life. But that's not what I wanted.

Sometimes it's hard to pinpoint how and exactly when these things start to go wrong, but it's like weeds. It might start with just one. But leave it unattended, and that one multiplies. They spread like wildfire and before you know it, they've taken over the entire garden.

I knew I needed to end it, but how do you do that sensitively to minimise the level of pain felt by someone you really care about? That's why, for the past week, I'd been mentally rehearsing how best to phrase it:

We have to end it?

It's time to end our relationship?

I think we need to move on?

None of them seemed quite right. Then I remembered what I always said to my team: keep it simple. Get your point across and then stay quiet. Don't ramble on. Be succinct. So I'd settled on two simple words: It's over.

Then I'd practised my delivery. Like I would for a new

business pitch. Trying to perfect the intonation of the words and my facial expressions. I needed to convey sadness, but also sincerity and conviction. Get across the fact that it had to be done and I was sorry about it, but no matter how much he tried to change my mind, I would remain steadfast and stick to my decision.

So here we are. After not finding the right time on Thursday or Friday either, it was now a cold, grey Saturday morning—the weekend. Which surely had to be a much better time to do it anyway. No work to worry about (well, maybe a little, but neither of us were compelled to go into the office today) and at least thirty-six hours to feel like shit before having to drag ourselves back out to the real world again on Monday morning.

Rich had been out late last night with his friends and had slept in, so I'd woken up at 8 a.m., showered, then gone for a walk on Clapham Common to get my thoughts together and psych myself up. Now I was on my way back home, I was hoping Rich would be making himself a fry-up or maybe sitting in front of the TV and we could have this very difficult conversation calmly…

I shut the front door gently behind me and poked my head into the living room. There was no sign of Rich, so I headed to the kitchen. He wasn't there either. The house was eerily silent. *He's got to be here, though, because his keys are still on the glass table in the hallway. Perhaps he's upstairs?*

I padded up the steps and headed for the bedroom. *It's gone 11 a.m. He can't still be sleeping?* I opened the door. *The bed's been made, so…*

I heard the shower in the en suite switch off. Oh, there he was. Perhaps I'd just wait in the kitchen. Maybe I'd make him breakfast. Soften the blow a little. As I turned around, ready to go back downstairs, I heard the en suite door open.

'Morning, Soph!' Rich said, flashing me a smile as he finished tying the towel around his waist.

Shit. I need to do it. If I don't say it right now, I'll bottle it.

'Soph, what's up?' he said, frowning.

I froze. I needed to say it. Actually, he'd just asked me how I was. So that could be the perfect in. By saying it's over, I'd be telling him *exactly* what was up. *Do it.*

Do it now*!*

'It's over.'

I did it.

I said it.

Fuck.

'What the fuck, Sophia?' snapped Rich, nostrils flaring. 'What do you mean it's over?'

As I stared into his hazel eyes, I started to ask myself the same question.

My mind went into a trance. You know how people who have a near-death experience say their lives flash past their eyes? Well, as soon as I'd said those two words, it was like my brain started playing a film of my life with Rich. When we'd first met at college, when we'd bumped into each other years later at a party and he'd asked me out for a drink, our first date at Browns in Covent Garden, our first kiss and how we'd moved in together literally months later. Then how supportive he was when I'd decided that after just a couple of years working in PR for other people, first at a fashion and beauty agency on the King's Road and then in-house at L'Oréal, I wanted to take the plunge and go it alone. Ever since then, he'd been there cheering me on and supporting me, yet here I was fifteen years later, breaking his heart.

'Earth to Sophia!' screamed Rich, stomping his feet.

I snapped out of my thoughts. Rather than reminiscing, now would probably be a good time to start explaining myself.

'Rich, I'm so, so, sorry. It's just…I mean, you must know it's not right. We've…' Jeez. What the hell was wrong with me? I'd spoken at conferences in front of thousands of people, been interviewed live on national television, yet now I was finding it hard to string a sentence together. And tears? *I know it's difficult, but get it together.*

I took a deep breath.

'We've grown apart, Rich,' I said, regaining my strength. 'We don't have that connection anymore. We've just let the relationship slide for too long. Gone past the point of no return. I'm sorry, but it's over.'

Even though it felt like my heart was physically being ripped to pieces having to say those words to him, I took my own advice and stood there firmly in silence. No rambling, just quiet.

'Why now?' Rich replied, face contorting. 'Where is this coming from? I know we've had our challenges in the past, but I thought we were fine.'

'First of all,' I said, crossing my arms awkwardly, 'we're both guilty of working too much. We don't get to see each other as often as we should, and when we do, invariably we end up talking about work.'

'Well, I'm *so* sorry for trying to be a good listener,' he said sarcastically. 'I thought I was being a good boyfriend by always asking you how your day was every night when you got home from work and giving you time to get things off your chest.'

'Yes, it's true, you *are* a supportive boyfriend,' I added. 'I'm not disputing that. You've been there from the beginning, through thick and thin, and have always been a shoulder for me to cry on during the tough times when I was building the business. But as terrible as you may think it sounds, it's not enough. "Fine" isn't okay. I need more from my life.'

'What do you mean, you need *more*?' he said, frowning as he crossed his arms.

'After what happened with Albert, I realised that I'm just existing, not living. We're together because it's easy. It's convenient. It's safe. Think about it, Rich.' I paused, trying to gather my thoughts. 'We've known each other since college—close to twenty-three years—and been together for fifteen. That's a *long* time, and yet we're not married, we don't have children, we don't do *anything* remotely fun together anymore. We're more like brother and sister than boyfriend and girlfriend. I mean, be honest: when was the last time we had sex, or even had a proper kiss?' I said, looking him straight in the eye.

'Um…well…' he muttered sheepishly as he looked down at the cream carpet. 'I know it's probably been a while, but come on, Soph, we've both had a lot on our plates.'

'Yes, you're right,' I said, placing my hands on my hips, 'but it's more than that. We've just grown apart. We used to laugh and go out. Now on the rare occasions that we actually are together, we don't do anything other than watch TV. We've become different people. I want to travel, you like staying at home. I love eating out and experimenting with food, you'd be happy to have steak and chips every day for the rest of your life. I want to have fun and experience new things and meet new people. Your idea of a good time is binge-watching multiple seasons of *Game of Thrones* or playing games on your iPad in bed.'

'It's not playing games per se. It helps me relax and think strategically,' he protested.

'If that's what floats your boat, Rich, that's fine. But I don't want to waste my life anymore. I owe it to myself to do more. Not because I'm being greedy, but because I'm *alive*. I'm healthy, I'm successful, I'm lucky enough to have so many opportunities that other people would only dream of, but I'm not making the most of them, and that's got to change.'

'But we've been together for so long!' he said, running his hands through his cropped brown hair. 'Surely you don't want to throw it all away, just like that? Let's talk about it,' he pleaded as he stepped forward and placed his hands on my shoulders. 'Maybe we can cut back on work hours so we can spend more time together.'

'I don't think—' I replied before he interrupted me.

'I can *try* the travel thing if you want,' he suggested. 'As long as it's not anywhere too hot. And I guess I'd be up for eating out *occasionally*…I'm not one to experiment with exotic dishes, though, as I can't afford to get food poisoning or take time off work, especially if we win this library pitch, but…I'll try. Just tell me what you want me to do, and I'll change!' he said, now squeezing my shoulders and giving me his puppy-dog eyes. 'I love you, Sophia, and I don't want to lose you.'

Dammit. He's pulling on my heart strings. I can feel my resolve weakening…

No. I had to trust my gut. As hard as it was, it was time for this chapter to end. I needed to move on. I knew it was the right thing to do. I had to stand firm.

'Rich,' I said, stepping back and removing his hands from my shoulders. 'I love you too. I will *always* love you, but like I said, it's not enough.'

He paused as he glanced at the carpet once again. I sensed he was lost for words and trying to think of a solution.

'Are you not attracted to me anymore?' he said, glancing down to scrutinise his stomach. 'Is *that* it?'

His looks weren't the issue. Six foot four and in good shape, I still found him attractive, but yet somehow the sexual connection was no longer there. Technically it didn't make sense, but it's how I felt, and it was really hard to explain. Even on the very rare occasions that we did try to get physical, it was, well, awkward. It didn't feel right. Whatever we'd had in those early years had gone.

'Rich,' I said gently. 'You're a smart, handsome, amazing guy…'

'Well, if I'm *so* amazing,' he snapped, 'then why do you want us to break up? Is there someone else? Is that it?'

'*No!*' I yelled. 'Of course not! Where would I find the time for that? I can't explain. It's just…'

'Well, that's a relief at least, I guess,' he interjected. 'I don't know how I'd cope with knowing that you'd been with another man. Well, maybe we can work on getting that spark back, then,' he suggested. 'What about trying counselling again?'

'We tried that already. Twice. Each time, we said we'd work less, try going out and having fun and being more intimate. And each time, things would change for a couple of weeks and then they went back to normal.' *Stick with your gut. Stay strong, Soph. Stay strong.* 'No, Rich,' I insisted. 'I'm sorry. It's too late.' His face fell.

'You mentioned that we've been together fifteen years but aren't married,' he said, perking up like he'd suddenly had a brainwave. 'I didn't think you were into the whole fairy-tale wedding thing, but if it helps, we can get married…'

'Seriously?' I said, eyes widening with disbelief. 'You think getting married is going to solve this? Getting married would be a *disaster*. Look, I know you're trying to think of a solution, and believe me when I say that this isn't at all easy for me, nor is it a decision I've taken lightly. If we're honest, we've both known for years that things haven't been right. That's why we tried the counselling, and when it didn't work, I just kept pushing my feelings to the back of my mind because I was too busy to process it properly and found it too daunting to face the thought of losing you. But I can't do it anymore. As painful as this is, I have to face the fact that it's over. I'm so, so sorry.'

He sat down on the corner of the bed in a daze. He looked totally crushed, like I'd just taken a pair of ten-inch Louboutins, plunged them into his heart and slowly rotated the heels round and around and around. On a scale of one to ten, with ten signifying feeling like a total and utter shitbag, I was currently off the scale at about a hundred. This was truly awful. I feel like the worst, most evil woman in the entire world.

Rich put his head in his hands, exhaled deeply and then got up, straightening his towel around his waist.

'Soph, like you said, I've known you a long time, and

when you get that look in your eye, you've made up your mind and you won't budge. So that tells me you're serious. This time, it really is over.' He paused again, as if he was searching deep down for the strength to speak. 'Despite me being totally and utterly devastated and feeling like everything I've known and loved for the past fifteen years has just come crashing down around me, even though I think you're making a mistake, I realise that I will just have to accept your decision and somehow find a way to move on. You don't want me anymore, so I will pack a bag now and go. I'll message you once I've got my head straight to arrange a time to come and get the rest of my stuff.'

He walked towards me, leant forward, then kissed me gently on the forehead.

'Goodbye, Soph,' he muttered. And then he was gone.

My reading on the shitometer was now rocketing into the thousands.

It was the end of an era.

No more Sophia and Rich.

I am free, I am single and I am officially way out of my comfort zone.

Fuck.

CHAPTER FOUR

So far, there were three key things I'd personally learnt about breaking up with a long-term boyfriend:

1) That as confident and kick-ass as I might seem at work, when it came to matters of the heart, I wasn't as strong as I appeared. The pain was real. Even when you were the one that made the decision to break up, somehow it was like *you'd* been dumped. You felt like total crap.

2) Throwing yourself into work really helped. I'd been so busy that when I was in the office, I didn't have time to scratch my head, never mind think about my new single status. But when I went home, it was a *totally* different story. My emotions were wobblier than a five-year-old trying to walk in their mum's heels. I hated it.

3) That M&S, Lola's, Hummingbird and all other purveyors of fine cakes should offer an emergency 2 a.m. cupcake delivery service for people going through a break-up, because sometimes a girl just needs to bury her face in frosted icing to feel better.

Rich had come round yesterday (thankfully whilst I

was at work) to collect more of his stuff. It was so weird to see his wardrobe empty. It was the little things that were strange too, like not smelling the scent of his aftershave in the morning or seeing his crumpled boxer shorts and socks on the en suite floor because he'd forgotten to put them in the laundry basket.

One positive thing about the whole situation was that, despite being together for so long, we'd both kept our own places. I'd bought this house ten years ago after landing three major clients, which had really propelled us into the beauty PR major league. And although it was where we'd both called home, it was still very much considered mine.

Rich had already had a two-bed house in Dulwich, which I'd moved into when we had first got together, plus a loft-style apartment on Bermondsey Street, which he'd bought long before the Shard and all the cool restaurants had come to London Bridge and the area had become all trendy. Now it was worth a fortune. He wouldn't be short of somewhere to stay. By a pure stroke of luck, the tenants had moved out a few weeks ago, and he'd put off renting it out straight away to give himself time to freshen up the décor, which would help bump up the rent even more.

Rich had his own car, his own savings, his own everything. He certainly didn't need anything from me, which I hoped would make things a lot easier. Fingers crossed we could have a clean break. No hassle, no legal wranglings— just consciously uncouple like Gwynnie and Chris. *Time will tell...*

When she heard how shitty I sounded on Wednesday night, four days post-break-up, Roxy, my best friend of one year, had summoned an emergency FTA. That's a

'Food, Therapy and Alcohol' session, aka a humble catch-up.

Roxy, or QOTA (Queen of The Acronym), as I'd started to affectionately call her, had an abbreviated phrase (often featuring expletives) for everything. From feeling TAF (tired as fuck) and HAH (horny as hell), no phrase was immune to being 'Roxified'. Sometimes she used so many code names that she'd leave even James Bond feeling CDC (confused.com).

I'd met Roxy at a welcome drinks party for one of the big industry exhibitions in Manchester. She'd just become the sales and marketing manager of a health and beauty tools company, and the event organiser had introduced us as Roxy was looking for a PR agency to launch their new Sonic Pulse Technology electric toothbrushes.

We'd literally only spent the first five minutes chatting about business, and then, before I knew it, Roxy started telling me all about her private life and the fact that she'd just got back on her feet after ending a destructive marriage with her SEH (Shithead Ex-Husband), which had caused her to lose her friends, her job and confidence.

I don't know if it was the tequila she'd been drinking or her no-holds-barred personality (probably a combination of both), but she really opened up to me and chatted for hours.

I could barely put one foot in front of the other at the exhibition the following morning as I was so exhausted, but it was worth it. I instantly loved Roxy's new-found spirit and the fact that after enduring such an oppressive relationship, she'd emerged a million times stronger and now gave zero fucks about speaking her mind. I knew I'd discovered a new friend. Winning the PR project was just a nice bonus.

Our FTA session was scheduled to take place at 'base', i.e., Hush, our favourite restaurant, which was tucked away in Lancashire Court, off New Bond Street. It was one of the few places that always had something on the menu that I would like (no small feat given how fussy an eater I can be), and critically, the glasses were also streak-free. Normally, when I didn't cancel, of course, we would have one on the last Saturday afternoon of every month, but given my current situation, Roxy had suggested we bring it forward a few weeks. Which kind of balanced out, as with Albert's funeral last month, it hadn't been possible to meet in January.

Roxy, myself, and Bella, my long-standing best friend of twenty-two years and counting, who I'd met at college, would sit on the comfy brown banquette seating in the special cove in the corner and discuss everything that was going on in our lives. Whether that was venting about our careers, man trouble, or trying to fathom why it took us a week to recover from staying up post 1 a.m., whereas in our twenties we could party until 6 a.m., sleep for two hours and go straight to work. It was like a therapy session, but with alcohol and no payment required. And boy was I in need of both therapy and a stiff drink right now.

Unsurprisingly, I was the first to arrive. I'd been up since 8 a.m. replying to client emails. Yes, I knew it was a Saturday, and I was supposed to be cutting back on work... but by 10 a.m., it was so eerily quiet without Rich there that I couldn't wait to get out of the house. Normally he'd have the TV blaring from the living room whilst he caught up with watching Formula 1. I showered, headed to my dressing room, put my face on, smoothed out my hair, pulled on my favourite black tailored flared Gucci trousers, a cranberry jumper and black heels, then jumped in a taxi.

I'd already ordered myself a G&T (not wise for a light-weight like me to drink on an empty stomach, or to start at 11.50 a.m., but I was sure they'd be bringing the bread soon, so that'd soak it up) and started scrolling through Instagram whilst I waited for the girls to arrive…

Mia, the twenty-five-year-old lead singer of that reality show girl band, had just announced she was expecting a baby with boy band guitarist Callum, and beauty writer Lydia's boyfriend had proposed to her in Paris over the weekend. All very happy news, but now was probably not the best time for me to be looking at this. Time to log off.

I heard Roxy coming before I saw her. I could recog-nise the click-clacking sound of her knee-high skyscraper-heeled boots from a mile off. She strode through the restaurant confidently, flicking her long fiery red hair, wearing her signature black leather short skirt (just above the knee to strike the perfect sexy, yet tasteful balance), off-the-shoulder red top and matching bold pillar box lipstick, looking every bit the glamour puss. When she saw me, her brown eyes grew bright and she smiled, revealing her gleaming white teeth. As I got up to greet her, she threw her arms around me.

'Hi, honey,' she said, pulling back to scrutinise my eyes for signs of dark circles and tears like a concerned mother. 'How are you doing, my love?'

'Ah, you know, Roxy,' I said, trying to stay strong. 'I'm okay. It's been tougher than I thought, but I'll survive,' I added as she sat down next me and wrapped her arm around my shoulder.

'Don't worry, darling,' she replied. 'By the end of this FTA, we'll have you feeling right as rain. Trust me. Now!' she said, changing the subject. 'What are we drinking? G&T? Let's get a bottle of prosecco too. Toast your fresh start.'

As she caught the attention of the waiter to order some more drinks for the three of us, Bella came bounding through the restaurant, looking flustered.

'Guys, I am sooo sorry!' she said as she plonked herself down on the banquette like she had the weight of the world on her shoulders. 'Paul decided to throw the mother of all tantrums just as I was leaving, and not even Mike could stop him screaming, so I had to calm him down before the neighbours called social services!' Her eyes weren't as bright as normal, probably down to lack of sleep. Taking care of her almost-two-year-old son whilst juggling lesson planning and teaching English to foreign professionals working in the city part-time was clearly no walk in the park.

'No worries honey,' said Roxy reassuringly. 'I just literally arrived two minutes ago. You're fine.'

'Oh, thank goodness,' said Bella as she stood up again to take off her green parker coat. At five foot eleven, she towered over Roxy, who was five foot two. Bella was dressed in a simple pair of skinny blue jeans and a comfortable orange cardigan, with her brown curly hair tied back in a practical bun. If Roxy was the poster girl for glamour, Bella was the doyenne of natural beauty. She didn't tend to wear much make-up. Just a flick of black eyeliner, a teeny bit of mascara and slick of clear lip gloss was all she ever needed to look stunning.

We ordered our starters and mains so that the waiter wouldn't interrupt us mid-conversation, then Bella reached over to give me a long hug.

'So sorry about you and Rich,' she said as she undid her scarf and stuffed it in the sleeve of her coat. As she'd had her hands full looking after Paul, I had only given her a quick summary over WhatsApp on Saturday evening, when I'd eventually peeled myself off the sofa.

'I know it was a long time coming, Soph,' added Bella, 'but I also know how hard it must have been for you to actually go through with it.'

'Thanks,' I replied as I scrutinised the glass, which thankfully was perfectly clean, before taking a sip of my G&T. 'You're right. Neither of us had been happy for a while, so the practical side of my brain absolutely knows it was the sensible thing to do. But the less logical and more emotional side is starting to freak out a little.'

'In what way?' asked Bella.

'Well, for starters, I'm going to be thirty-nine in less than eight weeks…thirty-fucking-nine. That's one year away from forty!' I said unhelpfully, as if she was unable to do basic maths. 'I know I should be strong and confident and believe that I *will* be fine, which I *am* ninety percent of the time. But then I'll read an article, or see Instagram posts with what feels like *everyone* looking loved up or pregnant, and I start fretting about the future and thinking I've made a mistake. I mean, *technically* Rich was such a catch, a guy in a million. Even at the end, when I'd crushed his heart, he was *still* understanding,' I added, hanging my head and hoping they didn't chastise me for being so weak.

'It's only natural to feel apprehensive about the future, but you've got to trust your gut,' said Bella as she put her hand on my shoulder.

'Of course,' I replied in agreement. 'Like I said, I *know* it's the right decision. And I *know* it's silly, but I get these visions of a sixty-year-old me, sitting in a rocking chair all alone with cobwebs growing from my vagina after decades of inactivity and then turning on the TV and seeing Rich named as the world's most successful architect with a thirty-year-old wife, three gorgeous kids, and they'll be living in between their homes in St Tropez, the Maldives and LA, whilst I'll be rocking away in a big empty house, regretting the day I'd told him it was over.'

'Oh fuck,' yelled Roxy. 'Bella, this is *much* worse than I thought. Thank goodness we met up today,' she added, slamming her hand against her forehead with despair.

'I know I sound like the most pathetic person on earth. But I haven't broken up with a boyfriend in a long time, certainly not one as serious as Rich, and sometimes I just have these moments where I just feel so shitty.'

'Wow…I've never seen you like this before,' said Roxy, picking up the bottle of prosecco and kindly scrutinising the glass on my behalf before pouring out a generous amount. 'Normally you're so together and so strong. But don't worry, honey. We'll help you through this.'

'Thanks, Roxy,' I murmured. 'Just listening to those words come out of my mouth is mortifying.' I vetted the glass myself, just in case, then took a giant glug.

'Firstly, remember: you're a strong, intelligent, resourceful woman running a PR empire,' replied Roxy. 'If you can take an idea and build it into a multimillion-pound business, you can definitely get over a man and take care of yourself. Secondly, step away from social media,' Roxy said, banging her hand on the table for emphasis. 'It's only going to make you feel like shit seeing all those *he liked it, so he put a ring on it* or *we're expecting* posts. Cool for them, but not helpful for you right now.'

'Totally agree,' added Bella. 'When you're feeling rubbish, looking at everyone portraying their airbrushed lives or scrolling through endless ultrasound scan pics can be toxic.'

'It stirs up so many different emotions,' I said, bowing my head. 'As much as you're happy for them and their amazing news, you also start wondering if it will ever be you, and then you feel bad for having those pangs of jealousy. After all, if it were me, I'd probably want to shout about it from the rooftops too, so why *shouldn't* they celebrate something so joyful? Lord knows there's enough doom and gloom in the world, so I should be happy to see something positive for a change.'

'I know you're sensitive, and things may appear to be shitty right now, but it *will* get better,' said Roxy, squeezing my hand reassuringly. 'When I divorced Steve, it took a long time to get over the initial loneliness and despair. There were days that I just curled up on the floor, crying my eyes out. We'd been married for eleven years, and as you know, he'd stripped away all of my confidence. I didn't know who I was. I felt completely useless.' She took a large gulp of her G&T.

'How did you get over it, Rox?' asked Bella.

'Initially with great difficulty. When I left him and moved into my own flat, I worried about silly things, like who would kill the spiders, change the lightbulbs or put up the IKEA furniture,' replied Roxy as she rested her glass back on the table. 'And the bed. That's one of the first things you notice. When you're sleeping on your own for the first time in years, the bed suddenly feels huge!'

'That's exactly how I feel each night,' I said, nodding. 'It just feels so empty.'

'Precisely. Sometimes I didn't think that I'd survive. But each week it got easier, and after I'd struggled through the first few months, I slowly got to know myself again and remembered that I *could* take care of myself. I'd done it before I'd met Steve and I would do it again. Sleeping alone meant I didn't have to deal with the duvet being pulled off me in the middle of the night. Handling creepy crawlies wasn't so bad, and as for self-assembled furniture, thanks to Google and some YouTube videos, I even smashed the shit out of putting up an IKEA wardrobe!' said Roxy, giggling.

'Ha-ha!' replied Bella. 'Now that's *definitely* an achievement. Sometimes assembling flat-packed furniture feels like bloody rocket science!'

'Totally! Soph, my relationship was extreme,' sighed Roxy. 'I was married to a controlling, abusive psychopath, so it took me a long time to get over that. You'll be much better, as your break-up is much more civil and Rich was always supportive, so your self-esteem should hopefully remain intact. But one thing I believe is that, like me, you won't look back. This is a new and exciting chapter for you, and nearly thirty-nine or not, it's going to be amazing, I can just feel it!' her eyes widened with excitement.

'I'd like to think that you're right,' I said cautiously as doubts flooded my brain.

'The truth is, Soph as lovely as Rich is, you were stifled in that relationship. Your youth and sexuality were wasting away. Now, you can be free to get out there and start living!'

'Well, as you know, Rox, I'm generally always a glass-half-full kind of person, but we can't deny the facts,' I said pragmatically. 'As a woman of a certain age, when I *am* eventually ready to get out into the world of dating again, my chances of meeting someone *will* be significantly reduced,' I added.

'Bullshit!' shrieked Roxy. 'You've been reading too much of that sexist, ageist crap society feeds us. I got divorced just before my fortieth birthday, and two years on, I'm having the time of my life! Like you, I assumed that becoming single at forty meant I'd end up like some boring cat lady—a spinster left on the shelf with no one but some seventy-five-year-old great-granddad interested in me. But it's been quite the opposite,' she said with a cheeky glint in her eye.

'In what way?' I asked, still not convinced.

'What I mean is that I'm not just attracting men in their forties, fifties and upwards, but also men in their twenties and thirties too. A lot of these young guys actually have a thing for the older woman,' said Roxy.

I shot her my best *yeah, whatever* look as the waiter placed our starters on the table and then left swiftly, grinning as if he'd caught the tail end of our conversation.

'O ye of little faith,' she replied. 'I kid you not, Sophia, I've never really gone into detail with you before as I know you're quite prim and proper and didn't want to shock you, but I've got hot twenty-seven-year-old guys wanting to get in my knickers!'

Bella nearly choked on her tuna salad.

'What?' I asked.

'Yep! Younger guys tell me women their age can be immature or play games, which they don't get with a mature lady like me. I'm much more confident and self-assured since my divorce, and I think that attitude gives off a vibe that men like.'

'I've heard that too,' said Bella in agreement as she stabbed her fork into another sliver of tuna. 'One of Mike's cousins is in his late twenties and likes to date women in their thirties and forties. It's not as uncommon as you think, Soph. Either way, younger or older, a smart, ambitious, beautiful woman like you is definitely *not* going to have a problem finding some male company again, trust us!'

'Tell her, Bella!' added Roxy. 'What you need to figure out first and foremost, Soph, is what you really want. Another long-term relationship? I mean, it's up to you, but surely the *last* thing you need right now is to tie yourself down. I reckon you should get out there and have some fun. At least for a while. You've worked damned hard for years and have spent so long withering away in that relationship. You need to let loose. Hit the dating sites hard: Tinder, Bumble, OKCupid—get on them all. Go out, meet people in real life and get your leg over. You don't want to be a MARGIN forever!'

Oh, here we go. Roxy and her acronyms.

'A *what*?' asked Bella, clearly reading my mind. 'What's a MARGIN, Roxy?'

Roxy rolled her eyes in a *how do you not know what it means?* fashion. She sighed:

'You know, a *MARGIN*?' Bella and I both shook our

heads in unison. Roxy sighed again before explaining: 'A middle-aged virgin. You know, the *M-A* stands for middle-aged, and the *R-G-I-N* is for virgin?' Her voice went up an octave in disbelief. Our faces were still blank.

'Oh, what am I going to do with you two?' she said, voice not dissimilar to a schoolteacher being forced to explain the alphabet to a twenty-year-old.

'A middle-aged virgin is someone in their thirties and forties—in fact, any adult who hasn't had sex for so long that technically, they're like a born-again virgin. It's a term normally reserved for those experiencing an extensive period of sexual drought, typically of six months or more,' she added matter-of-factly.

'Ah, I see…' said Bella as the penny started to drop.

'There are many reasons for MARGINITY,' added Roxy as she started cutting up her Carpaccio of Beef. 'And before you glaze over again, MARGINITY is middle-aged virginity. It's not just singles and divorcees that are MARGINS. It could be women who are in a relationship, but are so exhausted from looking after the kids that they just don't do it anymore, or they might have been married for a while and don't fancy their partner or vice versa. You'd be surprised how many couples sleep in separate rooms,' she said as she put a forkful of food into her mouth. 'It's not even just restricted to women. There are more MARGINS out there than you'd imagine!'

I devoured one of my sautéed scallops. This was actually fascinating, and it *definitely* applied to me.

'How do you know all this?' asked Bella as we both leaned in.

'Well,' replied Roxy as she repositioned herself, 'when I was finding myself again, I read a lot of books and studies, not just about healing yourself, but also about sex and relationships, and apparently, we're having less nookie in the 2010s than in the nineties. These days everyone's too busy on their phones tweeting and watching Netflix to get some adult time. Most people don't even have sex once a month!' she said, exasperated, as if it was the equivalent of a century.

'Pff!' I scoffed. *She thinks once a month isn't often?* It had been *at least* six months since I'd had any action. Probably more like nine, or maybe even twelve…? Shit.

'Well, Soph, you know better than anyone that when you're in a long-term relationship, one month without sex can quickly become two, then six, and before you know it, a year has passed,' said Roxy as if reading my thoughts. 'Hell, some people haven't had it for years. Those are the fully fledged, stalwart MARGINs.'

'Yeah, I can see how that can happen,' added Bella.

'The more you talk to people, the more common you see it is,' said Roxy. 'Particularly amongst women who may have married young, had their kids early and spent years raising them. Then they reach their forties, realise they want to start living their lives and get divorced, but then have to start navigating the whole dating scene all over again. It can be hard. But, Ms Huntingdon, you shall be a MARGIN no more!' she added excitedly.

'If you say so,' I smirked.

'Naturally, you probably need to take a bit of time to find yourself again and get used to your new single status, but in a few weeks' time, I reckon you should get back on the horse and find a man with a giant duster to blast away the cobwebs down under!' She shrieked with laughter. Not only was Roxy the queen of acronyms, at times she was also the queen of crude.

'A few weeks?' I replied, surprise evident in my voice. 'This is a man I spent fifteen years with, not fifteen minutes. I think I'm going to need longer than that.'

'Like I said, if you had the emotional trauma and baggage I was carrying after an acrimonious divorce, then perhaps I'd agree with you. But you're *much* stronger than I ever was, and I reckon a wild night of passion with a hot guy will make you feel a *whole* lot better,' Roxy said, plastering a wicked grin all over her face.

'Roxy, I know what I said earlier about being nearly thirty-nine and worrying about turning into a spinster, but I don't want to rush into anything. I was just being weak. In truth, I know I don't need a man to complete me,' I said robotically. 'I'll be just fine on my own.'

'Hello? Soph?' shouted Roxy. 'It's me! You're not the keynote speaker at a women's lib convention. You can spout that independent stuff all you want and, yes, you are right—hence why I've not raced to shack up with someone. *But*, equally Soph, you are a *woman*, and sometimes a woman needs the touch of a hot man! It doesn't make you weak, or less of a feminist . It makes you *human*. Sex is recognised as a basic human need. And after the drought in your knickers, I'm guessing you need to lose your MARGINITY more than most!'

She wasn't wrong, and although experiencing passion *was* on my secret MAP list, the prospect of going through all the dating site rigmarole to try and meet a guy, or even getting physical with one, stirred up a new level of trepidation that I wasn't ready to address quite yet.

'I can't disagree that I *would* like to experience some

long-overdue passion, but right now, maybe I need to just focus on me and getting my head together. Perhaps I just need a bit of time out. I don't mean wallowing at home. I did enough of that last weekend. I mean perhaps a change of scenery,' I said, considering my next move.

'Yes!' said Bella in agreement. 'You need a holiday, or maybe one of your spa breaks?' Bella's mention of a spa break also reminded me of another MAP point and my plan to do something different and more educational this year.

Our main courses arrived, and Roxy wasted no time getting stuck in.

'I'm all spa'd out, to be honest, but you're right. I think I'll book a holiday. Something different this time, though, where I'm doing something productive and fulfilling, like photography or—'

'Mmm,' interrupted Roxy as her eyes rolled with plea-sure. 'This pasta is absolutely divine. It's *almost* as good as an orgasm, I swear. Taste it!' She stabbed a piece of lobster then twirled the tagliatelle around her fork and pushed it towards my mouth. She was right. How had I not ordered this before? The food here was always *so* good.

Food...

Yes. I love food...

'I know,' I said as if a thousand-megawatt lightbulb had just been switched on in my head. 'I'm going to book myself onto a cookery holiday. It's my birthday in a couple of months, so that's what I'll do. I won't go to a spa. I'll go away somewhere beautiful and learn how to cook gorgeous food.'

'That's a brilliant idea,' agreed Bella. 'Where are you thinking? France?'

'Italy!' interjected Roxy. 'Go to Italy. You can learn how to cook fresh pasta, and then you can come round to my place and make me a divine lobster tagliatelle like this!'

Italy. What a good idea.

That's why I loved our FTA sessions. I definitely needed to make time for them in the future. I always came away feeling inspired and a million times better.

Sod all this self-pity and wallowing. As soon as I got home, I was going to research cookery holidays.

I'd go to Italy, have fun, and emerge stronger, happier and ready to embrace my single life and everything this new chapter might hold.

Bring it on.

CHAPTER FIVE

Ahhh…the sound of silence. It was so strange. It was 9.30 a.m. on a Sunday and I'd just stepped through the grand glass double doors of our Covent Garden office. If this had been a weekday, there'd have been the buzz of the team discussing projects, plus the excitement of journalists, celebs and bloggers coming in for meetings or to get a sneak peek at our clients' latest beauty launches. But today it was just me.

Now that there was less than a week until my birthday and my trip to Tuscany, I was trying to get as much done as possible before leaving so that I could *try* and relax a little whilst I was there.

Yes. I was going to Italy. After my last catch-up with Roxy and Bella, I'd gone home and spent hours researching cookery holidays. I'd found a small business called Taste Holidays who did package deals to Italy that welcomed people like me who were flying solo. There was no hotel as such, which ruled out a lot of my normal checks. Instead you stayed in an authentic Tuscan villa with other single travellers and got daily cookery lessons from the onsite Italian chef. All food, booze, accommodation and a couple of excursions, such as a trip to Florence, were included in the price.

It had amazing press reviews, and having quizzed the founder on the phone about the number of people on the holiday, their gender and age range, what their rooms were like and a million other questions, I'd decided to bite the bullet and book it.

Was I terrified? Definitely. But although I was taking a leap into the unknown, this would allow me to tick the educational holiday goal off my list. So I was going to feel the fear and do it anyway.

Although coming in on a Sunday didn't *appear* to demonstrate that I was making progress with my goal to achieve a better work-life balance, I actually was. How? Well, rather than working for several hours, which I would typically do on the weekends, today I would be leaving at 1.30 p.m. and going to Bella's for Paul's second birthday party. Usually I'd say I was too busy, but this year I thought I'd make more of an effort to be a better godmother and take time out to attend.

Seeing the office peaceful like this gave me a rare moment to take stock and think about what I'd achieved. When we'd moved here four years ago to celebrate the business' tenth anniversary, Rich's architecture firm had helped design the office to bring my vision to life and they'd done an incredible job. This was the glamorous yet down-to-earth working environment I'd always dreamt of creating, and even now I still had to pinch myself to check it was real.

As you entered the reception area, individual free-standing illuminated yellow letters of the company name, BeCome, stood on a platform, flanked by large, lush indoor palm trees in white stone pots either side. I'd never wanted to name the agency after myself. So instead I had chosen something that would convey both our specialism (*Be w*as taken from the first two letters of *beauty*) and what we did for brands. Every company wants to *become* something—whether it's the market leader or the most luxurious salon in London. And we could help them *become* whatever they wanted to be.

I scanned the area again. To the right sat a grand red sofa in the shape of giant lips, and on the left was a glass reception desk with the words 'hello *beautiful*' imprinted at the front. There was always a stunning display of bright fresh flowers in a tall, elegant glass vase. This week it was a pretty peach-and-cream arrangement.

The walls were adorned with prime editorial features we'd secured for clients in *Vogue, Cosmopolitan, Stylist, Grazia* and everything between. There were celebrity front covers, quadruple-page spreads and certificates displayed in platinum frames highlighting the multiple accolades secured for the brands we represented, as well as awards the agency and I had won in our own right. It was a hall of fame that never failed to impress everyone who came to visit.

I walked across the solid oak floor and followed the corridor round to the main open-plan office space, which was flooded with natural light coming from the large oval windows that were surrounded by exposed brick. There were rows of glass-and-chrome desks, which I'd had designed and made especially for us, and on each one sat a shiny MacBook laptop or iMac.

I headed to the centre of the room and began to climb one of my favourite features: the eye-catching floating glass staircase that led to the mezzanine directors' floor. I had my own individual glass office there, as did Harrison, my younger brother and the head of our digital division; Robyn, my senior account director who'd been with the company for almost a decade after joining us as an intern when she'd graduated; and Joe, the financial director. The beauty of the unique design was that the front panel of each office was also created to be a large sleek sliding door, so that we could slide it across to feel part of the open-plan atmosphere but could also close it for privacy.

My office, the largest on this floor, was quite minimalist. Exposed whitewashed brick walls, glass desk, charcoal Herman Miller Aeron chair, solid oak drawers, a small glass cabinet proudly displaying some of our clients' hero products, small rectangular glass coffee table with a matching vase that was always filled with bright cheery flowers, and a comfy two-seater mustard-yellow sofa.

As I often went to events after work, I'd also had an en suite installed to allow me to have a shower, get changed and do my hair and make-up in privacy. It also meant that the loo was only ever a few steps away, which as a workaholic, or I should say a *reformed* workaholic, meant that I could spend more time working and less time going up and down the stairs to get to the main toilets.

I pulled up my chair and fired up my iMac Pro. This morning I wanted to spend a few more hours working on the MIKA Cosmetics lipstick launch campaign.

As their target audience was females aged eighteen to thirty-five who were very social media savvy, several months ago, we'd handpicked two key influencers with a huge following and flown them to MIKA's beauty lab in New York to create a lipstick in their own custom shade. Céline, from *Aspire* magazine, the UK's biggest glossy, was one of the most influential beauty directors in the industry, with an Instagram following of 200K, and she'd developed a wearable pretty pink-nude shade. Amelia, who, with a gazillion followers (well, over 5.5 million), was a big-deal blogger, had gone for a nude-beige hue. She literally could post a photo of a slice of burnt toast and get thousands of likes in less time than it takes to boil a kettle.

We'd planned a launch at Harvey Nichols, where both influencers would invite their followers to come along to meet and greet them, discover their beauty tips and, of course, buy the limited-edition lipsticks. Now the date was confirmed, I needed to go over the details today to be sure that everything was in place before I jetted off to Italy.

Right on schedule at 1.30 p.m., I locked up the office and then jumped in a taxi to Hampstead for the party. I would've preferred to spend a couple more hours working on a few other campaigns, but this was the *new* me, and the new me would no longer spend all weekend working.

Repeat after me: it's all about balance, it's all about balance...And who better to spend my new-found down-time with than my best friend of over two decades and my godson?

I'd met Bella at the bus stop on the way home from college when I was sixteen. For weeks I'd seen her getting the same bus as me to the main garage in Croydon, and when we found ourselves huddled under the shelter in the rain, waiting for what felt like hours, we'd struck up a conversation. We vented about the weather (we wouldn't be true Brits without having a meteorological moan), then found ourselves chatting about everything from *The Jerry Springer Show* to the gruelling homework and our plans to learn to drive the second we turned seventeen to avoid having to rely on public transport.

Even when we had gone to separate unis, we still used to speak daily. We went clubbing and took our first 'adult' holiday together (i.e., without parents, not *that* kind of 'adult' holiday). Plus, when I lived in France, because we didn't have our own email, and On Demand TV hadn't been invented, she used to send me ten-page letters with comprehensive updates on what had been going on in *Home & Away* and *Neighbours*. Now if *that* isn't the sign of a good friend, I don't know what is.

We'd been there for each other through first jobs, first proper boyfriends, first mortgages, and also when she'd first met Mike at her uni freshers' week. At the time, they were both going out with other people, so they didn't get together until they saw each other at a ten-year reunion. They got married a few years later, and now she was enjoying bringing up their first child. We'd both been through ups and downs in our lives, but the one thing that had always been constant was our friendship.

Yes. After far too much time focusing on work, taking a few hours out of my day to attend Paul's party was the least I could do for such an amazing friend.

'You came!' squealed Bella with delight as she opened the door. 'Look who's here!' she said, signalling to Paul. Dressed in a long red-and-black patterned top with light blue fitted jeans, a slick of pink gloss, mascara and eyeliner, and her long curls tumbling past her shoulders, she was glowing as always. 'It's Aunty Sophia! Come and say hello!'

'Hello, gorgeous!' I said as I held my arms open for Paul, who had grown significantly since I last saw him, to run into. Paul, however, had other ideas. Sporting a full head of cute brown curls, dressed in a long-sleeved white t-shirt imprinted with a multicoloured 'It's My Birthday!' slogan and the cutest blue jeans, he stared at me as if to say, 'Who is this woman?' Then he paused and ran off into the living room to play with his friends.

'Ah, don't worry,' said Bella, trying to make me feel better about the fact that my godson saw me so infrequently that he didn't even recognise who I was. 'He'll warm up later and will give you a big hug. Come, come.' She gestured me inside.

In the homely-looking living room and adjoining dining room, which were both decorated with blue helium balloons and 'Happy Birthday' banners, there were about a dozen little people running up and down and a scattering of adults both seated and standing.

'Bella!' I recognised Mike's voice coming from the kitchen.

'Sorry, Soph,' said Bella, looking flustered. 'It's all go at the moment! I'll be with you in a sec. Come and take a seat.' She scanned the room, then directed me to a space on the green sofa near the patio doors. 'Soph, this is Felicity. Felicity, this is Sophia,' she said, introducing me to the lady who was dressed in a cute floral dress with her dark blonde hair cut into a neat bob. 'I'll be back in a mo,' added Bella before she rushed off into the kitchen.

'So which one of these little ones is yours, then, Sophia?' asked Felicity excitedly.

'None of them, actually,' I replied as I pulled the bottom of my fitted navy jersey dress down over my knees. Maybe I should have worn jeans too. I might end up catching my leg on one of the toys on the floor and laddering my tights.

'Oh?' she questioned, face perplexed, like I'd just asked her to divide 1.3 million by 13, then multiply it by 27 without a calculator. 'Why, where are your children?'

Oh dear, here it comes. The *kidterrogation*: when 'well-meaning' individuals, often those with children, interrogate women *without* kids about the status of their ovaries. This is exactly why I dreaded coming to kids' parties…

Now, predictably, as Felicity tried to find some common conversation ground, she'd dropped the K bomb.

'I don't have any children,' I replied, hoping unrealistically that she'd accept my response and just talk about the weather instead. Wishful thinking. More chance of London having a thirty-degree heatwave on Christmas Day.

'You don't have any children? But *why not*?' If I thought she looked confused before, now she had the kind of horrified face you'd expect to see on Mariah Carey if she was asked if she wanted to stay at a Travelodge rather than the penthouse at London's swanky Corinthia Hotel.

Now, don't get me wrong. I understood that because we were at a kid's party, it might be a fair assumption that every adult in the room was here to oversee their offspring. However, asking someone *why* they don't have children is a very personal and intrusive question and most definitely isn't okay.

For all Felicity knew, I could have been struggling to conceive for years. How did she know I wasn't on my third round of IVF and was riddled with worry that it wouldn't work again? What if I'd recently suffered a miscarriage, or just been told I couldn't have children at all? Or, horror of horrors, I might have even made a conscious decision *not* to have kids, like Roxy. Now *that* would blow Felicity's mind! But as many women over thirty without children will attest, people like Felicity don't actually *think* about the implications and emotions that can be evoked by casually asking someone they met less than five minutes ago something that is frankly none of their business.

I wonder how she'd react if I asked her how often she had sex with her husband or what colour knickers she was wearing today. Ha-ha! Now *that* would be funny. I was almost tempted to ask, just to see her reaction.

Anyway, because I knew Felicity probably didn't mean any harm by what she wrongly considered a perfectly innocent question and was just trying to make conversation, I trotted out my standard response:

'Oh, you know, Felicity. It's just not something that has happened for me yet, but perhaps in the future,' I said, complete with fake smile. *That's it. Keep it short and sweet.*

'Right,' she muttered, still unconvinced. 'But what about your husband? Does *he* not want kids now, then?' she added, firmly pushing the second of my buttons. As well as being an outcast if you didn't have children, I was also learning that being single in your thirties was also a crime to womankind punishable by something terrible like suffocation by wedding veil.

Keep calm, Soph. She doesn't realise what she's saying. Pretend you're at work. Be professional.

'Actually, I'm not married, Felicity,' I replied confidently, and she suddenly became overcome with utter disbelief. In the past few minutes, her face has gone through more expressions than an impressionist on *Britain's Got Talent*. And as for what she was thinking, I'd imagine the current headline in her brain read something like:

BREAKING: 30-Something Woman Discovered Living in 21st Century <u>WITHOUT</u> Children or a Husband!

Ever persistent, Felicity was clearly not going to let this go until she discovered what led me to lead such a *terrible* existence.

'Oh..! Good heavens!' she said disapprovingly, struggling to think of something constructive to say. 'Um…erm, well…you're still young, I suppose, so you have a *little* time. Not much, but some at least. What are you? Around thirty-two, I'm guessing? It's only when you get to thirty-five that you *really* need to start worrying, because *boom*! Your fertility nosedives faster than the *Titanic*,' she added solemnly.

Now I'd consider myself a patient person, but she was pushing my buttons harder than a teenager typing a text message. Oblivious to this, she continued:

'That's why it was a race against time to have Billy, my third child, before my thirty-third birthday. Phew!' she said as she gestured wiping imaginary sweat from her forehead. 'Just pushed him out in time. I mean, Bella was incredibly lucky. Having a baby at thirty-seven—I tell you, it's a miracle. Any older and, let's face it, it would have been curtains!'

Is she for real? Yes, I've done enough research to know fertility decreases with age, but that is *not* an appropriate thing to say to someone you've just met. And as for the husband thing, seriously. Was this the 1800s? Didn't she realise that not every woman has to get married?

'Well, in that case, Felicity,' I said, my face getting hotter by the second, 'I'm fucked, then, aren't I? I mean, seeing as I'm not thirty-two—thanks for that compliment, by the way—I'm actually almost thirty-nine.'

'Sophia!' screamed a clearly horrified Felicity. At first I thought it was because she couldn't believe I could *possibly* be in my late thirties and wanted to know what anti-ageing face creams I used, but then I realised this was *not* a happy scream. This was a *you've just told my child that Father Christmas doesn't exist and shattered their dreams* angry scream.

'The children!' she gasped again. 'You cannot *swear* in front of the children!'

Right on cue, Billy, who had been playing with a small red toy Ferrari on the floor beside us, then proceeded to innocently and repeatedly shout, 'Fucked! Fuck! Fucked!'

Crap. She did have a point about the swearing. I wasn't used to being around children, but in fairness, I wasn't accustomed to being irritated by some insensitive, self-satisfied ignoramus whose views belonged in the Natural History Museum either.

'Billy, stop saying that!' pleaded a rattled Felicity. 'Bad word!'

'Fuck, fucked, truck,' he trotted out calmly as the other parents looked on, trying to work out whether this two-year-old was in fact dropping the F-bomb. But Billy continued rolling the Ferrari backwards and forwards along the wooden floor, clearly oblivious to the meltdown poor *Felicity the self proclaimed fertility expert* was currently having.

Come on! You can't tell me that was the first time little Billy had heard that word. He said it far too fluently. Bet Mrs Baby Making Machine used it at home constantly!

'Yes, Billy!' I added, thinking on my feet. 'Have you ever played with a truck? I was just telling Mummy that I *love* trucks! Trucks, trucks, trucked. Can you say *truck*, Billy?' I paused as I waited to see whether I'd salvaged my fuck faux pas.

'Yes!' cried a now-excited Billy, his bright blue eyes widening by the second. 'Trucks! Mummy, can I have a truck? Billy wants to play with truck!' he said, tossing the car to one side.

And with that, Felicity shot me an evil look, took Billy by the hand and hurried over to the toy box at the other end of the room, I suspected not just to find a truck but to get her darling son as far away from the potty-mouthed single childless weirdo as quickly as possible.

She needn't have bothered. I decided to go for a walk and clear my head.

Felicity had struck a nerve. The baby decision weighed heavily on me. On the one hand, I believed women shouldn't need to be married or be mothers to be complete. However, on the other, the older I got, the stronger the yearning to be a mum became.

Not because I felt the pressure to conform to society's 2.4-children-with-husband-dog ideal, nor because I wanted someone to look after me when I was too old to do it myself. But because I would genuinely like to nurture a child, help him or her grow up to achieve amazing things and make a difference to society in their own way. And I'd like to think I would be good at it too.

As I wandered down Hampstead High Street, I thought

again about how quickly the years had passed. I'd spent my late teens and early twenties desperately trying *not* to get pregnant so that I could focus on my education. Then came work, and after launching the agency at twenty-five, that had become my life. So when most of my friends had started having kids in their early thirties, my baby was the business. And although the kidterrogations had become more frequent, I was so overwhelmed with building the company, plus taking care of clients and the team, that procreation had been inadvertently placed on the back burner.

I was also conflicted. Realistically, would I have the time to look after a child as well as myself *and* the business? When I looked at my friends with kids, they were often exhausted. Desperately trying to juggle working with waking up at the crack of dawn to make breakfast and get the little ones ready, doing the school run, ferrying them to after-school clubs and birthday parties, making dinner, attending parents' evenings, homework…the list seemed endless. Whilst they'd never be without them, raising children is definitely not child's play.

Then there was the guilt. Full-time mums were made to feel 'unworthy' for being 'just a mum' (clearly bonkers seeing as it's the only role in the world which involves you being available to work 24/7, 365 days a year for at least two decades). Then women who *did* work were chastised for not being with their child at every moment, yet were also berated for taking time off to spend with their family or leaving work early to attend a school play. It was nuts.

As annoying as she was, maybe I could understand Felicity's surprise (but not her intrusive grilling). After all, most of my friends had had kids by the time they were thirty-five, and whilst not as many were married, the majority had settled down, so I clearly didn't conform to 'normal' standards. Then again, I never had.

It wasn't normal for someone in my family to go to university or to graduate with a first-class French degree. And it certainly wasn't normal for a twenty-five-year-old with no prior business experience to set up her own PR agency from scratch and go on to create a million-pound company from it.

No. I was anything but normal. And career-wise, so far it'd worked well for me. My professional life was good—great, even. But now I really needed to work on getting my personal shit together.

CHAPTER SIX

W ow. Last few moments of being thirty-eight. In approximately ten minutes, I would be thirty-nine. Otherwise known as one year away from the big 4-0.

As I sat in my bed clutching a glass of chilled prosecco, I did a mental scan of my achievements so far, which had become a kind of pre-birthday ritual:

Professional Life:

Turnover and profits: up by 27 percent compared to this time last year. Check.

Team: amazing. Staff retention remained high. Check.

Clients: I had my dream portfolio of clients. Good mix of beauty, fragrance, hair and well-being brands. We'd even been approached by a few multinational communication agencies who wanted to buy us. The figures they'd been mentioning sounded very attractive. Sounded a bit too good to be true—there were probably lots of clauses and catches. I hadn't studied the offers in enough detail, as I didn't think I could ever give it all up. This business was my baby.

Anyway, in short, career was great.

Personal Life

Hmm, I didn't think I even needed to go through a checklist to know this wasn't going to be good…

Personal life in general: poor, but set to improve… (let's think positively)

Relationship: non-existent…

Children: non-existent…

Non-work-related happiness: yet to be discovered…

Fun: currently hovering around the zero mark. *But* in twenty-four hours' time, it could all be different as I reckoned I'd enjoy learning how to cook authentic Italian dishes…potential check?

If this was a school report, I'd be getting an A* for my professional life, but my personal life grading would probably read 'D' with comments such as: *Room for improvement. Sophia shows great potential, but she needs to apply herself more.* Surely the first step to recovery, though, was recognising that you had a problem, and I was actively taking steps to rectify it.

For example, rather than staying in a country hotel like I always did, tonight (well, I was literally seconds away from it being my birthday), I would be having a dinner party at my parents' house. Then Saturday morning would be when the real fun would hopefully start, as I would be flying out to Tuscany for my long-awaited cookery holiday. I was really excited.

At exactly one minute past midnight, my phone pinged. I picked it up from the duvet and read the text message flashing on the screen:

From: Mum Mobile

Happy birthday, darling! See you this evening at 7 p.m. sharp!

I LOVED that Mum always messaged me at the same time every year.

On the subject of my birthday, I know I'd said on my MAP plan that I'd have a party, but as I had been so busy at work and was also still trying to get my head around my break-up with Rich, there was no way I would have had time to organise a proper one this year. So I'd decided to do it next year instead. I know I was supposed to be living my life now and ticking everything off the list. But rushing it, or not doing it the way I'd like to, would only make me unhappy, which was the opposite of what the plan was designed to achieve. Also, I reasoned that would make more sense, as it'd be my fortieth, so it would call for an even bigger celebration.

Right. Lots to do today, so time for bed.

LEAVING the office at 6 p.m. when you're about to go on holiday for four days and need to tie up loose ends was no mean feat for a workaholic like me. I was supposed to be at my mum's in an hour and hadn't even gone home to get dressed yet, never mind the fifteen-minute journey time to their house in Streatham.

I had a quick shower, then stepped into one of my favourite parts of the house: the dressing room. Like most of this property, my dream of the ultimate walk-in wardrobe had been brought to life by Rich and the expert team at his firm. I had a lot to thank him for.

The dressing room was connected to the bedroom. Once I opened the frosted glass double doors, it was like entering my own personal clothes, shoes and handbags paradise.

It had been fitted out just like a mini department within Selfridges. At the back of the room was an illuminated shoe wall with no fewer than fifty pairs of the finest footwear, including everything from strappy sandals to more practical, yet still glamorous boots and courts.

Either side and above the shoe wall were mini coves housing a display of handbags. There was a bag in a colour, size and style to suit every occasion.

And then there were the clothes: Armani, Burberry—a million miles away from the geeky getups I used to have stuffed into my teeny wardrobe during my student days. Everything here had been organised to military precision. First according to occasion, e.g., evening wear, daytime/work, casual; then by type, e.g., all dresses within that category together and also by colour, making things much easier to find.

In the centre of the brightly lit white room was a square island. The top had transparent glass drawers where I kept my jewellery and accessories, and in the ones underneath was an underwear drawer, another for tights, and also a separate section for belts.

By the window was a silver dressing table where I sat every morning to get ready. The drawers below were filled with all the make-up, skincare, nail polishes, products and tools I needed to ensure my hair and face look immaculate. I also had shelves either side showcasing some of my perfumes (one of the perks or running a beauty PR agency) —just like a mini Space NK display. I always enjoyed getting dressed in here. It was where the 'magic' happened. Where I transformed myself.

This was definitely a pinch-me-is-it-real kind of room. Sometimes I couldn't believe that I had all of this stuff. I still had moments where I felt like that naïve twenty-five-year-old starting out in business who didn't have a clue what she was doing but pretended she did. *Fake It Until You Make It* had been my motto. But now I was doing okay (I don't know if anyone can ever truly say they've 'made it'), and the feeling of faking it hadn't gone away. Dressing up to look the part does help, though. It's like you're getting into character, ready to play the role of 'businesswoman'. My clothes were like my armour. The shield that protected me. They told the world that I was a success and worthy of acceptance, even if inside, I often didn't feel like I was.

On the subject of dressing, I needed to pick out something for tonight. I headed over to the evening wear section, scrolling through the options.

Nope, too formal, too long, too sexy...hold on. *Too sexy*? Aha. Yes. I'd forgotten about this one. I pulled it off the rail and held it up. It was a daring black mesh dress I'd tried on in a little boutique in Fulham. Across the boob area, it had a black bandeau, and then a little skirt sewn in that just covered my bottom, leaving the midriff and leg area exposed except for the mesh.

At first I'd thought it might be a bit too much for a woman in her late thirties. But when I'd tried it on, it had fitted perfectly and I'd instantly loved it. As if to solidify my decision, whilst I was in the changing room, I'd heard another woman asking the sales assistant where the black mesh dress was, which was clearly the one I was trying on. I knew it was the last one and that I liked it, so I went ahead and bought it.

Yes, I thought, running my fingers over the mesh. Although tonight I'd be at my parents' and not at a glamorous event, it was my birthday, so it was the ideal time to give it an airing.

I headed to the shoe rack and selected my favourite blue suede Louboutins, then grabbed a black clutch bag from the shelf. Twenty minutes later I was good to go.

When I arrived, Harrison was in the living room chatting to Dad. Seeing them together just reminded me of how alike they looked. Both were six foot four—although Dad might be an inch or two shorter, now I think about it —with dark cropped hair, brown eyes and well-groomed beards. As always, they looked dapper in dark blue jeans, and tonight, both wore navy-blue jumpers. I wondered who'd sent the uniform memo to whom.

My elder sister Marilyn, also blessed with the tall genes—at five foot seven, I took after my mum, who was a petite five foot four—was looking glamorous with her signature red lips and Carey Mulligan-esque pixie-cut black hair as she brought the food into the dining room with my seventeen-year-old niece, Jasmine. Bella and Roxy were already standing in the corner laughing with Monique, a straight-talking New Yorker I'd met through work about a year ago and struck up a friendship with.

I whipped out my phone from my clutch and started taking some photos. With her tall model physique, dressed in loose black trousers and a zebra-striped top, as always Bella was towering over Roxy, who was wearing a fitted red mini dress and of course her favourite knee-high boots. Monique was sandwiched in between the two, her platinum-blond cropped hair and striking green dress reflecting her confident, spirited personality.

I surveyed the light and airy room, which had old family photos in gold frames on each of the deep burgundy walls. As always, Mum had ensured that everything was *just so*. The oval pine table was hosting a generous spread of dreamy dishes, including everything from fried rice to noodles, and the aroma of the sweet-and-sour sauce that accompanied my favourite tempura prawns filled the air. Mmmm.

I started making the rounds, hugging everyone and thanking them for their birthday cards, gifts and best wishes and taking lots of photos along the way. Then Mum, who was looking beautiful as usual in a ruffled gold dress, almost matching the golden highlights scattered through her long brown hair, which she'd pulled into a chic bun for the occasion, shouted from the kitchen:

'Dinner's ready! Everyone at the table now, please. And don't worry, Soph,' she added reassuringly, 'I've checked all the glasses and washed them twice, so they're perfectly clean.' *My mother knows me so well.*

I took my normal seat at the end of the table. The others filtered in at a steady pace. It would be a little more cosy than usual, as we didn't normally have nine people eating at one time, so a few extra chairs had been added to fit everyone in.

After taking some pics of the spread, I started helping myself to the food, piling everything sky-high onto my plate. As the guest of honour, surely I had the perfect excuse to eat like a pig.

On the whole, I'm a very healthy eater. My diet in general consists of eating lots of oily fish like sea bass as well as seafood (especially prawns) and chicken, with lots of vegetables, salad and typically potatoes, brown rice and occasionally pasta. For a weekend treat, cake is definitely my vice.

There are a few things I'm not so keen on, though. I don't really like cheese (unless it's melted on a pizza, of course). I like eggs, but only the egg white—not the yolk. Eggs in cake and ice cream, etc., are obviously fine. I don't really do red meat often either, so I generally steer clear of burgers, sausages and pork. Although an occasional bacon sandwich is okay. I like salmon, but only sometimes…

Thinking about it, there wasn't much logic to my food preferences. Some might call it fussy, but that's just me. I like what I like, and my friends and family are just used to it. My mum had definitely come up trumps tonight with prawns cooked in multiple ways, plus some lovely chicken, rice and noodle dishes. I couldn't wait to get stuck in.

I'd barely sat down and thanked everyone for coming before the interrogation started.

'So, Sophia,' said my mother, resting her hand underneath her chin. 'How's it all going on the man front?' Oh no, not again. I already didn't like the direction of this line of questioning…

'Umm,' I said, trying to keep my cool. 'Well, it's not really, Mum. As you know, I've only just broken up with Rich.'

'Come along, darling,' she scoffed. 'That was what, three months ago?' she added as if twelve weeks was more than enough time to get over a long-term boyfriend.

'Remember, you're thirty-nine now. There's no time to lose if you want to find a man. It's not going to be easy, so don't waste time getting back on the horse. *Especially* if you're still even contemplating kids—although, it's probably too late for that now.'

'That's exactly what I've been trying to tell her, Gloria!' said Monique, jumping in. 'Honey, take it from a fifty-four-year-old single woman like me. The older you are, the harder it becomes, and you're not getting any younger, sweetie. You need to start pushing out some babies.'

And so the kidterrogation began. *Again*. For fuck's sake!

'Come on, ladies,' Dad chipped in as if he'd heard me screaming in my head. 'I'm sure Soph will be just fine.'

My father was always very protective. The most affectionate of my parents, he never tired of saying how proud he was of me. I was the first person in his family to go to university and the only one to run their own business. Before he'd retired, his office, where he'd been a foreman for a building company for forty-five years, had been a bit of a shrine. He'd collected dozens of articles on me, like the one from the Sunday *Times* business section and displayed them on his walls. In his eyes I could do no wrong, so he was going to be firmly in my corner for this debate.

'Pfft!' fired back Monique. 'That's a typical male response! It's okay for *men*. They have no biological clock. Look at Ronnie Wood, Mick Jagger and all those other horny old men still shamelessly getting girls knocked up in their sixties and seventies. Sophia, trust me, girl. You need to find you a man fast and get reproducing.'

'Seriously, guys,' I huffed. It had been bad enough being quizzed by Fertility Felicity at Paul's party. 'Give me a break. It's my birthday, for goodness' sake. I wish everyone would stop bloody quizzing me about my love life, or lack thereof, and the status of my ovaries. Even if you *are* right, it's not that easy. I can't just step out on to the street and grab the first man and ask him to impregnate me. Well, not without getting arrested for harassment, anyway.'

'Listen,' replied Monique, running her fingers through her vibrant hair. 'I'm not saying it's a walk in the park. But, honey, you're a successful businesswoman. You're used to making shit happen. Pulling rabbits out of a hat. This will be child's play in comparison.'

'Oh, you think so, do you?' I replied, curious to hear the magical solution that she was going to propose that would result in the imaginary Mr Perfect knocking down my door.

'You've got to stop waiting around and approach this like a new business campaign. If it was work, how would you deal with this? You'd put together your credentials and a proposal, and you'd draw up a list of potential targets from searching online, speaking to different contacts in the industry or getting out there to research the hottest brands. So do the same for your personal life.'

'That's a great way of looking at it, Monique,' said Roxy in agreement.

'Thanks, Rox. So, Soph, here's what I suggest: first of all, look hot at all times, which should not be a problem for you as you're always immaculate. But remember, it's not just about looking smart. We're dealing with red-blooded men here, so turn up the sex appeal too. For example, I am L-O-V-I-N-G that dress you're wearing tonight.'

'Thank you,' I replied whilst awaiting the next tip from her *How to Magic Up a Perfect Man* manual.

'Secondly, join dating sites,' she suggested. 'I always tell my friends to do this if only for practice getting back into the dating world again. Network like you would for work, get friends and family and ask them to set you up on dates. This cookery holiday you're going on tomorrow is a good start. But you need to join clubs, do activities and meet new people. You've got to put yourself out there and go and get yours!'

She wasn't entirely wrong. I could see there was potentially some mileage in what she was saying. But I still wasn't convinced it was that easy.

'Yes, Monique,' I replied, still considering her suggestions. 'Roxy's already given me the lecture about going on to dating sites, so I'll look into it, but even if I were to meet someone, it'd still take years to get to know them properly, and by that time I'd be too old to have children anyway.'

'Hell no!' she fired back. 'The older you get, the quicker things can happen. We know what we want and are more confident, so we just go for it. My friend Arianna was forty-three. She met a lawyer one afternoon, and a year later she was pregnant and married. I'm *telling* you, girl! It *can* happen. But not if you're sat on your butt at home, watching Netflix with a tub of Häagen-Dazs every night.'

How did she know I'd been doing that?

'See, Soph!' said Roxy. 'Like I keep saying at our FTAs, it's all about getting some experience. You've been out of the game for a while, so you need to practice flirting with guys. Kissing them. Honing your bedroom technique. It's been soooo long you need to check that everything's still working downstairs.'

Whilst Roxy was giggling, in contrast, Jasmine's cute face was now contorting as she held her hands against her ears, squashing her curly black hair against her flawless skin.

'La, la, la, laaaa!' Jasmine screeched. 'This conversation is getting *waaaay* too cringe for me. I do *not* need to be listening to you guys talking about my auntie getting some action.' She got up from the table and pulled her phone out of her pocket. 'I'll be in the living room... eeeeurrrgh. Gross!'

'As I was saying,' Roxy added, rolling her eyes at Jasmine's reaction and sudden departure, 'I know you say you need more time to get over Rich, but the trick is just to do *something*. Get yourself off the starting block. Find someone to flirt with, snog their face off and see where it goes. He doesn't have to be perfect, Mr Right or the love of your life. Just find someone you like the look of and stick your tongue down their throat, goddammit. It'll be fun. And it will get you on the pitch again. If you're not on the pitch, Soph, you can't score. Simples.'

Who knew Roxy was into football? It was an interesting analogy.

Whilst my dad's eyes were fixated on his plate to avoid showing his feelings of awkwardness, my mum's jaw was on the floor. Bella and I had been friends since college, so she was already considered part of the family. I'd only known Roxy for just over a year and Monique just shy of that, so my parents hadn't had that much contact with them, and they were obviously taken aback by their frankness. Particularly Mum, who was a bit more, how can we say? Traditional. She certainly wasn't one for 'sexy talk' around the dinner table.

In fact, my whole world was a bit alien to both my parents. They were simple, humble people. Not into flashy things. A car is just to get you from A to B. Clothes were just to keep you warm and protect your modesty, so as long as they looked smart, that was all that mattered. No designer tag required. Work was something you did to pay the bills. For example, up until a couple of years ago, when I'd paid off their mortgage so that my parents could retire early, Mum had worked as an office manager at a local insurance firm for decades. When we were growing up, she also took on various extra jobs, including bar work at weekends and childminding, just to make ends meet.

To my parents, the most important thing was family. And that's why my mum often struggled to understand why I had been so career-driven and not settled down properly years ago.

'Well, erm, I guess everyone has their own way of putting things,' said Mum tactfully in response to Roxy's 'scoring' suggestion, 'but essentially, darling, I think we all agree that it's time that you started courting again.'

'I think Soph is making good progress, actually,' said Bella supportively. 'It's only been just over three months since the sad passing of Albert, and she's dealt with that and taken the brave step of breaking up with a long-term boyfriend of fifteen years, which can't have been easy. She's having a super busy time at work, and we all know how terrible she is at taking time off, but she's actually going on holiday tomorrow by herself to stay with a group of strangers. How many of us have done that? She's taking some big steps. Soph's really trying, and I think it will lead to some exciting adventures.'

'Thank you, Bella!' I said, blowing her a kiss.

'It's true,' chipped in Harrison. Christ. It seemed *everyone* has something to say about my sad love life. I helped myself to some more prawns and took a large gulp of champagne.

'She wouldn't normally consider going away at such a busy time, but I think this break will do Soph good. That's if she doesn't spend the entire time checking emails, of course!' Harrison added, laughing loudly.

'Girl, switch that phone off as soon as you get on the plane and go and find yourself some hot Italian ass!' shouted Monique.

Oh dear God.

With that, I think my mother was about to faint. I had a feeling when I got back from this holiday, she'd be quizzing me not just on developments with my love life, but also on my choice of new friends.

After singing "Happy Birthday," cutting the red velvet birthday cake, toasting my thirty-ninth year with copious amounts of bubbly and taking even more group photos on my phone, I headed home to finish packing and prepare for my 7.30 a.m. flight.

Before I left, Mum pulled me to one side and handed me a large paper gift bag filled with some casual clothes she'd picked out for me. She knew I had a room full of clothes already, but she always tried to encourage me to loosen up with my dress sense.

'For once, Soph,' she'd said, taking my hands into hers, 'try to relax. Forget about your Gukey this and your

Dolce and Banana that. Just be like the *old* you. The you *before* you became successful and went all fancy. This is a *holiday*. A chance to forget about work for a few days. Switch off that bloody phone and go and enjoy yourself for a change.'

Gukey and *Dolce and Banana*... Typical Mum. Zero interest in designer names or their pronunciation. I thanked her for the birthday gifts, gave her a kiss on the cheek and promised to do my best.

I unzipped my suitcase and flipped up the lid, glancing over what I'd packed so far.

There was a lot of overly fancy stuff. Maybe Mum had a point. We were going to be cooking most days and staying in the villa, so that red Gucci skirt was probably not going to be appropriate.

I took everything out of the suitcase. Time for a rethink. *Let's think casual and simple*. I reached into the bag Mum had given me. There were leggings, some comfortable-looking cotton tops/mini dresses—all from the high street. Okay, I'd pop those into a *plain* black case. Not this Louis Vuitton one. I went to the 'casual' section in my dressing room and pulled out some jeans that only had a subtle logo at the back and a few plain tops.

The organisers had said that sometimes people liked to dress up in the evening for dinner, but maybe Mum was right. Maybe I could allow myself a few days to be 'off-duty'. I always had to wear fancy clothes for work and have my hair, nails and make-up and everything looking immaculate. For once, maybe I could just relax.

Think about it. I was going away with strangers. They wouldn't know anything about me or what I did for a living and wouldn't have any expectations. I didn't need to impress anyone. I could start afresh. This was the perfect opportunity to just 'be'. Return a little bit to the old me.

Before I'd started going out with Rich, I'd looked very different. It was the pre-ghd, keratin treatment era, so my thick, curly hair hadn't been as smooth as it was now, and my dress sense was very simple. I wasn't into fancy stuff at all. Even when we were at college, he'd always worn expensive clothes. So when we had begun dating, little by little I'd started getting sucked into that world. And of course, once I got into beauty PR, it was all about glamour and projecting the 'right' image, so wearing designer clothes became the norm. It was expected. It signified 'success'. I knew that so many clients said how much they loved my handbags purely because of the designer logo they'd spotted or had gushed about my shoes because the trademark red soles.

I looked down at my toes before I stepped into the shower. Bloody hell. It seemed I'd already started to relax my grooming regime before my mum had suggested I do so. They hadn't been painted for two weeks. *Very* unlike me, but I'd been so busy focusing on getting through everything before I went away that perhaps I'd let a couple of things slide.

I glanced further up my body. It would seem that my lack of grooming had also extended to my nether regions. Whilst my legs and underarms had been lasered and were fine, I hadn't waxed my bikini line since last month either, which was unheard of, and it was starting to look like an overgrown jungle down there. To be honest, it hadn't been top of my to-do list. After all, what was the point? No one but my dressing room mirror was going to see me naked, so on a scale of one to ten in terms of priorities, it ranked around minus twenty. I was meant to get a mani-pedi done that afternoon after my blow-dry, but then I'd had an unexpected conference call, so I'd had to cancel, and I didn't have the energy to sit here at 1 a.m. painting my nails when my taxi would be here to collect me in two and a half hours so I could get to Gatwick Airport nice and early. We'd be kneading dough and making pasta. The last thing I'd want is chipped bits of polish getting mixed into the flour. For once, naked nails seemed like the best option.

Yes. I was going to take my mum's advice and go to this holiday and relax. No flashy overtly designer clothes. No one-hour-plus make-up-and-hair regime. No airs or graces. I was going to chill out and be the me I'd secretly wanted to be for ages. A bit more laid-back and free.

I didn't quite know whether I could loosen up and let go, how I would cope for four days without my ghds, or if I was going to get on with a group of complete strangers, but I was certainly going to give it a bloody good try.

CHAPTER SEVEN

Well, this is weird.

Here I was sat on this British Airways plane all on my own. Even when I travelled for work, I'd have someone with me—Harrison, Robyn or a group of journalists. So the idea of flying solo today was definitely pushing me out of my comfort zone.

The reality of the trip was starting to dawn on me. I was on a plane by myself. I would be staying in accommodation that wasn't five-star, with a group of three other strangers that I'd never spoken to or met in my life. And I had to live with them for four whole days.

What if we didn't get on? What would we even talk about? What if I just wanted to sit in silence, but I had to listen to them droning on about some mind-numbing subject I had no interest in, or I was forced to engage in dull small talk?

Come on. Think positively. If I just approached it in the same way I would attending a networking event, I'd be fine. Then again, after being in the industry for so long, it was rare for me not to know most people at one of our dos or not to have things in common with them, so this wasn't quite the same…

Where's that drinks trolley? Do you think they'll serve G&T on a 7.30 a.m. flight?

IT WAS NOW 11 A.M., and I'd landed safely in Pisa. Our driver would apparently be meeting us here at the arrivals gate at 11.30 a.m. local time as we were all arriving on different flights but would be collected together and then taken to our villa.

As I stood against the back wall opposite the airport exit/entrance doors, I felt a flutter of butterflies in my stomach. I'd never been on a blind date before, but I was guessing it felt a lot like this.

I scanned the people around me, wondering whether anyone else here would be living with me for the next four days. I stared at a slim blonde lady. *Is it you?* Then a tall man with short wavy hair. *Are you staying with me?* Was it that couple over there by the leather shop? This was driving me crazy. I wasn't used to not being in control.

Actually, was I even in the right place? They did say arrivals, didn't they, and not outside? I fished the paper-work out of my plain black canvas bag and read over the meeting instructions:

Itinerary
Saturday 9th April
Benvenuti! Welcome to Tuscany!

Our transfer driver will meet you in arrivals at Pisa Airport at 11.30 a.m. As we have guests arriving from different flights, a transfer at 12.30 will allow everyone to be transferred together. Our driver will be holding a sign that says 'Taste Holidays'.

Good. I was in the right place, then. I just needed to look out for the guy with the sign.

I did another scan of the area. *Oooh, hello. I hope you are coming to live with me…*

Stood near the exit was a hot guy with beautiful olive skin, dark hair and the cutest, tightest little bum (well *of course* I was watching him as he turned around). I wouldn't be averse to the idea of *him* being one of my fellow housemates. Nor would I object to indulging in a wild holiday romance with such a fine specimen. Mm-mmm.

Reality check. I couldn't see any luggage with him, and he looked Italian, so doubtful he'd be coming on a cookery holiday when he could just learn from his mama.

Aaaaargggh. I just wanted to know where everyone was! Well, depended on *who* they were of course. These butterflies were still there, and now I was hot. As well as my dark blue jeans and white Converse, I had on a rose-pink cashmere jumper. It wasn't particularly warm, hence why I'd thought knitwear would be appropriate, but now I was thinking I should have worn a thinner coat, like my Burberry trench. Then again, the trademark checked lining would be instantly recognisable as designer, and I didn't want to look flashy. This dark grey wool Armani coat was much more subtle.

It was 11.29 a.m. One minute away from the official meeting time. *Is everyone here? The suspense is too much…*

Ha-ha! It was 12 p.m., and the cute guy that I hoped

would be one of my housemates was actually our driver. He just held up the 'Taste Holidays' sign. Half an hour late in doing so, I might add. Didn't he realise that there was a control freak in the building, desperate to know who she was going to be living with? The guy with the wavy hair was also part of the group, I reckoned, as he looked like he was heading over to the driver now. Well, at least that's one person I knew was coming.

Next, I spotted a cool woman who I guessed was in her early sixties, with a trendy silver bob and vibrant green jeans, heading over to the meeting point. She looked lovely.

You know what? Screw all this worrying. Remember MAP point number 7? I'd promised that I would embrace things. So that's exactly what I was going to do. Whoever the guests were, whatever they were like, I was just going to make the most of this trip.

I headed over to the group and as I did, a second lady with striking green eyes and longish blonde hair joined us, completing our foursome.

Mr Cute Bum (he told us his name, but I was too busy ogling to remember) signalled to us to follow him to the people carrier. He might look divine, but he seemed a little moody. Oh well. No holiday romance for me this time.

I climbed into the back seat right in the corner, and the others followed behind me. Time to get my PR networking hat on and embrace the situation.

'Hi, everyone,' I said warmly. 'I'm Sophia, lovely to meet you.'

Introductions swiftly followed. There was Grace, the cool-looking lady with the stunning grey hair, who was sixty-five and from Australia; Francesca from Berkshire, a nurse and happily married mother of two sons, one who was a teacher, and the other was travelling around Asia, who'd booked the trip to celebrate her forty-ninth birthday. Then the honorary male was Daniel, an engineer from Kent who would also be celebrating his forty-first birthday during the trip.

From the second we started talking, it was clear that I had been worrying for no reason. They all seemed adorable. We chatted so much that the journey time to the villa flew by. Before we knew it, we were surrounded by beautiful vineyards, admiring the expansive grounds of the place we'd be calling home for the next four days.

As we made our way out of the people carrier, our host, Erica, a cheery Italian brunette in her early thirties, greeted us and led us to the doorway.

Holy fuck! Who was *that*?

'Everyone, meet Lorenzo,' said Erica. 'Lorenzo will be your chef during your holiday and will be teaching you lots of delicious authentic Tuscan dishes.'

It took every ounce of energy I had to stop my eyes flying out of their sockets and straight into his gorgeous face.

He is a vision.

You know that saying, tall, dark and handsome? Well, he was that personified. He was a Tuscan dish I'd definitely like to sample. Six foot two, dark unruly (in a sexy way) hair, beautiful thick beard you just wanted to stroke, a killer smile and deep, deep come-to-bed eyes you could get lost in for hours. Luckily, I caught myself swooning just before it was about to get awkward.

He flashed me a warm smile.

Jesus, Mary and Joseph. I think I'm about to wet my knickers.

Sorry. TMI.

'Ni–nice to meet you, Lorenzo,' I stammered embarrassingly as I walked through into the dining room, desperately trying to keep my composure.

I couldn't help it. I started grinning from ear to ear like a bloody teenager. Monique had bluntly said I needed to find myself some hot Italian arse…*I think I just did.*

I was only a couple of hours into my holiday, but I already had a feeling I was going to enjoy it immensely.

CHAPTER EIGHT

Snooker, darts, golf. Snooker, darts, golf. Snooker, darts, golf…

I was reciting the most boring sports over and over in my head so I could try and take my mind off the Italian god who was now sitting directly opposite me in the living room of this stunning Tuscan villa. He looked hot in his fitted black chef's jacket and blue jeans. Good Lord. Even thinking about sleep-inducing sports couldn't stop the tingles that were racing through my body right now.

Katherine from Taste Holidays had, in my opinion, dramatically undersold the beauty of this place. The pictures on the website and in the brochure must be years out of date, as contrary to the old-fashioned décor and furniture that was in those photos, this place was airy, welcoming and beautifully maintained.

The rooms were spacious, with wooden beams going across the ceiling; there were lovely ceramic tiles adorning the floors, bright white walls, and the views—oh my goodness. From every window there were endless acres of vineyards, olive groves, woodlands and rolling lush green hills. It was breathtaking.

Much like this Italian stallion Lorenzo.

Francesca, Grace and Daniel were also seated on the sofa, and whilst we waited for Erica to return from the kitchen, we started chatting amongst ourselves.

Erica bounded into the room, skilfully clutching six champagne flutes, which she laid on the coffee table in the centre before returning to the kitchen and coming back armed with two bottles of prosecco.

Her short brown hair was tucked neatly behind her ears. She wasn't wearing a scrap of make-up, but her olive skin still glowed.

'So, everybody,' said Erica smiling warmly. 'Welcome to Taste Holidays. We are delighted to have you here with us. I hope you all love this beautiful villa that will be your home for four days and that you are ready to learn how to cook lots of delicious Italian dishes.'

She popped open the bottles and poured a generous amount of prosecco into each of our glasses.

'*Saluti!*' she said, raising her glass in the air. 'To a fantastic holiday, great food, great wine and great company.'

'Hear, hear!' added Daniel enthusiastically as he also raised his glass.

I picked up mine. *Oh shit. It's dirty.* My annoying cleanliness OCD was kicking in again.

If I was at a restaurant, I could just ask for another one. But this was different. I clinked my glass with everyone and put on my best forced smile whilst I worked out my next move. I had to live with these people for almost a week. If I started getting all weird now and asking for another glass, they'd think I'm a diva and it would dampen the mood of the holiday, which I didn't want. Once again I reminded myself of point number 7 and what I'd said at the airport. I would embrace *everything*. That meant all my tics, OCD and fussiness needed to stop here.

I rotated the flute so that the 'dirty' bit was on the opposite side and swiftly took a large sip before I changed my mind. *Mmm. That tastes so good.* Well, what do you know? I'd drunk from a dirty glass and I was still alive. Progress.

Erica sat down next to Lorenzo.

Oh.

Hold on. How did I not notice this before? They must be a couple or married or something, as she was sitting very close to him (don't bloody blame her) and she just touched his leg. Silly me, thinking a hot guy like him would be single. They weren't wearing rings, but maybe they took them off to cook? *There goes another hot Italian arse fantasy.*

'So, in a moment, I will show you to your rooms and give you some time to settle in,' explained Erica. 'There are four bedrooms in this building. One next to the kitchen and three upstairs. Lorenzo and I will stay in the building opposite this.'

See. Knew it. They're definitely together.

'Oh?' exclaimed Francesca a little too loudly. 'So you guys are together, then?' *Francesca, you goddess. You totally read my mind.* I'd wanted to ask but would never have done it so brazenly.

'No, no, it is not like that,' said Lorenzo emphatically in his sexy Italian accent.

Wait. I think he just said they're not together, didn't he?

Praise the Lord. Prosecco all round.

'No, we are just friends,' Erica added. I couldn't help but think that she wasn't entirely happy with the whole 'friends' thing, and who would be with a guy like that?

'We have known each other for a long time and worked together for Taste Holidays for several years. We are like…like, brother and sister,' said Erica, bowing her head.

Hmmm. I think there's more to this story than meets the eye…

And just like that, Francesca and I both glanced at each other with a sly *yeah, yeah, whatever you say* look. We were thinking the same thing. Could this be a classic case of unrequited love?

Keen to change the subject, Erica continued. 'After you have settled into your rooms, in half an hour, we will have a lunch that Lorenzo has prepared for us in the dining room. Then at four p.m., you will have your first cookery lesson.'

Gosh. Her English was very good. Just as well, really, as 'prosecco', 'Prada' and 'Armani' pretty much covered the extent of my Italian vocabulary.

'Sophia, we start with you? Let me take you up to show you the rooms,' said Erica. Oh, how I wished it was Lorenzo who was suggesting that to me…

As I lifted the handle of my suitcase to wheel it along, I wondered if Katherine's assistant had passed on my request to be given the best room. I knew it was bad of me, but I couldn't resist calling ahead a few days ago to ask if, given my fussiness and penchant for all things five-star, they could do that for me. Katherine had been 'unavailable' (probably exhausted by my constant questions), so her assistant, Alison, reassured me that it would be taken care of.

To be honest, though, as I walked through the hallway and up the wooden staircase, I could see that I had worried needlessly. This place was amazing.

'So, as you are first upstairs, you get first choice of the rooms,' said Erica.

I did a mini mental fist pump as I strolled down the corridor, peering in each of the three bedrooms. Katherine was right. All of them were equally beautiful.

The room at the end of the hall had a bath as well as a shower, green décor and a view of the outdoor pool, which had been covered over until it warmed up for summer. The next one along had a shower room, its own mini corridor and blue décor. Then the room nearest the staircase had a lovely shower room, wonderful views and a yellow theme. *This is the one*. To me, yellow equals sunshine and happiness. I'd found my little sanctuary.

'I'd love this one, please, Erica,' I said, positioning my suitcase in front of the pine wardrobe. 'Thank you.'

'*Prego*,' she replied, smiling.

I'm guessing that means you're welcome?

Erica headed back downstairs to show the others to their rooms. I overheard Francesca and Daniel looking around next door, which meant Grace must have opted for the fourth bedroom downstairs.

After I'd WhatsApped everyone to let them know I'd arrived safely, it was time to go back down. Thank goodness it was a Saturday. It meant that at least I wouldn't have to worry so much about checking emails. I was determined not to even glance at my inbox until Monday lunchtime. *Okay, let's not run before we can walk. Let's say 11 a.m. on Monday, which would be 10 a.m. UK time. Perfectly acceptable.*

Grace was already seated at the dining table with Erica when I arrived. Francesca and Daniel swiftly followed, as did Lorenzo, who put one final platter on the table and sat down next to me.

Snooker, darts, golf. Snooker, darts, golf…

Half of my mind was doing the running man over-whelmed with joy, whereas the other half was thinking, Shit. I am not going to be able to concentrate, never mind steer a fork of food in my mouth with him sitting next to me. Just look at those solid thighs. I slyly scanned his body whilst he was chatting to Grace, who was seated to his right. *Ooh, I would love to get my hands on those.*

Snooker, darts, golf. Snooker, darts, golf…

I don't think this is working.

I was beginning to regret my decision to be carefree by not bringing a case full of make-up, painting my nails and styling my hair meticulously as I normally would. I wasn't wearing any eyeliner or mascara, and rather than my normal foundation, which gave me full coverage, I was only wearing a light tinted moisturiser. And as for my hair, although I'd had it freshly blow-dried for my birthday yesterday, as I was going for comfort, today I had thrown it into a ponytail, something I only ever did when I was at the gym or at home where no one would see me.

In short, after taking my mum's comments on board, today I was a million miles away from my normal on duty, flawless *just in case I bump into someone* look, and I admit, I was so used to my routine that being practically bare-faced made me feel a bit exposed.

I had contemplated using the half an hour before lunch

to top up my make-up, give myself an emergency coat of quick-dry nail polish that I'd put in my bag at the last minute and attempt to smooth my hair down with my hairdryer. But then I thought, that would be *so* obvious. Everyone would realise straight away that I was trying to impress the hottest guy in Italy (not that I'd seen all of the guys in Italy, but this one must be on the podium and in the running to win gold, silver or bronze). Plus, I reminded myself that I needed to relax a bit more and start to feel as confident without make-up and all my beauty bells and whistles as I did with them.

I surveyed the table. Oh dear. If my birthday dinner last night was food heaven, then this was surely close to food hell. There were two types of salami (I hate salami with a passion). Chicken liver pâté (I hate pâté and I really, *really* hate anything to do with liver) and all different types of cheese. Yep. Unless it's melted mozzarella on a pizza, I hate cheese too.

Not a problem. This was the *new* me. I'd drunk from a dirty glass and if I could do that, I could do anything. As much as I detested literally everything on the table, I was going to give it a try. After all, I'd watched enough episodes of *Come Dine with Me* to know how much fellow diners will take an instant dislike to people who whinge about not eating this or that without even having the courtesy to try the food first. So, with much trepidation, I loaded my plate with a bit of everything on the table and got stuck in.

Mmm. I was pleasantly surprised. The salami was actually really nice. Nothing like what I'd tried in the UK. The cheese was lovely, and the pâté…well, I wasn't in love with it, but at least I'd given it a go.

I was proud of myself. And despite the nerves that came from sitting next to Lorenzo without my hair and make-up looking flawless, I didn't drop any food on my clothes or dribble pathetically when he caught my eye. More progress.

In around one hour's time, we would be starting our first cookery lesson. Which would mean spending more time in close proximity to lush Lorenzo. How the hell was I going to keep my cool?

Snooker, darts, golf. Snooker, darts, golf...

Forget having a disco nap when I get to my room. Looks like I had sixty minutes to find a phrase to prevent me from fantasizing about him that will actually bloody work!

CHAPTER NINE

W *ell, this looks very official, doesn't it?* I stood at
the doorway of the dining room, which had been
transformed into a mini cookery school.

Four individual cooking 'stations' had been created on
the table. Each one had a large wooden chopping board, a
red plastic chopping board and cream branded Taste Holidays apron on top, plus a big silver chopping knife to the
right-hand side.

Then, in the middle of the table, a selection of ingredients including eggs, sugar, chopped tomatoes, sponge
fingers, flour and different vegetables had been neatly laid
out. There were also silver mixing bowls, a whisk and
various other cooking paraphernalia. I was excited to find
out what we would be making.

We all took our places, standing at individual stations. I
opted for the bottom end of the table.

Moments later, in walked Lorenzo, which surely must
mean 'god of chefs' in Italian (completely shallow obser-

vation, considering I hadn't actually tasted his cooking—the few slices of salami and cheese we'd had earlier hardly qualified). Either way, I'd decided his sexiness alone earned him godlike status.

'So, this afternoon, we will be making classic tiramisu, and also we make de tagliatelle al ragu. Okay?' he asked, looking at us one by one for confirmation. '*Bene*. We start with tiramisu. I need one of you to separate six eggs and put the yolks into the bowl.'

'I'll do it!' Daniel volunteered excitedly.

'*Bene*. After, you will add nine tablespoons of sugar,' said the god of chefs in his sexy Italian accent as he passed the bag to Daniel.

Lorenzo talked us through each of the steps, and we divvied up the tasks. I was responsible for soaking the sponge fingers into the coffee and marsala liqueur mixture that Francesca had created. I layered the soaked biscuits in the baking tray, then covered them with the mascarpone cheese and egg white mixture Grace and Daniel had whipped up.

'No, not like that,' said Lorenzo as he looked over at the tray, disappointment clear in his voice. 'Too thick, too much.'

Great. I never claimed to be Jamie Oliver, but I thought I would at least be capable of spreading cream over some biscuits. Evidently not.

'Is that better?' I said, seeking confirmation after scraping off a thin layer and transferring it back to the cream bowl.

'Is a little better,' he muttered, barely looking me in the eye. 'Continue.' I admit I was finding this a little difficult. I was used to leading my team and giving other people feedback about their work, not the other way around. And when I did receive comments from clients, they were almost always positive.

Earlier he'd hailed Grace's whipping as *buonissimo*, Francesca's mixture was *perfetto*, and now my layering and spreading was basically *shitto* (I didn't know the Italian for shit yet, but seeing as everything seemed to end in an 'o' over here, I figured it was bound to be something like that).

I carried on with my biscuit-then-cream layers until they were all used up. I then smoothed the surface neatly and dusted the top with cocoa powder as instructed. I thought it looked pretty good, even if I did say so myself.

Lorenzo looked at it and grunted.

'So now, I will put this in the fridge for a few hours and we eat for dessert later.' Well, I was guessing that's the closest I was going to get to an approval from him, then, if he was taking it from the table to chill.

'Next we make ribs with olives, and then tagliatelle al ragu,' he said as he took the tiramisu dish into the kitchen.

I'd always wanted to know how to make my own pasta, so moody Italian chef or not, I was determined to enjoy learning this.

Once we'd prepared the ribs, which involved veg and herb chopping ready for Erica to brown, then add to the meat with the wine, tomatoes and olives, we got cracking with the ragu. This called for yet more chopping. Each of us opted for different vegetables. I went for carrots.

'Finer, finer,' instructed Lorenzo.

Oh, for goodness' sake. First I couldn't spread cream, now I couldn't chop. Christ.

When he was satisfied that everything was diced finely

enough, it went into a saucepan with cold olive oil. The meat, he told us, would be added later once the veg had been fried slowly, and then we'd add red wine, tomatoes and salt and pepper. So whilst that was doing its thing, it was on to make the pasta.

We tossed the flour from the bag out on the wooden board, made a well and carefully added the eggs into the middle.

He then told us to gently mix them together to form a dough, but according to Lorenzo, mine wasn't smooth enough. He took my dough and worked on it himself.

'Here,' he said, patting the dough he'd perfected. 'This is better.'

Well, clearly! You've done this a billion times, whereas I am a home-made pasta virgin.

He was beginning to irritate me. Was mine *really* that different to everyone else's?

Next we had to roll it out with the rolling pin. This was hard work, but like with everything I do, I gave it my best shot.

'*Bene*, Grace,' he said, flashing her a giant smile.

Oh, here we go. He's making the rounds. Once again, he had nothing but praise for the others. As he arrived at the foot of the table to view my efforts, I braced myself for more criticism.

'Thinner, thinner. Keep rolling. Dough must be thin so you can see through it.'

Grrrrr. Am I that crap?

Okay, chill, Soph. Stop taking it personally. He's trying to help you. Just try a bit harder.

I carried on whilst the others progressed to the next

stage of rolling the dough, then cutting it into tagliatelle strips.

Eventually I caught up, but again it seemed like my strips were a little too wide or too thick. What was wrong with me today? I just couldn't seem to do anything right.

We put all of our tagliatelle efforts into one large bowl, and off it went with Lorenzo to the kitchen next door. The old me would have worried about the fact that so many people had been handling the pasta and wondered how well everyone had washed their hands. But I was determined to be strong and continue to try and shake off my uptightness and cleanliness OCD.

I glanced at my watch. Wow—it was nearly 8 p.m. We'd been cooking for at least three hours.

'That was fun!' said Daniel.

'Yeah, it was, but easy for you to say, Daniel. You took to it like a duck to water,' I said, still feeling disappointed that I hadn't performed better.

'Well, I do all the cooking at home, so I get a lot of practice. Oh, and call me Dan. We're all mates here!'

'So, apparently dinner will be ready around eight forty-five,' said Grace. 'Dan, I know you need to call your wife, so would you ladies like to go for a little walk around the grounds whilst it's still light?'

'Love to!' replied Francesca.

'Count me in too,' I added. 'Let me just run upstairs and grab a shawl.'

The grounds were even more beautiful than they'd appeared from the window. I couldn't resist snapping another dozen photos on my phone. As we disappeared into the walkways, which were alongside the rows upon rows of olive trees, the air felt deliciously fresh. I took a deep breath and I swear I could feel my lungs expanding. This was a million miles away from the smog-and-pollution-filled surroundings I encountered in London every day.

We all took it in turns to talk about how we had come to find ourselves here.

Sadly, Grace had been recently widowed. She had been married for forty-five years to Robert, who sounded like he was the most adorable husband and father a woman could have asked for. For the past four months, she had been visiting her daughter in Cambridge and helping her look after her three grandchildren whilst her son-in-law was working overseas. Her daughter had suggested this as a well-deserved getaway to give Grace a break from the cooking, cleaning and babysitting she'd been doing for them.

Fran, as she told us she'd preferred to be called, was a relative newlywed who had married the love of her life, Andy, just nineteen months ago. Having spent twenty-three years being a doting wife to her first husband, Nigel, once her kids had gone to uni, she realised she no longer had anything in common with him and that she'd lost her identity. So Fran had got a job and saved up for a few years. By the time she was forty-four, she had enough to be independent and left her husband to start her new chapter. Five years on from taking the leap, she couldn't be happier.

I told them all about my break-up with Rich, and they both nodded sympathetically.

'So now, like it was for me, it's your time to discover the new you, then,' said Fran.

'Yeah. I'm not expecting it to be easy, but now that I've got my head around becoming single again, I'm up for the challenge,' I replied.

'Good for you, girl! That's the spirit,' said Grace.

'Have you thought about what you want now?' Fran asked. 'Another relationship? Kids?'

'Well, I'm ready to meet someone. But nothing too serious to begin with. I feel like after coming out of such a long relationship, I need to have a bit more time to rediscover myself,' I said, reflecting. 'I want to start by having some fun. I'd love to have kids, although I'm not even sure if doing that naturally is still an option, with my age and everything,' I added, doubt evident in my voice.

'Yeah, that's true,' said Fran bluntly. Not exactly what I wanted to hear, but as she was a nurse, perhaps she might know more about whether these things were possible.

'Yes,' I said, now feeling even more certain of what I wanted. 'I'd like to start dating. Or maybe not even date as such. I haven't been intimate with anyone for a while, so perhaps a passionate snog or even more would be nice for starters, and then I'll just see how it goes. My friends keep lecturing me about how I need to get out there, flirt, practise and all that stuff. They keep trying to get me on those dating sites too,' I said, rolling my eyes.

'Oh, I don't envy you youngsters with all that Tittering you all have to do these days,' said Grace, grimacing.

Fran and I let out a little chuckle. We weren't sure whether she was referring to Tinder or Twitter. Either way it was funny.

'This walk has been wonderful,' said Fran enthusiastically. 'Such breathtaking views and wonderful company. I'm relieved everyone here is so lovely! I was terrified about it, and my son and husband have been messaging me constantly all afternoon, dying to know what each of you are like. We'll have to take some pictures at dinner to send to them.'

'I thought I was the only one who was a little nervous,' I said. 'I was convinced everyone would be boring and we'd need to force the conversation, but I feel so relaxed. It's as if we've known each other for years.'

'Exactly!' added Grace. 'When I got to the airport, I was thinking, holy far out! What if they all think I'm too ancient and don't want to speak to some strange old lady from Oz? But you've all been so welcoming,' she said, resting a hand on each of our shoulders.

I chuckled again. 'Holy far out?' I asked. 'I haven't heard that before! I'm guessing that means something like wow? Sorry, my Aussie vocab is limited to what I picked up from watching *Neighbours* and *Home & Away* years ago.'

'That'd be right. Stick with me, Stella,' she said, throwing her head backwards as she laughed. 'I'll teach you all the lingo!'

I didn't worry about reminding her my name was Sophia. She'd already started calling Lorenzo 'Luciano' and Dan 'Nathan', so I figured she just had a thing for renaming everyone.

We headed back to the villa famished and ready to devour the dinner we'd spent ages slaving over. For the first time since we'd arrived, I was starting to dread seeing Lorenzo. What criticism was in store for me this evening? Would he say I wasn't winding the tagliatelle around the fork properly? Or maybe not putting the correct ratio of ragu sauce on the spoon? Either way, I was sure to do something wrong.

What had I done to make him dislike me so much? And more to the point, should I graciously accept it (you can't please all of the people, all of the time) or make an effort to change his mind?

CHAPTER TEN

As my alarm sounded, I stretched my arms up towards the ceiling and exhaled. I'd slept like a baby. No doubt helped by our intense first cooking lesson, not to mention the copious amounts of prosecco we'd enjoyed at dinner.

The tagliatelle and ragu sauce was divine. We were all proud to be eating something that we'd created. Home-made pasta was one thing I'd always wanted to learn, and now I could do it. So far, this trip was proving to be much more fulfilling than my normal hotel breaks.

Things were no better on the Lorenzo front. He hadn't sat next to me last night, choosing to be between Erica and Fran instead. I don't think he uttered a single word to me. I got the hint. I wasn't going to beg for his approval. I'm sure he was used to women falling at his feet, but that just wasn't me.

After a simple breakfast of fruit, yoghurt, bread and a selection of jams, it was time for our next lesson. Today, Lorenzo explained, we'd be making ravioli, a fish dish and something that sounded like it was going to a type of biscotti.

We started with the biscotti, again taking it in turns to do the different steps. Then we moved on to the cod with chopped leeks, and finally, the ravioli. And of course I needed extra assistance after being told that everything I did wasn't quite good enough.

After three hours of cooking, I was looking forward to going for another walk like last night. But surprisingly, lunch was pretty much ready straight away. The biscotti thing had been cooked in the oven ages ago, the cod apparently only needed fifteen minutes on the stove, and the ravioli took no time once it was put in boiling water, so Erica had called us to the table much faster than I'd thought. It was worth the effort. I'd definitely be cooking those dishes again. Well, perhaps everything but the ravioli, unless I felt motivated to dedicate an entire Saturday morning in the kitchen.

Later that afternoon we visited a vineyard nearby for some biodynamic wine-tasting and a tour. As we strolled around the grounds, it was interesting listening to Erica. Fran, ever the conversationalist and expert prober, asked her questions about Lorenzo: Was he single? What was his story? Etc. Once again, all the things I really wanted to know.

'Ah, Lorenzo, what can I say?' Erica said reluctantly. You could tell she wanted to spill but was trying to remain professional. 'Lovely guy, but he has, how you say? Issues...with women. His life, is very complicated right now...' Erica paused as if realising she'd already said too much, then left it at that.

Fran looked at me slyly. She was like a dog with a

bone, I could tell. She would let it go now, but I got the impression that this was a conversation she fully intended to continue at some point in the very near future.

The alcohol combined with our marathon cookery lesson made me feel a little bit tired, so I was quite relieved that we wouldn't have to make dinner this evening and we could just relax instead.

By the time we returned to the villa I was famished.

No way…?

I'm in over my head
I'm out of my depth
I'm head over
I'm head over
I'm head over
I'm head over heels in love with you
I'm head over…

It can't be?

As soon as I stepped inside, I heard the music blaring loudly from the kitchen. I'd recognise those lyrics anywhere. That's 'Head Over Heels' by the Eclectic Detectives!

I peeked my head around the door and saw Lorenzo in front of the stove, strumming an air guitar to the thumping beat whilst belting out the chorus and clearly getting into it.

Wonders will never cease. He was rocking out to one of my favourite bands. If they were a famous, chart-topping group, it would be no big deal, but the Eclectic Detectives, who I'd discovered randomly on Spotify, were relatively new and definitely not well known. Certainly not amongst any of my friends. And yet, here was Lorenzo, the normally surly Italian chef, singing along to every word. Wow.

I pulled my head back, not wishing to disturb his moment. It was nice to see him in good spirits for a change. Music has the same effect on me too. Even if I'm feeling down, it always has a way of making me feel better and taking me to my happy place.

'Lorenzo!' Erica called out as she bounded into the kitchen. 'Why so loud?' she shouted! I then heard them engaging in a heated exchange in Italian, and seconds later, everything fell silent. Shame. I was really enjoying that.

'Dinner we hope will be around eight or eight-fifteen,' announced Erica as she stepped into the living room. 'Is okay with you?' We all nodded in agreement, then I headed upstairs to my room.

I caught up on WhatsApp, sending Roxy and Bella loads of pics of the dishes we'd cooked, which attracted lots of thumbs-up emojis, and after about an hour, I went back downstairs for dinner.

Well, he might be a moody arsehole who had developed a passion for critiquing my cookery skills (which, to be fair, was his job, so really I should stop taking it so personally…), but whilst I'm stating the obvious, he definitely did know how to cook. I tucked into a delicious mushroom risotto that he'd served us, and I could have sworn I'd died and gone to heaven.

I polished it off in no time and was desperate for seconds.

'I have more,' he said as if reading my mind. He picked up the pot on the table and tilted it so that we could see inside. 'Anyone like?'

I stared around the table, politely waiting to see who would take him up on his offer.

'Oh, I couldn't possibly,' said Fran, rubbing her stomach. 'It was lovely, but I'm stuffed, thank you.'

'I wouldn't mind a little more, thank you,' I said. 'It was delicious.' He nodded at me in acknowledgment.

'Go on, then, Luciano. I'll have a few more spoons,' added Grace, giving him a wink.

'Lovely woman!' he exclaimed as he scooped out extra into her empty bowl. 'I love that you like my cooking.' He gave her a warm smile and then squeezed her shoulder.

Er, hello? Favouritism much? Did I not also say I liked his food and that I wanted more? FFS!

As he moved towards my chair, his smiley expression changed to stone and he spooned out an extra portion for me in silence, then returned to his seat on the opposite side of the table.

Wow. What a dickhead.

By the time we were tucking into the panna cotta for dessert, the wine and conversation began to flow. And after a couple of hours had elapsed, you could tell that everyone was feeling much more relaxed, including the surly chef.

Flirty and persistent Fran didn't miss her opportunity to get some goss and went in for the kill.

'So, Lorenzo,' Fran said, smiling cheekily, 'tell me. Is there a special woman or even *women* in your life?'

Go, Fran! Like a female Columbo, once she had her mind set on a line of enquiry, she didn't give up.

Lorenzo started to blush and wriggle in his chair. 'Um, is, it is complicated…'

Come on, Lorenzo. You know that Detective Fran won't accept that *as an answer.*

Like a bulldozer, she continued: 'In what way? Do you have a girlfriend, or *multiple* girlfriends? Have you just broken up with your girlfriend, or are you looking for a girlfriend?' Bless Fran. She was about as subtle as a sledgehammer.

More blushing and chair shuffling ensued. Everyone's eyes were now squarely focused on him, itching to hear his response.

You could tell he wasn't at all comfortable with talking about himself or his love life to a bunch of nosey English people he barely knew. However, sensing correctly that Fran would keep probing until she received an acceptable reply, he relented.

'I am in a...I have been in a relationship a long time, but it is not working. I know things are not right, but it is...difficult.'

'Tell me about it!' screamed Dan. 'Women are just a complete mystery, aren't they!'

'I beg your pardon, Dan. We are very simple creatures,' protested Fran. 'Well, Lorenzo, you're a young man in your prime, so if something isn't working, don't waste your life. Get back out there. I'm sure there'd be women queuing around the block to get a piece of a hot man like you!'

He frowned, not initially understanding what she said, and then as the penny appeared to drop, he blushed.

'*Grazie*, Francesca.'

'*Prego*, Lorenzo. It's a bit like Sophia,' she added slyly.

What? Why is she bringing me into this?

'You know, she's newly single and *totally* gorgeous, so Grace and I were telling her yesterday that she needs to get herself out there more. There's a lot of guys that would *love* to spend an evening with her too.'

'Fran!' I exclaimed. What was she doing? This wasn't bloody *Take Me Out*. Her attempt to matchmake à la Paddy McGuiness made me feel awkward. Particularly when it was so obvious he wasn't remotely interested. It was safe to say that if I was the last woman on earth, he wouldn't even spit on me, never mind snog me.

Seems like I wasn't the only one feeling uncomfortable, as Lorenzo started squirming in his chair again and then jumped up.

'It is getting late,' he said, changing the subject. 'I must go and tidy the kitchen.'

Wow, I hadn't realised that the prospect of spending some sexy time with me would cause him to leave the room so quickly. As much as it shouldn't bother me, no one likes to be considered undesirable, which is exactly how he made me feel.

'Ah, yes,' said Erica, glancing at her watch, clearly not enthralled about the suggestion of the man she obviously fancied potentially being paired up with another woman.

'Tomorrow we visit Florence, so we leave early to make the most of the day. Perhaps it is better that we go to bed now. We have breakfast at eight and then leave by eight forty-five. Is fine with you?' Everyone nodded in unison and also looked at their phones to check the time. It was fast approaching midnight. The evening had flown by.

We said our goodnights and headed up to our room. I avoided Lorenzo in the kitchen to prevent any further awkwardness. Yes, it was good to know that he was on the verge of singledom (well, good for everyone except his girlfriend). But at the same time, it was pointless even considering it could go any further.

He'd made it very clear that he didn't fancy me. I just had to realise that I couldn't be everyone's cup of tea and get used to the fact that this was going to be a man-free, romance-free holiday.

What a damn shame.

CHAPTER ELEVEN

Hard to believe it, but today was our last full day here.

I felt so relaxed. The combination of the idyllic surroundings, great company, fantastic food and learning new skills (although Lorenzo would say not quickly enough) made it a great getaway. Albert was surely presiding over everything to help me enjoy myself.

Monday was a working day, which meant I should be checking my emails... no. *Stop!* The deal was 11 a.m., wasn't it? And it was only seven. With breakfast at eight, that gave me a full hour to get ready.

I'd enjoyed being more low-key with my dress sense, wearing less make-up and, as we were working with food, putting my hair up in a loose, 'undone' ponytail these past few days—something I'd try to do more often when I was back. However, because we'd be venturing outside of our cosy group to Florence, and it was our last full twenty-four hours together, I decided there was no harm in making a bit more of an effort on the appearance front today.

After my shower, I painted my toes so that they could dry whilst I was brushing my teeth. I applied my make-up, then smoothed out my hair with my hairdryer so I could have it down.

What to wear? I wanted to keep the clothing comfortable, but I was sure I had a little something more smart casual.

I opened the wardrobe and sifted through the rail of clothes I'd neatly hung up when we'd arrived to ensure they didn't get creased. Starting from the left, I pulled out a black slogan t-shirt. Nah.

Next I came to a black Karen Millen jumper, which I'd packed to look more high street and less Bond Street. Nope.

I continued trawling through the hangers. Ah yes. *This* could work. I pulled out a vibrant orange mini dress—one of the items that mum had given me for my birthday. Whilst she comes across as regal and always looks immaculate, she loves nothing more than a good rummage at TK Maxx and refuses to spend lots of money on clothes. And she thinks the amounts I pay are ridiculous.

Once, when she spotted the price tag on my Victoria Beckham V-neck dress whilst she was nosing through my dressing room, she almost fainted. '*How much?*' she'd shouted. 'You could buy three hundred dresses in Primark for that—literally a new one for every day of the year!' As well as trying to encourage me to look more relaxed, I think she's convinced that if she keeps giving me high street clothes, I'll realise the error of my ways and stop buying designer altogether.

I held the orange mini dress up to the light and checked the label. Top Shop? I'd always considered them as a younger brand, but it still looked good. Yep. This was the one.

I took a fresh pair of leggings off the hanger to wear underneath. Yet another gift from Mum. Leggings were not something I'd normally wear unless it was for Pilates. I checked the label. Atmosphere? Hadn't heard of them. The tag was still on. £2.50 from Primark! That's practically the same price as a coffee at Pret. Wow. I knew Mum had always gone on about it being cheap, but that was crazy. This would be at least £60 in Whistles or Joseph. It'd be more stylish, but you can't argue when something's that inexpensive.

Right, footwear: now my toes had been painted, I could wear my sandals. A lot more feminine than the pair of white Converse I'd been living in for the past few days. I grabbed my phone and checked the weather. A quick search for Florence revealed that it would be a sunny eighteen degrees until 6 p.m., when it would become cloudy, followed by heavy rain at eight. That was fine. We had our last cookery lesson later this afternoon, so we'd be back before then. Black and gold sandals it was.

I stood in front of the long mirror on the wardrobe door. That's better.

I'd scrubbed up okay. It wasn't full-on work-mode scrubbing up—just a more comfortable version. How I'd wanted to feel when I went out, but I'd always been paranoid about bumping into clients without heels or being completely done up to the nines.

As a beauty PR, I felt that I need to look glam at all times. That I'd be misrepresenting my brands or letting them down if I wasn't a walking advert for their products. But today I was off-duty, so I decided to wear make-up, but nowhere near as much as normal. No primer, concealer, blusher, highlighter, lip liner or eyeshadow. Just eyeliner, mascara, a bit of eyebrow pencil, a little base and a nude lipstick with a slick of pink gloss on top.

I was ready for action. Well, not quite *action*, as we'd established that I didn't have a cat in hell's chance of that happening, but I was ready to face the day. Whether that involved more criticism and scornful looks from Lorenzo, I didn't care. I was feeling great, so screw him (if only…).

I walked downstairs and glanced in the kitchen. Mr Moody was there, making coffee.

'*Buongiorno*,' I said cheerily.

He looked up, and maybe it was just me, but I could have sworn that his eyes momentarily popped out of his head. Okay, maybe they stayed in their sockets and didn't extend *all* the way, but there was definitely a hint of surprise in his eyes. Perhaps even *pleasant* surprise tinged with a touch of *desire*?

'*Buon–buongiorno*,' he stuttered. And, wait: I think he just strained a smile.

No way. Either that or he had wind? Wonders will never cease.

'*Buongiorno*, Sophia. Wow!' said Erica as she bounded into the kitchen, heading for the fridge. '*Che bellezza!* You look very beautiful today!'

'*Grazie*, Erica,' I said graciously.

Well, that's a promising start isn't it? Lorenzo had actually spoken to me and even tried to smile, which was probably such a painful experience that he might shortly need medical attention. Erica said I looked nice too. I know as a confident thirty-nine-year-old woman, I shouldn't need validation from others, but hell, I'm human, and who doesn't like to be complimented?

After a quick breakfast, we all bundled into the people carrier and nattered the whole way to Florence. It dawned on me as we arrived that it was now approaching 11 a.m. —email checking was on the schedule.

Fuck it! I'm on holiday. For once in my life, I would *not* be checking my messages. Time for a mini digital detox. Whatever it is could wait until I got back.

Even more progress.

The driver dropped us off just outside the perimeter of the centre, so within minutes of walking, we were at the Piazza del Duomo. The Cattedrale di Santa Maria del Fiore was breathtaking. The exterior was a decorative mix of pink, white and green marble. I'm not the most cultured person and was never one to do the whole museum/monument sightseeing thing when I went away (I'm more of a beach holiday kind of girl—well, I would be, if I actually took proper breaks), but even *I* could appreciate the beauty of this city.

Erica was the perfect tour guide, taking us to all the famous sites including the Ponte Vecchio old bridge, the Palazzo Vecchio town hall with the copy of the David sculpture and lots of other butt-naked statues in questionable poses (is it just me who wonders why some of them are in such compromising positions? Sorry, I told you I wasn't very cultured).

As we wandered around the busy streets, Fran disappeared ahead with Erica. She was up to something...

Moments later I heard her exclaim, 'No! Really?'

What were they talking about? Not long afterwards, Erica stopped and turned around to check that we were all visible and that no one had got lost whilst Fran had distracted her. Then Erica took her phone out of her bag.

'I will just call the restaurant to check that they are ready for us to come for lunch. *Un momento.*'

Fran rushed over to me, eyes wide, and pulled me to one side.

'You'll never guess what? I knew it!' she yelped. She was trying to whisper, but she couldn't contain herself. Any minute now she was about to spontaneously combust with excitement.

'What?' I asked. '*What* did you know?'

'Erica and Lorenzo. I *knew* they had history! Like brother and sister my arse! It took some digging, but I was determined to get to the bottom of it! She was always complaining far too much about what a womaniser he is and how he doesn't do this and doesn't do that. Those are the words of a woman scorned. I know the signs, my friend,' she said gleefully like a detective who'd just cracked a ten-year case.

There was no point in denying it, though; I was desperate to know more.

'So are they together now?' I asked eagerly.

'No!' Fran said, eyes widening. 'That's the thing. Apparently, they had a night of passion years ago. She was all loved up, hastily planning marriage and the fairy-tale ending, but a week later, he slept with one of the guests! Can you believe it? And not a pretty young thing, either. The word is, she was a very average-looking, generously proportioned fifty-two-year-old. Get in! It seems he likes older women!' She fluttered her eyelashes flirtatiously.

'Fran!' I said. 'You're a married lady!'

'I know. Doesn't stop me from ogling, though, does it!'

She let out a raucous laugh. I raised my eyebrows and tried to signal with my eyes that Erica was now approaching and we needed to cut the conversation or change the subject. Shame, really, as it was getting kind of interesting.

So Lorenzo had slept with a guest...hmm.

We walked to the restaurant and had a beautiful lunch. After a few hours of sightseeing, it was also a relief to take the weight off my feet for a while.

Erica explained that we could now split up and have free time on our own. I could tell by the fire in Fran's eyes, she was not even going to *think* about shopping when there was more gossip to be gleaned.

As Dan and Grace filtered off separately into the centre, Fran said, 'Erica, why don't you walk around with Sophia and me? Unless, of course, you want to be on your own.'

'Oh, yes,' replied Erica. '*Grazie*, that will be nice. I have done this tour millions of times, so I am very happy to walk with you both.'

'Wonderful!' said Fran, clapping her hands together with glee. She wasted no time getting back to delving deeper into the story.

'So...you were telling me all about Lorenzo,' said Fran.

Erica looked a little startled. You could tell she was a professional and took her job seriously, so she didn't want to be seen to gossip. But at the same time, I got the sense she enjoyed having some girl-talk time and the chance to vent.

As if sensing her trepidation, Fran assured her, 'Don't worry—Sophia's fine. We're amongst friends here. So,' she said, resuming her line of questioning, 'Lorenzo slept with a fifty-two-year-old guest a week after you'd been together. How awful!'

'I know,' said Erica, bowing her head. 'I was heartbroken. I thought we could have a real future together. We are similar age. I am thirty-four, he is forty. We have similar background and job. We could have been perfect, but he ruined everything. He is just a sex addict. If he wanted more sex, he could have just asked me. I would have given to him. But instead he went with *her*. And she is not the first. There have been others. He just cannot help himself. Some of them are not even special. If they are female, are breathing and they let him know they are interested, he does not hesitate.'

Fran was literally chomping at the bit. I think even she was surprised about the amount of information she'd managed to coax out of Erica about Lorenzo the lothario.

'So is that why he's breaking up with his girlfriend, then?' asked Fran. 'Because he can't keep it in his pants?'

'Ah. Like I say,' continued Erica sheepishly, 'things with Lorenzo are complicated, and I said already too much. He told me last night they have broken up, but who knows how long they will stay apart or if they will get back together? I give up,' she replied dismissively.

Fran was still trying and failing to suppress how widely her eyes were expanding.

'He sounds like a horny little devil!' said Fran. 'I'm surprised he hasn't tried it on with you, Sophia, seeing as you're young, hot and single!'

Well, he'd have to not hate me first, Fran, I thought. But I'll admit, this insight I was getting was making my vivid imagination go into overdrive. If he offered himself to me, I wouldn't say no, but I wasn't about to tell them that.

'Who, me?' I said, feigning innocence. 'I'm a sensible girl…'

'Yes, Sophia,' warned Erica. 'Stay away from Italian men. They are *cani*: dogs. You are newly single. Best you spend time on your own. Don't get involved with these stupid *uomini*,' she insisted.

Uh-oh. If there's one thing that's sure to make me determined to do something, it's being told *not* to. As we drove back to the villa, I started to evaluate everything I had now heard about Lorenzo.

So, he was a sex addict, who had previously slept with guests, was an equal opportunities womaniser who didn't discriminate in terms of age, looks or size and was quite literally happy to shag anything that moved.

Hmm. This is interesting. I wondered if his services extended to guests that were rubbish at rolling out pasta thinly, had initially found achieving the correct sponge-and-cream ratio for making tiramisu a challenge and hadn't yet mastered the art of producing glossy dough.

As I was still relatively young and in good shape, surely that would give me an advantage—no? I started to weigh it up in my head. What if I were to take control and proposition him? The chances of rejection must be quite slim, seeing as he was a sex addict and all. And even if he rejected me, we would only be at the villa for a few hours tomorrow before being driven to the airport, so he should be easy enough to avoid and then I'd never have to see him again.

Hmm. Maybe, just maybe I was still in with a chance of sampling some hot Italian arse after all…

CHAPTER TWELVE

T he more I thought about it, the more I was warming to the idea. I'd always been a proactive, go-getting person who hadn't waited for things to fall in my lap, and the whole essence of MAP was about seizing the day and living life. So if I fancied Lorenzo, I should just go for it.

Just think, if I did, and assuming he didn't laugh in my face, I'd also be able to tick goal number three, 'experience passion', off my list.

The slight spanner in the works was that, for some reason, he didn't seem to like me. But let's think positively: if he could like all of those other women, I must be able to persuade him. Yes, yes, I know ordinarily, you shouldn't have to persuade a guy to like you. But I had a goal which I was determined to achieve, so this was purely a means to an end...

My job was all about promoting people and products and convincing men and women of different ages and backgrounds to buy into something. So with all my experience, whipping up a mini *I'm going to fall madly in lust with Sophia and snog her face off* campaign in the next few hours should be a walk in the park.

Well, in life there are no guarantees, but as Roxy so eloquently put it the other day, in order to score a goal, you must first be on the pitch. Therefore tonight, I would act like I'd been firmly and unequivocally superglued to the grounds at Old Trafford.

I had half an hour until we were due back downstairs for the final cookery lesson. So firstly, I'd dial the glamour up a notch. We already discussed as a group that we weren't getting changed for dinner, so I wouldn't put on anything new, but I *would* reapply my make-up, zhush up my hair, and spritz on my favourite perfume—and I *would* prepare a plan of action.

When I went downstairs, I would be bubbly, I would be outgoing, I would lavish Lorenzo with attention and even though I couldn't entirely remember how to, I would flirt. What's more, if he gave me steely, stern, mean looks, I would kill him with kindness by smiling and fluttering my eyelashes.

I would be so irresistible and charming that he would feel ridiculous and silly to be frowning at someone who was so lovely and warm to him.

Pep talk over. Let's do this.

By the time I had to head down to re-join the group, I was pumped full of energy and ready and raring to put my plan into place. Setting my sights on a man and being determined to make him mine for the night felt a little naughty, but why shouldn't I try? Nothing ventured, nothing gained.

I picked my phone up off the wooden bedside table, as I wanted to take lots of photos tonight. Not just of the food we were making which I'd been doing constantly since we'd arrived, but it would also be great to get some more nice pics of Grace, Fran, Dan and me altogether, and somehow, I also had to get some snaps of Lorenzo so I could show Roxy and Bella how hot he was.

I arrived at the kitchen, where Lorenzo was preparing some bowls of ingredients for our lesson.

'Hello, Lorenzo,' I said warmly.

He looked up, his eyes widening as they had done this morning and he smirked a little.

'*Buonasera.*'

Well, well. I actually got a reply this time. That's progress.

'So how was your day?' I said, flirtatiously cocking my head to one side. He seemed a little surprised that I was engaging in conversation with him, but he answered anyway.

'Was good, thanks,' he said in his gorgeous accent. 'And you?'

'Very nice, thank you. Or should I say *bene*?' I said, pleased that I was able to remember a whole word in Italian. 'I enjoyed visiting Florence. I'm really looking forward to this cookery lesson tonight, though. Can't believe we'll be going home tomorrow as I'm having so much fun. You've been *really* patient with me and are teaching us *so* many amazing dishes, so thank you.'

Hold up…he actually cracked a smile. He's even blushing a bit…

'*Grazie*,' he replied, his smile widening further. 'You are a nice group. I enjoy cooking with you too.'

And just as I was getting warmed up, Fran, Grace and Dan spilled into the kitchen. Dammit. I smiled again, gave him another breezy flutter of the eyelashes and headed to the other corner of the room.

Erica then came in from outside.

'Okay, so our lesson starts in five minutes,' she announced.

'That's great, actually. I thought maybe we could take some pictures now, whilst we're all still standing,' I said, reaching for my phone. 'I'm imagining as it's our last night, the prosecco will be in full flow, so we won't be looking as photogenic later!'

'Great idea!' enthused Fran. With that, I flicked left on my iPhone to bring up the camera screen and encouraged Fran, Grace and Dan to huddle together so I could take a shot of the three of them. Perfect. Now, I needed a group shot.

'Erica, would you mind taking a photo of the four of us together, please?'

'No problem,' she said, holding her hand out to take my phone.

I handed her my mobile, then joined the group as she snapped away. I had a quick flick through the pictures on the screen. Yep, there were some good'uns in there.

Now I needed a photo of the chef. *Gotta play it cool, so I'd suggest a photo of him with Erica.*

'Now we need a photo of our *wonderful* hosts. Erica, would you mind posing with Lorenzo for a picture?' I asked.

Is the Pope a Catholic? Of course she bloody wouldn't.

She blushed and then also tried to act casual. She wasn't fooling me, though. 'Oh, okay, yes,' she said, feigning nonchalance.

She snuggled up to Lorenzo, who pulled various faces

and struck different poses in front of the camera as I snapped away. *Ah, I see. This is a man who clearly knows how good-looking he is, has practised in front of the mirror for hours and likes having his photo taken. Note to self.*

Right. I needed a picture with him too. On my own would be too suspect, though. One with the girls would be a good idea.

'Fran and Grace,' I said, calling out to them. 'Let's have a picture with Lorenzo too.'

Didn't need to ask them twice.

I handed the phone to Dan to do the photo-taking honours, then positioned myself on Lorenzo's right-hand side at the end, and Fran made a beeline for his left whilst Grace stood next to Fran. We also seized the opportunity to wrap our arms around his waist as Dan snapped away.

Pictures mission accomplished.

'Do you want to have a look at my handiwork?' said Dan, referring to the photos he'd taken. As he repositioned his hand around the phone, he clicked on the lock screen button on the side by mistake. When he tried to touch it again, my screensaver wallpaper flashed up.

'Wowzers! Is that you?' he said, eyes widening. 'That's a bit of a racy dress! You look *hot*! Look at those abs!'

Everyone looked over curiously, desperate to know what Dan was gawping at.

Ah, yes. My screensaver was a photo of me in the daring black mesh dress, posing with my dad at my birthday dinner.

'Let's have a look!' said Fran.

Dan held the phone up so everyone could see.

'*Che bella donna!*' said a startled Erica. God bless her.

He then held it up in Lorenzo's direction.

'Look at that, mate,' said Dan. 'I would!' he added cheekily as if I wasn't even in the room.

'Damn right!' added Fran.

'Nathan!' exclaimed Grace. 'You cheeky little thing!'

I glanced slyly over at Lorenzo to gauge his reaction and was pleased to see his eyes were wide once again and he was smiling and nodding vigorously in approval. Nice one, Dan.

'That was at my birthday celebration a few days ago,' I explained.

'Well, you look gorgeous, my darling. Is that your dad with you?' asked Fran.

'It is indeed,' I confirmed.

'Oh, he looks lovely too,' Fran added. 'There's no doubt about it: you are hot stuff. This lady won't be single for long, that's for sure. The men are going to be hunting you down. Look at that body. Wow! I'll have to set you up with some of my friends when we're back in England.'

I felt myself blushing.

Lorenzo looked over at me and smiled. He was thawing, I could feel it…

We made more delicious dishes, all whilst sipping on prosecco. A Tuscan beans and pulses soup (or *zuppa*—yep, the Italian vocab was building nicely…) and guinea fowl with mushrooms. Then for me, the pièce de résistance (yes, I know that's French rather than Italian) was that we were making one of my absolute favourite things: cake. I'm convinced it's all my mum ate when she was pregnant with me, causing me to develop some kind of sponge addiction.

Not only had we made a crushed Florentine cake,

which I could already tell was going to taste delicious, but also tonight, a major miracle had happened as there was *zero* criticism from Lorenzo during the lesson. In fact, I think I even got a *molto bene*.

Once Lorenzo popped that in the oven, it was time to be seated at the table as the other courses had been cooking whilst we were making dessert. He started transferring the soup into six bowls, and we each carried them into the dining room.

I took my normal seat at the end of the table nearest the door. Suddenly the chair beside me was pulled out and Lorenzo sat down, giving me another cheeky smirk in the process.

Wonders will never cease. More miracles were happening: a) he'd chosen to sit next to me, b) he'd smiled at me (again), and c) something told me that he was starting to like me. So far, so good…

I gave him a flirty smile, playing with my hair as I did so and tilting my head to one side seductively. This felt sooo weird. I wasn't used to all of this coquettish behaviour, but it appeared to be having the desired effect. He smiled back again.

'So, where are you from?' he asked, turning to face me.

'London,' I replied, surprised that he was actually making conversation. 'Have you ever been?'

'Ah yes, many years ago. To meet a girl,' he said, smiling mischievously.

'To meet a girl, eh?' I said, returning the smile. 'How did that work out?'

'Long story,' he said, smirking again.

'Oh, I bet. You seem like a *very* mysterious man,' I said flirtatiously. 'Full of surprises…'

'Mmm, maybe,' he added suggestively whilst holding my gaze.

'Well, *maybe* later you'll tell me more…' Eyelash flutter, more smiling, hair playing and head tilting. I was throwing everything at this. Then the alarm on the oven went off for the cake. Dammit.

'I will be back,' he said. 'I will just check the cake and get the fowl.' He grinned again and headed to the kitchen.

My imagination was already running wild, thinking about how the evening could end if things continued in this direction. By now, thanks to the drinking I'd been doing whilst cooking, I was already on my third glass of prosecco, hence why I was more than a little relaxed, but I still had to maintain some focus if I was going to see this through.

He returned to the table with the plates of food. When he did, everyone was deep in discussion, and it felt awkward to continue a private conversation on our own. After the main course, he returned to the kitchen to get the dish I'd been waiting for: the cake.

In honour of Dan's birthday tomorrow, he'd made it into a birthday cake adorned with candles. So kind. We sang 'Happy Birthday' in English (our vocab didn't stretch to the Italian version), and then it was time to cut the cake.

'Can't wait to taste this,' I said enthusiastically. 'I absolutely *adore* cake.'

Lorenzo smiled, then cut off an extra-large slice and transferred it straight to my plate. Could this be miracle number five? I was losing count. Either way, by feeding me big portions of cake, he was shaping up to be my kind of man.

'Thank you, Lorenzo. You certainly know how to make a woman happy,' I said flirtatiously. *Go, Soph.*

He smiled and then licked his lips.

Oh dear God…

Once everyone had devoured their cake, he pulled the remains towards him. He cut himself a slice, stared deeply into my eyes again and then reached back over to the cake, cut me another generous slice and then placed it on my plate, still holding my gaze seductively.

Something might be brewing here…

I needed to move this to the next level. Tricky as we were at a table with four other people, so if I said anything too suggestive, they'd hear.

Roxy's and Monique's words buzzed around my brain: *Get out there. Flirt. Practise. You need to practise.* They were right. I seemed to be doing fine on the flirting side of things, so now I just had to move it on a little. He seemed like he liked me a bit, but what if I pushed it too much and he said no? Nobody enjoys rejection. Least of all when it's their first time dipping their toes back in the man-waters after so many years.

Fuck it. Was I going to go back home filled with *if onlys* and *what ifs*, or was I going to grab this opportunity by the balls (quite literally) and just go for it?

I'm going to go for it, dammit.

I started to brainstorm. I couldn't make suggestions verbally, but what if I typed something on my phone and showed it to him subtly without the others seeing?

Yes. That could work.

Okay. I needed to think of what to say. I was now on prosecco number five and limoncello number two, so my copywriting skills were likely to be a little cloudy…

Well, the objective was to practise, right? He was a chef who had been teaching us to cook, but now I wanted him to teach me how to feel passion again. So I kind of wanted extra lessons.

Got it.

I started typing on my phone under the table.

I need help with something later when the others have gone to bed. Would you like to help me?

I gently touched his thigh and pointed to the message on my phone, which I was holding to the right-hand side of my leg, in between our chairs.

He read it, then looked up at me, eyes wide like a kid that's just walked into Hamley's for the first time, and started nodding eagerly.

Great! He's up for it...

I started typing slyly on my phone again.

But you don't even know what I need help with yet.

He turned to me and mouthed seductively, *I will do whatever you want.*

He licked his lips again.

Fuck...

I carried on typing:

Well, as you know, I'm newly single, so I need some practice as it's been a while since I've been with a man. Do you think you could give me some extra lessons...?

I can't believe I just wrote that... I showed him the screen.

His eyes widened, and he was now grinning so much I thought his face was going to shatter.

He leant over to me, his thigh now brushing against mine, and whispered in my ear, 'I am very good teacher.'

Oh, Jesus. My body began to tingle. He was really starting to turn me on…

Suddenly the rest of the table seemed to sense that we were having our own private conversation. Fran, ever Mrs Perceptive, did a false stretch and completely overexaggerated yawn.

'Oh, I'm *sooo* tired,' she said. 'I think it's time to go to bed. Don't you, Dan and Grace? I think we should be heading to our rooms now.'

Dan frowned, looking confused, then Fran subtly tilted her head in our direction as if to say, *I think these two have some private business to attend to.*

'Yes, yes, right, yes,' said Dan. 'I'm *very* tired too. Erica, shall we take the plates out into the kitchen?'

'I'll help too,' added Grace, grinning widely.

I sure had lucked out with these lot. Lorenzo and I remained at the table, now seemingly rooted to the spot and gazing at each other. It was obvious that there was a magnetism drawing us together.

'It's okay. We will clear the table. You can go to bed,' offered Saint Lorenzo, recognising that the sooner we emptied the room, the sooner we could get up to no good.

Fran gave me a wink as she herded everyone out like a flock of sheep. Erica looked a little crestfallen but, ever the professional, still mustered a 'goodnight' before disappearing outside and over to the building opposite the main house.

When the room was clear, Lorenzo stared into my eyes.

'So…' he said, patting his sexy, solid left thigh, signalling for me to sit there. 'What would you like to practise first?'

CHAPTER THIRTEEN

As I climbed onto his thighs, a combination of nerves, adrenaline and excitement pulsed through my body. I had no idea what was going to happen next, but I was ready to find out.

Lorenzo looked at me intensely and leant forward. His lips were now less than an inch away from mine, and his woody, masculine scent flooded my nostrils. Before I'd even had time to catch my breath, he pressed his mouth firmly on mine, thrust his tongue inside and started kissing me passionately.

My heart began to thump like a heavy baseline and my stomach started doing backflips. *Now* I remembered how this felt. The sensation of a man's delicious, soft lips against yours. The fiery flicks of their tongue, the shivers down your spine…the tingles. How had I survived for so long without this?

It had been years since I'd kissed someone properly, but as it turns out, you don't forget. It all felt so natural. Like breathing.

As I ran my fingers through his thick, wavy hair and stroked his jet-black beard, the kisses became more intense. Damn. If this was what kissing was like, imagine how it was going to feel when he touched me.

He'd read my mind. Just as the fantasy drifted out of my head, his hands began to wander. First lightly brushing against my nipples, then slowly down to my thighs. My cheeks began to burn and the tingling between my legs grew stronger with every second. *This is unreal.*

With our lips still locked together, Lorenzo began to stand up slowly (and let's just say he wasn't the only thing standing to attention).

'Come,' he said, lifting me up, wrapping my legs around his waist and carrying me into the living room.

He laid me down on the sofa, straddled me and started showering my mouth with more hot, steamy kisses before moving down to nibble my neck and then gently sucking my earlobes. My whole body turned to jelly. *Good Lord...I cannot cope...*

As I struggled to catch my breath, Lorenzo reached for the bottom of my mini dress and pulled it up and over my head.

'Mmmm,' he said, licking his lips whilst scanning my body. '*Che bella donna.* You are a beautiful woman.'

Lorenzo reached behind my back, skilfully unclipped my bra in one seamless move and tossed it to the floor before diving his head into my chest. He wrapped his mouth around my left breast and sucked it slowly, then gently flicked his tongue before licking all around my nipple. *This man is making me so wet. I literally feel like I am about to explode.*

He sat up briskly, undid the top three buttons on his

chef's jacket and whipped it off to reveal the most magnificent chest. Bronze and sculpted like a Roman statue, it was covered in beautiful, thick dark hair and looked so manly. I couldn't resist. I began to caress it slowly. It felt so fucking divine.

I'd never been with a guy with a hairy chest before as all my exes had had very little body hair. But right here, right now, stroking Lorenzo's felt so damn sensual...

Jesus. I have literally been sleeping through my life. I cannot believe I have reached the age of thirty-nine without experiencing the sensation of touching a man's hairy chest. This, I supposed, was the cold reality of not being more sexually experimental in my late teens and then going into such a long-term relationship in my early twenties. And of course, focusing on work for too long. Forget being a MARGIN. Right now, I felt so green I was more like a bloody virgin.

Whilst I continued stroking his chest and started rubbing my hands against his large rock-solid rod, his hands glided slowly down my stomach, past my belly button, and rapidly headed further and further south. This felt soooo damn good...

But as his hands slipped below my leggings and then over my knickers, I flinched as the realisation hit me.

Oh fuck.

I'd just remembered. In my attempt to be carefree, I hadn't pruned my lady garden before I'd left, and it was like a jungle down there. I wasn't expecting visitors...

'Are you okay?' said Lorenzo, frowning. 'You want me to stop?' My body screamed 'hell no!' but my mind was freaking out. What was I going to do? I wanted this man inside of me, but what would he think when he saw what lay beneath? He'd probably run out of the room screaming!

Maybe I could say I needed the loo and run up to my room to sort myself out? If I checked my toiletries bag, I might have a razor? I wasn't sure how long it would take to get it looking decent down there, but...I could give it a try. Then again, getting up now would *totally* kill the moment and I didn't want to do that because I was really, really enjoying...*oooh!*

Whilst I was considering my hair removal options, Lorenzo had wasted no time in sliding his fingers underneath the front of my black knickers. I held my breath sharply, waiting for his reaction of shock and disgust...but it never came. Instead, he gently rubbed his finger over my clit, and I could have sworn I'd stopped breathing.

'Oh my *God*!' I screamed, gasping for breath. Even if I'd wanted to play it cool, it was impossible. I couldn't hold it in.

'Mmm, you like?' said Lorenzo, looking up at me and licking his lips. *I love it when he does that.*

'Fuck yes!' I said, wondering how much longer I'd even be able to speak.

He pulled my leggings and underwear down past my toes before throwing them over his shoulder onto the floor and once again leant back to admire the view.

'Mmm, mmm, mmm,' he said, running his hands across my naked body before stroking me between my legs. 'Perfetto. You are perfect.'

Wow. His eyes, wide with desire, said it all. He didn't give a fuck whether I'd shaved down there or not. He wanted me, and I definitely wanted him. No, scrap that. I *needed* him so badly. Right now.

He plunged his fingers inside of me, and I melted.

'You are so wet, Sophia. I love it.'

My body shuddered. This was unbelievable. *He* was unbelievable. 'Now we have had lesson number one,' he said, stroking my clit with his thumb whilst his two fingers continued to thrust in and out of me, 'it's time for lesson number two, no?'

If I could speak, then I would have said *absolutely*. But by now, I was hanging by a thread. I could feel the wave building. The feeling that for so long I'd only been able to achieve through necessity with my own hands. But *this* was different. *This* was on a whole different level. The sensations were so much more intense.

My breathing grew faster and heavier. My body began to shake. The blood rushed through me, I couldn't control it. The wave went higher and higher and then…

'*Ohhhhhhhh… Lorenzo! Fuck!*' I screamed.

My whole body collapsed.

I closed my eyes. I was powerless. I couldn't move. I would pass out any second now. I was sure of it.

He pulled his fingers out slowly and lay on my chest.

'Mmm. I love that you came, Sophia. That makes me so happy,' he said, lifting his head to kiss my neck. I wanted to respond, but I was still struggling to catch my breath. 'Do not worry,' he said as his lips travelled across my shoulders. 'You do not have to talk. Just relax and let me please you.'

I was floating. I could still feel my clit pulsing and the blood rushing through my veins. I could easily lie here forever, but as lightheaded as I felt, I wanted to give him pleasure too. I mustered up every ounce of energy I had left to force my eyelids open. I began to unbuckle his belt and then unbutton his jeans before pulling them down to his knees.

Wow. What a sight to behold. His thick rod was throbbing from underneath his charcoal-grey boxer shorts. If I'd been concerned before that he wasn't into me, then his hard-on was definitely saying otherwise.

'I'm ready for lesson number two,' I said, running my fingers slowly down from his tip to the base, 'And it would seem that you *definitely* are too.'

'*Sì, Sophia. Decisamente.* Definitely,' he said, holding my gaze as he reached down into the back of his jeans pocket, pulling out his wallet and then a condom.

I could feel the excitement pulsing through my body. In just a few seconds, he would be inside of me, and I couldn't fucking wait.

Just as he began to peel off his boxers, a loud knock vibrated through the room.

We bolted upright, then turned towards the kitchen to see Grace edging slowly out of her bedroom door, shielding her eyes with both hands.

'Apologies, Luciano and Stella,' she said, creeping towards the kitchen as I grabbed my dress to cover my naked chest and Lorenzo quickly pulled up his jeans. 'I know my timing is *terrible*, but I'm absolutely *gasping* for some water and I've been trying to hold off for *ages*, but I *really* need to take my medication and the darn pills are so bloody big that I'd probably choke to death if I tried to swallow them with just my spit. I'll only be a sec, then you can get back to the action! So sorry, darl. And I'm not looking, I promise!'

She darted into the kitchen, we heard the fridge door

open and close, then she re-emerged, clutching a bottle of water.

'Still not looking!' she said, covering her eyes with her free hand. 'You can get back to it now. Sounds like you're doing great, Luciano! Keep it up! Oops, I didn't mean that…actually, yes, why not? Keep it *all* up, son, and keep showing Stella a good time. Help loosen her up a little. Mind you, from that scream, it seems you've already done that! Anyway. Enough from me. Better go and take those pills. I'll leave you young'uns to it!' she said, closing the door behind her.

Lorenzo and I looked at it each other and both burst out laughing.

'Talk about a passion killer!' I chuckled.

'My God! She has taps in the bathroom. She could have used the water from that sink, no?' reasoned Lorenzo before laughing again and flashing a gorgeous wide smile I'd never seen before.

'True,' I said whilst secretly thinking that like Grace, given the choice, I probably would have opted for bottled rather than bathroom tap water too. *Still working on my issues…*

'It is a shame,' he said, stroking my face. 'I was looking forward to lesson number two…'

'Mmm, me too,' I said as he rested his head on my chest.

'I hoped that tonight we would be together, and it would have been better to make love to you, but I am still happy.'

'Wait, what…?' I said, jolting my head forward. 'So you wanted to be with me all along?'

'Well, yes,' he said matter-of-factly. 'I like you. Why

do you think I sat so close to you at dinner, started talking to you and gave you extra cake? You didn't notice?'

'Of course,' I added. 'I showed you the messages about the lessons…'

'Yes, but that was *after* I had already made it obvious that I liked you,' he said. 'I did not know for sure if something would happen or how, as you cannot plan these things, but now that I am single and there was not much time left before you went home, I thought that I would see if you were interested and wanted us to spend the night together.'

Well, what do you know? All that time I'd thought that *I* was hatching a plan to seduce *him*, he'd already set his sights on me.

Strange to hear him say he liked me, though. Clearly our chemistry tonight showed that, but since I'd arrived, he'd been so surly. I was curious to know what had changed.

'If the last couple of hours hadn't just happened, I would have been convinced that you didn't even like me. In the lessons, you were always so cold towards me, and it was always *bene, Grace, buonissimo, Fran…*'

'Sorry about that,' he replied sheepishly. 'But I like you,' he said as his fingers circled my nipples again. 'I was always telling Erica that I think you are a beautiful woman.' The tingling resumed between my legs. 'Ask her. When I first saw you when you arrived here, this morning when you came down to breakfast, this evening when I saw your picture on the phone. I always talk about you. But I have also had a lot on my mind recently. And beautiful women can be bad for me too, so maybe I was nervous.' His voice trailed off.

'*You?*' I said cynically. 'Nervous? I find it hard to believe that *you* would be nervous around women. From the way you touched me, I can tell that you've had a *lot* of experience. And from what I've heard, I'm not the first guest you've been intimate with either. Apparently there have been several…'

'No, Sophia,' he said reassuringly stroking my hands. 'You must not believe everything people tell you. Especially if that woman likes the person they talk about and is upset that man does not want to be with her.' No doubt he was referring to Erica…and I couldn't imagine she was best pleased with him saying he liked me, given their history. 'I slept with maybe two guests in seven years, when I was single. It is not many. When I have a girl-friend, I behave myself. And until yesterday I *had* a girl-friend. Now I am single again. That is why this has happened tonight.' He leant forward and pecked me on the lips.

'Mmm,' I said, reciprocating his kiss. I think I actually believed him.

The fuzzy feelings were returning. I was horny and wanted to experience everything that had just happened all over again and more…

'So,' I said, placing my hand between his legs, 'lesson number two?'

'*Sì*,' he confirmed. 'But we must be careful. Grace could come out again. Let us go to your room, yes?'

Hmm. With Fran the eagle-eyed detective next door? She'd surely have a glass to the wall, listening out for every move.

'Fran will hear us, and Dan's room is close by too…' Dammit. There was no point pretending that I could stay silent. If his touch could make me scream, God knows what I would do if he was inside me. I'd probably be so loud they could hear me from London.

'Well, if we cannot have sex, maybe we can just go to sleep together in your room,' he suggested. 'We do not have to do anything. We can just hold each other and fall asleep.'

I looked at his gorgeous face and body with flashbacks of our time together this evening and knew there was no way I could just lie down beside this beautiful specimen and do nothing. Especially after realising how badly my body had been craving a man's touch. It just wouldn't be possible. It would be akin to being locked in the M&S bakery aisle overnight and *not* burying my face in a Victoria sponge.

'There's no way we could be on the same bed and not end up ripping each other's clothes off again,' I said. 'Impossible. Like you said, the connection between us is strong. You mentioned you'd been to London before for a girl. So why don't you come to London to see me? If you do, then we can do lesson number two, three or even one hundred.'

'Mmm…' he muttered, mulling over the idea whilst running his fingers through his hair. 'Maybe. It is a busy time here. Are you sure you do not want to do it tonight?'

My whole body was screaming 'yes!' but my head reluctantly said no. He started kissing my neck, and I didn't have the strength to stop him.

'You have no idea how much I want to, but…'

'Okay,' he conceded. 'Next time. Well,' he said, pulling away slowly, 'I must wake up early to tidy up the dining room and prepare breakfast, so if we cannot fall asleep together, I will go to bed now.' He stood up, then pulled me out of the sofa and into him before pressing his mouth firmly on to mine.

I could feel his heart racing and his hard-on against my thigh.

Ohhhhhhhh. I *really, really* wanted to take this further...

'I must go,' he groaned as he gently stepped back. 'You make me want you. And if I cannot have you, I must go now. It is too much.'

Aaaargghhh! Why oh why couldn't Grace have waited longer before interrupting us?

'Okay, goodnight, then,' I muttered, my insides crashing with disappointment.

'Before you go,' he said, 'please hold me.'

Strange request from a guy, but I was happy to oblige. He pulled me towards him again, wrapped his arms around my waist and rested his head on my shoulder. We stayed there for a few minutes before he finally stepped away.

'*Buona notte, bella Sophia*,' he said, his eyes fixated on me.

'*Buona notte, Lorenzo*,' I replied.

And with that, he opened the door and disappeared outside.

Did that really just happen?

After years of suppressing sexual desire in every form and being lost in a non-physical long-term relationship, I, Sophia Huntingdon, had just experienced the first stages of spine-tingling passion with a hot Italian god. And do you know what? It felt fucking amazing!

CHAPTER FOURTEEN

I crept up the stairs like a sixteen-year-old with a midnight curfew sneaking in at 2 a.m. Even though I knew that super-sleuth Fran probably had her ear to the ground all night trying to listen in on what we were up to downstairs and no doubt was sleeping with one eye open to check what time I'd returned to my room, I tried my best to unlock the door as quietly as possible.

I flicked on the bedside lamp, flopped onto the bed and stared at the large wooden beams on the ceiling.

No way. Had I fallen asleep hours ago and dreamt the whole thing?

I'd had rather a lot to drink, and so it was quite conceivable that I'd made the whole thing up.

No, no, I reasoned. *I do believe that this* did *actually happen.*

I felt so *alive…*

I was on the pitch.

I'd done Roxy, Monique, Bella and myself proud. I'd

experienced some passion and ticked another goal off my list.

And it was funny. Somehow, despite not knowing Lorenzo, without having a full face of make-up, being clad in overtly designer gear (not to mention the lady garden situation and the fact that I hadn't been this intimate with anyone for ages), I'd still felt remarkably comfortable with him.

Whilst I was frustrated that we hadn't gone all the way, perhaps it was better to ease myself into this new world gently. I'd already done far more than the uptight, prim and proper MARGIN who'd arrived in Tuscany four days ago would have done.

In fact, who the hell am I? Where has Sophia gone?

I undid my sandals and curled up on the bed. I would certainly have sweet dreams tonight.

My alarm sounded at 8 a.m.

After barely four hours sleep, I was feeling groggy. Then, like a thunderbolt, it hit me:

Oh my God...

I wriggled around on my bed in excitement. It *had* happened. A million thoughts flashed through my mind. The taste of his lips, the sensation of his warm, sweet breath all over my body, the feeling of a highly aroused and ridiculously hot man on top of me...

My, my, my...

I wondered how he'd act towards me at breakfast. Would he pretend it didn't happen and go back to being cold or would he be nice? I'd soon find out as I had got an hour to shower, put on a hint of make-up, quickly smooth out my hair (after last night's antics, it had become more than a little dishevelled), get dressed and pack my suitcase.

'*Buongiorno*,' I said as I approached the kitchen. Erica was in there with Fran and surprisingly gave me a warm smile.

'*Buongiorno*, Sophia,' she replied. Well, I wasn't expecting her to be so nice to me, given the fact that she must know I had gotten up to no good with Lorenzo last night.

A flash of guilt ran through me. I'd known how much she liked Lorenzo, yet I'd still pursued him. Whatever happened to the sisterhood?

Fuck it. Remember what Albert said: Life is short. You only live once. You have to go for what you want. Lorenzo's single, I'm single. We're both free agents. And Erica lived over here, so she could see him any time. But I was only staying for a few days and had to try and seize the opportunity.

As I entered the hallway, I saw the vision that was Lorenzo glide through the dining room doors from outside.

Wow…

He was wearing those sexy dark blue jeans again, with a fitted blue jumper that showed off the shape of his magnificent chest. Yes. I remembered that chest…

He flashed his killer Colgate smile, and I felt my body tingle all over. *He is so damn hot.*

'*Buongiorno*,' he said as he approached us.

'*Buongiorno*, Lorenzo,' I replied innocently as he entered the kitchen. My stomach did a giant backflip.

I attempted to hold it together as I made my way out to the dining table and sat down.

I overheard him speaking to Erica, checking that everything he'd set up for breakfast earlier that morning met with her satisfaction. When she agreed that it was fine,

I heard his footsteps pad into the dining room. Then he stopped, sat down and moved his chair so close to me that our bodies were almost touching.

I tried very hard (and failed) to focus and to push the memory of what had happened the last time we were seated at this table out of my mind. *Oh my God...*

'So, Sophia,' he said, looking me straight in the eyes. 'Last night. Did it really happen, or did I dream it?' His accent was so frigging sexy.

'Yes,' I said, holding his gaze and smiling at the flashbacks of his head between my legs that were now buzzing through my brain. 'I believe it actually *did*, Lorenzo...'

'Mmm, good,' he replied, stroking my thigh.

This man...

'I *really* enjoyed my lesson,' I whispered into his ear. Partly to avoid Fran and Erica hearing our conversation from the kitchen, and partly to assume my new role of seductress. 'You're an *excellent* teacher,' I said, now stroking his inner thigh upwards and purposefully just missing his manhood, which seemed to be expanding by the second. 'Do you think we could have another lesson before I leave?'

I didn't know what had come over me. And this time, I couldn't even blame the prosecco...

He started grinning wickedly again.

'Mmmmmm. I would *love* to give you another lesson,' he said, his hands travelling further up my left thigh. 'But how? Everyone is here and it is daylight. People will see.'

Good point.

Think, Sophia, think.

'Well, maybe before we leave, I *might* need help bringing my suitcase down or something, and being a gentleman, *maybe* you might need to come up to my room and help me?' I said suggestively.

He laughed.

'But of *course* I help you,' he said, licking his lips. 'Beautiful woman must not carry heavy suitcase herself.'

Oh, yes. It's on…

Just as we were probably about to get ourselves into hot water (which, with the way I was feeling, could have quite conceivably ended with me clearing the table in a fit of passion and pulling Lorenzo on top of me), Erica and Fran came into the dining room.

I spun my chair forward and moved it a little to the right to create a more acceptable distance between us and then reached for the toast in a bid to try and play it cool.

'Where's Grace and Dan?' I asked Fran casually.

'Oh, they've already had breakfast and are in their rooms, packing their suitcases,' she replied. 'I did mine earlier this morning, so I'm just going to go for a quick walk around the grounds before we leave. What time is the driver coming, Erica?'

'In about forty minutes. Maybe less,' she replied solemnly as if sensing the rising sexual tension between Lorenzo and me. 'I have something to do in my room,' she said, walking towards the door. 'So I will come back in a minute.'

'I'll walk out with you,' said Fran.

We'd managed to clear the room again.

Within seconds, I'd grabbed hold of Lorenzo's hand and was leading him through the living room and up towards the staircase. I stood on the second step, making us just about equal height-wise, and leant forward and started kissing him. He responded without hesitation.

As his tongue flicked against mine, I felt the electricity pulsing through my body all over again. He was such an amazing kisser. I still couldn't believe this was what I'd been missing all of these years. Passionate kissing. Something so basic, but yet so powerful in how it can make you feel.

I should never have left it this long. There must be so many women my age or older in unhappy, loveless relationships who dream of this, but think it's too late. Or maybe think that as much as we still desire it, passion is something that disappears when you hit your thirties or forties, settle down and become overwhelmed with the pressures of work and life in general. I certainly had done. But now that I'd put myself out there and was very much enjoying the touch of a man again, I could definitely confirm that it wasn't just a huge turn-on; it was also giving me a new sense of energy. I felt happy. On cloud nine. *Alive.*

Within seconds, our hands were going everywhere. Then we heard a noise and he pulled away.

'We must stop,' he said, looking worried. 'We must not do this here.'

Awww. He was trying to be good and responsible, but he'd awoken my naughty side…

I took his hand again and we treaded gently up the stairs, then darted across the hall into my room. He pushed me up against the wall, pressed his body against mine and kissed me on my neck and across my shoulders, then lifted up my black t-shirt and started petting my stomach, licking inside my belly button and then planting kisses downwards until he met the top of my jeans.

'I want you,' he said, gasping for breath.

'I want you too…' I replied, pushing my hand down the front of his jeans.

He lifted me up swiftly and carried me the few steps towards the bed before laying me down gently and climbing on top of me.

'Condom,' I said, panting. 'We need a condom.'

'I have,' he replied.

He reached into his back pocket, whipped out his wallet and fished out the square packet from a side compartment. Just as he was about to unbutton his jeans, we heard footsteps on the staircase.

'Lorenzo! Dove sei?'

It was Erica. *For fuck's sake! Why does everyone have to keep interrupting us?*

He jumped up, grabbing the condom, stuffing it in his pocket, hastily smoothing out his jumper, straightening his jeans and widening his eyes to signal for me to do the same.

'Quick, quick,' he whispered, hurrying me to make myself look presentable as he leapt over to grasp the handle of my suitcase.

Thankfully, by the time he flung open my bedroom door, I was on my feet, had pulled my t-shirt down, fixed my hair the best I could and was trying to look innocent whilst Erica's eyes burned through me as she padded up the final few steps and approached the doorway.

'*Ma che cosa fai, Lorenzo?*'

I'm guessing she was asking him what he was doing…

'Sophia called me to help with her suitcase,' he attempted to explain. 'She bought a lot of things in Firenze which made it heavy.' Hmm, not sure that he was a very convincing liar. Particularly as Erica was walking with

Fran and me for much of the afternoon in Florence and would have seen that I'd only bought a couple of small leather bags, plus some truffle oil. Nevertheless, I just had to go with the story…

'Yes. *Grazie*, Lorenzo,' I said, playing along. 'You're such a gentleman. I think that's everything. If you're able to take it downstairs for me, that would be amazing.'

Erica shot us both an *I don't believe you, but I can't be bothered to argue* look.

'Well, the driver is coming soon, so better you wait downstairs,' she demanded.

'Great, thank you, Erica. And thanks, Lorenzo, for taking it down for me,' I said, continuing the act. 'I just need to check my room again and pop to the loo, so I'll be down in a second.'

They both left the room, Erica shooting Lorenzo a dirty look, but once she was out of sight, he turned back to face me and gave me a cheeky smile.

I closed the door once again and sat down on the bed. Oh…it could have all ended so differently. First Grace last night, and now, when we were just about to get down to business, we were disturbed again. Dammit. Erica's timing sucked. I guess we just weren't meant to sleep together. But I *really* wanted to. The connection I felt between us was undeniably electric.

Seconds later I heard footsteps running up the stairs and my door flung open. It was Lorenzo!

He pulled me towards him and gave me one long, hard kiss, then gently stepped back.

'The driver is downstairs, so Erica ask me to come and get you,' he said.

'Will I ever see you again?' I asked a little too eagerly. 'Will you come to London?'

He paused.

'I do not know,' he said, bowing his head. 'It is the truth. My life, it is very complicated. I have problems with my girlfriend—well, she is now my ex-girlfriend. It is stressful. I wish she was a wonderful woman like you. It is busy season. I will work for the next six weeks without any breaks and then over the summer too. It is difficult. I do not want to tell you lies.'

Although I'd achieved what I'd set out to, and seeing each other again hadn't been part of the plan, I couldn't help but feel disappointed. Typical me. I always wanted more…

Lorenzo reached into his pocket to take out his wallet again and this time pulled out a business card.

'Here,' he said, placing the card in my hand. 'WhatsApp or email me. We stay in touch, no?'

'Okay, sure,' I replied.

'Can I have a hug, please?' he asked, wrapping his arms around me, and I put mine around his waist. Although I barely knew Lorenzo, I already sensed that I was going to miss him. Definitely needed to nip those feelings in the bud. This was just a bit of fun. To get myself back on the pitch. I couldn't start getting all mushy.

We stayed there together for a good minute.

'Come,' he said, pulling away. 'Erica will look for us again if we are not quick. Let's go.'

We hurried down the stairs, through the living room and dining room and out to the front of the building, where Erica was standing and the door of the people carrier was open, waiting for me to take my seat.

'*Ciao, Sophia*,' she said, smiling, leaning forward to give me a kiss on each cheek. Still found it strange that she was being so nice to me. Maybe she didn't know and really *did* think he was helping me with my suitcase? Okay, probably not..

'*Ciao*, Erica, and *grazie mille* for everything. You've been a wonderful host,' I said, meaning every word, as she really had been great.

'*Prego*,' she replied, the smile now becoming a little more strained. A pang of guilt flashed through my mind again.

I turned to Lorenzo. Now this was awkward. How did I say goodbye to him? Well, we'd kind of already done it inside, so I supposed a formal, *no we haven't just been snogging each other's faces off* approach would be best.

'*Ciao*, Lorenzo,' I said as he also planted friendly kisses on my cheeks.

'*Ciao, Sophia. Volo sicuro.*'

I'm guessing that meant something innocent, like *have a safe journey*, rather than the *I wish I could have made sweet love to you* thoughts that were racing around my head right now.

I smiled at them both, then climbed into the back seat of the people carrier and shut the door.

Oh, how I wished we weren't leaving...

The driver had barely got into second gear before Fran spun her head around in the seat in front to face me.

'So, Sophia the seductress. What have *you* been up to?' she squealed with excitement. 'Tell me *everything!* I want to know all the gory details, you saucy little minx!'

CHAPTER FIFTEEN

'Don't be shy, Sophia,' said Fran, feigning innocence. 'Come on, you're amongst friends here.'

For the last ten minutes, she had been using every trick in her extensive arsenal to get me to dish the details on my night with Lorenzo, but I wasn't having any of it.

I'd seen how she'd skilfully coaxed information from Erica and even Lorenzo himself. But as much as I was bursting to share every detail because I was still on such a high from what had happened, I wasn't about to do it in front of this new driver, who would no doubt report everything to Erica and the rest of the Taste Holidays team. I didn't want to get Lorenzo into any trouble.

'You came up to bed at three twenty-seven a.m.,' Fran stated, giving a knowing smile, 'so he must have been an *excellent* lover for you to be downstairs for so long together…'

I knew she'd be listening and checking her watch. Forget the NHS. I reckoned Fran was one of M15's top agents. Her speciality was sure to be interrogation. Who needed waterboarding or the threat of chopping your fingers off? Just send in Fran and she'd get even the most hardened criminal to talk.

I could tell she wasn't going to give up, so I thought I'd throw her a bone. Make her *think* I was giving her something, but not actually tell her anything. It probably wouldn't work, but it was worth a shot.

'Francesca,' I said formally, 'as you know, I am a *lady*. And a *lady* never tells,' I added virtuously. '*Especially* in a car full of people which includes a driver that could go back and blab to all and sundry. But what I *will* say is that I had a *wonderful* time last night, and let's just leave it at that.'

Fran raised her eyebrows as if to say *seriously?* There was no way I was going to get away with my PR spiel.

'Oh, come on, Soph,' she said, rolling her eyes and crossing her arms to show she meant business. 'You're not at bloody work now. Stop feeding us that spin shite. Don't worry about the driver, he probably doesn't even speak English.'

Right on cue, the driver, a man in his early sixties who had been smiling to himself throughout Fran's interrogation, suddenly went all stony-faced as he pretended to play deaf and dumb.

'Trust me, Fran, our lovely driver probably understands *everything* we've been saying,' I said, nodding my head in his direction, hoping she'd catch a glimpse of his 'busted' guilty face in the rear-view mirror. 'Let's save this story for another time, shall we?'

'No!' Fran screamed in frustration. 'I've been itching to find out what went on since you came up to bed at all hours, and I can't wait any longer!' she said, eyes widening like a crazed gossip junkie who desperately needed her fix. 'You *owe* me, madam,' she huffed. 'If it wasn't for me spotting that something was going on and clearing the room for you, you probably wouldn't have got any action at *all* last night.'

She had a point, but I wasn't going to be broken.

'So you guys actually did the deed last night, then?' asked Dan brazenly. 'Get in there, my son!' he shouted, thrusting his hips backwards and forwards suggestively. 'I knew that Lorenzo would score. He's a filthy one, he is, I can just tell! And I bet you're a bit of a screamer, aren't you, Sophia?' he added crudely. 'You know what they say about the quiet ones! I *thought* I heard noises downstairs. Grace? Can you enlighten us? You must have heard *everything!*'

So bloody cheeky…

'I'm with Stella on this one, Nathan,' said Grace respectfully. 'What happened between her and Luciano is a private affair. The only thing I *will* say on the matter is that they seemed to be having a *lovely* evening with each other.'

'Thank you, Grace,' I said. At least someone knew how to act tactfully. Then again, she also owed me one after interrupting us. 'Dan, happy birthday by the way,' I said, changing the subject. 'Got any plans for celebrating with your wife tonight?'

And just like that, I managed to steer them away from asking about my love life. As if it wasn't bad enough having my mum, Roxy and Monique grilling me at home, now I had Fran and Dan submitting me to an interrogation on my holiday too. I had to admit, if the shoe had been on the other foot, I'd want to know all the goss. I would tell them, but just not right here and right now. In any case, I wouldn't have a choice as, just like Liam Neeson in *Taken*, you could guarantee that Fran would track me down and tie me up until I'd revealed every last detail.

I watched from the window as the plane soared higher into the clouds. *Ciao, Italia.* I'd certainly had fun. I took a moment to reflect on everything that had happened over the past four days. It was nothing short of a miraculous transformation for me.

I'd come on holiday on my own, lived with three strangers who I now believed would become lifelong friends, learnt to cook dozens of amazing dishes, eaten food I previously would never have touched with a hundred-foot bargepole, and drunk from a 'dirty' glass (not an achievement for most normal people, but a major one for me). I'd also put my obsessive fear of germs on the back burner and had happily eaten food cooked by many different hands without freaking out about how clean they were. And guess what? I was still alive.

I'd stayed in accommodation that didn't have a spa attached and that wasn't five-star. I hadn't checked my emails since Saturday—a whole four days. I'd worn very basic clothing (much of it high street, which I hadn't done since my uni days) and zero pairs of high heels, had applied at least seventy percent less make-up than I normally would, and on the whole, I still felt confident and had received dozens of compliments.

Oh, and of course, there was also the small fact that I'd hooked up with a hot Italian chef...

I grinned from ear to ear. I was finally allowing myself to have fun and starting to live my life a bit more.

I pulled my handbag from underneath the seat and

rummaged around to find my notebook. I flicked through the pages until I got to the MAP section.

1) Stop being a workaholic…

Probably a half check. Four days without checking emails had to count for something. More to be done, but we were making progress.

2) End my relationship.

Yes.

3) Experience passion.

Check! Although, definitely to be continued…

4) Go on an educational holiday.

Hell to the yes.

5) Throw a party.

No, but definitely next year.

6) Look into adoption.

I was just starting to rediscover myself, so whilst time was against me, it still felt a bit too soon. Rain check…

7) Have fun/live life to the full.

Certainly felt like I was doing that. Check.

In just three months, I'd ticked off four and a half out of seven challenges. I was over halfway there. But as the cliché goes, life's a journey not a destination, so experiencing passion once, for example, wasn't going to cut it. I had a taste for it now, and I wanted more…

My thoughts turned to Lorenzo. Would I see him again? By the sounds of things, it wasn't looking likely, but never say never. When I got back home, I'd organise drinks with Roxy and Bella and see what they thought.

I couldn't wait to tell them. They were not going to *believe* what Little Miss OCD Workaholic MARGIN Sophia Huntingdon had been up to.

CHAPTER SIXTEEN

I t'd been almost forty-eight hours since I'd arrived back in London and—shock horror—I had *not* yet returned to work.

Normally, I would have gone straight from the airport to the office, or locked myself away in my study at home and stayed there until midnight, frantically trying to work my way through hundreds of emails and feel like I was up to speed with every single thing that had happened whilst I was away.

But that was the *old* me.

The *new* Sophia had decided to ease herself back into real life gently instead. And I was *so* glad I did. Naturally, I'd called the office on Tuesday afternoon when we'd landed and again this morning to check that everything was okay and confirm someone had been taking care of my emails (come on, I couldn't let go completely. Rome wasn't built in a day). But after Harrison and Robyn had assured me that everything was totally fine and under control (and cheekily praised me for switching off from work for a change), I wasted no time snuggling back under my duvet.

Ah yes, sleep. I'd never been one for long lie-ins, particularly on weekdays, as there was always so much work to do. But I'd discovered it was the best way to try and avoid thinking about Lorenzo and our wonderful night together. Every time it flashed into my mind, I'd get the tingles.

Another reason why it was great that I hadn't gone straight back to work was because I'd been in constant contact with Fran, Grace and Dan. As we'd all taken extra time off, Dan had set up a WhatsApp group, and we had exchanged about fifty messages back and forth over the past twenty-four hours alone. Unlike me, who had been pretty much whiling away the hours either sleeping or gazing at Lorenzo's Facebook photos, Dan was more productive and had got stuck straight into recreating the dishes we'd learnt, plus had sent us a flurry of pics to prove his culinary prowess.

Grace had been doing the same, as her grandchildren were eager to taste all the food their nana had been cooking and couldn't wait to help her recreate them. The photos she'd sent through were adorable. Fran had also been whipping up some amazing meals for her husband.

In fact, the only one who hadn't cooked anything yet was me. I couldn't let the side down any longer. I locked my iPad screen to prevent me from logging back on to Lorenzo's Facebook page, peeled myself off the bed, had a quick shower, then headed downstairs to the kitchen.

I picked the recipe sheets that Erica had given us up from the worktop. Thankfully, my Ocado delivery had turned up last night, so I had all the ingredients I needed.

Super-fine 00 grade pasta flour, eggs, butter, oranges, cod fillets, leeks, chopped tomatoes—I was ready to go.

A few hours, two Spotify dance playlists and one very messy kitchen later, I was done. I carefully arranged the finished dishes on the glass dining table, then captured my creations on my iPhone before getting stuck in.

Whilst the strips weren't perfectly uniform, the tagliatelle tasted nice (though I'd learnt that it was even harder to roll out the dough without a chef to do most of the hard work for you). My orange cake wasn't as light as the one Lorenzo had helped us make, but it was still really tasty and great for a first attempt. And I made no apologies for blowing my own trumpet, because the cod with leeks was bloody amazing, plus, most importantly, a doddle to create. I'd *definitely* be making this every week.

I loaded the dishes in the dishwasher, went to the living room and curled up on the sofa, feeling pleased with my new-found skills. A week ago, I hadn't known how to make any of these dishes, and now look—first solo outing and pretty good all round. I picked up my phone and sent a string of photos to the group chat. Within minutes, they'd all replied, praising my work. But of course, they soon shifted their focus to ask about Lorenzo…

Fran: *So, have you heard from lover boy Lorenzo yet?*

Dan: *Have you been sending lots of saucy nude pics and sexting Lorenzo all night?*

Grace: *How's it all going with Luciano, Stella?*

They were like a bunch of persistent tabloid reporters.

Sensing a different approach was required, Fran switched tactics. She took the conversation away from the group chat and messaged me directly. I'd filled her in on what had happened with Lorenzo late last night as, in true

Fran style, she'd been messaging me from the moment we'd landed to find out the details. I knew she also wanted to genuinely check I was okay, and she said that she was there for me if I needed any advice.

Whilst I didn't yet know what I was going to do next, what I *did* know was that, far from enjoying that night together and just moving on, which had been the plan, I was now completely and utterly smitten. I couldn't help it. I logged out of WhatsApp and back on to look at his Facebook page. Again.

In between the millions of food pics and all the fancy dishes he'd cooked for and with other groups were old holiday photos. There were beautiful topless ones of him on the beach with tight swimming trunks and even some dodgy budgie smugglers, which ordinarily I'd report to the fashion police, but in this case, it was a *joy* to look at…

Two hours later, I'd gone through several years of photos and seen him with at least four different hairstyles: head completely shaved, mohawk, big curls where he'd not cut his hair for months and it had grown into a mini Afro, and his current 'do. There were clean-shaven snaps, photos with a thick beard, a moustache, a goatee. He definitely liked to change up his look, and as I'd suspected when he'd posed for the photos on our last night, he loved having his picture taken. Not that I was complaining, of course. It had given me hours of pleasure.

By 4 p.m., the voice of reason, who lately was popping into my head so frequently that I had decided to call her *Reasanna*, piped up again:

Stop this now, Sophia, she scorned. *You are becoming* obsessed. *Step away from the iPad, close down Facebook and get a grip. Either bite the bullet and contact him or just forget about him, but stop sitting on the fence. You'll get splinters.*

She was right. So now it was Thursday and I was weighing up what to do. I didn't want to be too keen. Yet at the same time, I didn't want to leave it so long that he'd forget about me either. But as hard as it was to admit, because it made me sound weak, I was nervous.

If I didn't contact him, I could still exist in this fantasy world. But the minute I stepped out of this bubble and got in touch, I risked rejection. What if he didn't reply? Or if he replied and said, 'We had fun but, now you're back in London, I'm not interested?' It was too daunting to think about. *Time to take my mind off him.*

What else was going on in the world? I clicked on the News app, and before I knew it, I'd got sucked into reading the sidebar of shame: the black hole I *always* avoided at work because logging on to this newspaper's website was akin to taking valuable hours of your day and quite literally flushing them down the toilet. You could *never* read one story and log off. One story turned into ten and before you knew it, what felt like an entire afternoon had evaporated.

After skimming the story about the squeaky-clean TV star and his addiction to prescription drugs, I then started reading about a Hollywood actress who had announced her pregnancy, aged forty-seven. This, declared the journalist, was a *miracle baby*. Admittedly, I was also surprised. Particularly as women are constantly told it's curtains for our ovaries post thirty-five.

Given the fact that I was still contemplating what options were going to be open to me if I was going to have a baby, either by seeking out a sperm donor or adoption, I was intrigued. I Googled 'celebrities baby over 40'. Multiple stories flashed up. There was Susan Sarandon, who had been told she'd never have kids due to her endometriosis but had gone on to have two boys—one at forty-two and another at age forty-five; Gwen Stefani, who had given birth at forty-five; Céline Dion: forty-two; Madonna: forty-one; Geena Davis, aged forty-six; Janet Jackson: fifty…the list went on.

Did this help? I wasn't sure. In a way, I felt like I was perhaps being given a false sense of security. It was all very well looking at a headline on a website and assuming it was simple and that because it happened for them, it could happen for me too. But just as with fertility, unless you know each individual's circumstances, it's impossible to comment. They might have been trying for several years, the child might have been conceived via IVF or they might have had help from a surrogate. Only they knew their journey (and rightly so, as it was no one else's business) and making assumptions about the ease or difficulty of their child's conception would be foolish.

I thought about what Monique had said at my birthday party about women she knew having a baby in their forties. Perhaps that would be more realistic. Rather than looking at what went on in the showbiz world, what was the reality for the average woman? I did another search and came up with more stats:

The number of women aged over 40 having babies has now overtaken those under 20 for the first time in almost 70 years.

Sounded encouraging enough…until you got to the bit that said:

As well as it potentially taking longer to get pregnant,

later maternity can involve a greater risk of miscarriage, a more complicated labour, and medical intervention at the birth. Conceiving does take longer the older you are, and that is a reality—you have fewer quality eggs towards your later 30s, so each month there's a lower chance the mature egg your ovaries produce will be good enough to fertilise. So at 40, you have a 5% chance of conceiving per cycle, compared with a 20% chance at 30. Furthermore, treatments such as IVF don't work for everybody, and success rates also decline with increasing female age...

Oh, great.

Not looking good for me, then, was it (as Fertility Felicity had also 'kindly' pointed out), seeing as I was single and knocking forty? Nope. This was not helping me at all...

Speculation was the worst thing to do. The only way I was going to know for sure was to go and see an expert myself. I couldn't face it right now, though. I needed to sort my head out first. All this Googling and Facebook stalking I had done today was toxic. I locked the screen of my iPad and went back to sleep. And it was 6 p.m. This wasn't good.

I woke up at 8.37 p.m., feeling a bit more positive. I needed to get out of this destructive obsessing/over-sleeping cycle. First things first: I started by arranging an FTA catch-up next week, as Bella and Roxy were both busy over the coming days and I preferred to see them in person rather than chat on the phone.

Next, Lorenzo.

Maybe I'd message him tomorrow...

No! screamed Reasanna. *Has Albert's passing taught*

you nothing? Why put off until tomorrow what you can do today?

True. Okay. Right. I needed to think about what to say: *I can't stop thinking about you and drooling over your beautiful pictures on Facebook.*

Definitely not.

It was true, though. I don't think I'd stopped thinking about him since I'd got back. If men think about sex every seven seconds, then I must have been thinking about Lorenzo every five. In fact, no. Make that four. I kept thinking about his lips all over me and replaying *this time two days ago we were…* thoughts in my head. Bloody hell.

Those four days had shown me so much. I got it now. I understood how fun life could be. How you could lose yourself and feel happiness and joy. How people got married after knowing each other for just a few weeks.

Oh yes. That was another thing I had shamelessly been doing. Practising how our names would sound together (*Sophia Rossi* did have a nice ring to it…), imagining us getting hitched (even though, despite my parents being married for forty-five years, I had never really been into the whole marriage thing myself), planning how many kids we'd have if I was still able to conceive (two), which was debatable after this afternoon's gloomy online research, and what we'd call them (Florence for a girl as a tribute to where we'd kind of met, and Angelo for a boy—a strong Italian name) and mentally decorating the dream family home we'd live in together after he moved to London to be with me.

Why do women like me who are normally sensible and intelligent have these crazy thoughts after knowing a man for five minutes and before we've even found out how they like their coffee? Next thing you know, I'd be scrawling *S loves L.* over press releases and my notebook like some lovesick thirteen-year-old. So embarrassing.

I started jotting down my thoughts as a draft email:

Hi, Lorenzo,

Really enjoyed our lessons together. You're an excellent teacher. I think we've mastered lesson number 1. Still available for lesson no 2...?

There. Nice and light. Not too full-on, with a hint of flirting. I'd put my mobile number at the bottom. And if I didn't receive an email or message back, at least I'd know he wasn't interested and I could just move on.

I'd considered going for a walk to let my thoughts marinate and to check that I was one hundred percent happy with what I'd written, but I needed to continue the relaxed approach I'd adopted in Italy and stop overthinking things.

It's not like I was submitting an official announcement from a client for publication in *The Times*. It was just supposed to be a casual email. Not too contrived. Just natural.

I read it one more time. *That's fine.*

I typed in his email address, skim-read it again and then hovered my finger over the send button.

Once I click this little blue button, everything could change.

I was apprehensive, but I had to do it.

I pushed my thumb down.

That's it. Gone. Nothing I can do about it now. The ball is firmly in his court.

Right. Time to take my mind off things. Mum had messaged me earlier about coming round for dinner one evening this week. I messaged her back to say tomorrow or Sunday would be best and to let me know.

I was feeling peckish so went to the fridge, took out the leftover cod with leeks, ready to reheat, and just as I was closing the door, my phone chimed. Then pinged again.

That's good. Mum's getting better at replying to text messages. Normally it took her at least twenty-four hours before she even remembered she actually needed to take her mobile out of her handbag more than once a day to check whether someone had been in contact, rather than waiting for the house phone to ring (who even used a fixed phone anymore?).

But as I touched the screen, I saw the WhatsApp logo flash up, along with a number I didn't recognise.

That's not Mum's number. If it was, it would have come up with her name.

That's a very long number. A foreign number.

Wait. That was an *Italian* mobile number.

It couldn't be. It'd only been ten minutes—fifteen tops —since I'd sent the email. He couldn't have got back to me already.

My heart was racing…

I unlocked the screen and clicked the WhatsApp logo.

Holy shit. Lorenzo had replied…

CHAPTER SEVENTEEN

I'd put so much focus on potentially being rejected that I hadn't even thought about what I'd do if he didn't blank me and *did* actually reply.

I clicked into the chat. Sure enough, there were two new messages from an overseas number, and next to them was a photo of none other than Lorenzo…

Lorenzo
Hi, Sophia
Lorenzo
Prof here…

I took my plate of food out of the microwave and carried it along with my phone into the living room, sitting down on the sofa.

I glanced down again at the screen. Yep. His messages were still there, and he was still online—perhaps waiting for me to reply. Now might be a good time to snap out of this daze and do exactly that…

Me

Hey there, teacher…

The double ticks on my message turned blue. He'd read my reply…

Lorenzo

How are you?

As tempting as it was to say, *I'm missing you like crazy and want to fly back over to Florence right now and rip your clothes off*, instead I simply settled for:

Me

Good, thanks. How are you?

His reply came quickly:

Lorenzo

Good, thanks…new group tomorrow, so early start.

I fired a message back:

Me

Oh, that's a shame.

Right. Enough of the niceties…

Me

So, are you just messaging me to say hello or something else…?

Lorenzo

typing…

typing…

Come on. What's taking so long?

Getting impatient, I put my feet up on the chaise longue and plumped up the cushions behind my back. I guess I had to remember that English wasn't his first language.

Lorenzo

Yes…to say hello

Lorenzo

And to give you a kiss

We're getting warmer. Still, best to play it cool.

Me

Awww

Lorenzo

I am working on some new recipes too

Me

Wish I could taste them. You're a great chef. I tried making the tagliatelle yesterday. It was good, but I don't think my pasta was rolled thinly enough. It's not the same without your help.

Lorenzo

Don't worry

Lorenzo

I will help you soon

Me

Are you offering me another lesson?

Lorenzo
typing…

Stop teasing…hurry up and answer.

Lorenzo
More than one
Me
Lesson 1 or Lesson 2?
Lorenzo
typing…
Lorenzo
One more one
Lorenzo
But after a lot of number two

I definitely liked the sound of that…

Me
Looking forward to it already…

And with that, he read the message and then logged off.

Shame he'd stopped messaging so soon. I was enjoying that. I looked at the time at the top of my phone. It was now 10.30 p.m., which meant it'd be 11.30 p.m. over there. Fair enough if he was working on new recipes, and he did say he had an early start.

I lay back on the sofa and started to think of him. The flashbacks of him kissing my breasts flooded my brain. Oh my God…

❦

IT WAS NOW SUNDAY. Almost five days since I'd been back, but it felt like five hundred.

I'd spent Friday and most of yesterday either thinking about Lorenzo, staring at photos of him on his Facebook page or sleeping to avoid thinking about him and staring at his Facebook page. It was *very* unhealthy. Thank goodness I was going to have dinner with my parents tonight. Lord knows I needed a distraction.

I hadn't heard from him since Thursday and was desperate to. So after deciding that three days was enough time to elapse and not appear too keen, I made the first move again and sent him a message. As before, I tried to keep it light and breezy:

Me
Good morning, how are you? How's the new group?

You'd think that messaging would have helped. It didn't. With every single second that passed, I started overthinking about what I'd written, wishing I'd said something better, funnier or sexier and wondering whether I should have messaged him first or waited for him to make the first move.

I know there's a million rules about this stuff. Hundreds of articles have been written about the importance of the man instigating everything and the woman not messaging first three times in a row, or is it twice? I couldn't keep up with all these theories.

In fact, now that I thought about it, did I really want

to? All this 'playing it cool' and 'not being too keen' was actually exhausting. Surely if there was a magic formula, then everyone would follow it and men and women would understand each other perfectly? I'd try just going with my gut, and if I felt like messaging, I would. Hmmm. But it's hard to be strong when you're 'lost in the sauce', which my niece Jasmine informs me is the 'hip' way of referring to someone who is lust-sick.

The next stage of my downward spiral caused me to log on and off WhatsApp every five minutes just in case he'd messaged and I'd missed the notification. What the fuck was wrong with me? The combination of having time off and being in lust was clearly kryptonite for me. I knew what I was doing was stupid, yet I couldn't seem to help myself. I looked at the message again. The ticks were still grey, so it wasn't that he was avoiding me. Just that he hadn't read it yet.

If I took a moment to think logically, I'd realise that it was around 11.30 a.m. their time, and he'd already told me that he was working with a new group, so he must be busy showing them how to make lunch or something. It wasn't realistic to expect a reply now.

I attempted to pull myself together, put my phone down to one side and went back to sleep. Yes. *Again.* If sleeping was an Olympic sport, this weekend I would have won gold. When I woke up two hours later, I made a beeline for my phone.

There was a WhatsApp notification. He'd replied with two messages:

Lorenzo
Not as nice as yours

Lorenzo
And no beautiful girl

What does he mean by the second message? Is he disappointed because there's no beautiful girls there?
I'd let that one slide and just keep it light-hearted.

Me
Ha-ha! Well, our group was pretty cool
Me
I've not seen any hot Italian guys in London
either

Now I was back to the waiting for him to reply. This was driving me mental…

No. I wasn't going to do it to myself. If I couldn't be trusted not to look at my phone, I was going to leave it in the bedroom and go into the living room and watch a film to take my mind off him.

Two hours later, I couldn't resist any longer, so I went into my bedroom and pressed the home button to wake up my phone. There was a reply from him, but it seemed to be just an emoji. I went into the app and clicked on his name to open the chat, and sure enough it just had the winking face with tongue emoji:

WTF? Was that *it*?

No *I miss you*? No flirting? Just an emoji? What the hell was I supposed to make of that?

I knew he was working, but I hated all this. I hadn't had to do all the will he/won't he call/message crap for over fifteen years and certainly didn't miss it.

I was out of my comfort zone again. I clicked on Fran's

image and messaged her, as she seemed to understand a lot about men and how their minds worked.

Me
Hey, Fran, how are you?

She replied almost instantly.

Fran
Good, hon. You? Heard much from Lorenzo?

That was the kind of quick messaging I liked. No waiting around for a reply…

Me
Well, not really…if I message him, he'll message back (but he's not very verbose). Otherwise, if I don't message, I don't hear from him. I can't work out whether it's because he's genuinely busy and I'm being paranoid/expecting too much or if he's just not interested…

Fran
Well, with men, if you don't know what to say or do, it's best not to do anything…

Me
Very true

Fran
You can either put it down to experience and enjoy the memories or do the whole long-distance thing, which won't be easy, especially as he still seems to have issues, notably with his ex, so worth taking that into account too…xxx

Me

Well, I'm not completely crazy, so not considering the long-distance thing. That wouldn't work for a million reasons.

Me

I'll give it some more thought and decide how I'm going to play it. I know we didn't get to chat last week, so can I still call you if I need another perspective next week?

Fran

Of course, hon xxx

It was amazing how comfortable I felt speaking to someone I had only known for a week. Although we'd only messaged briefly, somehow, I had greater clarity on the situation.

The long-distance relationship thing wouldn't work. But I wasn't quite ready to consign everything to the memory bank yet either.

That evening with Lorenzo had been amazing, but we had unfinished business. I wanted to progress to lesson two. I *needed* to know what it felt like to have him inside me.

I was at least a decade behind the curve. I was essentially a MARGIN trying to navigate my way around this man-minefield. But if we had a dirty weekend together, then I'd feel like we'd at least finished what we'd started. I would have had a more comprehensive experience, got some great practice in and would be ready to go out there and date more confidently in the real world.

And as well as being talented in the kitchen, after showing me how skilful he was with his hands and those lips, I was convinced that Lorenzo would be an expert in the bedroom too. The perfect professor to teach this willing student.

Yes. A naughty weekend. That's what I wanted to happen next. Two hot and steamy days and nights of passionate kissing and explosive sex.

And just like on that last night, where I'd set out a plan to make Lorenzo mine, I was prepared to do whatever it took to be with him once again.

CHAPTER EIGHTEEN

M onday morning. I could not wait to get to the office. Not just because I'd had a whole nine days away (a major miracle in itself), or because I loved what I did, but mainly because I *desperately* needed a distraction.

I was now thinking about Lorenzo approximately every two seconds—in fact, scrap that. *Every* second was more accurate. As much as I tried, I couldn't seem to stop him dominating my thoughts. I had to take control of my mind again, so if I could reduce that to every three seconds at least (let's not run before we can walk), I'd be making huge progress.

I made my way to the dressing room to pick out an outfit. I felt different. More relaxed. I wanted my clothes to reflect that. To show the new me. Today I was going to dress a little less formally. Normally it'd be all about the structured dress. But right now I was drawn to the other end of the spectrum. No, not a tracksuit. I was thinking a pair of fitted dark blue jeans, a crisp white shirt and a smart black blazer. I might even wear *flats*. *Very* unlike me. Well, very unlike the *old me*.

I got dressed and gave myself the once-over in the mirror. Yes. I felt *great*. Was I missing something? Wow. I'd been so used to going au naturel these past few days that I was about to leave without wearing any make-up or styling my hair. How times had changed.

I wasn't in the mood for a full face of make-up. The time off and the fresh Tuscan air had done my skin good. A little tinted moisturiser was all that was needed. In fact, I was going to keep my make-up light again like I had in Italy. No contouring, blush, eyeshadow, etc. Just eyeliner, mascara and a nude lipstick, finished with a slick of gloss. Done.

Hair? I was going for the loose, effortless, undone ponytail like I'd seen Daniel, our A-list hairdresser client, create hundreds of times at fashion shows. Ironically, it took more effort than it appeared, but I'd tried it in Tuscany and it had looked cool, so time to give it a more public airing.

Rigid, uptight Sophia had gone. And she'd been replaced by a cooler, more fun, younger sister.

As I strutted through the corridors up to my office, greeting my team as I went, the gasps were audible. Anyone would have thought I'd come to work naked. Well, I supposed they were used to me looking like I'd just had my make-up done for a photoshoot and dressing as if I was about to be interviewed for ITV News. And a pony-tail? Undone and cool or not, the Sophia they knew would *never* dream of having her hair anything other than all down and swooshing around like I was auditioning for a shampoo advert.

Well, people. *This* was what a bit of time off and some rolling around on a sofa with a hot Italian chef did to you...

I knocked on Harrison's door. 'Come in,' he said as he looked up from his computer and then did a double take.

'Wow! Sophia!' he said as I walked over to his desk to give him a hug. 'Get *you* looking all relaxed.' He looked me up and down. 'No way!' he said in disbelief. 'Are those *jeans* you're wearing to the office? And hold on...' he said, walking around to look at the back of my head. 'You've put your hair in a *ponytail*? And your make-up— you're wearing make-up, right? Are you? Yes. But it's more... natural. What *happened* over there?' he asked, raising one of his thick, dark eyebrows.

If only you knew, Harrison, I thought to myself. Those were details I wasn't planning to share with my younger brother any time soon...

'Ah well, you know,' I replied coyly. 'Time off, the fresh Tuscan air...'

'Well, whatever it was, Soph, I'm loving the new look!' he said.

'Thanks, bro. Just felt like trying something new, you know. Switching up my style a bit,' I added innocently.

'Well, sis, it suits you,' he said, standing back to look at me once again. 'Mum said you seemed different, happier, when you came round.'

'Oh yeah, how was your reunion?' I asked remembering that he couldn't make dinner at my parents as he'd met up with some old friends from uni.

'It was good, thanks. I hoped I'd get back in time to see you but, you know, it'd been a while since we'd all caught up, so...anyway,' he said, switching topics. 'Back to you. I can't get over it! The power of a holiday, eh? And as you can see, the company is still here, still standing and still thriving, despite you having a few days off. I've been telling you to do this for *years*.'

'Yes, yes, I know,' I said, rolling my eyes in anticipation of his *I told you so* speech. 'You were right, Harrison. I did need a break and it was *wonderful…*'

'I thought I heard your voice,' said Robyn, walking into Harrison's office wearing a smart grey knee-length dress which showcased her long, slender legs and skyscraper black heels, 'but I just didn't recognise you. You look so different!'

'Oh…how I *love* the word 'different'—*not!*' I said, smiling sarcastically. 'It can mean *so* many things and not all of them good…'

'Ha-ha, yeah. I know what you mean, Soph. But in this case, I mean *good* different. Relaxed, happy, *glowing*,' she clarified.

Robyn also looked great as always. Her thick, almost waist-length rich chocolate-coloured hair accentuated her piercing green eyes and her cute doll-like features.

'Well, thank you,' I said, smiling. 'I'll take that kind of different.'

'And congratulations,' added Robyn.

'Congratulations?' I asked, wondering if I'd won the lottery but no one had told me.

'Not only did you manage a whole nine days out of the office, which is technically only five working days, but you also managed to stay off Instagram and all social media. And whilst we saw you reading them, as far as Harrison and I can tell, you haven't actually *sent* or *replied* to most emails either,' said Robyn.

'Yes, I managed to restrain myself!' I said, laughing. 'You guys have done an amazing job of taking care of everything. I admit, it was difficult at first, and I was tempted to start replying to everything, especially when I got back home and was just pottering around, but I saw your responses and they were spot-on, so thank you.'

Robyn blushed. I could tell she realised what a big deal me saying this was. She knew how much of a control freak I was (or *used to be*?), so for me to trust her to take care of things without micromanaging was major.

'Well,' she said humbly, 'that *is* what we're here for. As we've been trying to tell you for years, you know Harrison and I, in fact the whole team, we've got this. You trained us. I've worked side by side with you practically every day for almost a decade. I know how you like things done. I know what this business means to you. It means a lot to all of us too, so we wouldn't ever want to let you down.'

'Awww. Thank you again, Robyn. Right,' I said, clapping my hands together. 'I've got about fifteen hundred emails to sift through, so I'd better get back to work. Can we catch up later re: the MIKA launch and also the numbers for the press trip to Paris that Gail is managing?'

'Absolutely,' confirmed Robyn. 'Although, when you get to email one thousand, four hundred and ninety-nine, sent about ten minutes ago, you'll see that a full update on the launch, the press trip numbers and all the important stuff has already been sent to you.'

'I'm impressed,' I said, smiling. It was great how well Robyn had once again perfectly anticipated my needs. 'Thank you. Maybe I should go away more often.'

I had quite a productive day at work. Of course it was

overwhelming coming back to all those messages, and so much had been happening that at first it felt like I'd been away for nine weeks rather than nine days. But once I'd got up to speed with everything, I felt so reassured. So *comfortable*. It was such a contrast to the feelings of doubt, paranoia, uncertainty and second-guessing that had been plaguing me when I was at home trying to get my head around this whole understanding men thing.

As I'd hoped, work was a brilliant distraction. I'd had so much to do that I barely even thought about Lorenzo every hour. But now that I'd decided to continue the progress I'd made and achieve a better work-life balance by packing up and leaving at 7 p.m., that was sure to go out the window, as I'd be at home alone with plenty of time to fill fantasising about him. In actual fact, thoughts of him began flooding through my mind the minute I stepped out of the office door.

Whilst I was off, I'd been thinking about my next move. I knew what I *wanted* to do. I *needed* to see him again. But what I hadn't quite worked out yet was how best to go about it. Perhaps I should wait until my catch-up with Bella and Roxy on Saturday to get a second opinion?

They were both chomping at the bit to hear about my trip. I'd been teasing them all week by alluding to the fact that I had so much to tell them, but then saying it would be better to do it in person, rather than messaging on Whats-App, which annoyed them no end. Hopefully they'd agree that the story of my mini Italian adventure was worth the wait.

Just as I was considering running my next move past them before I acted, a flash of clarity—or should that be Reasanna's loud voice?—hit me.

Sophia, Sophia, Sophia. Why should you wait to speak to other people first before you act? When it comes to your career, you've always gone for what you wanted without seeking validation or approval from others, so your personal life should be no different. You know what you want. You said you wanted a dirty weekend, so what's stopping you? Just go for it!

She's right. If I waited to speak to Roxy and Bella, almost another week would have elapsed. Why waste time? If I liked to travel, if I wanted to experience more of life and have fun, what was there to think about? Why did I need to ask for someone else's opinion?

Of course, I was apprehensive. Concerned that he might reject me—especially seeing as I was the one who always instigated the messages. But I couldn't let pride stop me. Plus, if there was a more definite 'goal' of us meeting on a specific date, then he might be more inclined to message.

The butterflies were back…

Screw it. I needed to at least try.

As soon as I got home, I kicked off my shoes, headed straight to the living room, pulled out my phone and clicked on WhatsApp.

Me

Hi, Lorenzo. I'm planning another trip to Tuscany in a couple of weeks. Would you like to work on those lessons we spoke about…?

Done.

Now, before I started obsessing and overthinking, I'd have my shower, make dinner, and then and only then would I look at my phone, which I would put on silent and leave here buried deep under the cushions, to avoid the temptation of rushing to look at it as soon as it chimed. I was thinking positively that he *would* of course respond…

Ninety minutes later, the curiosity was killing me. I retrieved the phone from the sofa…

He'd replied after forty-five minutes:

Lorenzo
Mmm-mmm. Of course!

Well, that was encouraging. I launched iCal to check the dates of the next bank holiday weekend, then tabbed back to WhatsApp and began typing:

Me
I had Thursday 26th–Sunday 29th May in mind.
Are you free? Not sure what days you work, so let me know…

An hour later I received a reply. Must be after 11 p.m. in Italy now.

Lorenzo
OK, baby, I will check and tell you as soon as possible

Checking sounded good. I'd rather he did that and be sure than respond with a blasé 'yes' without really knowing if he could or not. On the other hand, it meant I now had to wait for his response…

Aaaaargh! This went against the person I had been for

so long. The old me would never *dream* of chasing a guy or doing this running and waiting around. But as frustrating as this whole single thing could be, at times it was also a little bit exciting. It would be good to have something to look forward to over the bank holiday weekend for a change, rather than just staying at home working.

As the saying went, no pain, no gain. So, if waiting for him to respond meant I got to achieve my objective of having that naughty weekend, then so be it.

CHAPTER NINETEEN

'So, madam: spill!' said Roxy the second we sat down at the table and settled into the comfy leather seats of our favourite booth in the corner of Hush. 'You've been teasing us for ages, and we need to know what you've been up to!'

Before we got caught up in conversation, we ordered our starters, mains and drinks, then after the waiter had left, it was time to begin the storytelling and reveal all about my Italian shenanigans.

After they'd both gushed about how much they loved my more relaxed look, I started by elaborating on the things I'd touched on during my WhatsApp messaging the weekend I'd arrived. How lovely Fran, Grace and Dan were, the cookery lessons, the fact I'd drunk out of a dirty glass and only worn minimal make-up, the villa, etc. And I showed them the pics I'd taken on my phone.

'Oh, they all look lovely! So, that must be Fran, and that's Grace, right?' said Bella, pointing at each of their faces on the screen.

'Yep,' I replied.

They swiped through the pics of Florence whilst sipping on their G&Ts, then arrived at the shot of Erica and Lorenzo together.

'Holy fuck! Who is *that*?' screamed a clearly impressed Roxy. 'Is *that* your chef?' she said, eyes growing wider by the second. 'You lucky cow. And who's she? Is that his wife?'

Roxy grabbed my phone, positioned her thumb and forefinger on the screen and started sliding them outwards to blow up the image and zoom in.

'He is mighty fine,' she added, giving her seal of approval as she continued scrolling through the photos. 'Are there more pictures of him? He is *hot*!'

'I have to agree,' said Bella, leaning in to take a closer look.

'Oooh, nice one,' added Roxy. 'You got a picture next to him here. Wait,' she said, looking at me suspiciously. 'You didn't answer my question. Was that woman his wife? And what did you say you wanted to tell us again…?' she asked.

I tried to play it cool for a bit longer to maintain the suspense, but I couldn't help it. I started smiling uncontrollably. Roxy put two and two together and correctly made four. I began to blush.

'You *didn't*!' Roxy screamed again. 'Did you screw the chef? You dirty dog! Tell us *everything*!'

I smiled again slyly, still remaining silent. Both Bella's and Roxy's mouths were quite literally on the floor, and their eyes now looked wider than a seventy-five-inch flat-screen TV.

'Well, no, not *exactly*,' I said coyly, finally breaking

my silence. 'But let's just say we spent a *very* pleasurable evening together kissing passionately, touching, caressing, coming…'

'I don't bloody believe it!' shouted Roxy. '*You*? Ms Uptight OCD MARGIN, frolicking with the married chef right under his wife's nose?'

'No!' I protested. 'He's not married! She's just his colleague. And excuse me, I'm not uptight and I don't have OCD, thank you very much. I'm just *particular* with some things, that's all.' Of course, Roxy's description of the old me was in fact spot-on.

Bella and Roxy both looked at each other as if to say *yeah right* and laughed.

'Soph,' said Bella as she smiled and lifted up her glass, gesturing a 'cheers' motion. 'Well done, girl. Proud of you!'

'So how did it happen?' asked Roxy. 'I'm pretty sure you mentioned on WhatsApp that the chef thought you were *shitto* or something and that he didn't like you. So I don't get it,' she said, looking confused.

'I know!' I said, still not quite believing it myself. 'It's crazy. But Erica—our host—the lady in the photo that he works with, started telling me and Fran that he'd slept with an average-looking guest and that he was a bit of a nympho. So I thought it was worth a try. Plus, I had your voices in my head, telling me I needed practice and to get myself back on the pitch, so that spurred me on to find a way to make things happen.' I paused to take a sip of my G&T. 'And so I propositioned him on the last night. He said he was up for it, and the next thing I know, we were rolling around on the sofa…'

I recounted the story in such a matter-of-fact way, like

I was telling them a tale about popping out to M&S for a pint of milk.

They were both dumbfounded. If they didn't pick their jaws off the floor pronto, I was worried that the waiter, who was now approaching with our starters, would crush them with his size 11s.

'Well, say something, then!' I said impatiently.

'I'm speechless, Soph!' said Roxy, still surprised. 'I can't bleeding believe it! Come here.' She leant over and gave me a massive hug.

The waiter smiled as he rested the plates of tiger prawns, Korean spiced chicken and avocado salad down in front of us, then made a swift exit.

'You did it!' said Roxy proudly. 'You got yourself on the pitch. How did it feel? More importantly, how did *he* feel?'

'Roxy…' I said, starting to picture his body in my mind, which gave me the tingles. 'He felt fucking amazing!'

'I bet!' added Bella, leaning in to hear more of my story.

'So how come you didn't sleep with him?' quizzed Roxy, mouth half-filled with chicken.

'We were just about to, and then Grace interrupted us. It's a miracle it even went as far as it did, as I was feeling a bit self-conscious because I hadn't, erm, tended to my lady garden, so it was a teeny bit overgrown down there,' I added sheepishly.

'Ahem. *Excuse me?*' said Roxy, now almost choking on a prawn. 'Let me get this straight: Miss Prim-and-Proper Beauty PR, who preens more religiously than a Christian goes to church on a Sunday, was not groomed to perfection downstairs? I don't know what's harder to believe: you practically having a one-night-stand, or you having more than a single strand of hair out of place.'

I laughed as I nabbed more than my fair share of the plate of prawns.

'I know!' agreed Bella.

'First you rock up to this restaurant looking all casual, then you tell us you've drunk from a dirty glass and have eaten not just salami but pâté too. Next, you drop a bomb-shell that you spent less than ten minutes on your make-up and *weren't* dressed head to toe in Armani, and now *this* bombshell? Seriously, Sophia,' said Roxy, running her fingers through her hair, 'there's only so many surprises a woman can take in one afternoon!'

'Stop taking the piss!' I said, laughing. 'I don't know what to tell you. This holiday, *this man*, the whole experi-ence has kind of changed me…'

'Understatement of the century!' added Bella. 'So, where are you at now? Have you messaged him since you got back?'

'Well, I'm planning to go over there in a few weeks' time for a dirty weekend,' I said confidently.

'No fucking way!' screamed Roxy. 'Bella? Who the hell is this woman sitting at our table? This is *not* our friend Sophia. She has been kidnapped and replaced with some sort of floozy impostor. I refuse to believe the words that are coming from this stranger's mouth!'

'Roxy's right, Soph,' said Bella, nodding in agreement. 'The transformation is incredible. Well done, you! So is it all booked? What stage are you at?'

'Well, annoyingly, I'm waiting for him to get back to me to confirm dates, which I hate as it makes me feel like

I'm in limbo,' I said as I cut a piece of chicken in half, ready to devour. 'It's not helped by the fact that he's not very verbose on messages and so far I've led the way, always being the first one to message, which I can handle, just about, provided he's interested. He said on Monday night that he'd let me know re: dates and I still haven't heard back from him. That's almost a full five days, so I think I should start to chase. I don't like feeling like I'm being dangled on a string.'

'Maybe give him until Monday?' suggested Bella. 'Then it's a clear week? What do you reckon, Roxy?'

'Message him now!' shrieked Roxy. 'Why wait? Sounds like you're on a roll. Better to know sooner or later if he's interested or if it was just a little one-off fumble.'

'You're right. It's a little daunting, though,' I said, covering my eyes with my hands. 'I feel like a fish out of water, and I'm trying to address my fear of rejection. I keep thinking, what if he says no? Or he does say yes, and then I end up going and he doesn't show up or something? I know I should think positively, but he hasn't really done anything to instil confidence in me and make me feel like he's definitely interested.'

'That's a lot of *ifs*. If this or that happens, then you just deal with it,' advised Bella sagely. 'There's so many wonderful places to visit in Italy, so you'd just go and explore. See the places you don't get to see when you go there for work. Worst comes to the worst, it wouldn't have to be the end of the world. I say give it a try, but be pragmatic at the same time. Don't go with any big expectations of this being the love affair of the century. Just enjoy the ride.'

'Yeah, quite literally!' added Roxy, sniggering like a

teenager. 'I cannot believe you had that hot totty in front of you and didn't sample the goods properly, as I would *not* have let that slip through my fingers. But for you, as someone that's been out of the dating game for so long, I get that this is a giant step, and like Bella said, we're so proud of you.'

'Thanks, Rox—that means a lot,' I said, smiling.

'You've got to keep the momentum going, though, and get your arse back to Italy,' she added firmly. 'If you leave it too long, he'll move on to some other guest and forget about you. So first thing in the morning, chase him up about dates and then book that ticket pronto!' she said, letting out an excited squeal. 'And by the way, when we get the bill later, you are not paying a penny for this meal. I feel like I've just been to the cinema and watched a chick flick. What a show you've given us this afternoon, young lady!'

Ah, bless my friends. It was great that they understood me and the steps I was taking to try and enjoy living my life much more.

Like Roxy said, though, I couldn't wait around. I needed to find out whether lesson number 2 was still on the cards, which meant taking charge again and messaging him.

This time tomorrow, would I be preparing for a weekend of fun with Lorenzo or cursing him for not replying?

CHAPTER TWENTY

I think deep down when I sent my message to Lorenzo on Monday asking about dates, I knew that he wouldn't reply without me having to chase. Oh well. *Just keep the objective in mind. You're not looking for a reliable husband who will be there to bring you tea and a hot water bottle when you've got your period. You're looking to hook up with a guy who is so hot, he would make the gorgeous Channing Tatum look like Quasimodo, for a weekend of no-strings-attached sex.* Thus, lengthy WhatsApp chats and punctual messages weren't really part of the deal.

Relax. This is all probably normal in the dating game.

Right. Time to send that message. It's 10.15 a.m. here, so 11.15 a.m. there. Perfectly fine.

I sat up in bed, plumped up my pillow and began typing a WhatsApp message:

Me
Hello, handsome. Any news on those dates? As it's

only two weeks away, the flights are getting
booked up, so I need to be quick. Can you let me
know today? Grazie mille xxx

There. I kept it light, squeezed in a compliment (they
say flattery gets you everywhere), and showcased my
Italian vocab skills. How could he resist?

I was still guilty of checking to see when he was last
online, whether he'd read the message or not and how
many hours had elapsed since I'd sent it. I couldn't seem
to help myself.

Three hours and fifteen minutes later (not that I was
counting…), he replied:

Lorenzo
I can be with you on the 28 and 29, but unfortunately I have to work until the 27.

Couldn't argue with that. Two nights of passion had
always been my objective. And I'd rather him let me know
that he was working on certain days now so I could book
the flights accordingly. I typed out my reply:

Me
Great! I'll let you know once I've booked my
tickets.

A wave of excitement flashed through me once again,
just like on the last night at the villa, when he'd first
confirmed he was up for *helping* me. I grabbed my iPad,
typed in the dates and checked for the available flights to
Pisa.

The flights were triple the cost I'd paid before. Understandable, I supposed, seeing as it was a bank holiday. Maybe I should shop around and do a bit more research?

Here comes Reasanna…

FFS, Sophia. Are you really doing this shit again? Are you going to spend hours going through all your cost analysis bollocks like the old you, or are you going to take a leap of faith and go for it? You're already on the flights/hotel price comparison site you and the team use for all your work bookings, so you know it's good. And it's not like you don't have the money! You should just bloody well book it. Seriously, woman!

So pushy…but she was right.

I checked the dates again to be sure, selected the times and then clicked confirm quickly. Even a seasoned PR like me couldn't resist all the threats of *there's only one seat left at this price* and *five gazillion people have booked onto this flight in the last five minutes* that flashed up on the booking page.

Done. This bank holiday, I would not be sitting at home like I normally did, working on my laptop and staring out the window as the rain poured down, lamenting why the weather was always so shit in England during bank holidays.

Nope. This time, I would be jetting off to Tuscany for a shagathon with an Italian stallion.

I reached for my phone and sent Lorenzo another message:

Me
All booked. Arrive Fri 27th May (5.30 p.m.), leave

Mon 30th May (afternoon). Is Florence city centre the best place to stay?

A record twenty-seven minutes later (of course I was *still* not checking timings…), he replied with:

Lorenzo
Nice

He would *not* be winning any prizes for literature. And he didn't answer my question about where to stay. Never mind. We could deal with that another time. For now I just wanted to take a moment to reflect on the fact that I was returning to Italy. What's more, I had booked a flight in around forty-five minutes as opposed to multiple hours, which is the time it would traditionally take if I was going through my normal checking and analysis procedures. Bella and Roxy were right. I really was a new woman.

I clicked on to our group chat.

Me
So, ladies…what are you doing the weekend of 4th June? I've thrown caution to the wind and booked flights. As I'm not normally this spontaneous, forward or…just not like this at all, I'm bricking it a bit!

Me
I chased in the end because as predicted, I hadn't heard back re: dates. He said Sat/Sun would be good but not Thurs/Fri due to work. So I'm going Fri–Mon. Worried that I may be wasting time/money if it falls through. Hence may need

moral support the following weekend to take my
mind off any disappointment…

Now *that's* what you call a verbose message. Lorenzo,
take note.

Bella fired back a message. Paul must have been
having an afternoon nap.

Bella
Bricking it is good!!! Feel the fear and do it
anyway. Don't forget to pack certain items… Sat
4th June is in the diary!!

Next Roxy messaged:

Roxy
Yay! Go for it! You'll have an amazing time! Sat
4th June is fine with me too. Can't wait to have a
front-row seat for the sequel to your exciting chick
flick. But this time, can you bring popcorn? Preferably the salt/sweet mixed packets from M&S.
(hehehe!) Proud of you! xxx
Me
Thanks, ladies. I'm apprehensive but also
excited…
Bella
Try not to worry, hon. Keep busy, not just between
now and when you go, but also put lots of stuff in
the diary for when you get back so that you're not
missing him too much when you get back to
reality.

Me

Great idea. You know how sometimes I do have a tendency to overthink…

Roxy

Ha ha! You? Overthink? Sometimes? Never!

Me

Not funny, Roxy

Roxy

Well, just saying, Soph! You do tend to obsess because you always want everything to be perfect, but you're definitely getting better…ish…

Me

Hey—cut me some slack. I'm much more relaxed than I used to be…

Me

M&S popcorn will be covered, Roxy. Alcohol is sure to be needed one way or the other too. Packing list will be also be sorted, Bella…

Roxy

By the way, Soph, don't fuck up this time with the lady garden situation. You need to be booking your appointments with the beauty salon to get everything ship shape pronto. Your nails, feet, all need to be on point.

Roxy

Hold on. I can't believe that *I* am telling *you*, Ms Beauty Queen Glamour Puss, about grooming. How things have changed!

Me

Don't worry…it was a one-off. I'm normally always neat down there. I'll be preened to perfection, and downstairs will be pruned better than a

row of bushes at Kew Gardens. It'll be like a work
of art!

Roxy

Glad to hear it. Now go and book those
appointments!

Me

Will do. Thank you, my darlings. You're the best x

And with that, we all signed off. Love those ladies. I
was feeling much more positive about my decision to go
there now. In fact, I couldn't wait.

Time to sort out those appointments: I booked a mani-
pedi and bikini wax (legs and underarms had been lasered
so all good there), eyebrow threading, messaged my
industry friend Annabel to check availability for her stylist
Josh to do my hair at her salon in Mayfair, then scheduled
an appointment with the hygienist to get my teeth cleaned.

That reminded me. Underwear. I'd get some new
lingerie too.

It was hard work gearing up for this whole sex thing.

Strictly speaking, I should keep my look low-key as
that's how I was when Lorenzo met me. But this time, I
want to be totally relaxed and not have to think about stray
pubes spilling out from my thong.

My sensible side told me I should exercise caution and
not get too carried away until I was there and we were
actually together, but I couldn't help it. The fact that there
was a possibility of some fun (and sex) in just two weeks'
time gave me something to look forward to.

As nervous as I was, I just had to try and relax and tell
myself it would all be fine.

CHAPTER TWENTY-ONE

With the MIKA influencer lipstick launch less than a month away and so many other projects on the go, it had been a hectic week. But I didn't mind, particularly as my weekend with Lorenzo was getting closer.

On Tuesday morning, I was surprised to receive an unsolicited message from him which said:

Lorenzo
Good morning, beauty..how are you?

We then messaged for a while about what he'd been up to, and he said he had been working hard. We exchanged various non-flirtatious messages, then I upped the ante a little by asking if he was looking forward to our lessons next week. He replied with a row of heart eyes emojis.

As there was now just a week to go, on Thursday I decided to book a hotel. I'd been trying to delay doing this, just in case he cancelled, but his impromptu message had helped to put my mind more at ease.

I'd done some top-level research on TripAdvisor (without going overboard like I normally would) and rather than going for five-star, I found a good four-star hotel just outside the centre with parking, as I assumed he'd have to drive to get there. Next I messaged Lorenzo to check that the location would be convenient for him.

Me
Good morning, honey, how are you? So I'm
booking my accommodation today. I'll be staying
in a nice place near Florence town centre in the
Porta al Prato/Borgo Ognisanti area. Is that easy for
you to visit?

He replied two hours later:

Lorenzo
Good morning to you
Yes I know the place…i lived there for one year
Me
Perfect!
Lorenzo
Kiss

I confirmed my reservation. Part of me wanted to book the flexible rate so I could cancel up to twenty-four hours before, but I'd already organised my flight, so I had to go. I needed to be positive and have faith.

∾

TIME WAS FLYING BY. I was still trying to get my head around the fact that this was actually happening in just six days. I took a quick look at his Facebook page. He was *stunning*. I mean, ridiculously so. What a way to get myself back in the saddle.

Despite my occasional flashes of apprehension, I hadn't even worried about the fact that I was going to stay with someone who was effectively a stranger for the weekend or thought about whether we'd get on (not that I needed anything else to start fretting about, of course). Strange how relaxed I felt about the prospect of spending time in his company.

I wondered how I would be feeling this time next week. I'd either be overjoyed after spending two full days enjoying mind-blowing sex, disappointed because he was busy working and forgot to meet me, or happy that he had come (in more ways than one…), but sad that he'd left straight afterwards rather than spending the whole weekend with me as planned.

Overthinking was pointless. The reality was, I wouldn't know until next week. Like everything on this journey so far, I just had to say 'fuck it' and roll with the punches. It was out of my hands. All I could do now was send him a message on Wednesday to let him know the hotel details and what time I'd be there and to confirm final details. Until then, I would not obsess. I repeat, I would *not* obsess over this.

AFTER ALL MY grooming and prep appointments it was good to finally lie back on the pedicure couch. I closed my eyes and exhaled. In just two days' time, I'd be in Florence. Which meant that, as well as helping to take my mind off my feet getting touched (I'm very ticklish), now would also be a good time to send that confirmation message to Lorenzo:

Me
Hi, how are you? Two days to go…just sending over details of where I'll be staying:
Hotel Firenze
Via Garibaldi, 9
50123
Florence—Italy
What time do you finish work on Friday? I'll be there from 5.30 p.m., so let me know if lessons begin on Friday night or Saturday morning…

I hit the send button. He normally replied in two hours, so by the time I finished this pedicure and then travelled home, I should have a response.

As I headed back from the salon, I heard my phone chime. It was probably approaching the two-hour mark, so it must be him. I pulled my phone out of my handbag. It was indeed.

I tapped on the WhatsApp icon and then into his chat.
Nooooooo!
It can't be!
I fucking knew this would happen…
Bastard!

CHAPTER TWENTY-TWO

A nd the award for prize plonker goes to…me!
I had spent the last half an hour lying on my bed, repeating, *I am such a fucking idiot*, over and over again.

As well as being a fool, it appeared I was a clairvoyant too because the outcome I'd predicted days ago had come true. His lame message read:

Lorenzo
Sorry, Sophia, I apologize so much but I cannot. I have to work.

What a wanker.

Well, you couldn't say I hadn't tried. I'd tried *so* hard. Too hard, in fact. I would never normally have done that. Chased a guy. Offered myself on a silver platter. Never. But I'd thought: *Be more adventurous. Throw caution to the wind.* So I had. And whilst it had paid off in the short term on my last night at the villa, because I'd just *happened* to be in the same room as him and it had required minimal extra effort on his part, it hadn't in the long term.

My head was spinning. I *knew* this would happen! Deep down in the bottom of my soul (in fact, not even that deep, practically surface level) I had seen the unreliability, the lukewarmness, the unresponsiveness. But I'd ignored it and thought I knew better. That I'd win, just like I always did at work. That he believed I was different. Special.

He had probably taken two seconds to write that shitty message and then carried on with his work or screwing some bimbo without giving me another thought. My first reaction was to write to him and try and make a suggestion or find a way around it. But the fact that he didn't volunteer a solution showed he clearly wasn't bothered. I even considered deleting him from my contacts altogether, or blocking him. But I'd just leave it. I wouldn't even reply.

What could I even say? *Oh, don't worry about pissing all over my emotions, or the grand I've spent booking flights, accommodation and buying sexy underwear. It's no biggie.*

At the end of the day, this had been my choice and I had known the risks, but had been living in such a dream world that I had gone ahead with it anyway. Stupid.

Maybe I should stay here and focus on the MIKA Cosmetics launch... No! I was supposed to be getting more balance in my life, not working on bank holidays again. It'd be better for me and my well-being to explore Florence for three days than simply do the same old thing I always did in London.

So, much like I had done a month ago, I just had to get on the plane and be prepared for the unknown. It might not be as exciting as my last trip, but what could I do? Somehow, I would just have to find a way to get through it.

I launched WhatsApp. I needed moral support and knew Roxy and Bella would make me feel better.

Me
Evening, ladies. How's it going?
As I'd feared, the dirty weekend plans have fallen through. Sent a pre-check message today and got a reply saying 'so sorry but I can't now as I have to work'. Should have put money on that happening. Old me would have never gone ahead with something like this when my gut sensed flakiness/unreliability, but I was trying to be more spontaneous and step out of my comfort zone. Trying to be pragmatic about it, but it's hard because I was really looking forward to it

Roxy replied straight away:

Roxy
Aww, darling, can't believe it, what a fucking arsehole. What you going to do? You still going?
Me
I bloody can! So annoyed with myself as it was what I thought would happen all along.
Yep, have to—everything is already booked. Don't fancy just sitting around here all weekend, so may as well go and make the most of it. Grrrrrr.
Suppose I have to start getting used to this sort of thing with this new being single malarkey. x

Roxy

Yup, it sure is part of the joys of being single!
Well, you go, girl. Love that you're going. Try to
fill your day up with walking tours and stuff so you
get to see the place and you're around people too.
You're so bloody strong and already seem to have
everything sorted in your mind and are thinking
positively, so I know you'll be fine.

Me

Thanks, Rox. Well, needs must and all that. I'd feel
silly and wasteful just to say I'm not going.
I do feel like shit. Don't even think I'll reply to the
message. Was even thinking of deleting and
blocking him altogether.

Roxy

Yeah. I'd probably send a message saying 'fuck
you, arsehole' and delete him. Trust me, honey.
You get used to this shit after a while!

Roxy

BUT there is the biggest positive…you had an
amazing time on your last trip, you braved what
you wouldn't have three months ago and have good
memories of your breakthrough to the new you, so
give yourself a pat on the back. You had a night of
passion and with an Italian stallion…just like an
amazing chick flick. Minus the soppy happily ever
after this time round…

Me

You're so right. I will focus on the positive
elements, see it as a fun experience and try to move
on (easier said than done, though…). Thanks, hon.
Speak soon x

I climbed out of bed, dragged myself to the kitchen, opened the fridge, took out a bottle of gin and some tonic and poured myself a generous glass.

I could do with some cake too. I opened the cupboards. Nothing. That lonely looking chocolate bar lurking at the back would do nicely though.

I retreated back to my bedroom, plonked myself on the bed, took a large swig of G&T and checked my phone. Bella had replied.

Bella

Dammit!!! I know it's disappointing, but without sounding soppy, I'm sooooooo proud of you and I think you mentioned that you picked a hotel where you could pop off to Rome for a day? You know our motto, that things happen for a reason? I really think he's served his purpose and maybe his function was to awaken the sleeping lioness within. There are many more fish in the sea (truly there are!) and what a wonderful talking point, eh, when you next go to a dinner party? Just put certain things in a safe place, ready for the next reveal!!

Bella

I'm away to Cornwall with Paul and Mike this weekend and I'm not sure what the Wi-Fi will be like where we'll be staying, but will try to check messages, so keep in touch. P.S. still got 4th June in the diary x

Me

Thanks. I'll try my best to make the most of it. Also, better that I know now rather than when I get there, but wasn't ready for that story to end just yet

—especially as the lioness within truly was awake and ready to roar! But hey-ho. Out of my control, and like you said, everything happens for a reason. Let's hope there are more fish. It has been a fun chapter, though. Too short but relatively sweet. I'll keep you posted. Have fun in Cornwall xxx

Bella

Will do. xx

Thank goodness for my friends. Whilst I was still feeling like crap, on the scale of shittiness, with 10 being the worst, I was now hovering around the 6/7 mark, whereas before messaging them, I had been more like 20 (I know that's not technically possible, but…).

I downed the rest of my drink, stripped off my dress and underwear, threw them on the floor and pulled the duvet over my head. Screw having a shower. Screw throwing my clothes in the laundry basket. Screw packing. Screw Lorenzo (well, I was hoping to, but that was never gonna happen now). Screw everything. I was going to bed.

SO HERE I WAS AGAIN. Back in Florence. I put the key in the door of my hotel room and opened it to reveal a very grand yet minimalist room with dark wooden flooring, huge windows, white furniture and a ginormous bed. What a shame.

I put my suitcase by the white wardrobe and then sat on the edge of the bed, which was clearly created with orgies in mind. It could literally fit four or five people (now I know I'd come here for a dirty weekend and to lose my MARGINITY, but that would definitely be too much of a stretch for a vanilla girl like me). It would have been perfect for the two of us. We could have rolled around on here for hours…

Whilst I hadn't quite worked out exactly what I was going to do on this trip and was apprehensive about being completely solo this time around, I'd have been disappointed with myself if I'd just sat at home. That would be giving Lorenzo too much power and letting him control my life, and I'd already done enough of that by waiting for his messages. As everything was already paid for, I had nothing to lose by being here, but potentially lots to gain. Who knows? I might even have a good time. I had zero expectations, so any enjoyment I got to experience will be a bonus. In honour of MAP point number 7, whatever happened, I would embrace it.

I was starving, but first things first. Better let the ladies know I was here.

Me

Hey. Arrived safely. Still quite warm here and it's just before 9 p.m. Currently in my hotel room lying on a ginormous bed all on my own. Oh, what could have been…gutting.

Me

I'm okay. I go from feeling shit and wondering why he didn't meet me to thinking 'sod him, I don't need a man to have a good time'. Will probably venture out to a restaurant around the corner with a good book, order some delicious food, get a nice bottle of wine, do some people watching and try and take my mind off things. I'll also go to the

concierge and book some excursions. Enjoy your
weekend and see you next Sat xxx
Roxy
Aaaah buonjourno (sorry don't know how to spell
it!) my gorgeous…glad you arrived safe and sound.
That's the spirit. Now go find food! And keep
messaging x

I went around the corner to a cute little family restau-
rant I'd driven past in the taxi on the way from the airport.
It was busy, which was a good sign, but not too noisy.
Perfect.

'Table for one, please,' I said to the ridiculously good-
looking waiter with floppy dark hair, clean-shaven olive
skin and greeny-brown eyes who greeted me with a beautiful smile as I stepped through the door. Seriously? What
was it with these Italian men? Why were they all so hot?
And more to the point, why couldn't they all up sticks and
come and live in London?

In the end it wasn't so bad dining alone. I'd flicked
through the literature that I had picked up from reception
with details of all of the organised trips and made a short-
list. Then I WhatsApped some photos of my dinner to
Roxy and Harrison, caught up on reading some articles
whilst enjoying a glass of chianti and of course some
dessert: an orange Florentine cake. Whilst it was nice,
annoyingly, I had to admit, it wasn't as tasty as Lorenzo's
recipe.

After dinner I went to the concierge with renewed optimism and booked myself on a pizza and gelato-making
class for tomorrow and a day trip to Cinque Terre, which
apparently was a collection of five lovely fishing villages

tucked away on the Italian Rivera, for the Sunday. The coach would leave at 5 a.m. and then we wouldn't get back to Florence until about 8 p.m. Perfect. That would take my mind off things for an entire day. Then on Monday it would be time to go home.

I NEEDED an early night if I was going to be up at 4 a.m., ready for the coach to collect me at 5 a.m. Roxy had been messaging throughout the day to check up on me, so now I was back from my cookery lesson, I typed a summary of what I'd been up to:

Me
Hi. How did the wedding go? Any single guys? What was the food like?
Today I went into Florence but tbh, I'd seen it all before when I went last month. I'd booked on to a pizza and gelato making course which was good. The pizza I made didn't look as good as it could have but was tasty. Another dish to add to my growing Italian recipe repertoire! The chef was cute (the amount of good-looking men per square mile in this country is ridiculous!). Will send pics shortly.
Me
Tomorrow I'm booked on an all-day excursion to Cinque Terre (means something like 'five lands'), which has beaches and looks interesting. Didn't fancy Rome in the end. I've seen a lot of the attractions during press trips and just not cultured

enough to do it all again right now. Then on Monday it's home time.

Still get moments where I think about what could have been with Lorenzo…but I guess that's what happens when you take a gamble. Sometimes you lose… xxx

Roxy

Gorgeous pics and adorable man!!

Was a very long day at the wedding (and zero hot guys—clearly they're all in Italia!).

Good luck with the trip tomorrow. Keep me updated and stay positive—you really are amazing! xxx

NORMALLY GETTING up this early on a Sunday was a struggle, but I was relieved to be doing stuff and was looking forward to going to the beach and feeling the sun on my skin.

I popped on my jean shorts, a khaki t-shirt and also a black jumper, as it might be a bit chilly this time in the morning. I packed the leggings I'd worn on the Taste Holidays trip in my bag for later this evening and headed downstairs. As I waited at reception, I glanced at the weather forecast on display on the desk. Rain? Surely not?

'Excuse me,' I said to the stocky, suited man behind the desk, who was typing away on the computer in front of him. 'It says on this forecast that there will be rain in Florence today. But is it likely to be raining in Cinque Terre too?'

'Possibly, madam,' he replied.

Don't know if it's just me, but being called 'madam' always made me feel about ninety.

'Oh…I thought it would be sunny at this time of year,' I said. 'Do I have time to run upstairs and grab a brolly, I mean an umbrella?'

'*Sì, signora*. If you are quick,' he said.

I hurried to my room, unlocked my case, pulled out my umbrella and locked it again.

Should I bring my coat? Nah, it'd be too heavy to carry that around all day, and as I had packed sandals, snacks, water and a book for the journey, my bag already weighed a ton. This was beautiful Italy, not England, so if there was a little shower, it probably wouldn't last long.

Oh dear…first the rain started trickling gently down the coach windows, but within five minutes it became torrential. *You have got to be kidding me*. All of the women in their spaghetti-strapped tops and cropped shorts started to look *very* nervous. Like me, they must have thought that, as we were visiting beach towns in Italy, somehow it automatically guaranteed sunshine.

The rest of the day could only be described as being like a school trip from hell.

Luckily for me, I had my leggings to wear over my shorts (not a good look, even for the new me), a thin scarf, which I tried to use to cover my hair in a bid to stop it exploding into a ball of frizz, and my umbrella. But the rain was so heavy, even that was futile. We scrambled to the nearest tourist shop to buy flimsy plastic ponchos, which helped marginally, but we were in the middle of a storm. Why oh why hadn't I packed my bloody coat! Had living in London not taught me anything? Never leave home without preparing for every conceivable meteorological possibility.

I had a flashback to when I was a student and had gone up to Kings Cross to do some research at the British Library. When I left the house, it was sunny, but I got out of the tube station it was raining, and then when I left the library a few hours later it was snowing. And this was in March! Three seasons in one day. Only in the UK, right? Well, evidently not...

My blue canvas shoes were now black and completely soaked through—it was like walking in a bath with slippers on. If I'd known I would be auditioning for the role of a drowned rat, I would've asked to attend the casting in London and stayed at home.

Not only was it raining, but it was windy and freezing cold too. Frankly, it made the British weather seem tropical. What's more, it was only 11 a.m. and the coach wouldn't be picking us up until 5 p.m., so I had six hours of this nightmare still to endure. Aaaarrrgghh!

First, after getting drenched in Manarola, we went to a train station, where we stood freezing our butts off on the platform, waiting for a train to Riomaggiore, which of course was late. I thought commuting in London was bad, but try waiting on a platform with a hundred other tourists in wet shoes, in an ill-suited outfit without a coat, as the wind and rain give you a serious lashing. It was about as much fun as having a tooth extracted without anaesthetic. But if I thought the train was bad, next we had to get a boat—yes, a boat—to Monterosso, an ancient fishing village. Cue rough seas, a bumpy crossing that was akin to being on the Stealth roller-coaster ride at Thorpe Park, feeling like I was either going to throw up or, worse, drown, and you kind of get a taste of the experience.

As we approached the shore, the sun started to come out. Thank fuck. We went to the restaurant and had some gorgeous pasta, seafood and fresh fruit salad with ice cream for dessert. At least the weather was finally looking up. Or so I thought.

The minute we stepped out of the restaurant, the heavens opened again. *This can't be happening!* I went back into the bar and ordered a glass of prosecco so that I wouldn't have to wander around for an hour until we were due to meet to get the train to Vernazza.

As positive as I'd been trying to feel throughout the trip, this excursion from hell had brought all of my emotions and sadness to the surface. *Why, Lorenzo? Why did you stand me up?* In fact, why did I do this to myself by putting my precious heart and emotions in the hands of a man who clearly didn't deserve it? If I hadn't gotten carried away with stupid dreams of having this amazing weekend together, I wouldn't be here freezing cold, wet and feeling sorry for myself.

Why didn't he want to meet me? Was it really because he was working, or something to do with me? Maybe it was someone else? Had he got back with his girlfriend? Were they getting married? *Shit…maybe it's because she's pregnant?*

There I went again. Overthinking…

I glanced over to the other side of the restaurant. Oh, great. A couple kissing. Would I ever kiss a man, ever again? Maybe I should have just stayed with Rich. This single life was *sooooo* hard…

What the fuck is wrong with you, woman! screamed Reasanna in my head.

Pull yourself the fuck together and stop letting this man take control of your thoughts. You are a smart, successful and beautiful woman, and if he can't see that, that's his loss. Rain or no rain, you're away from London for once, in a beautiful country on a bank holiday weekend, and you're not *working—this isn't just another miracle. It's an opportunity to actually do something different, discover new places and experience more of life. So don't waste it.*

Remember, when shitty Italian men like Lorenzo throw you lemons, make Limoncello. Drink up and enjoy!

Hell to the yes, Reasanna.

I called the barman over, ordered a shot of Limoncello, downed it in one and made my way to the meeting point at the station full of positive, don't-give-a-fuck gusto.

We got a train to La Spezia, where we boarded the coach back to Florence. And of course, five minutes later, the sun started to come out! I laughed to myself. What a day. It had certainly been an adventure. Not one I'd wish to repeat, but this was all part of my growth and another experience to add to the memory bank, that's for sure.

I settled back into my seat, took out my phone and scrolled through the photos I'd taken earlier. Despite the rain, the colourful houses suspended on the cliffs overlooking the sea and the surrounding scenery still looked beautiful. I bet when the sun was shining, it was even more amazing. Shame that wasn't to be today though, but that's the way stuff goes sometimes. Things can't always be perfect. And would you believe it? When I messaged Roxy earlier, she told me it was twenty-one degrees and sunny in

London. Typical! I laughed again. Life really is funny sometimes.

MONDAY MORNING. After an eventful few days, I was at the airport and was finally returning to London..

As my flight was delayed for an hour, that gave me three hours to kill. It was a nice warm, sunny day (*why wasn't it like this yesterday?*), so I sat out on the grass outside Pisa Airport.

It wasn't long before I got bored. Should I message him? Part of me said, *No, why the hell should you? Especially when he hasn't even messaged to check you're okay or to express any real remorse for leaving you in the lurch.* But then the other part of me—you know, the weak, irrational, but *oh-so-persuasive* part, which makes smart women like me do stupid things when it comes to attractive men—started to cave. Before I knew it, I'd drafted a message.

I wanted him to know that I hadn't cancelled my trip because of him, that I'd had a good time (even if that wasn't entirely true). To feel remorse about standing me up. And to regret missing the opportunity to spend time with me. Childish, I know, but it was hard to be logical in these circumstances.

Me
Afternoon, Lorenzo. Well, I decided not to waste my money/time, so I came to Florence anyway and had an amazing few days. Love this country, the friendly people and the delicious food. And the

hotel was great (HUGE bed)! Hope work wasn't too awful? You should have told them you were busy and joined me instead. You really missed out, and who knows if you'll ever be lucky enough to get another chance...

I clicked the send button.

Would he reply? And if he did, what would he have to say for himself?

If past timings were anything to go by, in roughly two hours, I would find out...

CHAPTER TWENTY-THREE

Naturally, the minute I stepped off the plane at Gatwick, I switched on my phone to check whether Lorenzo had messaged. Sure enough, he'd replied within the golden two-hour window with four messages (still never understood why he couldn't just put everything in one):

Lorenzo
Sorry, Sophia, you have reason
Lorenzo
It is a bad time right now but maybe your smile would have helped me
Lorenzo
Good for you…glad you enjoyed your time in Florence without me
Lorenzo
Have a safe flight

Awww. *He sounds so sad*, I thought to myself. Then I

started wondering whether he'd found my message too harsh, confident and *screw you*? Without thinking, I messaged back quickly:

Me
Are you okay?

As soon as I'd sent it, I realised what a ridiculous question that was. Clearly he was *not* okay. That's what he'd said, right? So why had I asked him that?

Then I came to my senses and wondered why the hell I was even considering *his* feelings after *he'd* stood *me* up. At that point, I switched my phone off and started flicking through *Psychologies* magazine to try and take my mind off things.

And now here I was back home, annoyingly still with thoughts of him in my mind, but feeling glad that I'd been brave enough to go to Florence on my own and make the most of what could have been an awful trip if I'd allowed it to get me down.

This time around, I was actually relieved that I couldn't feasibly take any extra time off work tomorrow as, in addition to all of the campaigns we had running at the moment, I had a new business meeting with one of the top facialists in Chelsea, who wanted us to manage a project to promote her new facial. Then I was seeing Monique for drinks as I hadn't had a catch-up with her since my birthday and she'd be heading back to America for six months soon. Plus I was following Bella's advice and trying to keep myself busy.

'So that's where I left it. I stupidly asked if he was okay and I haven't heard from him since. Normally he replies within a few hours.' I'd recounted the whole story to Monique whilst she glared at me, rolling her eyes so hard I thought they were going to come right out of their sockets.

Oh dear. Take cover, people. I fear fire will be shooting from her mouth imminently.

'Girl, well, first of all, I think you done messed up,' she said, scowling. 'I'm sorry, honey, but as a career woman running her own business, how can you condemn a man for working? Surely you of *all* people must understand how these things go. Sometimes things come up at the last minute and you have no choice but to go take care of your shit.'

'I hear what you're saying, Monique, but—' Before I even had a chance to finish my sentence, she butted in again.

'You could have tried to see if you could have met him briefly whilst you were there,' she scolded. 'Or you could have changed your flight. But *oh no*, you got struck down with that whole Independent Woman Syndrome, decided to ghost him and just go anyway because you *so* strong and you won't let *no* man dictate your life. And *then*, if *that* wasn't enough, you send him a message which basically says, "I don't need you. I can go to Florence all by my damn self and have an amazing time *without* you".' I could tell her frustration was building with every word.

'Well, Monique, I *can* go to Florence and have a good time *without* a man,' I replied defensively.

'Sophia,' she continued, this time softening her voice a little, 'you gotta realise that men are very sensitive souls and you have damaged his ego. It sounds like he's going through a tough time and you've just pissed all over him.

And then you ask if he's okay? I don't even know what to tell you right now!' She crossed her arms and leant back in her chair.

I was dumbfounded. As usual, Monique didn't hold back. True. I had never thought about it from that point of view, but surely she couldn't be saying it was my fault. *Come on!* If I hadn't contacted him, who's to say he would have even bothered to tell me he was working? Anyway, the past had gone. What I needed to figure out was how best to move forward.

'I see what you're saying, and I know it's a casual thing, so strictly speaking, he didn't owe me anything. But at the end of the day, he essentially stood me up. And it's not like he made suggestions to meet another time, or showed any kind of real remorse, so you don't really expect me to feel sorry for him, surely?' I snapped.

'Honey, I know you think I'm being hard on you, but it's only because I've made those same mistakes and seen my friends do it too. I'm just saying, keep an open mind, and sometimes you need to be gentle with a man's ego. I know so many women who think that liking a man or doing things to please him makes them weak, and so they put their guard up and act all tough. But too many of them are also alone. It's okay to be vulnerable, and sometimes you need to give people the benefit of the doubt. You don't know about their lives and what they're going through.'

'Yes,' I said, interjecting. 'Maybe, but *he* could have handled it better!'

'Agreed,' she added. 'But I really don't think you've considered it fully. Okay, think of it as an employer, from a business perspective. You need one of your key workers to come in at the last minute. How well would it go down if they turned around and said, "*Sorry, I can't, Sophia. I've got to go and fuck some girl I've only known for a couple of weeks*"? It ain't gonna happen, sugar. Then think of it from Lorenzo's position. No man, especially one that hot, who probably has pussy on tap, is going to risk his job just for some sweet British apple pie.'

Hmm. As much as I hated to admit it, whilst I didn't agree with everything, she'd made some valid arguments.

'Okay, point taken,' I replied, 'but I still don't see why I have to worry about his feelings when he didn't give a shit about mine.'

'Honey, you don't,' Monique said before taking a sip of her cocktail. 'You don't have to do a damn thing. Hell, you can take your phone out right now, delete his number and never speak to him again. It's your call. But I can tell by the way you're getting all worked up that you like this guy. So if you do, consider keeping your options open with him in case you decide to give him a second chance, which, even if you want to, won't be possible if you make him feel like shit and act like you don't need him.'

I mulled her comments over in my mind once again. My objective hadn't changed, so maybe I could give him the opportunity to redeem himself?

'Okay. The benefit of the doubt. I guess that's possible,' I said. 'I was thinking—there's a big food festival called Savour London taking place in a few weeks. Maybe I could invite him over here to come with me to that?' She leaned in a little. 'When I was Facebook stalking Lorenzo, I saw that he'd done a bit of travelling and had worked in Singapore and LA in different restaurants, so clearly he likes to get international experience. That's why I thought if he came, maybe he could do some networking. What do you think?'

'Honey, it's worth a try,' she said calmly. 'What have you got to lose? Invite him, and if he's up for it, then great. If he says he's working, which based on what you've told me seems pretty likely, but suggests an alternative option, pursue it. If he doesn't, then leave it.'

'Yes, agreed. I already think I'm being generous, but I'll give him one more shot. Only because I genuinely felt a connection. But maybe it was just in my head. It'd be a whole lot easier if I just knew what he was thinking. Is he interested, or does he just consider it a one-night thing? I'll just be direct and ask him if he's into me or not.'

'Oh God, honey. This isn't how it works. Don't ask him if he likes you—it isn't the tenth grade!'

'Why the hell not? I'll see how I feel later, but I wasn't into games and this "women should do this and say that" bullshit and all the dating rules I'm supposed to follow. If you don't know something, the easiest way to find out is to ask, right? What's the point in guessing? Just ask the question, get the answer and save wasting any more time.'

'Look. It's up to you, Sophia, and I hate to break it to you, but when it comes to men, just because you *ask* a question doesn't mean you'll actually get a straight answer. I say keep it simple. He seems like he has a lot on his plate, as do you, so you don't have time for overthinking. Invite him to the event and see what happens.'

Well, Monique had certainly given me some food for thought. One thing was for sure—if I was going to message him again, this time, I wasn't going to rush into it. I'd put thoughts of him to one side, focus on my work and message him when I was good and ready.

IT WAS NOW SATURDAY AFTERNOON, and so it had been five days since I'd sent the 'are you okay?' message. I was meeting Bella in a few hours for dinner and wasn't working today, so it was a good enough time to message Lorenzo.

I drafted a message. Read over it once, and then again. It was a little gushy for my liking, but I was trying to take on board the fact that Monique said I'd probably damaged his ego. If I was honest, I still felt like *he* should be the one apologising to *me*, but I bit the bullet and sucked up a little and followed his multiple-message approach:

Me

Hey, Lorenzo, just thinking I messaged back to ask if you were okay but didn't get to reply to your other messages before I got on the plane. Whilst I had a good time in Italy, it would have been better if I'd seen you too.

Me

Sorry to hear you're going through a difficult time. Wish I could be there to give you lots of hugs and long kisses and make you feel better.

Me

You sound like you've been working really hard and need a break. Would you like to see me again? I felt like we had a connection. Do you feel the same, or is it just my imagination?

Me

There's a big food festival soon with lots of top chefs, so it might be good for you to network/see what opportunities there are to work at some of London's best restaurants—I'm sure they're always looking for talented people like you. I'll send you some links. Let me know if you'd like to come...

I fired off some links to the website, which showed the different chefs and restaurants who would be at the festival, dates, etc.

I knew Monique had said not to ask if he wanted to see me again, but I needed to know one way or the other. All this second-guessing was driving me mental.

At least I had a packed week ahead at work, and then Roxy had suggested that rather than her coming along tonight, I could come and stay over at her house next weekend. I was definitely up for that. Too much time alone for me lately equalled overthinking...

Bella hadn't got a chance to read my WhatsApp messages properly as reception was poor at the place she was staying at in Cornwall and the Wi-Fi was rubbish too, so we'd agreed to discuss everything tonight.

We went to Berner's Tavern, another favourite spot of ours. Despite being very glamorous, with its grand stately home-esque dining room, giant chandeliers, intricate plasterwork, zillions of gilt-framed photos and paintings of varying sizes adorning the grand and towering walls, it wasn't at all poncy and had friendly staff as well as a down-to-earth yet chic feel. We liked it here.

By the time we'd ordered our mains, I'd brought her up to date on everything, including Monique's controversial take on the situation and my recent message (which I'd sent four and a half hours ago and was yet to receive a reply...).

'I see what Monique's saying,' she said, taking a sip of her prosecco, 'but like I said in my WhatsApp message, at the end of the day, Soph, I just think some people are there to serve a purpose. And Lorenzo was there to show you that you are desirable and to remind you what you've been missing. So now he's done that, personally I think you should move on.'

'Hmm,' I said, pondering the two conflicting pieces of advice I'd received about Lorenzo this week. 'But I have an objective. And when I set my mind to something, I don't like to stop until I achieve that goal.'

'I know you wanted to use that weekend to build on your experience, but from what you've told me, his life seems complicated. He works a lot, which I know you can understand, but he also doesn't seem entirely reliable, so maybe draw a line under him, and if you really want to achieve your 'objective', as you call it, and get some action, look closer to home. Join some dating sites like Roxy suggested. You don't have to get on a plane and travel thousands of miles to do that.'

I took a moment to consider her suggestion. 'Yes,' I said. 'Maybe it's time to bite the bullet and get on those apps, as I'm definitely ready to meet someone. Tomorrow I'll have a lazy day in bed and sign myself up. No point hanging around. Need to be proactive. I feel so much better now, thank you. Have you ever thought about being a professional agony aunt or a counsellor? You'd be so good at it!'

'Ah, stop it!' laughed Bella. 'What with looking after Paul and counselling you, I barely have time to scratch my head!'

'Sorry! I know I've been a bit of a neurotic basket case

lately. These men can really fuck with your sanity. Maybe I'm a glutton for punishment, opening myself up for more of this by jumping into this online dating thing, but hey, gotta try! Brace yourself, Bella. This Lorenzo shit is probably going to be just the tip of the iceberg. Bet even you're wishing I was back with Rich so you could have some peace and quiet again,' I joked.

'Nooooo!' she insisted. 'You're better off being single than staying in an unhappy relationship. Honestly, I don't mind. For years you've held everything together as you're so brilliant at running your business, so I haven't really needed to give you any advice, so it's nice to be able to help,' added Bella. 'Plus, it's great to have an adult conversation once in a while, and without sounding bad, because I know you're the one going through it, your life is very entertaining right now. Like Roxy said, I'm saving a fortune on cinema tickets. It's like the start of one big messy romcom,' she said, letting out a wicked laugh.

'Thanks. Nice to know you're getting a kick out of my trials and tribulations!'

'I know, sorry!' she said, laughing again. 'But even you've got to admit that as hard as it is sometimes, right now your life is waaay more interesting than it was six months ago.'

'Yes. You could say that!' I replied.

After catching up on Bella's news, I headed home and jumped straight in the shower. I should've messaged her straight away as she lived in Hampstead, North London whereas I was the complete opposite, in South London, so we always liked to let each other know we'd got home safely.

I unlocked my phone. There was a message from Bella, and *seven from Lorenzo?*

I quickly messaged Bella to let her know that I'd also got home safely, then clicked on to Lorenzo's chat:

Lorenzo
Yes i am very busy
Lorenzo
For two more weeks
Lorenzo
You are so kind
Lorenzo
I will think about it
Lorenzo
Until then i am sending you a big hug
Lorenzo
And a kiss
Lorenzo
Goodnight

Oh.

So I sent a gushing, heartfelt, sucking up message and *that* was his reply?

Had he answered my direct question about wanting to see me again? Nope. And the two-week thing. Did that mean he was busy for two weeks, but he'd like to see me after that? He said he'd think about the festival. Maybe that was positive? It wasn't an outright no... it was in three weeks' time, so that was after the busy two-week period he had coming up. And the big hug and kiss thing, was he showing enthusiasm or just being polite?

I'd hoped asking questions would make things clearer

in my mind, but actually it had done the complete opposite.

As much as I hated to admit defeat, I couldn't really see that there was much more that I could do. I typed a quick reply. I knew this was likely to be the last message I'd send to him and that the chances of him coming over were non-existent, but ever the optimist, I kept it upbeat and positive.

Me
Yeah, have a think and let me know. Could be good for your career. And after you've done your networking, we can go and have some fun... Good-night x

Done. In more ways than one.

No more chasing.

If Lorenzo wanted to come over, he would. If he didn't, he wouldn't. I couldn't sit around waiting for him. Like Reasanna kept reminding me, I was smart, successful and attractive. And if Lorenzo didn't want to grab the opportunity to be with a woman like me, there must be other men that would.

Online dating: here we come.

CHAPTER TWENTY-FOUR

According to self-proclaimed dating expert Roxy, the best way to get over one man was to get under another. Now whilst she had an *interesting* way of putting it, and I didn't see why the saying couldn't be 'the best way to get over one man is to get *on top* of another' (why do we have to always be the ones underneath?), she did have a point. So, last Sunday after my catch-up with Bella, I'd decided to dip my toes firmly into the online dating waters.

Despite its reputation for just being a seedy hook-up site, I'd heard so much about Tinder that I decided to find out what all the fuss was about for myself. A week later, I could confirm that my first foray into the MAD (another Roxy acronym, for middle-aged dating) world had been an eye-opening experience. As far as I could make out so far, there appeared to be seven stages of Tinder:

Stage 1: The Set-Up

After downloading the app, I discovered it needed to be linked to Facebook. So I set up a fresh page, to avoid my dating escapades colliding with my professional life (yes, it was possible clients might spot me, but as long as I conducted myself 'appropriately', I didn't see cause for concern). I gave myself a new moniker: *Thea* (because it sounds like the 'phia' at the end of my name) and age. Not because I was ashamed of being thirty-nine—just because common sense said that if I shaved a few years off and said I was thirty-five, I'd widen my pool of opportunity. These little white lies, I was reliably assured, were the premise based on which online dating existed. The truth could be revealed if all went well during the first date...

Whilst I was fine to alter my name and age, I drew the line at uploading heavily photoshopped/filtered pictures or snaps taken a decade ago, as that would be *really* dishonest. Plus, it's a false economy. If you blow up the size of your boobs because you think that's what a man wants to see, it's only going to lead to disappointment when you meet in real life. They'd just need to accept me as I was.

Following some photo vetting with online dating expert Roxy, I uploaded a selection of real, untouched pics which fitted the 'triple S' image I wanted to project: 'sophisticated, sexy and sense of humour'. Said images included the shot of me in the outfit Lorenzo had gone crazy for from my birthday dinner and one of me wearing a very fitted blue dress which showed legs and teased a tasteful amount of cleavage. After all, I wanted to leave *something* to the imagination.

I kept my profile simple—you know, standard stuff about my love for good food and travel. Whilst not entirely original, this at least was also true. A thirty-kilometre radius seemed reasonable, and as for age preferences, I opted for males between twenty-nine and forty-nine—ten years either side of my own age. Set-up done.

Stage 2: The Swiping

This was the fun part. Well, initially at least. For the first few hours I enthusiastically swiped away at high speed, casually rejecting hundreds of photos without giving the blatant shallowness of this app a second thought. You'd be surprised how many things you can think of in a millisecond that cause you to swipe left.

Yes, there's the obvious things, like the fact that you're not attracted to them because you feel they're too short, look too young, too old, have too much hair, not enough hair/bald, look too serious, too smiley, not smiley enough (yep, like I said, the premise of this app is totally shallow). But in my opinion, the photos men post are also nuts. These also fall into several 'turn-off' categories. For example:

a) *I'm so hot I only need one photo.* Seriously, guys. Everyone has that one killer photo. But I need to see a few of you in different settings to be sure that pic isn't just a fluke and to check the attraction is there—don't put all your eggs in one basket with just one.

b) *Look at me I'm sooo hot* pose-y photos. You know, the ones of them flexing their muscles at the gym in the mirror, showing off their six-packs, etc. Photos with celebrities, selfies in bed…I know, on a site which is based purely on looks, you have to sell your best assets, but really… although, to be fair, in their defence the above are probably *exactly* the kind of photos to use if you want a hook-up.

c) *Look at me I'm soooo rich* photos. The blatant flashiness—posing in front of sports cars, flaunting a giant

Rolex type activity. Again, I guess they're selling the dream…it's a no from me though.

d) *Totally trashed* pics. Why would you post a photo of you looking shit-faced? There's a difference between having fun and looking like a total drunken dickhead. Unlike the flashy/pose-y photos which self-promote, these pics are the opposite of selling yourself.

e) *I'm with the hot girl* pics. You're supposed to be *attracting* a girl, so why are you posting pictures posing with one? Also, being surrounded by a bevy of beauties doesn't make me think you're an irresistible catch. It just makes me think you're a ladies' man.

f) *Don't worry, the kid isn't mine* pics. Why include photos with babies and children if they're not yours? Is seeing you with kids supposed to make my ovaries explode with excitement? Doing this only then requires you to use up valuable characters in your profile explaining that they are your niece/nephew/godchild/borrowed for the day. Not to mention the fact that posting images of children on Tinder is just wrong.

g) *Shady* pics. Yeah, we know you look cool in your sunnies, but that's kind of the problem. Most people look better in sunglasses, and so I need to see what you look like *without* them. As they say, the eyes are the windows to the soul. But who am I kidding? No one goes on Tinder to see someone's soul…

h) *Hat* pics. I want to see your hair. If you've got a hat on in every photo, I will assume you are bald. A lot of women go crazy for bald men and find them sexy—think Jason Statham, Bruce Willis, etc. So if that's the look you're rocking, don't hide it. Be confident and own it.

i) *Sexual* pics. E.g., zoomed-in boxer short pics or dick

pics…say no more. Then again, I remind myself for the hundredth time that this is bloody *Tinder*—you know, the site renowned for hook-ups—so what the hell do I expect?

Before I knew it, it was fast approaching 1 a.m. and I realised that not only had I been swiping consistently since 7 p.m. but that I was on the verge of developing irreversible repetitive strain injury. What's more, having put my business head on, I calculated that if I'd swiped left for over two thousand men and right for approximately twenty because of the extensive and frankly ridiculously rigid criteria I'd been using, I was unlikely to get a satisfactory 'return on my investment'.

So, whilst attraction and maintaining some kind of standards were important, I recited the cliché that 'looks aren't everything' (yes, I realise the irony of saying this whilst using an app based entirely on appearance) and opened up my mind a little more.

Stage 3: The Match

Unsurprisingly, the more open-minded strategy worked much better. The first few times I received a match, I can't deny it did give me a buzz. *The guy I like, likes me back! How wonderful*, you naively think. Until you realise that a) most men that you match with don't actually message you back because b) horror of horrors, whilst women often only swipe right when they *genuinely* like someone, men use dating apps as a vanity exercise to boost their ego and prove that women find them attractive. Shocking.

Legend has it that men swipe right for practically *everyone* to see who matches with them first, and only then do they go through and 'vet', by either unmatching or ignoring the ones they're not really interested in. Worse still, some of them just do it for cheap thrills. They don't even want a date. Knowing they got a match is satisfying enough. Boo.

Stage 4: The Messaging

But no matter, I told myself. Not all men were like that. What's more, as an independent woman, I didn't *need* to wait for the man to make the first move. So after matching, I decided to kick-start the proceedings and message José—an *extremely* attractive specimen who, whilst not Italian, had the trademark dark eyes, hair and beard that I'd become addicted to. Perhaps he was Spanish or Brazilian? His profile was blank, so I was none the wiser. Still blissfully naive and sticking with the 'simple is best' approach, I innocently opted for a basic:

Hi, José, how are you?

I awaited his reply (more eagerly than I'd like to admit as he was a *vision*). My phone pinged as he fired back two messages at high speed. I was excited to see his response:

Hi, said the first message, swiftly followed by, *Good, but I go back home tomorrow morning, so we should meet and have sex tonight.*

Whoa!

Not quite what I was expecting. I was so stunned by his frankness that I didn't reply. Realistically, what could I have said? Ignore the blatant booty call, ask where 'home' is and what the weather's like over there? It's obvious I was once again way out of my comfort zone…

I also quickly learnt from stage 4 that the matches that *do* message you often fall into three categories: 1) very direct and overtly sexual (à la José's message), staying true to the hook-up reputation of the app; 2) boring and bland (akin to asking what your favourite colour is or writing a 5,000-word essay on the different shades of white paint

Dulux produce); 3) promising. These are the rare gems. The one-in-a-million matches (well, sometimes those odds feel accurate) where a decent-sounding guy that you like actually interacts with you and seems normal. Happy days.

Stage 6: The VCOD: Vicious Cycle Of Disappointment

All too often, stage five often leads seamlessly to stage six—the vicious cycle of disappointment. You've downloaded the app because you're ready to find someone and also, if you're honest, no matter how confident you are, it's nice to receive some reassurance that someone in the universe (or within your thirty-kilometre radius) fancies you.

Filled with optimism, you swipe away and then receive the 'validation' of a match, but of course, given the 'like-all-and-sundry' tactics men employ, you know a match means little without a message. Thus, when they don't message, you're disappointed.

Or you take the lead and message them, you're enjoying the conversation and then, just when you feel it's progressing nicely and you're in the midst of making plans to actually meet in real life, suddenly they stop messaging you altogether for no apparent reason. There's complete and sudden radio silence. Otherwise known as ghosting. *Was it something I said?*

When this happens, you get so fed up that you log off feeling worse than you did before you logged on and vow to delete the app altogether. It can really fuck with your mind.

But of course, it won't *always* end up this way. Like I said at the start, as a middle-aged woman dipping my toe into the dating world for the first time in nearly a decade and a half when most of my peers were all settled and had done all this in their twenties and early thirties, I wasn't expecting it to be easy. Nothing ventured, nothing gained, and whilst I felt like I wanted to give up altogether after day three of using the app, I knew that if I wanted to get to the seventh stage, i.e., the actual date, I would need to persevere. So I started taking a more structured, businesslike approach.

For the last four days, I'd committed two hours to swiping and messaging (squeezed in between meetings, whilst eating dinner, just before bed, and also under the expert eye of Roxy, when I stayed over at her house last night). As a result I had three dates lined up for next week.

I had no idea what the men would be like in real life—if I'd like them, if they'd like me, if I'd want to meet them again. But given that it had been so long since I had been on a date, whatever happened, it was sure to be an 'interesting' experience.

CHAPTER TWENTY-FIVE

I was on cloud nine right now. Even after being in PR for seventeen years, I still got a huge buzz from organising a successful launch.

Last night was the long-awaited MIKA Cosmetics Influencer Lipstick launch at Harvey Nichols, and it had gone even better than we could have anticipated. Not only did the store sell out of their stock in record time (despite ordering extra), but we had over a hundred women that hadn't managed to book tickets to the customer event in the evening, queuing outside the door, eager to meet and greet Amelia and Céline in person. The store had even had to draft in extra security.

The lipsticks had launched online this morning and sold out in seventeen minutes. Social media had also gone crazy. #MIKAbyAmelia and #MIKAbyCéline were still trending, and there were thousands of posts on Instagram. The boomerang post Amelia put online last night of her jumping for joy next to the giant illuminated poster of herself in the window of the store had currently been viewed 30,709 times—a figure that was increasing by the second.

As well as the sales and social media success, the floods of editorial were also coming through thick and fast, with articles already live on Vogueuk.com, Graziadaily.co.uk and the *Daily Mail* website. Sunday *Times* Style were running a big profile piece in this weekend's issue.

It was a huge relief. That campaign was one of the biggest and ambitious we'd run to date. Even though we'd planned every last detail, I still always worry about something going wrong. Until the event is over and you get the seal of approval from the client, nothing is certain.

As well as being major for the company, it was also significant in terms of my own personal progress on the control-freak front. Whilst I had been involved at every stage and had overseen everything carefully, Robyn had led this campaign from the get-go. She'd continued to impress me and was definitely due a promotion. Perhaps to associate director, or maybe even deputy managing director? I'd need to give it more thought.

Her incredible competency meant that I no longer needed to work late every night or at weekends. With this in mind, even though there would be post-event activity to take care of, my involvement would be minimal. Which meant, despite being a little tired from last night, I was able to be bold and keep this evening free to experience the seventh stage of Tinder: the actual dates.

As we've established, when it came to my career, I was fine. But this dating stuff somehow caused my confidence to turn to jelly. So the only coping mechanism that seemed to be producing any modicum of success was relating everything to a work scenario. In this way, dating was just a meeting and going for drinks was like attending an evening networking event. So on that basis, I'd arranged three dates back to back across one evening:

6.30 p.m.: Riccardo—a thirty-three-year-old lawyer

7.30 p.m.: Diego—a thirty-one-year-old accountant

8.30 p.m.: Bruno—a twenty-nine-year-old restaurant manager

And yes, the 'o' at the end of all of their names did mean they were all Italians. Pure coincidence. Honest…

Was I bothered about the fact that they weren't MDs? Not really. Whilst there's a school of thought which says you shouldn't date outside of your 'professional circle' as you won't have anything in common, as my main goal is to have fun and gain more 'experience', I wasn't fussed. As long as they were interesting, had ambition and could pay their own way, that was good enough for now.

I'd allocated an hour slot per date, to give us around thirty to forty mins to chat, at which point Roxy (who I'd also sent details of whom I'd be meeting, when and where, just to be safe), would call my phone and I'd have to leave *unexpectedly*. In other words, make my way to the next date. I had learnt the 'get out call' was, once again, standard practice in the new dating world.

I'd made sure my hair, make-up and outfit were on point and had even embarrassingly struck different poses in the mirror—practising how I would smile and act when I greeted my dates. Big cheesy, confident smile? Or act demure and sexy? I was nervous. Understandable, as it had been a while since I'd been on a date, so packing three into one evening with men I'd never met before only intensified those feelings. Even though I wasn't sure if they'd turn up or what to expect, it was also quite exciting.

I was looking forward to meeting Riccardo. From his messages, he seemed like an ambitious lawyer, and I loved anyone with drive. But I should have known it was too good to be true. The man who rocked up (ten minutes late, I might add), was *not* the man I'd seen in those photos. That sexy stubble I'd been drawn to was in fact a full-on beard that would give Father Christmas a facial hair complex, and that cute head of ringlets was tied up into an unkempt, greasy man bun.

Turns out he wasn't, in fact, a lawyer. He'd graduated from law school six years ago and currently worked part-time at Caffè Nero but would start looking for a job in the industry again 'soon'…which, judging by his lack of energy, didn't seem likely to happen any time this century.

In contrast to Riccardo, Diego surprised me. He actually looked just like his photos. He'd already told me he was five foot seven, so I was expecting that, and at first he seemed very interesting.

Then out of nowhere, he'd asked, 'How do you feel about being worshipped?'

Random. I was pretty sure he wasn't talking about religion…

'You're a beautiful, intelligent and clearly successful woman,' he'd added. 'Someone like you deserves to be worshipped. So I would like to be submissive to you. What do you think?'

Whilst the idea of a man pandering to my every whim did sound appealing for a few fleeting seconds, I quickly came to my senses. I didn't want some sort of bedroom slave. I was attracted to strong men with their own mind and would rather us be equal instead of me being dominant. Each to their own, but this wasn't for me.

Thankfully, right on cue, my phone rang. Roxy! She apologised profusely for missing the first get-out call, as she had been stuck in a meeting, but her timing now was spot-on. After ending the call, I told Diego I had to rush off to meet a friend.

To be polite, I reluctantly exchanged two friendly cheek kisses with him, but then his tongue licked the inside of my ear. 'Mmm…you taste *so* good,' he groaned suggestively.

Surely licking your *mistress'* ear without permission wasn't good sub behaviour? Gross. I wanted to go home and take a shower.

I hot-footed it to my next date, hoping it would be third time lucky.

Bruno…was a vision. Not as breathtaking as Lorenzo, but still stunning. Anyway, I needed to forget about him. Back to Bruno—he actually looked *better* in real life than in his photos. He had the most beautiful dark eyes, gorgeous full lips and a beard so perfectly shaped, it would make the most skilled barber give it a round of applause. Although, sitting in front of him rather than a phone screen suddenly made things feel very real, and I did wonder whether it was wrong for me to drool over him? *He's only twenty-nine, for goodness' sake. The same age as Harrison. Surely he's far too young?*

Unlike Riccardo, this was a man putting his goals into action by using the knowledge he'd gained from working at one of London's top hotels to launch his own concierge company.

Once he found out I ran my own business (I'd just said I worked in marketing on my profile), that was it. The questions about how he should promote himself came thick and fast, which was draining. When I was thinking about comparing the dating thing to work, I wasn't quite expecting it to feel like I was actually at a new business meeting. He was like an overexcited puppy with verbal diarrhoea, and any initial attraction I'd had started to evaporate. So when Roxy's call came after forty minutes, I told him I had to leave as I had an early start.

So that was it. My seventh stage of Tinder was complete. I'm sure there were an infinite number of steps after this. Perhaps Stage 8 was Hooking Up, but right now, I was exhausted and thought I'd opt for 'Tinder Time Out'.

At least for now, anyway…

Well, you know what it's like. Never say never, particularly as these apps are *totally* addictive…

CHAPTER TWENTY-SIX

I t was 10.30 a.m. on Sunday, and I was almost ready to leave for my appointment with super facialist Anoushka. As I'd hoped, we'd won the project to publicise her new £300 Caviar Facial. And because we never promote a treatment without trying it first, I'd booked in at her private clinic in Chelsea to test it myself (I know, it's a tough job, but someone has to do it…).

Normally, I'd jump in an Uber. But I was conscious that I hadn't driven my car for at least two months. In fact, as I always got a cab to and from work (another thing I vowed to do when I could, after years of commuting on the train with my head buried in someone else's sweaty armpits), I often questioned whether I actually needed a car anymore.

I headed to the dressing room and selected a simple black-and-white dress (after my trip to Italy, I'd been experimenting more with non-designer threads). *Think I'll switch up my handbag today too.* I picked a white bag from the shelf and transferred the essential items from my work bag into it. Keys? Check. Purse? Check. Make-up bag? Check. Phone? Charging—will grab in a sec. Umbrella? Check. Notepad? Check. Tissues? Check. Mints? Check.

I gave myself the once-over in the mirror. My hair was tied up into my now-signature undone ponytail to keep it off my face. No make-up today, obviously, as I was having a facial. Whilst my skin wasn't glowing right now and I looked a little tired from a few late nights last week, with the launch and then the Tinder dates, I wasn't concerned as I'd be hidden away in my car. Plus, after an hour with Anoushka I was sure to look a million times better.

Better go. My appointment was at noon, so I should arrive in plenty of time, but it was always good to get there early. Even though Anoushka had moved since I had last seen her, I knew exactly where she was based, as I remembered passing that road on the way to a furniture shop Rich wanted to visit during the January sales, so at least finding it would be straightforward.

I picked my car keys off the side table, set the alarm, stepped outside, then unlocked the doors to my black Mercedes SLK. I placed my handbag on the passenger seat and then started the engine.

As I set off towards the South Circular, my mind started to wander. I made a mental note to check in with Marie today to find out how she was coping. I'd been doing this every few weeks, alternating between her, Henri and Geraldine. Each time, I wished I could do more to help, but at the very least, I wanted to ensure they knew I was thinking of them. As you'd expect, every day was a struggle without Albert, but they'd all said that keeping themselves busy at work and having everyone's support helped to ease the pain a little. Yes, I'd message again later.

I spotted a new restaurant on the corner as I crossed Lavender Hill. My thoughts turned to the Savour London food festival I'd attended yesterday. Needless to say, I had gone alone, i.e., without Lorenzo. I hadn't heard from him since the last message I'd sent inviting him to the event, so although it had taken longer than I would've liked for the penny to drop, I realised that he just wasn't interested, so I wouldn't be messaging him again.

The festival was cool. I didn't stay long, as it doesn't matter how confident you are, sometimes it's just more enjoyable to have company, so you can marvel at how good the food/drink tastes or share the experience together. I walked around and tried a couple of prawn dishes from the pop-up restaurants. I was going to sit in on some celebrity chef demos, but I knew it would make me think about Lorenzo, so I headed home instead.

Enough mind-wandering. Better start getting myself into 'work' zone. You can never entirely relax when you're having treatments with clients. You need to be ready to answer any questions they're likely to throw at you.

Okay. Kings Road. If I remembered correctly, firstly, I needed to go down Sydney Street, which should be coming up shortly on the left. *Yes, here we go.*

So then, I do a right at the lights at the bottom of the road, then it should be a road on the right? I'll know it when I see it.

As the lights turned green, I made a right.

Great, so it should be somewhere…here. I put on my indicator.

Oh?

Nope. It's *not* that road. I took off my indicator. Must be the next one. I sped up, then slowed down as I approached the next right, indicated, then stopped again.

Damn! It wasn't that road either. I could have sworn that's where it was. I sped up, then slowed down as I looked at the next road on the right and indicated.

Or maybe it was on the left, if Rich and I came from a different direction last time I was there? I clicked off the indicator and started steering the car to the left.

BANG!

I felt a big thud at the back of my car, shunting me forward into the steering wheel.

Shit.

I braked suddenly, pulled my handbrake up instinctively and then spun my head around to see what had happened.

Ouch. My neck! What the fuck?

My whole rear window was blocked out by the sight of the front of the huge metallic grey Range Rover that had gone straight into the back of me.

Without even thinking about my neck beginning to ache, I jumped out of the car.

A tall floppy-haired blond guy slowly climbed down from his giant car, smiling.

'What the hell?' I shouted. 'You just ran into the back of me!'

'Terribly sorry,' he said as he looked at both cars to survey the damage. 'Thankfully, doesn't look like it's had a big impact on your car, so not too much harm done,' he said, stroking the rear of my SLK and then the front of his Range Rover. 'Shall we exchange details and either let the insurance company sort it all out or arrange for one of the garages I know to fix it privately?'

How was he so calm? Surely there should be some sort of heated argument or something or he should deny any wrongdoing. And what an earth was there to smile about?

'You rammed my car,' I said, irritated by his lack of reaction.

'Without wishing to be rude, *you* were behaving rather erratically. Stopping, then starting, switching your indicator on, then off, speeding up, then slowing down, indicating right and then steering the car to the left,' he said, smiling and running his hands through his floppy Hugh Grant–pre–*Love Actually* hair.

'Well…' I muttered, trying and failing to think of something sensible to say in my defence.

'I tried to keep a safe distance as I wasn't sure whether there was somebody under the influence at the wheel, but then before I knew it, I was in the back of you. Anyhow,' he added, 'let's not make a big deal out of it. Like I said, it looks like it'll be easily fixed, so if we just exchange details, then we can both be on our way.'

He had a point. I had been driving badly. I had been sure I had known where I was going. I should've just used the bloody sat nav. So embarrassing.

'Okay,' I muttered, recognising that it was indeed my fault.

'I'm Charlie, by the way,' he said, smiling again. 'I would say it's nice to meet you, although that feels slightly wrong under the circumstances.' His smile widened to reveal a perfect set of pearly whites. 'I'll just get my phone so I can take down your details.'

'I'll get mine too,' I said, walking around to the driver's seat to get my phone out of my bag.

Shit. My phone. Where is my phone?

It's on my fucking beside table charging, that's where it is. I forgot to put it in my bag. Aaaarrrgghhh!

My phone was my life. It had *everything* on it, including Anoushka's number and her full address. I thought I knew the name of the road, but after what had just happened, I needed to double-check and I definitely hadn't memorised what number she was based at. *What's the time?* Hadn't worn a watch either as I always used my phone.

'Excuse me…Charles.'

'It's Charlie,' he corrected me.

'Sorry, *Charlie*,' I said. 'Do you have the time, please?'

'Sure,' he said, pulling up the sleeve of his shirt to reveal a giant watch. 'It's eleven twenty-nine,' he replied.

Why didn't I just check the time on the dashboard? It was the whiplash. Clearly I wasn't thinking straight.

'Fuck!' I said, initially regretting my decision to swear in front of a stranger, but then reasoning that given the circumstances, it was justified. 'My appointment is in half an hour and I have no idea where I'm going. Well, I *thought* I did, but now I'm not so sure.' Cringe. Now I was really sounding like the stereotypical ditsy driver. Feminists across the world must be hanging their heads in shame…

'Can I help?' he said, sounding genuinely concerned.

'I've just realised I've left my mobile at home, and the location of where I need to be is on my phone, as is the phone number of the person I'm seeing, and I don't want to be late.'

'Where is the address stored in your phone? On a text? An email?'

'Yes, an email.'

'Well, can you access your emails remotely?'

'I *could*, but I'd need to remember the passwords. Harrison!' I said, having a mini brainwave. 'My brother Harrison will have access to my emails on his phone. But I'd need to call him…'

'Here,' he said, handing me his phone. 'Take mine and ring him.'

'Really?' I said, taking his iPhone. 'Thank you. That's very kind.'

'Yes, of course,' he said, flashing those pearly whites again. Definitely whitened. It wasn't natural for teeth to be that white. Unless of course he existed on a coffee-, wine- and basically food-free diet. 'He doesn't live in Australia, though, does he?' Charlie asked.

I frowned, confused. Oh! He was worried about me making an international call.

'No, no, no. Don't worry. He's based in London,' I replied.

'It's okay, I was only joking. I'm sure a quick call to Australia won't bankrupt me. Go on. Make your call.'

I racked my brain, trying to remember Harrison's number. I dialled it a million times a day, but that didn't involve typing in any numbers. I just clicked on his name and the phone took care of the rest. Apart from my parents' home number, which I'd obviously had to learn years ago, before mobiles were invented, I don't think I knew anyone's number off by heart.

After dialling three wrong mobile numbers, I conceded and called the house phone that I'd frequently condemned as being a waste of time and space that only deserved to be in a museum. Right now I was so glad my mum still insisted on having one.

'Mum, Mum, quick, emergency,' I said, speaking at a million miles an hour.

'What's the matter, darling?' she said, sounding worried. 'Are you okay?'

'I've had an accident, and I've—'

'An accident!' she interjected. 'Oh my goodness! Are you okay? Where are you, what—'

I jumped in quickly to avoid her panicking unnecessarily. 'It's okay, Mum. I'm fine, but I left my phone on charge at home by mistake, which is why I'm calling from someone else's. I've got an important appointment in less than thirty minutes, and I'm going to be late if I don't speak to Harrison and get him to access my emails, so he can give me the full address,' I said in a panic.

'Oh, thank goodness you're okay. Why don't you just Google it or ask someone on the street for directions, though, darling? Won't that be easier?'

'No, Mum,' I said. 'It's not like going to your local Toni & Guy. It's a private clinic, so the address isn't on the website. It's like a secret location because she has celebrities that go there and...anyway,' I said, fretting about losing time. 'Please, can you just keep me on hold, get your mobile, call Harrison and ask him to get the address for Anoushka from my emails, please. Sorry about this, Charlie,' I said, suddenly realising that it might take a few minutes and I'd be holding him up. 'I won't be long.'

'No problem, that's fine,' he said in his plummy accent.

'Oooh, he sounds nice?' said my mother, perking up. 'Who is Charlie, Sophia?'

'Mum!' *Honestly. Now isn't the time.* 'Please, can you get Harrison on the phone? Better still, can you just give me his mobile number and *I'll* call him? It'll be easier…'

I grabbed my notepad and pen from my bag and scribbled down the number. I then typed it into Charlie's phone. Luckily, Harrison answered straight away. It was *Sumner* Place, not Jubilee Place like I'd thought. He'd done a quick check on Google Maps, and it was a completely different side of the Kings Road. And I was going in the wrong direction. I ended the call and walked over to Charlie's Range Rover, where he was now sitting in the driver's seat, whilst trying to avoid the cars that were angrily having to manoeuvre around us.

I might not know a lot about cars, but I knew from the look of this one that this guy had to be loaded, as I remembered Rich looking at this model before and deciding against it as it was too pricey even for him. This was at least a hundred grand. Dark cherry with ivory leather seats (the rear ones were clearly reclining too), TVs on the back of the front seats like you get on an airplane with some remote control sort of panel by the armrests, a mini table… this had been customised to the nines.

'So,' he said, smiling. 'Panic over? Did you get the address?'

'Yes,' I said, relieved.

'That's good. So forgive me for asking, but are you late for some sort of life-saving operation?' At first I couldn't tell if he was being serious, but he started smiling again.

Then I remembered. I was currently wearing no makeup, and I mean *zero*. No tinted moisturiser, no mascara, no lipgloss. Nada. My naked face was being exposed to a complete stranger who, on closer inspection, despite not being my type at all, was quite cute. I started to feel a little self-conscious.

'Um, no, not quite. I'm seeing someone important—a client—and it won't be professional if I'm late.'

'I see,' he said as if satisfied with my answer. 'Sorry. You didn't tell me your name.'

Never understood why us Brits say sorry even when we've done nothing wrong, which he hadn't. I was the one who should be apologising.

'Sorry, Charlie,' I said. 'How rude of me. It's Sophia.'

'What a delightful name!' he said, running his hands through his ridiculously shiny, floppy hair once again. Clearly a man who used good quality professional haircare products. 'So, Sophia. Are you certain you know where you're going now?'

Grrr! Now he's talking to me like a pathetic, clueless woman driver. Sadly, on this occasion I had done nothing to prove otherwise.

'Yes, I need to get to Sumner Place, which I believe is back there,' I said, pointing in the opposite direction to the way our cars were currently facing.

'Oh, I know it well,' said Charlie. 'Listen, jump in your car, follow me and I'll take you. That way we can get you there on time without you having to call your VIP client. Then, as far as she'll be concerned, you'll have turned up as planned, thereby keeping your reputation and professionalism firmly intact.'

Now it was my turn to smile. Wow. What a nice guy.

'Thank you, Charlie,' I said, blushing. 'That would be amazing. Why are you being so nice to me? Especially considering I'm a crazy woman driver that's about to make you claim on your insurance and lose your no claims bonus?' I asked.

'Ah, well, it's no big deal,' he said, shrugging his broad shoulders. 'My Sunday was shaping up to be pretty boring, so if I can help a damsel in distress, albeit distress that was caused by her own fair hand, then I'm happy to help. All good karma too, so it's not entirely selfless,' he chuckled.

'Well, thank you,' I said, ignoring the 'damsel in distress' reference. Despite the fact that my actions had suggested I was guilty as charged, I didn't want him thinking I was some weak woman. At the same time, though, I was grateful for his help. 'That's really kind of you—I appreciate it.'

My car was still drivable, and when I re-examined it, the damage didn't look too bad. With the big grille protecting the front of his Range Rover, Charlie's car was almost unscathed.

Charlie led the way to Anoushka's with me following behind. Luckily we were only a few minutes away. Phew.

When we arrived, I parked a few doors down from the building so that she wouldn't see my slightly scratched car. He pulled alongside me and his automatic window began winding down.

'Are you sure you'll be okay?' he asked considerately. 'I'm just on my way to brunch with some friends, but if you have any problems and are able to use your client's phone, then call me and I can come back and help you. Have you got that notepad? Let me give you my number.'

I jotted down his details and also gave him mine. Strictly for insurance purposes only, of course…

'Charlie, I don't know how to thank you,' I said, letting

out a huge sigh of relief. 'I really, really appreciate your help and everything you've done to get me here. Look,' I said, pointing at the clock on the dashboard. 'I've still got five minutes to spare. It's a miracle.'

'My pleasure,' he said, grinning. 'Go on, you better hurry. I'll call you tomorrow, and we can discuss how best to proceed with fixing your car.'

'Sounds good,' I said, returning the smile. 'Enjoy your brunch and speak tomorrow.'

He smiled again, accelerated and his beast of a car sped off down the road.

Wow. What a lovely guy. And kind of good-looking too, in a hot, young Farmer Giles kind of way.

Mmmm.

Behave, Sophia. I might not even be his type, and he definitely didn't fit my dark hair, dark eyes, olive skin, Italian god template.

He was cute, though.

I wonder if he's single…

CHAPTER TWENTY-SEVEN

I'm impressed. I leant forward to scrutinise my skin in my bathroom mirror for probably the fiftieth time. It was smoother than a baby's bottom, and the *glow.* Anoushka had magic hands. The luxury beauty press were going to love this.

On the way home, as well as reflecting on my appointment, I couldn't stop thinking about Charlie.

He was so kind and thoughtful. And I was a complete stranger. Why? He could have been a total arse about the situation, but he wasn't. He had gone above and beyond the call of duty. He really seemed to care. And he was cute. Did I mention that?

Okay. Not my normal definition of cute. I mean, we've established that I had developed a penchant for Italian men. Just something I loved about that gorgeous olive skin, deep eyes and abundance of facial and body hair. Mmmm.

In short, tall, dark and handsome was definitely my cup of tea, whereas Charlie, on the other hand, was fairly pale and clean-shaven, with floppy blond hair and blue eyes. He looked like he'd just walked off an episode of *Made in Chelsea*. His dad was probably an earl or the Count of Sussex or something, and his mum is likely to be one of those ladies who permanently lunches and sits on the board of a gazillion charities.

Something about him screamed 'money'. You know, he looked like the type that are so rich that they didn't have Andrex in their bathroom, or even black toilet paper à la Simon Cowell. They probably wipe their bottoms with fifty-pound notes instead.

But his personality and aura seemed very warm and relaxed—not at all la-di-dah. I was intrigued. In fact, I was borderline excited about the fact that he would be calling me tomorrow.

Here comes the voice of reason again…

Don't get carried away, Sophia. Remember, he's calling you to discuss fixing your car and boring insurance claims. Not to whisk you off to his hundred-foot yacht in St Tropez.

And anyway, weren't you just infatuated with Lorenzo like five minutes ago? So fickle! It's as if any guy so much as speaks to you, you start planning the rest of your lives together. Calm the fuck down!

Noted, Reasanna.

He was sweet, though…

As I walked into the living room, I saw the answering machine on the house phone flashing (I swear I forgot I had one half the time). Mum had left about ten messages. Why she'd assumed that, as I'd left my mobile charging at home, it would be better to reach me on the landline, which was also at home, I had no idea. I listened to message one:

'Darling, it's your mother. Are you okay? What happened with this accident? Are you sure you're okay? Please call me and let me know.'

Message two:

'Mother again. You haven't called back and I'm starting to worry. Please call.'

Message three (even more rattled than message two):

'Are you at home? Let me know you're safe. Should I call Harrison? Please ring.'

Message four (concern levels on a scale of one to ten? A hundred. Bless her):

'Where are you? It's been over three hours since we spoke. Call me.'

Message five:

'And who *is Charlie?'* she asked slyly. Well, that concern was short-lived, wasn't it? *'I haven't heard you speak of him before. Was he with you when the accident happened? I assume it's a guy Charlie as I heard a male's voice in the background. Should I get excited about a new man in your life? Please call me.'*

I was just about to listen to message six (why, I don't know, as the message was likely to be exactly the same as messages one to five) when the phone rang again.

'Hello, Mother. I'm okay.' I knew it was her without even looking as she's the only person I knew in the universe that would still call this number.

'Oh, thank goodness!' she shouted. 'Why didn't you call?'

'Long story, but I'm fine. Sorry to have worried you. Can I call you back later? I'm starving and need to get something to eat, then when I'm more relaxed I can ring you.'

'Okay, darling. Let's speak later.'

I just didn't have the energy for the Spanish Inquisition. Especially now that she knew I was okay, she would turn her focus to the 'Who's Charlie?' campaign, where she'd grill me like a pack of bacon about what he looked like, what he did for a living, whether he was married, if he wanted to marry me, blah, blah, blah. My imagination running wild when it came to men had *nothing* on my mother's.

Ever since I'd announced my split with Rich, she was constantly trying to pair me up with every single man she encountered. There was Doug, son of Jean who lived across the road from my parents, who was so dreary it was a struggle not to fall asleep when he spoke. Zero get up and go, and physically it was a no. Not even my grandad wore jumpers like that.

On the other end of the scale was Luke, a banker who sadly lived up to the stereotype. Proper geezer, or wanker as I'd prefer to phrase it. Well dressed and handsome, but also flashy, fast-talking and bloody annoying. Mum must have been having an off day with that recommendation, as he was the complete antithesis to the people they like. *Oh, I get it*. She probably thought that because I was into fancy designer stuff, he'd be right up my street. Definitely not.

Whilst I knew she was trying to help, sadly none of her proposed suitors were remotely my type. If her friend's son could make me laugh like Ryan Reynolds or Will Smith, with the body of Channing Tatum, then it would be a different matter entirely…

But then again, maybe it was time to open my mind a

little bit more. Charlie seemed interesting. I hadn't looked to see if he was wearing a wedding ring, but maybe he was single?

Oh, stop getting carried away, Sophia, and go and make some food.

I WAS CURRENTLY in my office on a call to Martha, an old-school journalist who could talk more than a chat-show host, when my mobile rang with a number I didn't recognise. It was 1 p.m., and chances are I would be on the phone for at least another hour at this rate. Still, she was incredibly influential, and if she wrote about one of our products, it would make the sales go through the roof, so it was time well spent.

The phone rang out, and then about a minute later, a voicemail flashed up. When eventually my call ended, I played the message.

Sophia, Charlie here. Hope your appointment went well and you got home okay. I didn't hear from you, so I'm assuming you did. Er, right, so, regarding the repair of your vehicle, it all seems straightforward. I won't bore you with the details now. Give me a call back and I'll run through it with you then. Also, you said you didn't know how to repay me. Well, I was thinking, whilst repayment isn't necessary, if you do insist, then how about dinner? I'm going away to Australia on business tomorrow for two weeks, so perhaps when I get back? I'll leave that thought with you. Call me. Goodbye for now.

Dinner? Mmm. I couldn't help it. I started grinning. I

was kind of excited. *See*, Reasanna? Maybe it wasn't all in my head.

Now I'm sure there were rules on playing it cool, waiting X amount of hours and minutes before replying so I didn't appear too keen and all that nonsense, but I couldn't be bothered to play games. I checked my diary. Yep, dinner in two weeks could work. Friday would be best for me.

After my marathon phone call, I didn't have time to call him back right then, as I had a stacked afternoon. I launched WhatsApp and started typing:

Me
Hi, Charlie, thanks for your call. I've got a hectic afternoon ahead, but glad to hear it should be straightforward re: fixing the car. Maybe we can discuss later?
Dinner sounds lovely. How about two weeks on Friday?
Enjoy the rest of your day.
Sophia

There. Simple. Now back to work.

Well. Working *was* the plan. But I started getting carried away again...fuck.

First I began picturing his chiselled jaw, sparkling eyes and megawatt smile. Then I was thinking again about how lovely and kind he was. Oh, how much my mum would love him. *Such a nice, polite young man*, she'd say. He also seemed successful. I liked that. Driven, ambitious, kind and handsome. He didn't seem remotely weird, like some of the guys I'd met on Tinder. He was just so selfless and not at all sleazy. He seemed reliable, trustworthy, solid. Maybe even potentially good father, or failing that, sperm donor material…?

Jesus! What was wrong with me? I had barely known the guy five minutes and already I was thinking about the future. After Lorenzo, I *couldn't* go down this infatuation black hole again and waste hours dreaming about him, stalking him on Facebook, waiting for messages, then analysing messages. No fucking way. Not again. The whole point of making mistakes like that was to learn from them.

I would not, I repeat, I would *not* spend the next two weeks letting my mind get carried away with this fantasy of some stranger I'd met yesterday called Charlie, that I didn't know from Adam, being some sort of knight in shining armour.

I would not, I repeat, I would *not*…

As if it were a sign from above, my mobile rang.

Maybe it's Charlie, I thought before I'd even had a chance to check the screen.

FFS, Sophia! screamed Reasanna. *I thought you weren't going to obsess over this guy, yet you already think he's calling you one minute after you messaged him? Get a fucking grip!*

Reasanna was right. It wasn't Charlie. It was, in fact, Roxy. Even though I was supposed to be working, I answered the call quickly.

'Hi, Rox, how's it going?'

'I'm bored,' she replied. 'I'm supposed to be spending the afternoon working out the prices for a new range of tweezers we're launching,' she said, 'but frankly I'd rather use them to pull out my own teeth right now than do that.

I'm just not in the mood. So,' she added, her voice brightening, 'I thought you could cheer me up with some more of your Tinder tales. Come on, love, spill!'

'Sorry. You're all up to date. I told you all about last week's dates and haven't really messaged any of them since.'

'Oh, what?' she said, sounding disappointed. 'Things are a bit quiet for me on the romantic front too, so I was hoping to live vicariously through you until my current FWB gets back tomorrow'.

'FWB?' I said, confused at another one of her acronyms.

'Come on, Soph, that's an easy one. Friend with benefits? The twenty-six-year-old I've been screwing? Remember?' she said matter-of-factly.

I racked my brains. Nope. Nothing.

'Is that the one that plays football?' I asked, still trying to scan my memory for clues.

'No! That was Wayne. He was like two months ago. This is *Danny*. I mean actually, he's more of a FB than an FWB, because technically we're not really friends. And before you ask, FB is fuck buddy. More casual. We're always safe, of course, but it's purely fun, nothing less, nothing more.'

'I don't believe you've mentioned him to me. I really don't know how you do it. How do you switch off? How do you not get carried away and start planning your future and all that stuff that even the most sensible, logical woman might be tempted to do?' I asked, clearly with myself in mind.

'Fuck that future shit,' she shouted. 'Remember, been there, done that, worn the t-shirt. I have no intention of getting shackled again. I've got a lot of time to make up for, and I'm still having fun. So that helps me not to get carried away. But also, I keep my options open and see other people too. That way I don't have all of my eggs in one basket or waste time sitting around waiting for one guy to call me,' she explained casually. 'Why? You're not still pining over the chef, are you?'

'Oh God, no. That's done. Finished. I'm over him now,' I said as convincingly as I could. 'No, it's just this guy Charlie—' Before I had a chance to finish she jumped in.

'Charlie? Who the fuck is Charlie? You didn't tell me about him! I thought you said you didn't have any stories. Tell me now!' she said, sounding like a showbiz reporter desperate for the latest celeb gossip.

I recounted the story of what had happened.

'Oooh, this is exciting, Soph!' Roxy said enthusiastically. 'It's been, what, about a month since you drew a line under the whole Lorenzo thing? And you're picking up men left, right and centre, aren't you? Can't believe you've pulled a billionaire. Who needs Tinder? Just drive like a madwoman and a rich toff can be yours!' she cackled.

'Well, Roxy, we don't actually know he's rich, and I'm not bothered by that anyway—I've got my own money, and I never want to be one of those women who just goes out with a guy so he can pay for everything. Not my style,' I insisted.

'Chill, Soph—I'm only joking! A lot of the rich ones are arrogant wankers anyway, and that's the last thing either of us needs in our lives,' she said.

'I was just really taken by his kindness, and now I'm starting to get carried away, wondering if we will go on that date, how it will go, what will happen next. And I can't allow myself to get sucked in again,' I said like an addict on the verge of relapsing.

'Honey, the best way to avoid that is to keep those options open. If he's the only romantic prospect you have, you'll put all of your focus on him and that'll be disastrous. Especially if your goal is still to have a bit of fun. My advice is to get back on those sites and organise some more dates. You did well last week, but you've got to keep the momentum going.'

'Yep, you're right,' I said.

'Exactly. So keep the Tinder thing going, but also try some of the others. Maybe a paid one like Match.com. Or, I know…' she said like she'd just had a brainwave. 'Try Bumble. As a control freak and a lady who isn't afraid to take charge, that'd be right up your street, because only the women can make the first move. Stops a bunch of creeps you're not interested in from contacting you.'

'Hmm, that sounds like a plan. Thanks. I guess that's this evening's activities sorted, then. I'll get on those tonight, then message you later to let you know how it goes.'

'Good luck! Now stop all this gossiping, young lady, and get back to work. You've got a PR empire to run!'

Keeping my options open. Signing up to some different dating sites. Taking control. Yes. I liked the sound of that.

Let online dating *round two* commence…

CHAPTER TWENTY-EIGHT

So today marked day five of my new phase of online dating. It also showed that I was continuing to be brave and throw caution to the wind, as not only was I currently on my way to my first non-Tinder date, but said date had been arranged just ninety minutes ago. How's *that* for being spontaneous and grabbing life by the balls?

I could have very easily stayed at the office or curled up with my iPad in bed, looking over the team's plans for Anoushka's campaign, which is what had *almost* happened when I'd arrived home at 7.40 p.m. and found myself bored out of my mind by 8 p.m. But then Vincenzo had messaged to say he'd finished work earlier than expected and wondered if I wanted to meet for a drink. And like the spontaneous, social butterfly that I was (well, outside of work I clearly wasn't, but I was *trying* to be…), I remembered my MAP plan and said yes.

So here I was. It was 9.55 p.m. on a Friday night, and after throwing on a body-hugging sleeveless navy dress and some nude heels, quickly adding some loose waves in my hair, then swiping on some red lipstick in the back of the cab, I was now hovering inside the WH Smith's at Waterloo, waiting to spot Vincenzo, the guy I've been messaging for the past three days.

Since speaking to Roxy on Monday about keeping my options open, I was now managing three apps: Tinder, Match.com and Bumble. I was excited to try Bumble as it's touted as the one that allows women to 'take control', so I made a beeline (ahem) for that first. Once I'd uploaded my pics, then copied and pasted the profile I'd used previously on Tinder, I'd started swiping immediately and could not believe the calibre of men. It was incredible.

Whilst on Tinder, I'd be lucky to swipe right for one guy in every hundred (I know, very picky), on Bumble, I found myself liking literally every third guy. And it wasn't just for purely shallow reasons (although hello? The men here all seemed to be stunning specimens). The guys also sounded fascinating. There were company founders, directors, musicians, actors, scientists...wow.

Just like when I'd first started using Tinder, the swiping was addictive. Plus, if you swiped left too hastily, Bumble also allowed you to backtrack three times for free. Once I'd matched with someone, I was then able to message them and take control. Yes! *Here we go*, I thought. No more waiting around for them to make the first move. *I, Sophia Huntingdon, am in the driver's seat now*. And because each match expired in twenty-four hours, there was a speedy turnaround too.

I quickly matched with a gorgeous Italian (I know, I know) who loved food, films and music. Sounded perfect. I couldn't wait to craft my message:

Ciao, Pierluigi, come sta? I also enjoy good company, conversation, films, music and Italy (I've been twice in the last few months). If you fancy chatting/meeting, then drop me a line.

Nice, enthusiastic, light and not too long. Great.

And then it happened…

Nothing.

Rien.

Twenty-four hours passed and no reply. After this happened a few times, I quickly realised that whilst, yes, as a woman you do have the so-called 'power' to be the one to message first (which, let's face it, you could also do on Tinder if you chose to), as with any conversation, it still takes two to tango. Thus, it doesn't eliminate the fact that you still need to wait for the man to make contact by replying.

After a day or so, I did start to get some messages. And once again, it didn't take me long to see that just because you messaged them first, even if they *did* reply, it didn't stop the responses from being overtly sexual. For example, the response to *'Hello, Nathan, how are you?'* was *'You are sexy, I want to lick you.'* Okay, then… At that point, I decided it was time to try Match.com.

As it was a paid site and required you to fill out an extensive list of questions about yourself, your hobbies and the kind of guy you were looking for, I hoped it would attract a more *serious* clientele. After all, if you just wanted a quick shag, you probably wouldn't want to sit there answering questions about your religion and how important marriage was to you. Right?

I signed up for six months, which I thought demonstrated my commitment to the cause and recognition that I wasn't expecting to find 'the one' overnight. I uploaded the photos I'd used on Tinder as well as a couple of extras, diligently completed the questionnaire and was ready to go.

Initially, I was bowled over by the hundreds of favourites, winks and views I'd received within the first twenty-four hours of joining, but then my fast lesson was that quantity does not always equate to 'quality'—i.e., someone that you personally feel ticks your boxes.

I'd also received about thirty messages from guys of all ages, including Connor, aged twenty-one (whose message read: *'Hey, age is just a number, right?'*) and Reginald, aged seventy-two (yes, really—despite setting my parameters to ages thirty to forty-five). What was also interesting about the messages was that, whilst many were short, others went in completely the opposite direction by sending full-blown covering letters.

For example, 'Theperfectguy' (oh, that's another thing about this site, people can give themselves silly usernames), who revealed himself to be Roger, aged forty-three, clearly put a lot of effort into applying for the position of 'potential boyfriend':

Hi, Thea,
I have just come across your profile and I would love to get to know you.
Unfortunately my membership expires tomorrow and I do not plan to extend it.
If you would like to get to know me, you can contact me either via email at:

roger@rogergreen.com or call/text my
mobile/whatsapp at 07001 222 313
As I am leaving this site and I would love to get to
know you, let me disclose more about me in case
you would wish to contact me in the future. My full
name is Roger Green. You can find me on different
social media sites including Facebook and
LinkedIn. Please feel free to connect with me. If
interested in what I do professionally, you can visit
my website at www.rogergreen.com
If I do not hear from you, I wish you all the very
best in your search for true love and happiness.
Roger

Well, he'd certainly supplied a sufficient number of
'references' to verify his suitability for the position. It was
so polite, I was almost tempted to reply, but as I wasn't
attracted to him, it would be fruitless. I also found it hilarious that two days later, I spotted the green dot on his
Match.com profile, indicating that he was online. So much
for that expiring membership!

As well as the polite covering letter, just like Tinder
and Bumble, there were the sexual messages:

Javier:
HIM: wow I love your legs. Can I gift you
louboutins?
ME: Thank you for the kind offer of shoes,
however I already have a few pairs of my own so
I'm fine thanks. Tell me, what are you looking for
on this site? Just a hook-up?
HIM: Probably…your legs and feet excite me Lol

Aaaargggh! Clearly, it doesn't matter which app you use. Men are men. And whilst I was looking to lose my MARGINITY and wanted some fun, the direct, one-night-only hook-up wasn't really for me.

Then, just as I was about to tear my hair out, Vincenzo got in touch.

Although he wasn't my normal gorgeous, bearded type, I was attracted to his lovely warm smile, full lips—oh, and of course, the fact that he was Italian. Plus, I loved that his messages were respectful and attentive.

Through our frequent messages over the past few days, I'd learnt that he was thirty-seven, from Naples, had been living in London for five years, worked as a manager for a boutique hotel in Piccadilly, and loved wine, travelling and cooking. Crucially, he actually knew how to hold an online conversation. This was rarer than you might think as many of the conversations I had attempted to have on all three of these dating apps often went a little something like:

First contact
Them: Hey beautiful
Me: Hello, how are you?

(Yes, yes, ignore the fact that I'd responded to someone who had started the conversation with *hey beautiful*. I was trying to keep an open mind and not be so rigid. Don't judge…)

One day later…
Them: Good thx, u?
Me: Great, thanks. Whereabouts in London do you live?

The following day…
Them: Ealing. u?
Me: Clapham. What do you do for a living?
Two days later…
Them: Work in a bar. u?
Me: Marketing. What do you like doing for fun?
After yet another 24-hour wait…
Them: watching films, going out with friends,
sex…
Them: Where do you live?
Me: Noticed how you casually dropped the 'sex' in
there…
Me: I did actually already mention where I
lived…
What feels like ten years later
Them:
He he!
Them: oh yeah!
Me: DELETE

Should've known from his opening line and text speak
it couldn't go anywhere…

Unlike these guys who took an eternity to reply to a
simple message (probably because they were busy
messaging hundreds of other women) and would forget the
answers you gave to questions (that's assuming they even
bothered to ask a question to keep the conversation going),
Vincenzo seemed different. He took an interest in me and
what I was doing and remembered to actually ask about it
afterwards (e.g., How was your meeting? How did the fish
pie you cooked last night taste?). I know it sounds crazy to
think that a guy would get brownie points for remembering

what I ate for dinner, but that was a big deal in this new-age dating world.

I enjoyed our conversations. It was nice having someone to chat to in the evenings as the house was always so quiet, and even though I still had my friends and family, sometimes I just felt a bit lonely. We were both keen to meet, but our schedules kept clashing. He'd suggested going for a drink the day after we'd first started chatting, but I had a client dinner. When I'd asked about this evening, initially he'd said he couldn't as he was due to work until 11 p.m. However, as the hotel ended up being quieter than normal, he was able to leave early and messaged me and—well, here I am.

I'd hastily WhatsApped Roxy on the way to let her know where and who I was meeting (complete with description, his username, and mobile phone number). As I'd already set up my escape plan by telling him I could only go for a quick drink and stay half an hour tops because I had an early start, I didn't think I would need a rescue call this time round (I might regret that, but let's see). 'Don't worry, Roxy,' I'd said. 'I don't think I'll fancy him, so I'll be tucked up and in bed by midnight.'

'Thea?' said a heavily accented voice from behind me.

I spun around and…*oh!*

I hadn't been expecting that at all.

It was Vincenzo, looking *significantly* more handsome in real life than his photograph. He was wearing smart black jeans and boots, a light blue shirt and a beige trench coat. Nice. His dark eyes sparkled and his eyelashes were ridiculously long. Why, God? I've never understood why men are given long lashes whilst we ladies need to resort to layers of mascara or extensions to achieve the same length. And his lips. Mmm, they looked luscious in his photos, but now, just inches in front of me, they were even more tempting. I was suddenly feeling a lot more optimistic about being attracted to him.

'Vincenzo! Lovely to meet you,' I said, reciprocating his two kisses on the cheek. 'How are you?'

'Well, a little tired after a long day,' he said in his thick Italian accent. 'But I am pleased to see you, so I will be fine,' he added, flashing an enthusiastic smile.

We headed to the South Bank and grabbed a table outside Strada. He told me how he'd originally come here for a holiday but had liked it so much that he'd never left. We discussed our love of food, and he told me about all of the dishes he liked to cook and I attempted to share my limited Italian repertoire.

Although he showed no signs of flirting, which I took to mean that perhaps he didn't fancy me, I was definitely finding him attractive. I like that he'd made an effort for the date and he was able to hold a conversation here in front of me (so many people are good at chatting online, but struggle in real life). I guessed his job meant he was used to socialising and making people feel at ease.

As I took a last sip of my G&T, I glanced at my watch. 11.30 p.m. Shit. I'd only planned to stay until 10.30 p.m.

'I should be heading home,' I said, placing my glass back on the table. His face fell.

'So soon?' he asked.

'Well, I'd only planned to stay for half an hour, remember, because I have an early start in the morning…' My voice trailed off, and his pretty eyes began to look almost tearful. 'I'm just going to pop to the ladies'.'

As I washed my hands, checked my hair in the mirror

and touched up my lipstick, I started thinking. *I'm having a good time, aren't I? So why cut it short?*

Exactly.

I headed back outside to the table.

'Are you sure you can't stay out a little longer?' he asked.

'Well…I am enjoying your company, so—' Before I could finish my sentence, he jumped in.

'I am really glad to hear that, Thea! I am loving your company too. Come,' he said, standing up and then linking his arm in mine. 'I know a great bar called Las Iguanas just two minutes away, where they do great cocktails, have a DJ and dancing…'

Oh, what the hell. I didn't really have anything to do tomorrow morning, so why rush home?

'Okay. Let's do it!' I said.

He ordered a large glass of pinot noir and a cosmopolitan for me, and we grabbed a table in the corner next to the window.

I loved the vibe. There was a little dance floor area, which was packed with people dancing to a salsa song that I vaguely recognised. Vincenzo stood up, encouraging me to join him (I politely declined) and started swinging his hips left, then right, merengue style. With moves like those, I bet he could do some great things in the bedroom…

Focus…focus…

The conversation continued to flow, but the more I saw his juicy lips moving as he spoke, the more frustrated I became. Did he find me attractive, or was this going to become a 'friend-zone' situation? I hadn't stayed out late to gain another friend. It was time to take control and move this on a bit…

'So,' I said, staring him straight in the eyes and smiling cheekily, 'what made you send me a message? What did you like about my profile?'

'Well, I cannot tell lies,' he said as he unwittingly fluttered his eyelashes and blushed a little. 'I find you very sexy. You have a nice smile and beautiful body. I love the photo of you in the black dress with the high heels. I want get to know you more.'

Good! Now we were starting to make some progress. That was the same dress Lorenzo had liked. Certainly was a worthwhile investment.

'And you? What do you like about me?' he asked.

'Your eyes and your lips,' I said, gently touching his hand, which was resting in the centre of the table. 'Definitely your lips,' I said, cocking my head to the side.

And that was it. Before I'd even had a chance to finish my sentence, he'd leant forward, taken my face in his hands and started kissing me. There were no half measures. He planted his lips on mine with with full force and enthusiasm. These Italian men kissed so passionately—I *loved* it!

Despite the slight aroma of the cigarette he'd smoked whilst I'd gone to the loo, I reciprocated, flicking my tongue against his. Whilst my hand rested on Vincenzo's right cheek, his hands were excitedly exploring my body— brushing against my left breast, down to my bum, across my thighs and then…

'Mmm, perhaps we should save that for another time,' I said, gently pulling my lips away and steering his hand from continuing its determined journey up my dress.

'Oh, I am sorry, Sophia. I could not help it. You are so beautiful,' he said, his eyes drunk with lust.

'That's so funny,' I said, letting out a little laugh, whilst conversely he began to frown.

'Why do you say it is *funny*?' he asked, now frowning more intensely.

'It's just that I wasn't sure whether you found me attractive,' I said, smiling. 'This evening you've been so— I don't know, *professional*? Up until five minutes ago, I thought maybe after meeting me, you just wanted to be friends.'

'Ah, I am sorry!' he said as his face relaxed again. 'Perhaps it is nerves. You are so successful and even more beautiful in real life, and so I was not sure if you liked me like that. But then when you go to the bathroom and you come back with fresh lipstick, I think ah, perhaps she is interested...'

'Really?' I said. 'You saw the fact that I'd reapplied my lipstick as a sign that I liked you?'

'Well, yes,' he said casually. 'If you do not like me and you are going home, then there is no need for lipstick.'

Hmmm. That was certainly an interesting observation. I avoided pointing out that I also might have put lipstick on mainly because it needed topping up and I wanted to keep my lips hydrated, but this time I decided to let it go. Right now I was more interested in enjoying my first proper snog since Lorenzo.

I was right about those lips. They were definitely delicious and perfect for long kisses. On the few times that we came up for air, I worried about the intense display of affection—particularly as anyone I knew could walk past the window—but then I thought, *Fuck it, who cares? For once I'm going to let my hair down and enjoy myself.*

We chatted, salsa-danced and kissed for hours. When the bar closed, we strolled along the South Bank hand in hand. This was lovely. Good call to stay out rather than rushing back home like I was Cinderella with a midnight curfew.

We sat down on a bench, and Vincenzo placed his hands gently on mine. 'Sophia,' he said, now using my real name, which I'd revealed earlier. 'I want you.' He stared deeply into my eyes. 'Tonight. Come back to my place.'

I couldn't deny I wanted him too. Not as much as I wanted Lorenzo, but that wasn't meant to be, and after coming so close to having sex, then having the opportunity snatched away from me, I was definitely more than ready to lose my MARGINITY. But like this? Right now? Tonight?

I wasn't worried about the 'rules' about how many dates you should go on before sleeping with a guy. After all, it was my body, so I could do what I liked with it, when I liked. It was just that my gut was telling me I needed to press pause and exercise some self-control. And after only knowing him for barely six hours, I certainly wasn't going back to his place. He could be some crazy murderer.

'Vincenzo, I want you too, but not tonight,' I said before leaning in to kiss him again and then gently pulling away. 'I should go home…'

'Well, let me come with you. Sophia, there are so many things I would love to do to you…I know you will enjoy,' he said, licking his lips.

'Mmm, I'm sure I would, but not tonight,' I said, resting my hands on top of his.

He stared at me intently as if assessing whether there was a way to change my mind, but this time there wasn't.

'Okay,' he conceded. 'I understand.'

I ordered an Uber, which arrived in minutes, and we had one last kiss in full view on the main road. Once again his hands began to wander, but this time, I decided not to stop them. So much for self-control…

'Next time, mate,' shouted a drunk, dishevelled-looking man as he passed us, 'go to a hotel and fuck her!'

Charming. But probably true…

As I climbed into the back of the cab and waved good-bye, both my libido and I started hoping that 'next time' would be happening very, very soon.

CHAPTER TWENTY-NINE

I couldn't sleep. Every time I thought about Vincenzo kissing and touching me, my whole body would tingle and I'd wriggle around the bed in frustration. I was so horny. And it was *really* uncomfortable…

By 10 a.m., my frustration levels were off the scale. Self-control is all very admirable, but what was the point of making myself suffer, when this could very easily be resolved?

I searched for his number, which I'd added to my phone last night and fired off a WhatsApp message:

Me
Good morning Vincenzo. Tomorrow's your day off isn't it? Fancy meeting up and continuing what we started?

No point in waiting for things to happen. I wanted him, he wanted me, so why not just go for it?

Seven minutes later my phone pinged.

Vincenzo

Good morning, Sophia. I like your suggestion very much as I cannot wait to kiss you all over. Let's meet for brunch in Victoria at 1 p.m. and then we can go get to know each other better…

Done. The advice to treat dating with the same tenacity I used for my work was definitely wise. It felt good to take control of my romantic life.

Roxy was right. Keeping your options open definitely seemed like the way to go. Since I'd been speaking to Vincenzo, I'd stopped obsessing about Charlie. We didn't get to speak on the phone as he was busy preparing for his business trip to Australia and then when he was free, I had a meeting. But we'd exchanged several messages that Monday evening and also before he'd boarded the plane on Tuesday. Mainly to do with organising the repair of my car, but he'd also confirmed that we were on to meet when he got back, which was something nice to look forward to.

I admit, after I'd finished messaging Vincenzo, I did feel a tiny twinge of guilt about setting up a sex session with him, whilst knowing full well I would be going out with another guy in a fortnight. But then I came to my senses and reminded myself that I didn't owe either party anything. Likewise, neither did they. I barely knew either of them, and we certainly hadn't made any formal declaration of monogamy. And after knowing me for just shy of a week, I'm sure Charlie would be enjoying himself Down Under (possibly quite literally…) and would not be giving me a second thought. So my intention was to do exactly the same.

TODAY WAS THE DAY. After spending what felt like the entire morning primping and preening, I was ready for action. Nails and toes were done, make-up was looking natural, hair had been waved, plus the lady garden had been trimmed and shaped.

When I think about it, it's exhausting the regime that women go through. I often wonder why we do it. As much as I'd like to say it's all for me, I'd be lying if I didn't admit there is definitely a desire to 'please' a man. Of course, that statement opens up a whole can of worms in itself, but like Monique said, provided it's on your terms, it's okay. Despite it being a pain to do, I *did* want Vincenzo to desire me, so the rigmarole was worth the 'reward'.

I slipped into a red lacy thong with matching bra, then pulled on a red figure-hugging dress which skimmed the tops of my knees, and clung perfectly around my boobs and arse. I remembered reading an article about a study that revealed that wearing red increases a woman's sex appeal, which was exactly what I wanted to do today.

'Yes!' I said to myself as I looked in the full-length mirror, spinning around to examine both sides as well as my pert behind. Fingers crossed, with this outfit, my confidence and my flirting dial turned up to maximum, Vincenzo wouldn't be able to resist me.

Just as I was composing myself in the taxi to Victoria, my phone pinged. It was a message from Roxy.

Roxy
So, is today the day you're re-popping your cherry?

Ha-ha! Funny, but true, I hope.
I quickly replied:

Me

It is indeed! On my way to meet him now. We'll go for brunch in Victoria and find a hotel nearby…

Roxy

Woo-hoo! You go, girl!

Me

Any last tips for this MARGIN? It's been a while…

Roxy

Darling, just relax and enjoy! Losing your *MARGINITY* isn't as scary as losing your *virg*inity, particularly as you kind of had a practice run with Lorenzo. You'll be fine. Sex is just like riding a bike. You never forget. So just lie back and let your bodies steer you to Pleasureville!

Me

Ha-ha! Steer us to *Pleasureville*! Where might that town be, Roxy? Just off Junction 10 of the M25? Hilarious!

Me

I'll try! I'm hoping he'll guide me. Judging by the way he moved when he was dancing and all the things he's been saying he'd like to do to me, I reckon I'm in for an exciting afternoon

Roxy

Yay! Message me AS SOON as you leave the hotel. I want to know everything!

Me

Will do! x

By the time I stepped out of the taxi, I was bursting with anticipation. After the false starts with Lorenzo, all the hours of swiping, enduring the creepy messages and going on those weird first dates, I'd finally met a decent, smart, handsome guy and was ready to dust off the cobwebs downstairs and get my sexual mojo back.

On one of his messages earlier this morning, he'd asked me to dress 'sexy', so as well as my man-magnet red dress, I was also wearing nude suede open-toed high heels. Of course, in the interest of equality (and to stimulate my libido as much as possible), I'd asked him to dress sexy too.

As I strode confidently across the concourse of Victoria station, I scanned the exterior of WH Smith's to see if he'd already arrived.

He had, and oh dear...

That was his idea of sexy?

The suave, sophisticated look that I'd loved on Friday night had been replaced with an outfit that could only be described as 'try hard'. He was wearing a black biker jacket which had been zipped all the way up (and made him look totally uncool—probably the complete opposite of what he was aiming for), black sunglasses (even though it wasn't *that* sunny today), light blue jeans and black biker boots.

You know those old photos of James Dean wearing a black leather jacket and jeans, looking all mean, moody and totally hot on a motorbike? Yeah, well, Vincenzo did *not* look like that. Instantly turned off. Shit.

Reasanna piped up and told me not to be so shallow. *Once you see those eyes and those lips are on yours, Sophia, all will be forgotten.*

He clocked me walking towards him and began grinning.

'Ciao, Sophia,' he said, leaning forward to kiss me firmly on the lips. He'd just had a cigarette, so not the greatest aroma, but his lips still felt lovely. 'Mmm,' he continued as he took a step back to give me the once-over from head to toe. 'You look very beautiful. Very, very sexy.'

'Thank you,' I said, pleased that the red effect had worked, but also a little disappointed at his interpretation of the 'sexy' brief. 'Shall we go and get something to eat?' I asked, trying to change the subject in case he asked me if I liked his outfit.

'Yes, why not?' he replied politely.

We headed to Bills for brunch and the conversation flowed nicely as he told me more about his work. After five years managing the same hotel, he was ready for a change of scene. He was currently toying with the idea of going down the training route—so rather than being on the front line, he would spend his days visiting different hotels and training their teams instead.

Talking about work was fine for a while, but that wasn't what I was really here for.

I edged my seat closer to his and placed my hand on his thigh. He looked me in the eyes and leant forward to kiss me.

Mmmm. That's much better.

'So,' he said gently. 'Shall we get the bill?'

We entered the hotel room, making a beeline for the bed (which, unlike the one in Florence, was a normal king size) and started whipping off our clothes.

As I pulled my dress over my head, he undid his shirt

and then removed it slowly. His slim, smooth chest was much paler than Lorenzo's bronzed and beautifully hairy torso, but *different* didn't mean bad.

True to his word, he began kissing me all over, gently peeling off my thong as I raised my hips. I was definitely thankful that I'd taken the time to tend to my lady garden earlier.

He placed his head between my legs and began licking slowly.

Oh…yes. I like that…

I'd always enjoyed a man kissing me there…mmmm.

But as he finished and edged himself up my body with his manhood getting ever closer to my mouth, then took his hand and steered my head towards it, I froze.

There was no doubt. He wanted me to reciprocate. But, how can I put this politely? The aromas that were coming from his nether regions were not the sweet scent of my favourite Jo Malone Lime Basil & Mandarin candle. Far from it. This was more burger and fried onions. A kind of stale *this penis has not been washed today* sweaty type smell…

Should I say something? Maybe decline and say I don't do *that*? But he'd already been down on me, so he'd think I'm a prude and I'd look like a pillow princess if I didn't return the favour. *But how? It stinks!*

I could ask him to take a shower. But then that'd ruin the moment and I really, really wanted to have sex today. I *needed* to have sex today. Help.

Suck it up, Soph—literally, screamed Resanna in my head. *Just close your eyes, imagine it's Lorenzo, do it quickly, get it over with and then you can get what you want. I'm sure you've tasted worse things…*

My head was now millimetres away from his manhood. I took a deep breath, squeezed my eyes shut and opened my mouth reluctantly...

I think I managed about thirty seconds before recoiling, pushing his body downwards and reaching for a condom. I felt like I'd just done a bushtucker trial on *I'm a Celebrity*...

I cannot believe I just did that. Right now I just wanted to rush to the bathroom and wash my mouth out, but instead I said in my best seductive voice, 'Vincenzo. I want you inside of me'. I gently tore the edge of the condom packet, took it out then rolled it onto him.

He got into position. It was finally happening. He was inside me. There was a little discomfort at first, as obviously it had been a while since I'd experienced full penetration, but I didn't care. I was *so* ready.

We rocked forwards and backwards and the memories started to flood back to me. It *was* just like riding a bike. This felt good. Yes!

I picked up the pace, rocking more enthusiastically. I'd waited so long for this and now it was happening, I wanted to give it everything I had.

I began to gyrate beneath him, grabbed hold of his bum smacked it and then...

'*Oh, Sophia!*' groaned Vincenzo.

Noooooo...

WTF?

In less time than it took to say *Usain Bolt*, it was all over!

He collapsed on top of me.

That was it? You've got to be kidding me!

'Erm, Vincenzo?' I said, struggling to find the words (well, polite ones anyway). 'Did you come?'

'Yes,' he said, gasping for breath (not sure why when neither of us had had a chance to work up a sweat). 'I'm sorry,' he replied sheepishly. 'I was just too excited.'

Oh my goodness. After boasting about all the phenomenal things he was going to do to me, that was it? Five pumps and he's done?

Calm down, said Reasanna. *Shit happens, right? It'd been a couple of months for him, so like he said, he was probably overexcited. Be understanding. Give him time and round two will be much better.*

Except it wasn't.

We tried for what felt like hours afterwards and he just couldn't get it up. I even attempted oral again (after asking if I could give it a little rinse first, which made him blush with embarrassment. Sorry, but I *couldn't* endure that again). At first it seemed to help. But no sooner had he entered me than it was over. I think I counted ten seconds, but that may have been generous.

After realising that I was flogging a dead horse, I said I needed to get back and left.

I slumped into the seat of the black cab, closed my eyes and let out an almighty sigh. That definitely had *not* gone as I'd expected. All that build-up. All that excitement, and that was it? My first time back in the sack in pretty much a year amounted to a few seconds of mediocrity? Why, God, why?

I'd thought today, I'd feel like a fulfilled woman. That I'd be skipping through the hotel doors and humming a happy tune, whilst my skin radiated with a warm *you'll never guess what I've been up to* post-sex glow. That I had found another Italian to satisfy my sexual needs. I hoped I'd be so high on lust that Lorenzo would well and truly be a distant memory. But rather than making me forget about him, Vincenzo had just made my thoughts of Lorenzo and our night together resurface.

As the taxi headed over Vauxhall Bridge, I felt more frustrated than when I'd arrived. Seemed like losing your *MARGINITY* could be just as much of a let-down as losing your *vir*ginity. In fact, it was worse. At least when I was seventeen and had decided to finally 'do the deed' with my then-boyfriend Jeremy in his single bed one rainy afternoon whilst his parents were at work, I'd expected it to be awkward. It was the first time for both of us, so it wasn't realistic to hope for fireworks. But what now?

What if the earth didn't move with the next person I slept with? What if I was disappointed again? Was this why our generation had become MARGINs in the first place, because the act of having sex never actually measured up to the anticipation?

Surely I wouldn't have to settle for having bad sex at the grand age of thirty-nine? Would I?

If today's underwhelming experience was anything to go by, the future was not looking bright.

Shit.

CHAPTER THIRTY

When I'd first got home after the unfortunate encounter with Vincenzo, despite trying to stay positive and reassure myself that one man's performance was not representative of an entire gender, I was still feeling disappointed.

It was his overconfidence that irritated me. Why boast about his extensive bedroom skills if he knew he had problems performing?

I'd initially written him off completely. Don't get me wrong. If this was a serious relationship, then we'd work through it together as a couple. But we were *not* in a relationship. This was supposed to be fun. A mutually satisfying arrangement.

Roxy's response reinforced my thoughts:

Roxy
Next!
Sorry he was a flop, darling. No sympathy for him after he made himself out to be the world's greatest

lover. Get back on the app and find someone else who can actually keep it up!

However, Fran was much more sympathetic and made me question whether I'd been too hard:

Fran
You know what? I wouldn't write Vincenzo off totally, hon. These 'flops' happen. Even the most skilled lover can get nervous or excited. Especially if he's thinking he's with a beautiful, successful woman, has hyped himself up and realises he now needs to deliver. That can be a lot of pressure on a man. It may just be a one-off. In the absence of anyone else, if you enjoy his company, consider keeping the door open and meeting him again.

Hmm. She had a point. I'd enjoyed talking to him both on and offline, especially as it was a distraction from thinking about Lorenzo (well, most of the time) and keeping my mind off chiselled-jawline Charlie. I liked kissing Vincenzo too, and perhaps it was a little harsh to judge a person on one (well, technically two) poor performance(s). He'd been uncharacteristically quiet and avoided eye contact when I'd left the hotel. He'd probably been beating himself up about what had happened (or rather, hadn't) ever since. I started thinking I should show a bit more compassion and give him another chance. So I did.

By now it was Thursday, and we'd been messaging every day. I'd broken the ice on Tuesday by asking if he got home okay on Sunday night after I'd left.

We were now planning to meet up this coming Saturday. I was up for giving it another go as there had been no improvement in the options available on either of the three dating sites.

Rather than go out for lunch, he'd suggested that he cook for me instead. At first I was apprehensive about going to his place, as I'd only known him for just shy of a week, and when I'd told my mum the other day that I had signed up to a few of the dating sites (it was during one of her increasingly frequent *what's happening on the man front?* interrogations and I wanted to show her I was making progress), she'd started relaying a load of horror stories she'd heard of women who were killed after meeting up with guys they'd met online.

Great, I'd thought. *Exactly what I need to hear. Not.* But then I'd decided that I couldn't live my life in fear, so I pushed that negativity out of my head and accepted Vincenzo's invitation. Provided I kept my wits about me and gave Roxy and Harrison full details of where he lived, etc., I should be fine. Meeting in daytime also seemed a lot less sinister somehow, but I wouldn't let my guard down. I'd still take my personal alarm with me, ensure my phone was charged and tune into my gut when I got there.

I had noticed, though, that lately when we'd been messaging, the conversations had taken a slightly different turn. One minute the messages would be super polite and 'straight', and then the next, his would turn saucy.

He'd just messaged with directions to his place and had sent me the itinerary/menu for the afternoon.

Vincenzo
Hey, sexy…I'm going to cook for you, then I'll

take a hot shower and make love to you, then we'll
go for a walk. You'll turn me on so much that we'll
make love again and again, then we'll go out to
dinner and I will take you back to my place. Wear
those heels in that photo that I love…

Wow. Okay, then. I chuckled to myself when I read the
bit about the 'hot shower'. Clearly I'd given him a cleanliness complex. Good! Maybe I'd save another woman from
enduring the same ordeal in the future.

But he was overselling himself again. After his performance last week, was he *really* going to be able to get it up
that many times? Hmm. His next message was much more
'normal':

Vincenzo
So I will make you baked monkfish with potatoes.
Sound good? I will also choose a good white wine.

See what I mean? His messages had gone from saucy
to straight in seconds. I typed a reply:

Me
Sounds delicious. Thank you.

I *loved* monkfish. I was looking forward to it. Well, I
was, until I received his next message…

Vincenzo
P.S. I wanna lick your pussy for my dessert so pls
make sure it's completely shaved. Not with lots of

hair like last time. Can't wait to see you on
Saturday!

What the hell?

Now, whilst I understand that everyone has their
personal preferences, and like I said, I'm all for women
dressing up to please a man if they so wish, I *do* take
offence at being *told* to shave off my lady garden
completely. What a bloody cheek!

Would he do the same for me if I asked him to shave
his sack and crack? I *like* the way my garden is pruned,
thank you very much. Whilst I know many women love to
have it all bare down there, which is entirely their choice,
personally that's just not for me. I'd wanted to give
Cameron Diaz a high-five when she encouraged women to
keep a *'curtain of pubic hair'* in that book she wrote a few
years back. I fired off a reply:

Me

As much as I'd like you to enjoy your 'dessert',
I'm not into the bare look down there, I'm afraid. I
can go low, but it won't be shaved off completely.
Each to their own, but that look isn't for me…

Vincenzo

Okay. Sorry if I offend. At least you can still eat
my banana split for your dessert…

Eat his fucking 'banana split'? Really? I couldn't guarantee I'd be able to do *that* again. The first time was kind
of traumatic. I'd better manage his expectations.

Me

Maybe…we'll see. Can't promise.

HE READ my message and then logged off. Strange..
A few hours later he logged back on:

Vincenzo

Sophia, I think maybe I am not your type. I need
hot fun to fit my style. I think this can be an issue
for me.

For goodness' sake. He's acting like a baby. Now
seething, I shot him a reply:

Me

So what, just because I won't shave completely or
promise to go down on you, you don't want to
meet anymore?

Vincenzo

Is not about the shaving. When a woman says she
don't like to be hot, I lose attraction.

What the fuck is he talking about now?

Me

When did I say I don't like to be 'hot'? I was
looking forward to seeing you this Saturday. But if
you don't want to have fun with me anymore, then
no worries.

Vincenzo

I understand but I want to do naughty things with
you. I wanna make a porn with you, are you ready

for that? I wanna fuck you with that black dress on and those heels as you're so stylish and sexy.

A porno! Is he for fucking real? I knew I was supposed to be living life and embracing new things, but that was a step too far…especially for a casual date and a guy I barely knew.

Me
You're right. It sounds like you're looking for something a bit more adventurous. Definitely not into making a porno, I'm afraid. Bye, Vincenzo.

Wow. I had *not* seen that one coming.

I wasn't sure what was worse: the guys like Diego, Nathan and Javier, for example, who declared their sexual intentions and fetishes upfront, either within the first few minutes of messaging or on the date, so you could then immediately say thanks, but no thanks and move on quickly; or guys like Vincenzo, who give the impression of being a sweet man with 'straightforward' non-kinky sexual desires, but then dropped the bombshell that they wanted you to be a leading lady in their home video. Oh, and ordered you to shave.

Sweet Jesus. I wonder what Roxy and Bella will make of this at our FTA on Sunday…

'SO WHAT HAPPENED to Mr. Flop, then?' said Roxy, sipping on her G&T innocently.

'Roxy!' said Bella, as if springing to the defence of

Vincenzo, and all men suffering with erectile dysfunction. I wondered if she'd be feeling so sympathetic at the end of this story…

'Well, first he *told*, not asked, *told* me to make sure I shaved my fanny completely so that he could eat it for dessert,' I said, tearing off a piece of bread and dipping it in olive oil.

'Oh!' said Bella, cringing as she wriggled around the leather banquette in our normal spot at Hush.

'So you don't have a Hollywood?' said Roxy, widening her eyes. 'I have to say, when it comes to tackling fanny fur, I'm totally with Vicky B on that one.'

'What, when she said that she thought Brazilians should be compulsory at age fifteen?' I asked, surprised at her declaration. 'Well, if you're with Victoria, I'm definitely in support of Gywnnie and Cameron,' I said strongly.

'What did they say again?' asked Bella frowning.

'Some nonsense about rocking a *seventies vibe* down there, I think,' said Roxy, jumping in and rolling her eyes. 'Spare me the details, Soph, but I find it hard to believe that you, Queen of the Beauty PRs, with VIP access to every laser machine and salon in the country, are sporting a fully grown bush down there!'

'Ha-ha, Roxy. Well, I didn't say I was. I laser my legs and my underarms, but not my nether regions. Although I know they say it's safe, personally I'm just not comfortable having lasers beamed around down there, and it's nice to have a little coverage for my undercarriage. As long as it's neat, tidy and well trimmed, that's enough for me. Plus it adds a bit of mystery,' I said, smirking.

'You cannot be serious,' said Roxy in disbelief.

'Yes, Rox. I'm definitely *Team Hair* rather than *Team Bare* on this one. Cameron's right. Once you start lasering it, it's gone forever, and 'trends' change. Yeah, the Hollywood and Brazilian are hot right now, but will they always be? I did a lot of research into this when we were working on a campaign for a waxing brand, and you'd be surprised how much opinions have changed over the years.'

'Really?' asked Bella, leaning in.

'Yeah!' I replied. 'In the Egyptian times, women removed all their hair except their eyebrows and eyelashes because they thought it was more youthful. But in the 1500s a full bush was fashionable again. Then I think it was in the 1800s that lovers even gave each other pubic hair as gifts to one another.'

'You've *got* to be joking!' shrieked a horrified Bella.

'Nope,' I confirmed. 'Weird, right? It was only in the early 1900s that women's razors were introduced, and then when bikinis became more popular in the sixties, the pressure came to remove body hair. Then of course the Brazilian got invented in the nineties by some Brazilian sisters, and women went crazy for it. But there's still plenty of support for the bush. Remember Kate Moss showed hers in that shoot for *LOVE* magazine, and when American Apparel put those mannequins in the window showing their muffs?'

'I think so,' replied Bella.

'The thing is, Rox, women who went and lasered off everything are now spending thousands on bikini line restoration and pubic hair transplants to actually reseed their lawns,' I said.

'No fucking way!' screamed Roxy. 'That's a thing?'

'It is indeed a thing. We had a London clinic contact us

to do their PR to promote it earlier this year. Look,' I said. 'To have or not to have hair downstairs is up to the individual, but all I'm saying is that personally, I like to keep my options open, so you won't catch me booking in for a Hollywood laser any time soon,' I said.

'Yeah, I get what you're saying about lasering,' responded Roxy, 'but you can wax down there and still keep your options open.'

'I *do* wax! I shave too. But whenever I wax, it's just a short back and sides. I have to be particularly careful as my hair is super curly, so too much waxing could mean painful ingrown hairs, which surely would look much worse than a bit of extra female fur downstairs.' Bella cringed again. 'And, yes, of course I know there's loads of products to help prevent that, but the last thing I want to do is have to exfoliate and put loads of chemicals down there every day. Why should us women have to torture our fannies just because men want us to look like plucked chickens?'

'Excuse me,' said Roxy, slamming her glass down loudly, 'but I don't do it for men. I do it for myself. I just think it's cleaner and more pleasant for the guy who's going down on you because he doesn't have to worry about getting pubes stuck between his teeth or choking on a bloody furball.'

'Oh my God.' Bella winced. 'The mental images you're creating right now are seriously putting me off my lunch,' she said, putting her head in her hands.

'And another thing, Sophia. I do *not* look like a plucked chicken either. Just all smooth, lovely and kissable,' she said, giggling cheekily.

'Well, each to their own, Rox, but don't be fooled—it's

not necessarily more hygienic. The hair actually prevents dirt and other shit from getting in there,' I said.

'What, like dicks and tongues?' said Roxy, now cackling.

'Funny! I can assure you, no man who has an invitation to visit my garden party will have trouble gaining access! Lorenzo seemed to manage just fine. Like I said, apart from my pre-Italy lapse, I generally keep everything tidy down there. And *clean* too, thank you very much,' I said proudly. 'When I think of the hours I spent prepping for that date for him to tell me I still had 'all that hair' down there and he didn't even bother to shower before we met up, it makes me so mad!'

'Yeah, that was gross,' said Roxy, wrinkling her face in disgust.

'I cannot believe we are having a full-blown conversation about pubes and smelly willies,' said a bemused Bella.

'Yep, well, Bella this is our FTA session and *anything* goes!' I said, laughing. 'Anyway, that wasn't actually the reason why I didn't meet up with him in the end.'

'What, there's more?' asked Roxy, looking curious and excited in equal measures. 'Did he ask you to shave your hair on your head off too?' She threw her head back, cackling.

'Well, that would *never* happen!' I said, horrified at the thought of ever choosing to chop off my locks for a man. I definitely considered it my crowning glory. 'In a nutshell, he wanted to make a porno with me.'

'No way!' said Bella, her jaw literally falling to the floor.

'Yes, *way*!' I confirmed.

'Welcome to the new world of dating, Soph,' said

Roxy matter-of-factly. 'Doesn't surprise me in the slightest.'

'Well, it sure as hell shocked me. I even had nightmares about it afterwards. I know some guys just make them for themselves to watch at home, but could you imagine if he'd filmed me, put it online and then all my clients, my team, the journalists and—gosh, my bloody parents had seen it?' I shivered just thinking about how years of reputation-building could have been shattered in seconds.

'You're right,' said Bella.

'I mean, how would I be able to pitch to some of the biggest beauty CEOs knowing they'd seen my butt and boobs jiggling all over the place? I'd be ruined!' I said. 'And for what? A few seconds of frustration with a guy I was just talking to out of sympathy and, dare I say it, slight desperation? This dating is fucking scary shit.'

'It's scary times and a world away from when I was dating before I met Mike,' said Bella. 'Cameras are everywhere and any sleazy guy can film you without you knowing—on the train, in the gym, in your home. Technology can be lethal in the wrong hands. You had a lucky escape, hon.'

'Definitely! That's it, though, ladies,' I said, firmly planting my glass on the table. 'I'm taking a break from the dating sites. It's doing my head in. I've realised that men are men whether it's on a hook-up site like Tinder or a paid site like Match.com. I'm not saying there aren't decent guys on there or that I'm giving up forever, but I've had quite enough disappointment from swiping over these past few weeks to last me at least a few months.'

'Oh, that's a shame,' said Roxy. 'I was finding all of your dating disasters quite entertaining!'

'Bloody cheek!' I said, laughing. 'Well, you know me. I get bored easily, so you never know, I might change my mind about the apps. Fear not, though, my friends. Like I said, there may well still be at least one decent guy out there, as remember, all being well, I have my date with Charlie this Friday. Lord only knows what tales I'll have to tell during our next catch-up…'

CHAPTER THIRTY-ONE

Tonight was the night. Although I was trying to play it cool, I was excited about my date with Charlie.

Since he'd got back from Australia, we'd either messaged or spoken every day. At first it was a bit formal, discussing fixing my car. He'd suggested that we didn't go through insurance companies, explaining that his family used one of the UK's finest car and body repair centres and promising that because they gave them so much business, they would ensure that the car would look practically new by the time they'd finished.

I'd given him the green light, so they'd collected it on Tuesday afternoon. Then on Wednesday night when we spoke on the phone (I know, an actual telephone conversation rather than messaging—so rare these days), he'd asked if we were still on for that dinner on Friday night.

I was tempted to follow the 'dating rules', act all aloof and pretend I had forgotten, but instead I just said yes. We'd agreed to meet at Sexy Fish in Berkeley Square as he'd assured me that, despite the short notice, he'd be able to get us a table, so it was all arranged. He'd texted me this morning to check that we were still on for tonight and I'd swiftly confirmed. Now I was about to leave the office to see Josh at Annabel's salon for a pre-date blow-dry.

'So have you Googled him yet?' said Josh, who I'd just been filling in about my forthcoming dinner with Charlie.

'I thought about doing that this morning, but I couldn't remember his surname, other than the fact that it starts with a C. Christie? Chrombie? Something like that,' I said, racking my brain to try and remember what I'd written down during our conversation. 'All the notes I made about getting the car fixed are at home,' I explained. 'Also, after going on a load of failed online dates, this time I've decided to do things the old-fashioned way and just find out more about him by having a conversation over dinner. I don't want anything I see on Facebook or anywhere else online to taint my opinion of him before we meet.'

That and I also didn't want to lose precious hours social media stalking him like I'd done with Lorenzo. But I was too embarrassed to tell Josh about my past behaviour...

'Well, if you say so,' he said, rolling his eyes. I guess guys in their early twenties like him did everything online, so the old-fashioned way was far too alien for them. 'Personally,' he continued, 'I'd like to know that my dates aren't serial killers before I meet them, so I always search for them on Instagram, Facebook, Twitter, Snapchat, and LinkedIn, and see what pictures come up in Google too. Why else was the internet and social media invented?' he laughed.

'Really?' I said, raising my eyebrows. 'And you reckon that looking at a guy's Instagram page is going to tell you whether or not they're a nutter? Serial killers don't generally post photos of their victims after the fact. Plus, I'm pretty sure you've gone out with people from Grindr, and that's probably no better or worse than me meeting Charlie in the middle of a road,' I added.

'True,' he conceded. 'Oh well, either way it will be interesting.' There was that word again: *interesting*. 'Hmm,' Josh continued, 'at least he seems nice, and by the sounds of it he's loaded!'

'I'm not bothered about that. He'll need to have more than a fat wallet to impress me,' I said cheekily.

'You little saucepot!' he said, giggling as he added the last few waves to my hair.

'I don't know what you mean,' I replied innocently. 'Of course, I was referring to his intelligence, charm, ambition…'

'Yeah, yeah. *Whatever.* I think you're forgetting how well I know you. Remember, us hairdressers know our clients inside out. That includes your secrets and your sense of humour! There,' he said, showing me the back of my hair in the mirror. 'You're all done.'

'Perfect,' I said, smiling with approval. I stood up, and Josh started undoing the velcro strip at the back of my neck to remove my gown.

'*Yes*, Sophia!' he said, walking around me to check me out at every angle. 'Looking *hot*! So what are you hoping to get out of tonight? Snog? More?' he asked cheekily.

'Hmm…well, probably not 'more' tonight, but I definitely wouldn't say no to a lovely, long passionate kiss for starters,' I said, slyly letting out a loud laugh.

'Sounds like a plan!' he said as he went to the cloakroom area to get my jacket. He peered through the salon window. 'Looks like your taxi's outside, darling. Go get him, tiger!'

As the taxi dropped me off outside the restaurant, I started to feel the gentle flutter of butterflies in my stomach. Why was I nervous?

Remember, it's just like going for a work meeting. You've had a few dates now. You'll be fine, said Reasanna encouragingly. Roxy and Bella had both messaged me to wish me good luck too, which helped.

I took a deep breath and stepped through the door opened by the smartly dressed doorman in the bowler hat.

It had been a while since I'd been here, but it still looked as glitzy as I remembered, with sea-green onyx floors, Damien Hirst bronze mermaid sculptures, a glossy black crocodile slinking across the back wall, fish lamps 'flying' above the scarlet lava-stone-topped bar and super-soft leather banquette seats. I'd deliberately arrived twenty minutes early so that I could head to the swanky loos, with floor-to-ceiling back-lit marble, for a final outfit, make-up and hair check. I scrutinised myself in the mirror. The waves in my hair looked good –loose and effortless. Make-up was natural again, but with a bold scarlet matte lipstick.

I'd kept my outfit simple too: a fitted royal-blue bodycon sleeveless dress which just skimmed my knees and covered my breasts enough to be classy. All finished off with a pair of matching blue suede Louboutin shoes. Whilst I'd been dressing less designer lately, seeing as I already had them and this was a special occasion, there was no point them just sitting in my dressing room gathering dust. I was even tempted to message that guy Javier from Match.com who'd offered to buy me a pair every month with a photo captioned, *'See, I have my own shoes, thank you. I don't need a man to buy them for me.'*

Yes. I was happy with how I looked.

As I climbed the stairs, I saw him sitting at the bar. He spotted me too, smiled and rose from the stool.

'Sophia! Gosh, you look stunning!' he said, eyes falling out of their sockets. Well, considering he had seen me bare-faced with hair tied back when we'd met, I'd imagine for him, this was a bit of a transformation.

'Thank you,' I said.

'Our table is ready,' he said, giving a nod to the waiter and directing me to a table tucked away in the corner by the window with a full view of the restaurant. I spotted Naomi Campbell two tables down and a Hollywood actor whose name currently escaped me over on the other side of the restaurant. Clearly this place was still drawing in the celebrities, but right now, nearly three weeks after we'd first met, I was only interested in finding out more about Charlie. Oh, and desperately praying that he didn't turn out to be a) be some weirdo, b) have any strange fetishes, or c) have a penchant for making pornos.

As the starters and then the main courses arrived, the conversation flowed fairly freely. He mainly asked questions about me. What I did for a living, my family, what my hopes and dreams were for the future, which was quite deep for a first date. Well, that's if this was a date? At times it felt like I was being interviewed (in fact, perhaps I should have emailed Charlie a covering letter like that Roger Green had sent to me on Match.com), but he listened and nodded intently, and I figured that he was just taking an interest. Either that or I was indeed being

quizzed to see if I ticked the boxes on his seemingly extensive 'ideal girlfriend/wife' checklist.

Ever the cynic, I also knew that asking someone
endless questions about themselves was also a tactic to
avoid having to talk about yourself, so I was determined to
flip the script now and give *him* the Spanish Inquisition.

'So,' I said, tilting my head. 'Enough about me, what
do *you* do?'

'Um, I'm a director for a, er, a food company,' he
stuttered.

'Oooh, food. I *love* food. What type?' I asked.

'Oh, er, sweet things,' he added, avoiding eye contact.
'You know, like biscuits, cakes, that kind of thing...' For
some reason he was being coy and trying to downplay
things. I remembered Fran's tactics when quizzing Erica
about Lorenzo. Like her, I was determined to find out
more.

'Cakes are my *favourite* things in the world—beating
even prawns. What's the name of the company?' I asked.

'Erm,' he said, hesitating. Nana Cromwell's.'

'Ah, Nana Cromwell's!' I said with genuine affection.
'I adore their Ginger Dreams, and the Coconut Macaroons
are my favourite.' Charlie blushed again.

Oh, hold on a minute...that name rang a bell...

'Cromwell's?' I asked, frowning, trying to place the
name. 'What's your surname again?'

'Er, Cr-Cromwell,' he said, stuttering and avoiding eye
contact again.

'So, are you any relation to the Nana Cromwell family,
or is it just a coincidence that you're working for a
company whose figurehead has exactly the same name as
you?' I asked, doing my best Fran.

'Erm, yes,' he said before pausing. 'It's the, yes, it's the family business.'

'That's amazing!' I gushed. 'Nana Cromwell's is a British institution. They're hands down the best biscuits on the market. I remember when I got my first Saturday job feeling so pleased to be able to go into Waitrose and buy my own pack because Mum would never get them. She always said they were too expensive, so we had to get McVities instead. Now on the rare occasion I get biscuits for the house, I'd never buy anything else. I love the fact that's your family business. You should be very proud of your success.'

He was fidgeting nervously in his chair. You could tell he was feeling embarrassed about it all. See? I was right about him being bloody loaded. Nana Cromwell's was huge. As a fellow business owner (albeit not on that same ginormous scale), I understood what it must have taken not just to build a brand like that but also to maintain it, plus make it grow so phenomenally. *That's* what impressed me the most. Much more than the money that came with their success.

'So what do you do there at the business?' I asked, genuinely interested to hear all about it.

'Erm, well, I look after the retail relationship side of things, so dealing with the major retailers in the UK, but increasingly expanding our business globally. Hence my recent visit to Australia. We're currently in fifty countries worldwide and intend to expand that to seventy-five in the next two years, so ambitious plans.'

'Oh yeah, how was Australia?' I asked. 'You didn't say much about it on your messages.'

'It was fine, thanks. But business trips are never as

glamorous as they sound. You get off a long flight and barely have time to drop your bags off at the hotel and have a shower before the driver whisks you off to a string of meetings with retailers, who are all trying to squeeze your margins so they can make more of a profit for their stores. And then there's the negotiations to get the prime shelf space and secure the best promotions. It all gets a bit tiresome after a while,' he said, sighing loudly.

'I know what you mean,' I said, nodding in agreement. 'I travel for press trips several times a year too, and it can be exhausting.'

'Plus,' he continued, 'there's the terrible carbon footprint from all the flying. Just one return flight from London to New York produces a greater carbon footprint than the whole year's personal allowance that we need to keep the climate safe. It's not what I want to do.'

Oh, wow. I was surprised to hear him say that.

'What is it that you want to do, then?' I asked.

'I've always wanted to work for an organisation like Greenpeace,' he replied, sitting up straighter in his chair as if I'd ignited a fire inside him. 'There's so much important work that needs to be done to secure the future of our planet. Issues like fracking, protecting our oceans and, like I said, dealing with climate change. These are real problems. Selling biscuits is just so trivial and mundane in comparison.'

He certainly sounded passionate about green issues.

'Oh, I see,' I replied. 'So if you don't want to sell biscuits, why don't you just leave?' I questioned.

'If only it were that simple,' he said, bowing his head. 'The business means *everything* to my father. It was him who started the company after his mother baked the cakes and biscuits for a high-profile event he was organising and everyone went crazy for them. For the past thirty-five years, he's dedicated his life to the company, and as his only son, he's grooming me to take over when he retires in two years' time. It would break his heart if I left.'

His shoulders sank. He looked visibly upset just talking about it. *Can't be an easy situation.*

'Sorry. I don't even know why I'm telling you all this and we've just met,' he added.

'Don't worry,' I said. 'That must be a terrible burden for you, though. Just because it's your father's life, it doesn't mean it has to be yours too. You need to follow and focus on your own dream, not someone else's. If you don't want to do something, speak up and tell him.'

'I wish I could, but I can't,' he said, raising his voice slightly. 'You don't know my father. Anyway,' he said, clapping his hands together as if to indicate it was time to change the subject. 'Let's not talk about this. It will only depress me. Right. You said you like cake. I can personally recommend the caramelised pineapple and coconut cake for dessert. Or the cinnamon doughnuts.'

'Both sound lovely,' I said, respecting his decision to change the topic of conversation. In the end we opted for both and decided to share. On the subject of dessert of another kind, I was hoping that an end-of-night snog was still going to be on the cards, but I wasn't sure.

We were getting on well. He was certainly handsome, smart and very caring. Although he was likely to be worth tens of millions, he was very down to earth. There wasn't the same animal attraction I'd had with Lorenzo, but that was just pure lust, and that hadn't really gotten me very far before had it?

But at the same time, after a long relationship, I wasn't really looking for serious husband material. Right now, passion, great sex combined with relaxed companionship were at the top of my list. Could Charlie give me that?

The waiter gently placed the bill in between us, which Charlie swiped off the table faster than you could say 'Sexy Fish' and requested the card machine.

'Oh no! I thought *I* was the one who was repaying *you* for not reporting me to the DVLA or police for my erratic driving. You must let me pay, or at the very least go Dutch,' I suggested.

'I won't hear of it. I've had a delightful evening with you, Sophia. It's the least I can do. It's so refreshing to spend a few hours with someone fascinating and funny for a change. You really have no idea.'

I got it. Whilst many people might think: *Poor you! Must be exhausting flying business class everywhere, getting the best seats at London's top restaurants at the drop of a hat and being a multimillionaire to boot,* I understood that often that champagne lifestyle isn't all it's cracked up to be. One of the reasons he probably wanted to go out for dinner with someone like me was so that he could feel more 'normal' and not be reminded of his massively privileged lifestyle.

'Thank you. I've had a lovely evening too,' I said, smiling.

'I'm so glad to hear that. Does that suggest you'd be open to going out with me again?' Sorry, is that too forward?' he asked nervously.

'Not at all. Of course, I'd love to,' I said without hesitation.

'Wonderful! I will certainly be inviting you out again.

Now, I'm assuming you didn't drive here as there was no debris or collision signs on the road outside when I arrived,' he said, chuckling. *Good. I like a man with a sense of humour.*

'Very funny!' I replied. 'No. My car is still with your mechanic guys, so I took a taxi here.' Not that I would've driven even if it hadn't been, of course.

'Well, on behalf of London, we thank you for refraining from putting us in danger by getting behind the wheel.' He let out a snorty laugh. 'In that case, let me get a taxi for you.' He went over to the doorman and asked him to flag down a black cab as he helped me with my jacket. What a gent.

The doorman gave him a nod to signal that a taxi was outside.

'Back in a sec. It's Clapham that you live, isn't it?' he asked. Good memory.

'That's right,' I confirmed.

'I won't be a moment.' He headed outside and I could see him lean through the window of the taxi to speak to the driver. He came back inside.

'Your chariot awaits!' he said enthusiastically.

'Thank you.'

He opened the door for me and led me outside to where the taxi was parked and we stood beside it.

Well, this is a bit awkward. What now? Might be too public for a full-on snog. I'll let him lead.

'Lovely to meet—I mean, see you again, Sophia.' For a split second I could have sworn he was going to put his hand out for me to shake it, but then he remembered himself and went for a nervous quick peck on the cheek. I then went for the other cheek.

'Oh, two!' he said, sounding surprised. 'Gosh, I never know these days whether it's one kiss, or two or sometimes even three! Minefield! Right, then,' he added, opening the taxi door. 'Do send me a text once you're home, Sophia, to let me know you've arrived safely and I'll be in touch re: a drop-off time for the car on Monday, and of course, meeting up again. It's been truly delightful.'

'Thank you again, Charlie, for dinner and, yes, let's speak soon,' I said, managing to strain a smile. I climbed into the back seat and he closed the door behind me.

A handshake? (Well, he almost went to shake my hand).

A peck on the cheek?

Is that it?

I was hoping for a snog. This gentleman thing was all very well up to a point, but sometimes a girl just needed a good...

Behave yourself, Sophia.

Surely a man wanting to shake your hand or giving you a peck on the cheek couldn't be a good sign? I was so frustrated!

Never mind him thinking the number of kisses to give someone on the cheek was a minefield. This whole dating and understanding men thing was starting to feel more complicated than bloody rocket science.

CHAPTER THIRTY-TWO

I fluffed up the cushions on the sofa and chaise longue, checked my new photo canvases were straight on the living room wall, then went in the fridge to make sure the wine and prosecco were chilling nicely. All good.

Roxy and Bella would be round any minute. I'd called an emergency meeting. As much as I had tried to be independent and not continually ask them a million and one questions about men/dating/my love life, sometimes you had to admit defeat and rally the troops.

Thursday night was my third date with Charlie and we were *still* at the peck-on-the-cheek stage. I just didn't get it and wanted a second opinion from two of the people that I trusted the most.

We'd all been super busy these past two weeks. Bella with juggling Paul and her teaching, Roxy with the normal stresses that come with running a sales force, and me working on various projects. That meant that, apart from the odd 'good luck with your date tonight', 'what are you wearing?' and top-line-summary-of-each-date WhatsApp messages, they weren't fully up to speed on what had been going on.

The bell went. Right on time. I walked to the front door and let them in.

'Hello, Soph!' they said in unison as I gave them each a massive hug.

'Come in, ladies,' I said, directing them to the living room.

'Oooh, new photos!' commented Roxy instantly.

'That's a lovely canvas of your mum, dad, Harrison, Marilyn and Jasmine. Gorgeous. Was that from your birthday dinner?' asked Bella.

'It was indeed,' I replied.

'You might be bloody irritating, always asking everyone for photos, but I admit, you definitely know how to take a great picture,' said Roxy.

'Thanks, Rox. So what are we drinking?' I said, walking through to the kitchen and opening the fridge. 'Prosecco? As you're staying over, I've got plenty of booze. It's Saturday night, so we can let our hair down. No work tomorrow!'

'Speak for yourself,' said Bella, rolling her eyes. 'Two-year-olds sadly don't differentiate between week-days and weekends. They want to be entertained and waited on hand and foot 24/7. As soon as I walk through that front door tomorrow lunchtime, I'll be back on mummy duty.'

'Poor thing!' said Roxy. 'And, yes, to answer your question, Soph, prosecco sounds good.'

'Me too,' conceded Bella. 'Screw it! I will worry about my hangover tomorrow. Mike can help out if I need to sleep it off. Thanks, Soph.'

I picked up the bottle along with three glasses and headed back to the living room.

They filled me in properly on what had been going on in their lives. Paul had recently started nursery part-time, so Bella had increased her teaching to three days a week. Whilst Mike's job as an English professor meant he earned enough for her to stay at home and look after Paul full-time, as someone who had always made her own money, she'd always wanted to retain some financial independence. But at the same time, Bella admitted she was finding it exhausting juggling the demands that come with looking after a toddler, plus lesson planning and rushing from one big firm to another across London to teach each of the high-flying foreign city executives, who'd booked her to help them improve their English.

Roxy's work was going well. Colette, the MD of the company she worked for, who Roxy credited as helping her get back on her feet after her divorce by offering her a job and a place to stay, was expanding the company, so she had offered Roxy the role of senior sales and marketing director. In terms of her love life, or rather her sex life (Roxy doesn't do 'love'), she had called it off with the twenty-six-year-old fuck buddy because he was starting to 'catch feelings', which wasn't part of her 'no-strings' agenda.

When our Chinese takeaway was dropped off, we all got stuck in, shunning the dining table and just eating whilst sitting on the sofa instead.

'Sooo, Sophia,' said Roxy with a glint in her eye. 'Tell us about Charlie. What's the emergency, then? Not that we don't love to see you, but we rarely organise a catch-up with just a forty-eight-hour turnaround, so it must be pretty urgent.'

'Well. I'll cut to the chase. Would you consider it weird if you've been on three dates with a guy and at the end of the date, he's still just giving you a peck on the cheek?' I asked, still feeling confused.

Bella and Roxy both gave each other puzzled looks.

'A peck on the cheek?' clarified Roxy.

'Yep,' I confirmed.

'Maybe he's just being a gentleman,' suggested Bella.

'At first that's what I thought. On the first date, he nearly went to shake my hand, which would have been super weird, but he must have realised what he was doing at the last minute and then did the one peck on the cheek. I thought maybe it was because we were outside Sexy Fish and it was busy and he wasn't into PDA.'

'PDA?' queried Bella.

'Public displays of affection,' clarified Roxy.

'But then on the second date, it happened again. His ritual is that he flags down a taxi, pays them to take me home—which is very sweet and did take me aback the first time as I went to pay and the driver said it had already been taken care of—but then he just kisses me on the cheek. And for the second date, the street was very quiet, so that can't have been the problem.'

'So what happened on date number three on Thursday?' asked Roxy.

'Well, he took me to Rumpus Room—you know, the really cool rooftop bar at the top of the Mondrian that has stunning views of London? Anyway, there I was thinking that maybe he'd chosen a bar that was attached to a hotel because he thought it might be a nice neutral place for us to spend the night together. You know, have a few drinks and then subtly invite me to check out the view from his room downstairs. But nothing.'

'So there was no *rumpy pumpy* in the Rumpus Room, then! Ha ha' shrieked Roxy. 'Sorry—I couldn't resist! I love that bar, and there's plenty of places there or in the cosy lift going up to the rooftop for a cheeky little snog. That's so odd! And you've sent me quick pics of your outfits each time and you've looked hot. Are you sure he's not gay?'

'No—of course not!' I said, surprised at the suggestion. Then I started to consider her comment. 'Well, at least I don't think so…'

'For all you know, Soph, you could be his beard. Maybe he only gets full access to the Cromwell billions when he's married and produces a child. You hear all about that kind of shit going on in those mega rich families.'

'You're crazy!' I scoffed.

'Okay, maybe it was just in a film I watched ages ago where the guy had a month to find a wife or he lost his inheritance, but that doesn't mean it couldn't happen in real life,' suggested Roxy.

'Although he did say his dad would be stepping down in a couple of years and he'd expect him to take over, I doubt that's true in this case,' I reasoned.

'You never know,' added Roxy, reviving her conspiracy theory. 'Maybe he's on borrowed time, needs a wife and thought, "If I hook up with a pauper, she'll be so grateful to experience my ten-star champagne lifestyle that she'll forget about all the sex stuff as she'll be too busy shopping on Bond Street or Fifth Avenue".'

'That's a bit far-fetched, Roxy, and Soph is hardly a pauper!' added Bella.

'And as you well know, I've had plenty of practice buying my own shit on Bond Street. Not interested anymore, thank you very much!' I said.

'Sorry, love, but even with your million-pound business and swanky Clapham townhouse, compared to him we're all hard up. And frankly, the only way you'll know whether he's gay or not is if he can get it up when you're standing there in front of him butt naked.'

'Roxy!' screamed Bella. 'You're more direct than a bloody high-speed train from London to Manchester!'

'Just saying!' Roxy said, letting out one of her raucous laughs. 'Or, if that's too X-rated for you at this stage and you want something more PG or perhaps 18, then you need to get snogging, let your hands wander and see whether he has something stiff in his trousers and is happy to see you, or if it's limper than a dead fish down there. *Then* you'll know.'

'Fuck. Looks like I'm going to need to take the lead and make the first move yet *again*.'

'Call me old-fashioned,' said Bella, 'but have you ever considered *talking* to him and trying to gauge how he feels? For example, do you know what happened with his last relationship or how long they went out for or why they broke up? I know it sounds weird, but do you think he's even had sex before? Maybe he's religious and doesn't believe in sex before marriage or something.'

'What?' I said, shocked at the mere suggestion. 'He's forty-two. Of course he's had sex!'

'Good point,' said Roxy. 'Soph, have you never watched the film *The 40-Year-Old Virgin*?' asked Roxy.

'Years ago, but *come on*. He's handsome, loaded and sometimes he *is* forward and a bit flirty. Like he didn't seem nervous about asking me out in the first place. He only seems to get nervous and bumbly when he's talking about money stuff or work, as you get the sense he doesn't want to flaunt it. I *definitely* don't think he's a virgin. Or gay for that matter.'

'Well, then, like you said, Soph, once again you'll need to take the lead and grab the bull by the horn, quite literally.' She cackled again. 'In all seriousness, though, Bella has a point. Speak to him, try and find out a bit more about him and his sex life.' Bella and I frowned in unison. 'Okay, okay, his past relationships. And if you've also turned up the flirting dial and all that doesn't work, then when he goes for that ridiculous peck on the cheek that he probably gives his Aunty Mildred, turn your face so your lips meet and then go in for the kill. When are you seeing him again?'

'He wants to meet for brunch tomorrow. Hence why I needed to see you guys tonight, because if I don't get a snog or preferably more than that soon, I think I'm going to explode. Vincenzo left me feeling more sexually frustrated than ever, and there's only so much DIY a girl can do!' I added cheekily.

'Sophia!' shrieked Roxy before laughing. 'And you guys think *I'm* crude! I am with you on that, though. When you're having to charge your Rabbit more frequently than your mobile phone, you know you're in trouble!'

'Exactly!' I shouted in agreement. 'I'm absolutely *gasping* for some male contact, preferably for longer than ten seconds too. Like Bella said, Lorenzo awoke the lioness within me and not to put too fine a point on it, I've been dying for it ever since. It's been sooo bloody long since my engine has had a proper service. If I leave it any longer, it might cease up completely!'

'Hilarious!' said Roxy, cackling. 'Well, although your Vincenzo encounter was short and far from sweet, at least you got a seat at the table. First you had a selection of tasty starters with Lorenzo and then—well, I guess we'll need to say a mini-starter with Vincenzo too as we can't really call *that* performance a main course.'

'*Definitely* not!' I said, closing my eyes as I relived the disappointing encounter in my head.

'Don't worry, hon, you'll be fine,' said Roxy reassuringly. 'Oh, talking of Lorenzo, did you ever hear back from him?'

'Nope. Nothing. Last time we had contact was a couple of months ago, when I invited him to Savour London. He said he'd get back to me and never did, so that's that,' I said, feigning nonchalance when in truth my heart was sinking. 'Anyway,' I said, trying not to waste any more time talking about Lorenzo. 'Back to Charlie. So it's a case of taking charge, then, you reckon?'

'Yep. Looks that way,' said Roxy. 'Where are you going tomorrow?'

'He hasn't confirmed yet,' I replied.

'So now you've met him a few times and we know who he is and where to find him, why don't you suggest staying in?' said Bella. 'Either he comes to yours for an early dinner rather than brunch, or he could invite you to his mansion slash palace, slash stately home, or wherever he lives. That way he'll be more relaxed, you'll be alone and then you can talk and act freely. Maybe he's just shy.'

'Good idea,' I responded. 'Then he'll definitely have

zero PDA concerns. Maybe it's because he comes from a well-regarded family and he has to be seen to be acting a certain way in public in case he gets papped or lands himself in hot water à la Prince Harry in Vegas.'

'True, Soph, true,' added Roxy. 'Just make sure if you go to his house, you send us the address and message us at regular intervals so we know he hasn't tied you up or taken you down to his red room of pain or whatever it was called in *Fifty Shades of Grey*.'

'Come on.' I rolled my eyes. 'I'm pretty sure he's not into S&M,' I said confidently. But then when I thought about my recent dates and online chats, I reminded myself that I couldn't rule it out completely…

'You never know,' said Roxy as if reading my thoughts. 'It's not like he'd wear a sign on his back saying, "I like to whip women and have strange fetishes".'

'True,' I agreed.

'Like I said, there's only one way to find out,' added Roxy. 'Flirt outrageously, then go in for the kill, just like you did in Italy. In fact, why are we even telling *you* what you should be doing when you've done all of this already? Just channel whatever courage you had over there and apply it to this situation. Simples.'

'Yep, you're right. I just found it so strange, though. All the guys that I've been speaking to online and have been on dates with couldn't wait to get in my knickers, so this threw me a little—*especially* the almost-handshake thing.'

'Yeah, that was a bit strange, but it was probably just nerves,' suggested Bella. 'Funny, though, isn't it? We complain when guys are too full-on and call them weirdos, then, when they try to be respectful and gentlemanly, we also think they either must be weird, a virgin or gay. They can't win!'

'Good point, actually. Right, like Roxy suggested, I'll suggest a night in and try to find out more about his past relationships. On all our dates so far, he just asks loads of questions about me and tries to dodge questions I ask about him. We do have a laugh, but sometimes it does feel like I'm being interviewed for the "girlfriend" position. I know that's essentially what a date is, but—'

'Trust me,' interjected Roxy, 'for someone like him, at his age, and given the way you describe how he acts during the date, it *does* sound like you're being vetted. He probably wants to see if you're ready for the duties that come with being the potential wife of a multimillionaire who's second in line to the Nana Cromwell's throne,' added Roxy hastily.

'Well, I'm not ready for all that serious stuff,' I said. 'At the moment, I just want some bloody fun.'

'Does he know that?' questioned Bella. 'Like I said, you need to do a lot more talking, not just to find out more about him and what he's looking for, but to also see if you're compatible—you know, romantically, to put it politely—as that is important. So those need to be the goals for tomorrow to avoid either of you wasting anymore time.'

'Definitely. I'll take your advice on board and speak to him and then, Roxy, if he doesn't ravage me voluntarily or cart me off to his kinky room, I shall switch on full Sophia Huntingdon take-charge mode and go in for the kill.'

I took a large sip of my prosecco and leant back on the

chaise longue as I turned my thoughts to the plan for tomorrow.

Charlie Cromwell, watch out. There's a very determined, undersexed woman on the loose, who is on a mission to have a hot, long-lasting night of overdue passion, and she's coming to seduce you...

CHAPTER THIRTY-THREE

W ell, I knew it would be big, but I wasn't quite expecting *this*.

No, not *that*...I'm talking about Charlie's swanky riverside apartment.

He was in the midst of giving me a guided tour, and I was trying to keep my jaw from dropping, when all I wanted to do was gasp at the enormity of it all. I attempted to play it cool (gushing about how amazing I thought it was would be a bit too cheesy...), like I regularly hung out in five-bedroom, three-bathroom penthouse properties in Battersea which had a terrace the size of an average entire two-bedroom flat overlooking the Thames. Yep, just a standard Sunday evening.

'So, what do you think?' Charlie asked as if keen to get my seal of approval.

'Well, it's all right. A bit on the small side, though, if I'm honest,' I said, obviously joking.

'That's what my father said when he bought it, but actually, living here on my own, sometimes I find it can get a bit lonely...' His voice trailed off as it suddenly dawned on him (probably thanks to my stunned expression) that surprisingly, I *wasn't* being serious...

'Oh. Sorry. I see, you were jesting!' he said, penny finally dropping. 'Well, do you like it?'

'Of course,' I said casually as I stepped out on to the terrace, marvelling once again at the view. 'I mean, what's not to like?' In the distance I could see a host of landmarks. The London Eye, Big Ben...imagine waking up to this every morning and having a leisurely breakfast whilst taking in the views, or sipping on a cocktail out here in the evening after work. Yep, if you twisted my arm, I reckoned I could get used to it...

Don't get me wrong, I'd always loved my home. It'd taken years to get it exactly how I wanted it, and I was happy there. But this? Charlie's place was on another level. Even the new, more down-to-earth me couldn't fail to be impressed by this.

Inside it was decorated like a show home: all neutral, safe colours. Cream leather sofas like mine (although likely significantly more expensive), solid oak flooring and marble sculptures.

The dining area was stunning too. It was part of the huge living room, but the glass table was on a platform made from onyx marble.

As it was a split-level penthouse, the bedrooms were upstairs and followed the same wooden/glass/neutral colours theme.

All the rooms had wall-to-wall, floor-to-ceiling windows, so, as you can imagine, the views were breathtaking. Even in the main bathroom, the bathtub had been strategically placed so that you could take in the scenery whilst enjoying a soak. Wow.

When Charlie had called earlier this morning, I'd told him that I couldn't do brunch but would be free from around 6 p.m. I'd also said that I didn't fancy going out and would prefer a quiet night in. I had invited him to my place, but he'd voluntarily suggested I come round to his instead, which was the perfect scenario.

Charlie seemed relaxed. As always, he was dressed neatly. Clean-shaven, crisp white shirt and blue jeans with brown brogues polished to perfection. I wondered if he ever slummed it and wore a tracksuit and trainers. Probably not. Mind you, I was a fine one to talk. Six months ago I wouldn't have been seen dead without perfectly blow-dried hair, full face of make-up, designer clothes and four-inch heels. Oh, how times had changed.

That said, today I'd made an effort, as I was trying to be a temptress, so had worn a tight pink dress which, despite having legs, a hint of cleavage and bare arms on show, was still very tasteful, and a pair of black, open-toed heels.

As tonight, I was a woman on a mission, I'd come fully prepared. Everything was in order underneath this dress. I had even packed three condoms—you know, just in case. I wasn't holding out much hope, seeing as we hadn't even got to first base yet, but as we'd learned at Brownies (or was it Girl Guides?), it's important to always be prepared (although when they'd taught us that motto, I'm sure they hadn't had *these* kinds of adult activities in mind).

We sat down on his sofa with a glass of wine. I let him run through his usual questions. How's work? Any new clients on the horizon? I knew he was only taking an interest in my life, but tonight, it wasn't talking that I wanted.

'So,' I said, switching on my temptress button. 'I've enjoyed these past few weeks with you. I feel like you've got to find out a lot about me, but I don't really know that much about you. I mean, how long have you been single for, and what happened with your last relationship?'

I could tell he was taken aback by the deer-in-head-lights expression that now engulfed his face. That and the fact that he was now verging on the colour of beetroot.

'Um, er, well…wow! What an opening question,' he said, trying to compose himself. 'I wasn't expecting *that*.'

I stared at him intently and with my eyes I gave a look that said, *I'm not letting this go until you answer my question so come on: spill.* Sensibly, he continued:

'I've been single for about eight months,' he said as he started shifting in his chair. 'I was, erm, engaged to Zara, but, er, unfortunately, or perhaps *fortunately*, depending on how you look at it, she was, uh…involved with…extracurricular activities with another man, so, er…we, we—well, I…well, it ended.'

He looked at me like a knife had just been plunged into his heart.

'Oh, I'm so sorry. That must have been awful, really hard to deal with,' I said sympathetically. 'Although, like you say, perhaps it's better that you found out before you walked down the aisle. Sadly, it wasn't meant to be. And,' I added as I gently rested my hand on top of his, 'if you'd married her, then we wouldn't have met, so that's a silver lining too…' His face brightened and his shoulders appeared to loosen a little more. 'Seeing as you've just had quite a serious relationship, I'm guessing that if you were engaged, you'd been going out for a while. So what are you looking for now?' I asked. 'Another long-term thing? Fun?'

'Well, I think all relationships should be fun to a degree,' he said, sitting more upright in the sofa. 'Don't you think?'

'Yes, but, I mean, *what* are you looking for?' I asked. 'A girlfriend? A future wife? This is, what, the fourth time we've met? And clearly you're a gentleman as you haven't so much as tried to even kiss me. So do you see me more as a companion, or are you actually attracted to me?' I said.

Looks like the deer-in-headlights expression is back...

'Well, of course!' he said swiftly. 'You're a very attractive woman, Sophia. A man would have to be blind not to notice that. Why do you think I asked you out in the first place? I'm just more traditional. I'm trying to find a *genuine* connection with someone. It's terribly hard for a man in my position,' he said, wincing a little. 'Sadly, I've encountered a number of women that want to be close to me for the wrong reasons, so I'm always wary of that. I believe intimacy is something to be treasured. I *abhor* women that give themselves to all and sundry at the drop of a hat. This time I want to take my time and get to know someone first, before taking things to the next stage.'

Oh, Jesus. This doesn't bode well.

'So when you say you like to take your time, how much time are we talking here? Like six dates? Five, or maybe even *four*?' I said hopefully.

'I don't think it's something one can put a firm number

on,' he replied. 'It's just when it feels right. When the moment is there.'

Did that mean I'd have to spend another three weeks waiting to see if he'd like to go to the next stage? I didn't want to force him as clearly that wouldn't be right, but I was so sexually frustrated. Perhaps if he was being a gentleman, he also just wanted to feel sure that I was comfortable with him going further? Yes. Maybe that was it.

I uncrossed my legs and then crossed them again seductively, à la Sharon Stone in *Basic Instinct* (except my knickers were unfortunately still on), tilted my head and fluttered my eyelashes and leant forward.

'Charlie, you're a very handsome, smart and kind man.' I leant further forward. 'And tonight, I want to feel *closer* to you...' I tilted my head and as my lips gently pressed onto his, I could feel him freeze. 'Relax and kiss me,' I pleaded, briefly pulling back and staring into his eyes. 'Please. If you want to, of course...'

This time he leaned forward and kissed me.

Halle-fucking-lujah!

So we were *finally* kissing. His lips were soft. He was very gentle at first, and then he started trying to pick up the pace by nibbling my ear and kissing my neck. His hands even started to wander.

But...

Houston, we have a problem.

He seemed to be doing all the right things, but...I don't know how to describe it. From my side, there just didn't seem to be anything there. Nothing was *happening*.

Don't get me wrong, if he kept doing this for long enough, I was sure *eventually* I'd start to feel *something* downstairs, but there were no fireworks. There was no…I don't know? *Passion? Spark?*

Shit. And this was what I had been craving for weeks. And now I had been forward and initiated things and he was really getting into it. His hands were stroking my legs and he was nibbling on my neck like a squirrel that's just fallen headfirst into a Nutella factory, and I was feeling nothing!

He gently eased me down backwards on the sofa, his eyes filled with lust and desire.

What happened to all that *intimacy needs to be treasured* and *I want to take my time* stuff from five minutes ago?

So now you're upset because he's doing what you wanted? Relax and focus, Sophia. You haven't had sex since the dinosaurs walked the earth (well, proper sex anyway. Vincenzo didn't really count). This is your chance. Just do what they did in the olden days and lie back and think of England.

It's because you're overthinking rather than paying attention to what's going on in front of you. You have a handsome man who is smart and kind on top of you, and he seems like he's up for some hanky-panky, so what are you waiting for?

Yes, Reasanna…I can confirm that he definitely is. At least I could safely report back to Roxy that a) he was not gay and b) evidently from the rod that was now firmly resting very close to my inner thigh, he was *very* happy to see me.

'Oh, Sophia, what are you doing to me?' he said, stroking my face gently. 'I hadn't planned for this to happen. I wanted us to take our time, but you—then *you* started kissing me, and your lips are just so soft and delicious and irresistible. I can't help myself.' His fingers then began circling my nipples. You could tell he couldn't wait to remove my dress and bra to gain full access. 'I'm sorry,' he said, pausing again. 'Of course, if you prefer that I stop, please do say.'

'No! No,' I said enthusiastically, trying to convince myself. 'I want this, Charlie, I do.'

Yes, I do. I do. Come on. I can do this.

The moment those words had escaped my mouth, he launched at me again. Kissing my lips, then my neck, then he paused whilst he unbuttoned the top of his shirt and pulled it over his head.

A flashback of luscious Lorenzo with his gorgeous olive skin, hairy chest and firm abs flooded my brain. With his pale chest and slightly rounded stomach, Charlie's physique was certainly *different*. That said, considering he probably spent all day eating cakes and biscuits, I guess Charlie was in good shape.

Stop it, Sophia! Reasanna piped up again.

Looks aren't everything. Charlie's a good man, and you've been bleating on for weeks about wanting some action. Now it's right in front of you, and you're spending all your time thinking rather than grabbing the opportunity with both hands.

Yes, okay, Reasanna. This might not be ticking the 'experience passion' box on my MAP list so far, but it is part of point number seven. I should be embracing this.

'Oh, Charlie, I want you,' I said, deciding to throw myself into it.

'Oh, Sophia,' he said, looking so high on lust I thought

he was going to pass out. 'I want you too. Come. Let's go upstairs.'

He took my hand and led me up to his bedroom. *Looks like I am finally going to get some action!*

'THAT WAS *AMAZING*!' he said, panting and gasping for breath. 'Goodness me!' He flopped backwards on to the bed, then put his hands behind his head, as he rested back on the pillow. 'Sophia, that was incredible. Thank you.'

Well, it was okay I guess. He came. I didn't. Like before, I'd remembered what to do. Not that I really did much other than lie on my back, move about a bit and make the occasional noise here and there to reassure him I was still alive.

It was a bit awkward in parts. Once we'd got the condom on, he'd struggled a little with getting the right positioning, but after I'd guided him, that was sorted. But then the rhythm just didn't seem to be right. We couldn't get the 'flow'. A bit like dancing, and the person is stepping on your feet, or not in time. We managed to make it work eventually, though.

It wasn't that adventurous. We just stuck to the missionary position. It was all over in about five minutes anyway (so at least an improvement on my last encounter) as clearly, like me, it had been a while for him so he had a lot of pent-up 'emotions', shall we say, to release. I didn't mind too much, though, because unfortunately, as much as I tried, I still wasn't feeling it…

Quick, I need to say something.

'Glad you liked it,' I added.

'I most certainly did!' he gushed. 'That was tremendous! Did you enjoy it?' he asked keenly.

Shit. How am I meant to answer that?

'It's so good to be with a man again,' I replied a bit too quickly. That didn't come out right. *What do you mean, Sophia? As opposed to being with a woman?* Let me clarify: 'I mean, sex is a natural, basic human need and it's been such a long time, so it's good to be back, to be on the path to feeling like a woman again.' I saw him frown briefly, but I think I got away with it. Just.

'Gosh, all that action has made me really thirsty,' I said, thinking on my feet. 'Maybe I'll go downstairs and grab a drink?'

'I won't hear of it,' he said, jumping off the bed, clearly not shy about his bits flopping about as he did. 'You stay there.' He stepped into his white boxer shorts. 'I'll get it for you. Water okay, or something stronger?' he asked.

I was tempted to go for wine, so that I'd feel a bit more relaxed if he wanted to do it again, but I had work in the morning and needed a clear head. Oh yes. Work!

'Water will be fine. I've got work in the morning so can't be hungover,' I said. 'In fact, what's the time? I'll probably need to get a cab home soon.'

'Oh no, really?' he said, face falling. 'It's only 10.30 p.m. Why don't you stay the night?'

'I wish I could,' I said, sitting upright in the bed and starting to wrap the sheet around me so I could get up without exposing myself. 'But I've got a meeting first thing, and I don't have any clothes here…'

'That's not a problem,' he jumped in. 'I can arrange for whatever you want to be delivered here overnight, all ready for the morning. Just tell me your size and what you want to wear and I'll get everything sorted.'

Oh, to be so rich and powerful. What would he do? Send some minions to open up Selfridges in the middle of the night just for me?

'It's not just that,' I added, 'it's my make-up, my shoes and—'

'I can arrange that all too,' he interjected. 'I'll get a make-up artist—whatever you need.'

If I needed to, I could organise a glam squad myself, but I appreciated the gesture.

'You are so kind, but I've got my work notes at home, which I need to go through, and I need a good night's sleep. I had my best friends over last night and we were up until all hours, and now I've just had this unexpected workout and I'm tired. And I know if I stay here, I'll be up all night with you too…'

'Yes, you've got a point,' he said, grinning wildly. 'I don't think I'd be able to keep my hands off you!'

And with that, he came over to where I was standing and launched at me again, kissing me on the lips, on my neck, across my shoulders, and then slipping his hands through a gap in the sheet that was wrapped around me and starting to skim my breasts.

'Oooh, stop it! Right,' I said, stepping back quickly. 'I'd better go. I think I left my phone downstairs. I'm going to order a taxi.'

I picked my now-crumpled dress up off the floor, pulled it over my head, then swiftly put my knickers back on. Couldn't be bothered to fiddle about with my bra. I rolled it up into a ball ready to stuff into my handbag.

'Okay, okay, sorry,' he said, also taking a step back.

'When you haven't had sex for months, you forget how wonderful it can feel, so that enabled me to be strong and stop myself from being more forward with you. But now you've awoken my sleeping sausage, I can't help it. I want you. Can we do it again? *Please*?' he pleaded like an eager eighteen-year old who'd just lost his virginity. 'Just quickly, before you leave?'

Did he just call his dick a sleeping sausage?

'Patience is a virtue,' I said, stroking his face, secretly wishing he had a beard. 'If I go now, with the anticipation, it'll be even better next time,' I said, trying to convince myself.

'Okay. When will the next time be?' he asked eagerly.

'Well, I've got a busy week at work, but don't worry, soon,' I said, not answering his question fully.

I made my way downstairs. This was so hard. I didn't want to lie. And I felt awful. Like one of those men that gets his wicked way and then skulks off home faster than you can say *Speedy Gonzales*.

Great—there's an Uber five minutes away.

He reached the bottom of the stairs, headed towards me and leant over for another kiss. I reciprocated. I *did* enjoy the *action* of his kisses. But I just didn't *feel* any butterflies, or that spark.

'Right, I better head downstairs as the cab is only a few minutes away and it will probably take about half an hour to get the lift down from this penthouse to the ground floor!' I joked.

'Of course,' he said, still sulking a bit about the fact that I wouldn't stay. 'Would you like me to accompany you downstairs?'

So formal! He really is a gent.

'It's fine, but I appreciate the offer,' I replied.

'Do you need some money for the taxi?' he asked, being a gentleman again.

'It's all paid for on my account. Thank you so much for offering, though.'

'Well, thank you again. I feel so, so amazing,' he said, stretching his arms up towards the ceiling like he'd just finished a productive workout at the gym. 'I feel incredibly relaxed and less stressed. Do please say we'll do this again soon?'

'Sure,' I said quickly without making a firm commitment as I stepped into the lift. He flashed a bright smile at me and the door closed.

So there we have it. I had just got what I'd been hoping for. I thought I'd feel fantastic. But instead, once again, I felt empty.

In contrast, I could tell Charlie already had his head in the clouds. He was smitten. And as I'd instigated it, I couldn't very well start backtracking could I?

What on earth was I going to do now?

CHAPTER THIRTY-FOUR

I sat out on the terrace in the fluffy white robe Charlie had bought for me (which in true, posh style had my initials embroidered on). For the beginning of December, it was surprisingly mild. Charlie had been travelling a lot over the past few months to the US, Europe and the Far East on business (he'd invited me to join him, but I'd explained that I needed to be at work), so we hadn't been seeing much of each other over the autumn. But this was now the third weekend in a row I'd been here, and I was a little disappointed with myself. I was worried that because of Charlie's kind, sweet, nature, I was getting swept away with it all and was losing focus.

After we'd first spent the night together, Charlie had sent me two boxes of my favourite Lola's cupcakes and a giant bouquet of flowers with a note saying how much he'd enjoyed our evening and couldn't wait to see me again.

Even back then, whilst part of me said: *'Awww, how sweet. What a lovely message,'* the other part was niggling away, screaming, '*Shit! I'm not even sure if I want to continue with this.*' I couldn't shake the feeling in my gut that it didn't feel right. But then Reasanna had piped up:

FFS, Sophia, the man has just sent you your favourite cakes and had them chauffeur-driven to you at work, and you're still not sure? What do you want, woman? Diamonds?

And furthermore, this passion thing you keep harping on about isn't real life. Look where that got you with Lorenzo. A first-class ticket to Nowhereland. That's where.

Have you forgotten that you're fast approaching forty? You don't have the same options as you did when you were twenty-five. You must see by now how hard being single can be. I'm not saying to go out with any man who sends you flowers—anyone can do that—but don't rule someone out before you've given them a proper chance. You'd be crazy to end this without seeing where it could go. It was the first time you two had proper sex in ages, so it's natural that you both may be a bit rusty. Try again, and I'm sure it'll get better. And maybe the passion will grow. Look at people who have arranged marriages. They find a way to make it work.

So I listened to Reasanna and decided to persevere. After all, according to point number seven in my MAP plan, I was supposed to be embracing *all* opportunities. And before I'd met Charlie, if the universe had said to me: '*I can send you a guy that is probably going to fall madly in love with you, will be handsome, kind, success-ful, eager to please you, not a weirdo, financially secure (understatement of the century) and will want to have sex with you,*' I would have said '*sign me up!*' But now that I had that, strangely, it wasn't so appealing. Rich had a lot of those qualities too, and sometimes it just wasn't enough…

That's the thing. Getting into another routine relationship had never been my intention. That had been the problem with my life before with Rich, and I felt like I was falling into the same patterns again.

As lovely as Charlie was, now that he'd stopped travelling so much for work and we were seeing more of each other, it had become a little predictable.

Typically, on the Saturday, he'd send a car to collect me from home around 5.30 p.m., which would then take me to a fancy restaurant in Mayfair or Knightsbridge. We'd have an early dinner until about 9.30 p.m., then go back to his penthouse, where, after some polite conversation, he would give me a look, take my hand, lead me up the stairs to his bedroom and we'd have sex.

It was marginally better, and sometimes, if I could get my mind in the right place and concentrated hard enough, I enjoyed it a little bit, but not as much as him.

I knew exactly how my weekends with Charlie would be and what he'd do in bed. It was like he'd followed some kind of 'how to have sex with a woman' manual:

Step 1: kiss subject on lips for one minute
Step 2: then move to her neck and give sloppy wet kisses for precisely thirty seconds
Step 3: peck from her neck downwards until you reach her breasts
Step 4: kiss said breasts in a clockwise fashion for fifteen seconds, before sucking on nipples gently for ten counts
Step 5: repeat action twice before taking hand and

slowly moving downwards until you reach her vagina

Step 6: rub vagina gently and check for moistness

Step 7: if sufficient moisture is evident, you may now proceed with entry. If not, repeat steps 1-6 until desired effect is achieved, this time adding a generous sprinkle of platitudes such as 'you're beautiful', 'I'm so turned on right now' and 'I want you so much'…

Aaaaarrggghhhh!

Where was the passion? Where was the spontaneity? Why was it always the missionary position? Why did it always have to be in the bedroom? This was a 4,000-square-foot apartment, FFS. Why couldn't we do it on the terrace in the moonlight, on the marble kitchen worktop or even on the bloody sofa? Whenever I suggested this, he said he felt more comfortable in the bedroom, and every time I tried to go on top, he'd roll me back.

On a Sunday morning, he'd pop out get pastries from the little French bakery and then some dishes from M&S, or he'd go to a restaurant and ask them to make me a special meal with fresh prawns or lobster and bring it back home for us to reheat.

Despite his kindness, the more I thought about it, the more I realised that I needed to seriously consider taking time out or ending things completely. But was that the right thing to do? Was I expecting too much? Maybe, like Reasanna said, with time things would improve. Or perhaps if I explained my concerns, he'd be okay with something a little less serious and full-on. Hmmm. My thoughts were all muddled. This was one for the frienmittee. I needed my committee of close friends, i.e., Roxy's and Bella's wisdom.

I launched WhatsApp. *Great—they're both online.*

Me

Hey, ladies, how's it going?

Roxy

Hey, Sophia. All cool. Just chilling in bed with coffee number two.

Bella

A major miracle has happened. I have some time to myself. Mike has taken Paul for a walk!

Roxy

Ha-ha! Amazing. It's 11 a.m. on Sunday, so let me guess, Soph, you're on the massive terrace, waiting for King Cromwell to return with brunch?

Me

Correct…

Roxy

Cut to the chase, how's the sex? Any better?

Me

Nope. I'm still not feeling much. There's no passion. It's all a bit colour-by-numbers. I know it's bad, but sometimes I'm tempted to bring my Rabbit with me to use so I could remind myself what it's like to really come…

Roxy

Oh shit, that bad?

Me

It's not bad per se. He's a decent size, he does the right things in general. But whilst he's panting about how great it feels and how much he's enjoying himself, I'm thinking about what I need to order from Ocado. That can't be right.

Roxy

Hell no! If he's pushing the right buttons, you shouldn't even be able to *think* clearly. You should be overcome—pardon the pun—with desire and everything should feel fuzzy and just WOW!

Me

Exactly. But for some reason it's just not happening...

Roxy

Clearly you just don't have a sexual connection. What about kissing? Anything there?

Me

He only does it in the bedroom for a few seconds as part of his rote foreplay and I still don't feel anything...

Roxy

Well, kissing is important. I remember reading an article that said kissing allows us to see how compatible we are with a guy and that when we get close to them, their lips give off pheromones or a special smell. Basically, you can find someone attractive like you do with Charlie, but then when you go to kiss them, you don't feel a thing because their pheromones just don't float your boat.

Me

That would make sense...

Roxy

It's something to do with genes—apparently we're most attracted to men with genes or a smell that's different to ours. It also said women see kissing as a way to weed out boyfriends, so most would dump them if the first kiss felt wrong.

Me

Well, yeah, the first kiss wasn't mind-blowing, but I thought it would get better…

Roxy

Hmm. Well, it's difficult for a relationship to survive without frequent, proper down-and-dirty snogging.

Bella

Ladies, I feel like I need to chip in here. You're not being realistic. As someone who has been in a relationship for nine years, I can tell you that it's not all about swinging from the chandeliers 24/7. That's just not real life.

Me

I know. I was in a relationship for fifteen years. But surely if it's not good at the beginning, it can only go downhill…

Bella

True.

Me

I've been thinking that I'm going to have to consider ending it. Or at least taking time out. He's a lovely guy, but I don't feel ready for something serious and I reckon he is. I don't want to hurt him, but I need to let him know how I feel.

Bella

You're right. The thing is, most men will assume that women of our age are looking for marriage and kids. So if that's not the case, you need to make it clear.

Roxy

Agreed. I know it will mean being single again, but it's better to be single than to be in an unhappy marriage, and that's where this is heading. A big, fat public Hello! magazine, bells-and-whistles wedding. And fast. Stay with him any longer, he'll be getting down on one knee. And not to give you oral, that's for sure!

Me

Roxy! You're right, though. He's been talking about meeting his parents in a couple of weeks, so I have to tell him how I'm feeling before then, as I wouldn't want him to announce me as his girlfriend and then suddenly I disappear. No. I can't do that to him. I need to do it soon. Definitely this week. At the very latest. Thanks, ladies.

Bella

Just put the cheque in the post!

Roxy

He-he. Do people still even use cheques, Bella?!

I heard the lift doors open.

Me

Guys, I think Charlie's back. I better go. Bella, enjoy your time to yourself, and Roxy, let's catch up tomorrow. I want to hear all about that big meeting.

Bella

Will do. xxx

Roxy

Sure thing, lady. xxx

'I'm back,' said Charlie, shouting from the kitchen. 'I've got us a lovely lobster risotto for lunch, and fresh pastries from the yummy French bakery. Bucks Fizz coming up in a jiffy. But first,' he said, striding over towards me excitedly, 'all that walking in the crisp winter air has made me feel rather energised. I think we should retire to the bedroom and work up an appetite before we indulge in brunch.'

I'd admit, I was horny, but, given the decision I had just made about cooling things, we should probably have a talk...

'Um, Charlie,' I said as he started trying to kiss my lips, 'I was thinking we could have a chat first...?'

'Mmmm...' he said as he started moving down to kiss my neck. 'Plenty of time to talk later. Let's go upstairs...'

His kisses weren't as wet as normal, and as his hands started to wander south, I could feel myself getting mildly turned on...shit. I suppose we could talk afterwards? After all, I hadn't thought about how to broach the subject and I needed to do it delicately. Maybe I should carry on as normal today, go home tonight, plan what I was going to say and then call him tomorrow to arrange a time to meet up on Tuesday to tell him how I felt? Or I could do it tomorrow? Fuck. I just didn't know what to do...

Before I knew it, we were upstairs kissing on the bed and he was running through his foreplay routine. He climbed on top, stared at me longingly, then hurriedly reached into his side drawer, pulled out a condom, peeled off my dressing gown and went straight for it.

As we rocked back and forwards, my mind started to wander. If I told him how I felt tomorrow, this would probably be the last time we ever slept together. I could suggest we have something more casual, but I didn't think he'd agree. Anyway, I was missing the point. Even if it *was* more casual, why would I still want to keep seeing him when the sex was just okay and we didn't have enough of a connection?

Charlie finished with an almighty roar like he was coming for England, Scotland *and* Wales. We lay there for a few minutes, then he pulled out and lay beside me.

I don't think I can do it. I couldn't look him in the eyes at lunch and make polite conversation for the rest of the day, knowing that I was thinking about putting things on hold.

I glanced at him from head to toe. The condom was on the sheet beside him. He took that off quickly.

I stared at the ceiling. This felt wrong. We shouldn't have slept together. Horny or not, I should have insisted that we talk first. I couldn't delay this anymore. It wasn't fair to string him along. I needed to tell him how I feel. Not next week, not tomorrow. I needed to do it now. Planning what to say was nice, but I was learning that sometimes you couldn't control these things. No matter how I said it, it was going to hurt.

'Charlie,' I said, sitting up in bed and turning to face him. 'You know you've been talking a lot lately about meeting your parents?' I said cautiously.

'Yes!' he said, bolting up in the bed, clearly excited by the idea. 'I can't wait!'

'Well, you see, that's the thing,' I said, softening my voice. 'I'm just not sure it's a good idea right now.'

'Look,' he said, stroking my face. 'There's no need to be nervous. I know sometimes I paint them as being a little harsh and judgemental, particularly my father, but I'm sure they'll love you like I do and will welcome you to the family with open arms.'

Wait. Did he say he loved me? Probably just a turn of phrase. And welcome me to the family? That definitely sounds serious.

'I just…' *Come on, Sophia, spit it out.* 'What I mean is, it's, it's too soon. Premature, in fact.'

His face dropped. Then he froze as if his brain was trying to process my comments. After what felt like an eternity, but in truth was only a few seconds, he broke his silence.

'What do you mean *too soon*?' he scoffed. 'We've been dating for months, have amazing sex and we spend every weekend together when I'm not travelling. I've showered you with all your favourite things and lots of compliments and affection. What's the problem?' The confusion in his voice was now turning into irritation. 'I thought women liked to meet their partner's parents, so that they could demonstrate the severity of their intentions. The fact that one is ready to make a commitment?' he said, frowning. *I was right. He is definitely looking to settle down. Shit. I'm not ready.*

'That's not always the case,' I pointed out. 'Every woman is different. I'm just…I need time to think about what I really want. I feel like I've come from one long-term relationship and am leaping headfirst into another one too quickly. I don't want to hurt you, but I need to be honest.'

Silence. Once again, he seemed to be trying desperately to get his head around everything I'd said.

'Okay, Sophia. It's fine,' he said finally. 'I don't want to rush you. If you need time, I can give you that. Perhaps you should go. Lunch is in the oven. Take it with you. I'll arrange a car to drive you home.'

I saw tears forming in his eyes as he picked up his boxers from the floor, put them on hurriedly and scurried to the en suite.

My heart sank. I really didn't want to hurt him.

I picked up the clothes I'd left on the chair last night, pulled my dress over my head, stepped into my knickers and tights, then scrunched my bra into my hand. I walked to the bathroom door and knocked gently.

'Charlie?' I called. 'I'm going now. Are you okay?'

Still silence.

'Charlie,' I said softly. 'I'm so sorry. I didn't mean to upset you. I just thought I needed to be honest. It just wouldn't be right to meet your parents knowing I was feeling this way. Do you understand? I need to think about things. Try and work out if I'm ready for something serious. Charlie?' I called out again. 'Are you listening? Can you hear me?'

'Fine,' he snapped. 'I said I'd give you time, didn't I?'

I could hear anger and frustration in his voice. He'd never sounded like that before. He was always so calm, so nice, so sweet.

'Just go!' he shouted. 'The driver's downstairs waiting.'

'But I need to know you're okay,' I replied a little taken aback.

'I said I'm *fine*!' he snarled.

'Okay, Okay, I'll leave you alone. Sorry again,' I replied.

Silence.

I got the message. I'd hurt him and he didn't want to talk to me.

When I got home, I still felt twinges of guilt, but tried to reassure myself that it was for the best. Continuing would have been worse.

Had we ended things? I'd said I needed time, as I did need to think about what I want. If I was honest, it probably was over, but I was just too scared to close the door completely. What if I never found another decent guy again? Look at all of the men on the dating sites. In comparison, my experience with Charlie was so much better. Let's face it. He was the most eligible bachelor in London. Maybe my expectations were too high and he was as good as it gets. What if I never found someone that I clicked with?

What have I done? I'm probably going to end up sad and alone…

I'll feel better after a shower.

I dried myself on the bed, threw my towel to the other side, then flopped back onto the pillow. I was feeling a bit more positive. Some music would make me feel better still. I reached for my phone to launch a mellow Spotify playlist. I needed to feel relaxed.

I touched the screen.

No fucking way.

I bolted up straight, nearly hitting my head on the headboard.

Shut the front door, the back door, the side door—in fact, all the fucking windows too.

It can't be.

There's a WhatsApp message.

A WhatsApp message from Lorenzo.

Fingers trembling, I unlocked the screen, clicked on the app and then into his message.

WTF.

He's where?

In London?

OMFG.

CHAPTER THIRTY-FIVE

I read Lorenzo's messages again for what must have been the hundredth time.

Lorenzo
Hello, Sophia
Lorenzo
How are you?
Lorenzo
Sorry. I know it has been a long time. but I am in London.
Lorenzo
For work
Lorenzo
Would be nice to see you.
Lorenzo
Miss you.

It wasn't often that I was speechless, but…

He's in London?

Why?

Yes. I'd read the message enough times to know he'd said he was working, but I didn't get it. What about Taste Holidays? Why had he stopped working there? Had he been sacked for sleeping with another guest? Had he quit?

How long had he been in London for? Where and how long was he staying?

So many questions. My head was spinning.

Well, the only way to find out would be to *actually* reply. But it wasn't that simple.

This was a guy I hadn't heard from for months. Who'd stood me up in Florence. A man whose messages to me (which only ever seemed to come when I initiated contact first) were bland and demonstrated lack of interest. Yet now all of a sudden he missed me? What a fucking cheek.

He'd probably arrived in London today and thought, *Oh shit, it's been twenty-four hours since I last had sex. Where can I get some for free? I know. I'll message that desperate woman from the cookery holiday. She's bound to say yes if I string her some BS about missing her.* Well, I wasn't going to fall for his tricks. Not this time. Once bitten, twice shy. What's that quote I read somewhere? 'Make a mistake once and it becomes a lesson. Make the same mistake twice and it becomes a choice.'

Exactly. Fuck you, Lorenzo.

But shouldn't you at least reply to find out why he's here before you dismiss him and make assumptions?

Oh, Reasanna. Get the hell out of my head with your logic. Surely I'd be mad to even give him the time of day. Why waste my time and risk getting hurt again?

But aren't you a little curious, Sophia? Is there any harm in messaging him to find out? Nothing ventured, nothing gained, right?

Okay, okay, okay.

But I was *definitely* not bothering with that over-thinking or planning what I was going to say again. Let's just get this over with. I started typing out a reply:

Me

Lorenzo? Wasn't expecting to hear from you…how come you're in London for work? What happened to your job at Taste Holidays?

I tossed my phone on the bed, slipped on my night-dress, climbed under my duvet and glanced down at the phone screen. The ticks had turned blue. I wondered if he understood 'how come'? I should've said 'why'. That would have been easier to understand. *Tough!* I said, coming back to my senses. *That's how I speak and like I said, I wasn't planning my messages. He'll have to figure it out for himself.*

He was 'typing'. Annoyingly, I felt a little flutter of excitement. *Calm the fuck down, Sophia. Remember, you're still supposed to be angry with him…*

Lorenzo

Season finished

Lorenzo

Until next year

Lorenzo

You said to come to London. That good restaurants are looking for a chef like me.

I take your advice
Lorenzo
And I wanted to come and see you too

Wait, what? So he's come here to work because I suggested it? The season's over? That means he might be here for a while? That he *didn't* forget about me? That he's been *thinking* about me?

Given his radio silence, I'd never even contemplated that he'd given me a second thought or that I'd ever see him again. And after our last exchange of messages, I *definitely* had not considered that he'd come to London, never mind stay here.

And he said he wants to see me?

My head started spinning. My heart was racing. The flashbacks of that night together came flooding back. My body started to tingle. My imagination flew into overdrive.

I can't believe it.

I was trying to suppress my excitement, but I couldn't help it. *Stay calm. Stay calm. Stay calm…*

I attempted to compose myself. Rather than getting carried away, I need to take a deep breath and find out more about this situation…

Me
So do you have a job yet? How long are you
here for?
Lorenzo
Yes
Lorenzo
Passed my trial so I will start this week
Lorenzo

Not sure
Lorenzo
Maybe two months

Two whole months! Wow!
Don't act excited. Play it cool…
I thought you weren't into playing games, Sophia?
Pipe down, Reasanna. This is different…

Me
Congrats on your job! Where are you working?
And where are you living?
Lorenzo
Thanks
Lorenzo
Nice Italian restaurant East London
Lorenzo
Called Polignano
Lorenzo
Live in shordutch
Lorenzo
*shoreditch. you know where it is?

*He's landed on his feet there. I love Polignano. The
food there is amazing.*

Me
Yes, I know Polignano. Very good restaurant.
Shoreditch is also a very cool place to live.
Lorenzo
Yes, good restaurant. Learnt lots from chef already
Lorenzo

My place is not very special
Lorenzo
Just one room with a kitchen so I can cook and a
bathroom
Lorenzo
But I like
Lorenzo
Chef knows the landlord so he gave it to me for not
a lot of money to help so I can afford the rent
Lorenzo
You want to see me?
Lorenzo
I want see you
Lorenzo
It's been a long time
Lorenzo
I miss you

Some things hadn't changed. He still sent multiple messages with a few words, when it could just fit into one message and one sentence.

Focus. He'd just asked if I wanted to see him. And he said he missed me again. Shit. The plan was only to message him, not to meet. Surely I was playing with fire…

Come on, Sophia. Remember MAP point number seven, to embrace all opportunities?

Yes, Reasanna. But after the shit he pulled before, which resulted in me becoming a pathetic mess, was it worth giving him a second chance? He certainly didn't deserve it. And what about Charlie? Wouldn't that be wrong?

What have you got to lose by giving him a second

chance? It's not like you're flying to Italy. You can call the shots. Arrange to meet at a time and place that suits you. Give him half an hour of your time, and if you don't like what he's saying, then leave. And as for Charlie, technically you're on a break. Plus, you're only going to see Lorenzo to say hello and hear what he has to say for himself, aren't you? Okay, probably not... but if you meet somewhere public, then that will help keep you honest and out of trouble. At least temporarily...

Seriously? You're asking what I've got to lose? Erm, my sanity. My self-respect... Isn't that enough, Reasanna? As for public places keeping me out of trouble, I didn't seem to have any problems with PDA with Vincenzo, and he was nowhere near as hot as Lorenzo, so I wasn't sure I agreed with that. But, yes, I *was* on a break from Charlie and, yes, Lorenzo was in London and if I met him on my terms, then I *supposed* it could work, if it was only half an hour out of my day...

Me
Maybe we could meet. Let me know when and
where you had in mind and I'll check my diary to
see if it's convenient.
Lorenzo
Tomorrow I have a day off
Lorenzo
You free?
Lorenzo
Don't know. I am new to London
Lorenzo
You have ideas of where to go?
Lorenzo

I don't mind
Lorenzo
Wherever you want

Tomorrow? When I'd asked, I hadn't thought he'd want to meet so soon…

If this was six months ago, I would have jumped at the chance, but it had taken me a long time to get over things with him. Not that we were in a relationship or anything serious, but despite what Reasanna said about going and hearing what he has to say, I had to be careful about jumping back into something like that again and risking getting hurt.

Embrace life, Sophia. You owe it to Albert's memory. Remember: MAP.

Well, I *supposed* I *could* make it, then. The team were self-sufficient, so leaving work on time wouldn't be a problem. At least then we could get meeting up over and done with, and then I could just move on and forget about him again. I don't want to meet too late, though. And it needed to be fairly close the office to minimise inconvenience.

Me
Okay. I can meet tomorrow evening. I finish work at 6 p.m., so 6.30 p.m.? Do you know Regent Street?
Lorenzo
Good
Lorenzo
6.30 is good
Lorenzo

yes i know. I went there before on the metro
Me
Fine. Let's meet for one drink at 6.30 p.m. at All
Bar One, Regent Street.
Lorenzo
Perfetto
Lorenzo
i look forward to seeing you

I was careful not to show too much emotion. Last time I had been far too gushy. That's why the two times he'd said he missed me, I hadn't reciprocated. I typed out a reply, reiterating the time and location once again so there could be no confusion or excuses for not turning up.

Me
See you tomorrow at All Bar One, Regent Street at 6.30 p.m. Goodnight.
Lorenzo
Kiss

ALL DAY I couldn't concentrate. I didn't know what to expect. It had been so sudden. He'd appeared from nowhere. I hadn't even thought about him much for ages.

Okay, who am I trying to kid? I thought about him *a lot*. But it wasn't like those early days where I'd *obsessed* over him. I wondered what he was doing, if he'd thought about me. And I can't lie, often when I was with Charlie having sex, I'd dream that it was Lorenzo on top of me instead. I know it was bad, but as hard as I tried, I just couldn't shake the feelings I'd had that night.

And now he was in London? And I was going to be seeing him in just three hours' time? Seriously?

I wasn't as prepared as I would have been with a bit more notice. Although I had no intention of sleeping with him (well, that's what sensible Sophia said…), I wasn't going to make the same mistake twice, so I had woken up early (not that I could even *get* to sleep after messaging him) and had pruned everything within an inch of its life.

I had just showered at work and changed into a dress. I'd be leaving the office soon for an emergency blow-dry with Josh. Even if it was one drink, I wanted to look and feel my best (and also show him what he'd been missing—childish, I know, but I didn't care). Plus, I didn't want to have any grooming regrets like I did last time.

Forty-five minutes to go.

Josh styled my hair in record time, adding some sexy waves. Not dissimilar to my date with Charlie…I did feel a few pangs of guilt.

Unlike all my other dates, I was feeling quite nervous. This wasn't some posh guy I'd met near the Kings Road or a stranger from Tinder. This was the gorgeous Lorenzo whom I'd shared a night of passion with. Who had kissed me all over. Who, eight months ago, had made me come so spectacularly without us even having sex. And I had been madly in lust with him pretty much ever since.

Lorenzo was the man that made me lose my mind so much that I'd spent days, weeks even stalking his Facebook page. Dreaming about him. The hot chef that I'd sent embarrassing gushy messages to.

He was also the man who'd said he'd meet me in

Florence for a weekend together and then stood me up at the last minute. I'd then spent four days there all on my own and getting soaked on that never-ending trip to Cinque Terre, feeling sorry for myself. In fact, what the fuck was I doing going to see him after he'd put me through all that shit? How had I let Reasanna talk me into this? Imagine what the frienmittee would say if they knew I was meeting him.

In fact, I *should* let Bella and Roxy know, shouldn't I? For safety reasons?

Fuck it. They'll only tell me I'm crazy. This was my decision. Something *I* felt I needed to do. I would just trust my gut.

Thirty minutes to go…

Time to freshen up my make-up. I added a deeper, more prominent cat eye flick, a light dusting of powder to eliminate shine on my T-zone, and of course applied a seductive red lip…

I'm so fucking nervous!

I smoothed out the front of my dress with my hands as I stood back to examine myself in the bathroom mirror. Always harder to look sexy in December when it's cold outside. I'd opted for a knee-length black dress with three-quarter-length sleeves and cleavage tastefully on show. I'd brave the cold so that I could have bare legs and wear my scarlet peep-toe shoe boots. This look was smartish, yet casual and, most importantly, *sexy*.

Fifteen minutes to go…

Done.

Make-up, outfit and hair all *on fleek*, as my niece Jasmine says. The salon team gave me the thumbs-up and lots of encouragement as I stepped outside into the crisp London air.

It was now 18.23. No point jumping in a taxi—it would take an inordinate amount of time with all the traffic on Regent Street. In these boots, it'd take me a comfortable ten minutes to walk to All Bar One, which meant I'd arrive there just a few minutes after 18.30. He didn't strike me as the punctual type, so I should have time to pop to the ladies' for one last check up and still head back upstairs to be fashionably late at 18.40.

As I walked back upstairs, I scanned the area. The long wooden bar, which was in front of a huge wall with illuminated shelves filled with hundreds of different bottles of wine, was heaving with office workers having a drink after work as well as shoppers and tourists. All of the tanned banquette seating in the centre was full, as well as the stools at the back. By the window underneath the row of pendant white ceiling lights, there were a handful of wooden tables for two that were empty. But judging by how busy it was, they wouldn't be free for much longer.

What if he doesn't turn up? I asked myself probably for the eight hundredth time today. Of course I'd be livid, but at least I would have tried and wouldn't have travelled hundreds of miles to see him. It would cost me a fifteen-pound cab ride home rather than the grand I'd wasted last time. And for the sake of the price of a cocktail, it was worth a try. Because after all, what if he *did* turn up?

That's right. Think positively, Sophia.

I hovered underneath the hanging giant black-and-white clock near the bar and glanced out the window.

Holy shit.
Is that him?

A gorgeous guy who bore more than a passing resemblance to Lorenzo walked past the window, then past the door.

Oh? I thought it was him. That's a shame.

Wait…he's coming back!

Said hot guy walked back towards the door and then through it.

It is *him.*

OMFG—he is sooooooooooooooooooo hot.

He flashed that killer smile at me and it took all my strength to remain upright.

'Wow!' he said as he walked towards me. 'Sophia. You look even more beautiful than I remember. *Che bella.*' He stood back, looked me up and down, nodding with approval and smiling as he did.

'Wow *yourself*, Lorenzo,' I replied, trying to play it cool and failing miserably.

His hair has grown back, but had been freshly shaved down at the sides, leaving it slightly wavy and beautiful on top. Perfect for running my fingers through.

His beard looked thick and gorgeous. He'd grown it back. Beautiful.

His hypnotic deep dark eyes drew me in. I could get lost in them for days.

His smile…

His lips…I remembered those lips all over my body. I wanted to kiss them right now…

And he had on those jeans. The delicious dark blue jeans he had worn the morning after the night before…

He was wearing a jacket, but he had a fitted jumper on underneath, and I could see the outline of his taut, firm, sexy chest…

One drink? Keeping myself out of trouble? Fat chance. I was going to need an entire army to stop me from wanting to jump his bones right now.

Please, God. Give me all the strength you can.

Something tells me I am about to sin...

CHAPTER THIRTY-SIX

We sat down on the dark pleather seats at a table by the window. Even though he was opposite me, I still couldn't quite believe he was here.

God, he was *so* beautiful. His olive skin was glowing. Flecks of grey were sprinkled through his beard and hair. I freaking *loved* salt-and-pepper hair on a man. Even his laughter lines were bloody gorgeous. I could literally stare at him all day.

Now I remembered why I had to recite those boring sports, to keep my emotions under control.

Fuck snooker, darts, golf and whatever bollocks I'd chanted in my head before. I'd waited so long to see him again and I wasn't about to suppress it. I was going to flirt my arse off and let him know *exactly* how I felt. I never even thought we'd meet again, so what did I have to lose?

Ahem. According to you, Sophia, sanity and self-respect...

Button it, Reasanna.

'So, tell me about your new job,' I asked, leaning in and tilting my head a little. 'How did you get it?'

'Well, I looked on the internet for good Italian restaurants in London,' he replied in his thick, sexy Italian accent. 'I picked four and looked on Facebook to see who I liked and looked at their websites. Then I found the email addresses for the head chefs, sent my CV and asked for a job. I liked the head chef at Polignano. He said I could come for a trial. I have to pay for the flight and hotel myself, so it is a risk…'

I nodded, desperately trying to focus on listening to him rather than imagining his hands all over me.

'But I was confident. The chef sounded interested, so I took the chance, and he liked my cooking. I am excited.'

'That's amazing,' I said, bringing myself out of my fantasy and back to reality. 'I'm so happy for you.'

'I say thanks to you too, as is it was you that made me think about coming to London.' He flashed his infectious smile at me again. 'I worked before in LA and Singapore, but never in London. It is a good idea. I have already learnt new things to take back home. I like it. And you?' he asked. 'What you do here in London, Sophia, for work?'

'Oh, I work in PR,' I replied casually. He didn't need to know the ins and outs of my business at this stage.

'What is that?' he asked, frowning.

'Public relations. Basically, we promote hair and beauty companies—you know, skincare products—face creams, make-up, hairdressers…that kind of thing,' I said, gesturing cutting hair and rubbing imaginary moisturiser into my skin like I was playing a game of charades. 'We get them in the magazines so that people know about them and buy their products or visit their salons.'

'Ah, yes, I see!' he said excitedly. 'Like advertisements. You make them?'

'Hmm...sort of....I'll show you one day,' I said. It was hard enough explaining PR to my mum, never mind an Italian chef.

The waiter came over to our table and asked what we'd like to drink. Thank God we didn't have to get up and go to the bar to order, as I wanted to stare at this man without interruption for as long as possible.

'I'll have a gin and tonic, please,' I replied. 'Lorenzo?'

'Good choice,' he said, smiling again. 'I will have the same, thanks.'

The waiter nodded, then headed back to the bar.

'So you said you reckon—sorry, you think you'll be here for around two months?' I asked, trying once again to play it cool.

'Not sure. When you join this restaurant, the chef likes you to stay a long time,' he said, switching on his serious face. 'If I told him I stay for only two months, he may not agree to take me because it is a lot of work to train someone and then they leave.'

'Yes, I can understand that,' I agreed.

'I will stay for as long as possible, but I must be back for the Taste Holidays season next year, which starts in February or March. I will wait to see when I am booked. We are now in December, so maybe I stay this month, January and perhaps February. I will see how I like it. And if there is another reason to stay in London...' he said, flashing a flirty smile.

We sat there mute for a few seconds, just staring at one another. Then he broke the silence.

'You are a beautiful woman, Sophia,' he said. 'I

remembered you were beautiful, but not like this. You are very, very sexy…'

I may have just wet my knickers.

Of course I actually hadn't, but if he carried on like this, I just might…

Our eyes locked again and we said nothing. Just gazed. I knew what I was thinking. I hoped he was thinking the same.

How long had we been here? I'd look at my phone, but that would involve not staring into his eyes for a full two seconds, and right now, that was just too long.

I reckoned we'd been here about fifteen minutes. Maybe twenty? *So, how long do you think is reasonable to wait before suggesting we leave this bar and head back to his place? Is twenty-five minutes too soon? Would that be considered too slutty or desperate?*

Okay. Forty-five minutes. If I really, really tried, I could hang on for another twenty-five minutes. Just…

An hour? *Seriously*, Reasanna. That's pushing it. I mean, it's not like we've just met. Technically, I've known him for eight months. That's the equivalent to two centuries in this fast-paced, new-age dating world.

Furthermore, think about it: if that weekend in Florence had gone to plan, there would be zero waiting. We would have met and got straight down to it. So why torture myself? You only live once, right? If I see something I want, I *have* to go for it.

The waiter brought over our drinks. Lorenzo sadly had to break our gaze as the waiter put the bill down on the table.

I reached in my bag for my purse. I should at least offer to go Dutch.

'No, no. I will pay,' he insisted as he reached into his pocket, took out his beaten black leather wallet, slipped out his card and handed it to the waiter. Once he'd tapped it on the contactless reader, he turned back to me and gave me a sexy smile. Oh, I *loved* his smile.

I took a large gulp of my drink. He mirrored this. And then, holy crap.

He just licked his lips.

Oh my goodness. Just like in Italy, it sent me crazy. My heart was beating so fast and I could already feel the tingles of anticipation between my legs...

I took another giant gulp of my drink. I couldn't wait any longer. Who was I trying to prove something to or impress? This was *my* life. I didn't care what people thought. I answered to myself. And tonight, I was going to do what I damn well pleased.

'So,' I said, doing my tilty head seduction move. 'What did you say your place is like?'

'It is small,' he said, pushing his hands together with a tiny gap in between to indicate the miniature size. 'It is, how do you say? Studio? Bedroom, kitchen and sofa in one room. Then there is a little bathroom with a shower and toilet. But I like.'

'Shoreditch isn't that far from here in a taxi,' I said, part asking, part making a statement. 'How would you like to show it to me?'

Yep, bring on the head tilting, eyelash fluttering and sexy smiling. I placed my hands on top of his, which were resting on the wooden table, and started stroking them gently.

'Mmm, mmm,' he said, smiling, receiving my *I want*

you, now message loud and clear. 'I like *very much* to show you my place. You want to go tonight?' he asked.

I glanced at my phone: 19.07. Not bad. I'd held out for thirty-seven minutes. No, no. Never mind the fact that we hadn't sat down at the table until 18.40ish. That didn't matter.

'I would love *very much* to go tonight,' I confirmed. 'Why don't we go *now*?' I suggested as I seductively licked my red lips.

'*Now*?' he said, clearly surprised at my boldness. 'Mmm. Sophia, I like this idea very much.'

He downed his drink in one, slamming the glass on the table, and I did the same. We pushed our chairs back and stood up, all the while transfixed on each other, then rushed towards the door.

There was a crowd of people outside smoking, and once we'd navigated through them, I looked left, then right along the roadside to hail down a black cab. Perfect. One indicated and pulled over.

'What's the name of the road you live on?' I asked as I opened the door of the taxi and climbed in.

'Hanford Street,' he replied, getting in after me, his eyes fixated on my bum.

'Hanford Street,' I said to the driver. 'As quick as you can, please!' The driver glanced in his rear-view mirror and smiled. I think somehow he could sense the sexual tension and knew precisely why we were in a hurry…

I'd barely fastened my seat belt before Lorenzo's lips were planted firmly on mine and he'd started to kiss me.

Oh yes. Now that's *what I'm talking about…*

He began thrusting his tongue in my mouth, and he

tasted delicious. Just like in Tuscany, Lorenzo kissed me like his life depended on it.

He couldn't have been worried about safety as by now he'd unfastened his seat belt and half of his body was pressed against mine, whilst his left hand made its way up my thigh with a sense of urgency, until…

Ohhhhh…

He'd pulled the front of my thong to one side, allowing his fingers full access to what lay beneath. With everything exactly how I wanted it to be down there, this time there was no need for him to hold back.

He started stroking inbetween my legs, sending me out of my fucking mind…

How much longer until we arrived? I didn't think I could stop myself. I wanted this man inside me.

'Oh, Lorenzo, stop,' I groaned. But it felt *so good* I didn't want him to. 'Actually, no. Don't *stop*. Oh my God. I want you,' I muttered in his ear as his face brushed against mine. 'I *need* you. Now!'

He eased his lips away from my neck. 'You want do here?' he asked. 'In taxi?' He grinned. 'You naughty girl. I like.' And with that, he resumed nibbling my neck, then my ear as his hands continued caressing me.

I opened my eyes, reluctantly. Okay, we'd just passed Liverpool Street station. Couldn't be much further. I might *just* be able to hang on for another five minutes…I know I'm in a liberal mood, but not sure I'm up for sex in a taxi just yet…

The cab slowed down and pulled up outside a warehouse type building.

'We're here,' the driver shouted, guessing correctly that with all the slurping and moaning noises we were making in the back seat, we wouldn't hear him otherwise.

I popped open my purse and gave him a twenty-pound note through the passenger window. Fuck the change. Fuck the receipt. I had more pressing issues to attend to.

As Lorenzo opened the taxi door with his back to me, I crouched behind him, shamelessly running my hands over his firm chest and then downwards…

The minute he opened the front door of his flat, it was like a love scene from a film. It had barely closed before clothes began being tossed in the air and landing in a heap on the floor. First his jacket, then his jumper…

Oh, his chest! All hairy and gorgeous, and he was still in amazing shape. He started unbuckling the belt on his jeans, staring at me with excitement and desire.

Lorenzo unzipped my dress, threw it on the floor, scooped me up in his muscular arms and carried me to the edge of his double bed. He unfastened my bra, gently pushed me backwards, then straddled me.

Working down from my ears to my neck, shoulders and my erect nipples, he showered me with sweet kisses, lingering over my stomach then sliding his tongue around my belly button. As his mouth moved further south, I could feel his hot sweet breath tickling my skin. He was teasing me, and my body was groaning with excitement. I knew *exactly* where I wanted him to touch me next…

Lorenzo unpeeled my red thong, tossing it over his shoulder, leaving me completely naked. This time, I was proud to have it all on display for him. A wicked grin flashed across his face.

'Mmmm,' he said, licking his lips. 'Even more beautiful than I remember.'

My body trembled as he began licking from my knees, then up along my inner thighs. As he travelled further and further north, I started to tense a little. I couldn't wait to have his mouth on me, but would I *taste* okay to him? I'd had a shower before I'd left the office, so hopefully I should be fine, but…

'Beautiful, Sophia,' he said, clearly sensing that I'd lost focus for a second, 'relax. Let me give you pleasure. Open your legs fully for me, please.'

I didn't hesitate.

He buried his head enthusiastically between my thighs before using both of his hands to spread my lips and gently kissed inside. Turning his attention to my clit, he started sucking it softly, then began slowly flicking his tongue: first up and down, with a short pause in between.

'Mmm,' he said, looking up at me and licking his lips. 'You taste so good.'

He buried his head in me once again. *Oh, yesss!* Just when I thought it couldn't get any better, he glided his tongue round and round like he was drawing circles, switching between clockwise, then anticlockwise rotations.

I could not breathe.

Lorenzo was devouring me like I was the most delicious dish he'd ever tasted. It was as if he'd been starved for months and had just been presented with his first meal. He listened to my moans of pleasure and the way my body reacted beneath him and instantly knew what was working for me and kept going. I could feel my clit enlarging with every stroke of his tongue.

Unlike some men, who squirmed at the mere thought of going down on a woman or considered a quick peck there enough to satisfy you, Lorenzo was clearly an oral aficionado, approaching the task of pleasing me with gusto. I would have been delighted to have him continue all night, but he was turning me on so much that I had to have him either in my mouth or inside me. Immediately.

'Lorenzo…' He lifted his head up, and his mouth was wet with me all over him. 'I want you.'

I sat up a little and finished unbuckling his jeans. He stood up, pulled them off quickly, followed by his fitted black boxers to reveal an enormous erection.

Divine.

Just as I was about to lean forward, Lorenzo pushed me back down onto the bed and climbed on top.

'I wanted to take you in my mouth,' I said.

'I know, and I would like that,' he said as he slid his hand between my legs and then licked his fingers, 'but Sophia, I have waited so long for this moment. The first time we tried, Grace came in. The second time, Erica disturbed us. We have had many delays, and it has been so many months since we have seen each other. I cannot wait any longer. I want to make love to you now.'

There was no way I was going to refuse. My body was also crying out to have him. Every inch of him.

He reached back down for his jeans, pulled a condom out of his wallet, then skilfully and speedily rolled it on. He'd clearly had a lot of practice.

I opened my legs wide again and he positioned his between mine. As he entered me, I gasped for breath.

At last!

I'd thought this moment would never happen. And now that it was, I was going to enjoy every millisecond.

I wasted no time in rocking my hips back and forth beneath him, mirroring his rhythm. Just as I'd hoped,

Lorenzo was doing all the right things, and he clearly had the ideal equipment for the job. As I watched him sliding in and out of me, I marvelled at how perfect he felt. Like the Goldilocks of rods, Lorenzo's wasn't too big or too small. It was just right.

He played teasingly, switching between shallow and deeper thrusts. I wrapped my legs around his waist to pull him closer into me, and as I did I felt the delicious friction on my clit, which became more intense. I grabbed his arse firmly, then he lifted my legs up onto his shoulders so he could go deeper.

Oh God. Every inch of me was trembling. I wasn't sure how much longer I could last, but I *had* to hold it together. I didn't want this to end.

Our rhythm was perfectly in sync, flowing from one beat to the next effortlessly. Everything just seemed so natural. Our bodies merged seamlessly. It was like they were meant to be together.

'Do you like to go on top?' Lorenzo asked as he kissed my right foot, which was still resting on his shoulder.

'Yes!' I confirmed enthusiastically. At last, a man who knew about changing positions and wasn't afraid for a woman to take the reins a little.

'Come,' he said, placing my legs back down on the bed. We held each other close as we rolled on our sides and then Lorenzo rolled onto his back whilst still staying firmly inside me.

I gently lowered myself up and down and started to ride him as he caressed my breasts. I rocked back and forth, moved my hips from side to side and then round and round like I was dancing provocatively on the dance floor.

I was having the time of my life, and from the look of pleasure spread across Lorenzo's face, he was too.

'How does that feel?' I asked.

'Perfetto. I love the way you move,' he panted as he rocked beneath me and squeezed my arse in appreciation. 'You are amazing, Sophia. I want to come very much, but I will wait. I must let you come first.'

A man that wants the woman to climax first? Who puts the woman's needs before his own? Praise the Lord.

I had a feeling that I could actually climax any minute now…

As I leant all the way back, arching my body, Lorenzo took full advantage by stroking my clit. He placed his forefinger and middle finger over the top and rubbed it in circular motions varying the size and frequency of the circles. As he increased the pressure, rhythm and speed of his touch, I felt the contractions pulsing through me.

My heart was now beating so fast I felt like it was going to burst out of my chest. The wave was building again, and as much as I wanted to continue, I was powerless to stop it. I felt my toes curling and a surge of intoxicating sensations flooding my body.

I was losing control.

I was on the verge.

It's building…I can't. I can't…

'Lorenzo, please don't stop,' I pleaded. 'I'm about to come. Don't change a thing, keep going. Please. I'm coming…I'm coming!'

As he continued stroking my clit, maintaining the pressure and the tempo, the tsunami hit me, and I had no other option than to succumb.

'*Oh my fucking goodness! Lorenzoooo!*' I screamed. If

I was worried about being loud in Italy, that was nothing compared to this. I could only hope his neighbours didn't think I was being tortured and call the police.

This was the very opposite of torture. Never in my entire life had I experienced an orgasm so intense.

Just as I came, I felt Lorenzo's body stiffen below mine and he groaned loudly as he also exploded inside me.

I collapsed in a heap on top of him, our bodies both deliciously sticky from our workout. I was spent. But I was already looking forward to round two…

WE BOTH FLOPPED BACK on the bed, panting wildly. That was the third time, and it wasn't even midnight.

And I still wanted more…

I wasn't even sure I would be able to walk tomorrow, but I didn't care.

This, I repeat, *this* was what amazing sex was like. I felt like I'd been waiting my whole life for this.

I couldn't even begin to tell you all of the things we did. We just could not keep our hands off each other. I loved that he took charge. And it wasn't just the sodding missionary position either.

He threw me this way and that on the bed and stimulated every inch of me. We did more positions than an advanced Pilates class. Some I'd never even tried before, but each one felt damn good.

And as for that studio flat, let's just say he gave me the full guided tour. I saw the wooden floor as we rolled around on the rug. I sampled the springiness of the sofa and could even vouch for the black-and-white speckled

MDF kitchen worktops. Very hard and cold by all accounts. And not at all comfortable to lie on, but comfort was the last thing on my mind. I was too busy coming.

I know, I know, it's the kitchen and where food is prepared (thank God I was over my cleanliness obsession), but the new Sophia said surely that's what bleach was invented for?

By 2 a.m., I was exhausted after going another round. This guy must be some sort of certified sex stallion to manage it this many times in one night (either that or he'd popped a blue pill before he met me this evening, but I doubted it). And these weren't short five-minute sessions either. Clearly there were benefits to sleeping with an experienced man. He knew exactly what he was doing, which areas to focus on to maximise my enjoyment, and how to control his instrument to make it last.

Although down below and inside felt like I'd just sat on a cactus, I was so, so high on lust. I'd never taken drugs before, but I couldn't imagine a feeling that would be bigger and better than what I was experiencing right now.

This man sent me out of my mind. At some points I was so aroused, I felt like I was going to pass out. And I had no idea how many times I orgasmed, but I'd never experienced anything like it. *Rampant Rabbit. You have officially been given early retirement. I will* not *be needing you with Lorenzo around.*

I rested my head on his chest. We were both dripping with sweat. Never mind a fear of dirty glasses. This was the kind of thing that would have caused the old me to go into total meltdown. There would be no way I could have considered lying on him without sending him to shower with a hundred bottles of Dettol first. But right now, I couldn't care less.

Lorenzo was now sleeping. He had worked hard tonight and had earned a rest. My hair was fucked. My mascara and make-up had been wiped off long ago, but I felt fine. I was so relaxed. Lying on him, I felt like I was home. Safe, secure and content. This was more than worth the wait. I was just so happy.

Right now, nothing could bring me down from this high.

CHAPTER THIRTY-SEVEN

I t was 6.47 a.m. already?

I hadn't really slept. How could I? After our last session finished around 3.30 a.m., I'd spent most of the time just staring at Lorenzo and stroking his chest to check he was real.

When I thought about the roller coaster of emotions I'd been through when organising that failed weekend in Florence, it was crazy to think about how quickly and organically this had happened.

Less than forty-eight hours ago, I had been in bed with Charlie and hadn't heard from Lorenzo for, what, six months? And now, here I was, lying on top of him butt naked in his studio flat in London.

Yes, London: the city he'd planned to stay in for at least two months. Nuts.

And we'd had the most mind-blowing sex, no less than five times. I didn't even think I'd had that much sex with Rich in the last two years…

I'd always sensed that we'd had a connection that night

in Tuscany. But I'd never even dreamt it would be something this powerful.

I pulled the brake on my thoughts. I mustn't get carried away. Although he'd said yesterday that how long he stayed would depend on whether he had another reason to, alluding to me, for all I knew, he could have just been saying that to get me into bed and this could just be a one-night thing.

Anyway. As hard as it was to break away, better go to the loo and brush my teeth before he woke up.

I picked my handbag off the floor, reached into my make-up bag and pulled out my travel toothbrush, hairbrush and a mini face wash. No wonder my bag always weighed a ton. It was all this spare make-up and miniature toiletries I carried around just in case...

I headed to the bathroom. He was right. Like the flat as a whole, it was very modest. Plain white basin, toilet and single shower. Just as he'd explained when we'd met up last night, the rest of this place is small (but at least he kept everything clean and tidy). Magnolia walls (which were in need of a fresh lick of paint), cheap laminate flooring, a charcoal fabric two-seater sofa with matching cushions and glass coffee table, a kitchen with slightly discoloured cream cupboard doors, a double bed (which I was now *extremely* familiar with), a small pine mirrored wardrobe and that was it. *Very* different from Charlie's place, obviously. However, as last night proved, there were a lot of attributes Lorenzo brought to the table that Charlie didn't. And frankly, I'd take staying in a tiny flat and having a wild night of passion over swanning around a palatial penthouse and being bored in the bedroom any time.

Ah yes, Charlie...shit. I did feel a little guilty. If I

hadn't had that conversation with him on Sunday night, I'd be feeling much worse. But I'd made it clear that I wasn't sure if I was looking for something serious and that I needed time to think. Obviously, I'd had no idea at the time that this would happen with Lorenzo, but now that it had, there was no going back.

I always sensed that something was missing with Rich and with Charlie. I'd condemned myself for walking away from two guys who clearly had a lot to offer. Perhaps some people would think I was mad. And I knew I sounded completely deluded and I shouldn't get carried away because we'd only spent one night together (well, two if you included Tuscany), but somehow I was convinced Lorenzo is the man for me. I just *knew* it. I *felt* it.

There was a knock at the bathroom door. I'd finished brushing my teeth and had made myself look as decent as I could given the fact I'd had about three hours sleep, if that, plus had no make-up on as it had been smeared all over the bedsheets and sofa cushions…

Lorenzo entered, looking bleary-eyed but still so damn sexy. His hair was all ruffled too, and oh yes…he was still naked.

Give me strength…

'*Buongiorno, Sophia*,' he said, voice all croaky. 'You are beautiful.' He pulled me towards him for a hug.

Oooh, hello…something else had just woken up too.

'I want to kiss you,' he said, rubbing his nose against mine.

'Mmm, go ahead,' I said flirtatiously.

'I must brush my teeth.' He reached for his toothbrush, picked up the toothpaste and then faced the sink. I stood behind him and caressed his chest and muscular arms as he moved the toothbrush aggressively around his mouth. My hands travelled down to his abs and then…mmm…

He rinsed his mouth and put his toothbrush back in the cup resting on the sink.

'*Now* I can kiss you!' he said, spinning around and pulling me into him again and kissing me forcefully. 'Come,' he said as he directed me two feet towards the white plastic shower cubicle. 'I must wash and get ready for work,' he said, taking my hand. 'Come. I want make love to you in the shower.'

Now, *that* was an offer I couldn't refuse…

HE HANDED me a towel and we both dried ourselves off in the main room as it was a bit tight on space in the bathroom. It was in the shower too, but after some slipping and sliding, we'd soon found our rhythm. When it came to sex, clearly there was nothing this man did not know how to do…

'What time do you start work?' I asked, keen to know how much time we had left together.

'Eight thirty,' he replied. 'So…in forty minutes.'

'And finish?' I asked, this time thinking of how feasible it would be to meet him afterwards.

'Around eleven,' he answered, throwing the towel on the bed and opening the wardrobe to take out a pair of boxer shorts from the top drawer inside, then removing a fresh pair of dark blue jeans which were hanging on the rail to the left.

'At night?' I asked, frowning. That was over a fourteen-hour day. Surely not?

'Yes. It is long hours,' he replied as if reading my mind whilst he slipped on his fitted black boxers. Mmmm… 'Chef always long time work in kitchen,' he explained. 'The morning, you start early to prepare for lunch. In the afternoon, we prepare for dinner. And then it is busy all night especially, because it is almost Christmas, and Chef says there are lots of parties.'

'Wow, that sounds like really hard work,' I said, eyes now fixated on him stepping into his jeans, pulling them up past his solid thighs, then up towards to his taut waist. 'So when do you get time off?' I asked, bringing my legs up onto the bed and then crossing them.

'He says we will work five, sometimes six days a week. I think my next day off is Sunday. If I am lucky, perhaps I will have Monday off too next week, but after that, I am certain I will work six days a week until January,' he said, now reaching into the second drawer down, taking out a plain black t-shirt, pulling it over his head and then over his delicious hairy chest. 'I will check when I go today. Do you want to see me again?'

Do the Kardashians like taking selfies?

'Er, yes!' I confirmed. 'Would *you* like to see *me* again?' I asked.

'Of course!' he said as he leant forward to kiss me.

'I wish I could stay with you longer now,' he said, putting on his chef's jacket. 'But I have to work. And it is a new job, so I must not be late.'

'I understand,' I said, standing up to kiss him again.

'But you, Sophia, you stay, no rush.' He picked his keys up off the floor from where he'd thrown them down during our passionate entrance last night. 'When leave, just shut the door. It should be okay.'

'So when do you want to meet next?' I blurted out, realising that despite discussing it, we still hadn't confirmed anything. Yes, I could have been all coy, played it cool and then messaged him later, but I was finding being upfront and saying what I felt rather than thinking it over a million times first before acting was also working well for me.

'Up to you,' he said as he headed towards the door. 'For me, as soon as possible is good.'

'Tonight?' I asked as I followed him to the door. *Well, why not? Best to strike whilst the iron's hot.*

'Tonight is good,' he replied. 'But you know I don't finish until after eleven, so it will be late. And I perhaps I will be very tired after last night and then working a full day. You don't mind?'

'It's fine,' I said without hesitation. 'As long as you at least *try* to make it worth my while,' I said cheekily.

'What does that mean?' he asked, frowning.

Oh yes. Must remember to keep the language simple.

'It means, if I come and see you, do you promise to try and make sure we have fun again and that you'll make me feel good?'

'Yes, yes,' he said, smiling. 'Of course. I promise.'

He opened the door, then turned to kiss me.

'Goodbye, beauty,' he said, holding my gaze. 'Until tonight…'

'Goodbye, gorgeous,' I replied, running my fingers through his hair. 'I'll get a cab to your restaurant for around eleven thirty p.m., then, and wait outside for you?'

'*Perfetto.*' He gave me a long, slow kiss, flashed his cheeky grin again and then was gone.

I shut the door, then walked back to the bed and flopped onto it.

What an incredible thirteen hours. I didn't remember ever feeling so alive and happy. Perhaps the last time was in Tuscany.

There was no way I could go to the office like this. I was exhausted. How he was going to do a fourteen-and-a-half-hour shift after last night and this morning, I had no idea, but I had no intention of doing the same. I'd call Harrison and let him know I'd be working from home today, get a cab back, have breakfast, take care of any urgent emails, then sleep for a few hours before preparing to come back here.

As I travelled back home in the cab, I felt so naughty. Not just about what had happened last night or how forward I'd been *again*, but also because no one knew what I'd been up to, where I'd been and, most critically, with whom.

Even though the evening had been beyond amazing and I wanted to shout about it from the rooftops, I still wasn't ready to tell Roxy or Bella. Of course, I knew they only had my best interests at heart, but I really liked Lorenzo and I was having fun, so I didn't want to risk inviting their negative thoughts into my brain and bringing me down from this cloud. I just wanted to enjoy this high without judgement for as long as possible.

IT WAS NOW SUNDAY MORNING. Normally at this time, I'd be on the huge terrace overlooking the Thames and a host of famous London monuments. That was undeniably beautiful, but the sight I had in front of me was, in my opinion, a million times better.

As I lay in bed, at the other end of the room was Lorenzo in the kitchen, cooking up an amazing lunch. He'd said today, we would dine like we were in Italy. He'd brought home some fresh pasta they'd made at the restaurant yesterday and had just taken the delicious crushed Florentine orange cake that I'd fallen in love with in Tuscany out of the oven, so the scent of fresh baking filled the flat, and currently he was whipping up a lobster risotto, which smelt divine.

He looks hot, he's amazing in bed and *he can cook? What's not to love about this man?*

We'd seen each other every evening this week. I'd met him after work, and despite being exhausted, he'd still put on a stellar performance at least twice. The same when I'd met him last night, and so far he'd already given me a good Sunday morning…

Today we'd be able to relax as he also had tomorrow off, and I'd already planned to join him. The team had proved a million times over that they could hold the fort without me. Plus, what better way to demonstrate that I was putting my work-life balance plan into action than by spending a Monday with this Italian god?

After a long and delicious lunch, Lorenzo put on some music and we relaxed on the bed, just holding each other.

'So…' I said, humming along to the song I instantly recognised as 'Heartbeat'. 'You're a fan of the Eclectic Detectives?'

'Yes?' he said, frowning. 'You know them? They are a great band. I like them very much.'

'I *love* them too!' I said, giving him a peck on the lips in appreciation.

'You do?' he said, his eyes growing wide. You are the first person I have met who knows their music,' he said.

'Ditto! Who else do you like?' I asked.

As he rattled off a long list, I couldn't believe my ears. We loved the same music. Whilst he wasn't keen on some of my more mainstream pop choices, lots of the lesser-known rock, jazz and UK soul artists I adored were amongst his favourites too.

'This is lovely,' I said, stroking his chest. 'I could just lay here forever. Thank you for the amazing food. You are very talented. In more ways than one…' I laughed cheekily and kissed him again firmly on the lips.

'*Prego*,' he replied, stroking my face.

'And you don't mind cooking on your day off?' I asked.

'For me, cooking is my passion, so it is not like work,' he replied. 'If it was, it would be difficult to be a chef because of the long hours. And cooking for you makes you happy, so it makes me happy too.' He smiled, then leant forward, planting a kiss on my lips.

'You're amazing,' I replied. 'And also, much more relaxed than how I remember you in Tuscany. You were very, I don't know… at times, you were moody. The last night we spent together, you were lovely, of course, but apart from that, you seemed unhappy and stressed. Whereas now you appear much calmer.'

'It is because I am with you,' he said, grinning, then kissing me again.

Hmm. Whilst what he said was nice, I sensed there was more to it than that… I knew I should just enjoy the moment and the time we were having together now, rather than look back to what had happened in the past, but I just needed to know what had happened before and why he'd stood me up in Florence.

'Speaking of Tuscany and Florence,' I said, stroking his chest again to help relax him enough to open up to me, 'what happened that time we were supposed to meet? Why did you stand me up? Sorry, plain English: why did you not meet with me?'

I felt his body tense up as if he was uncomfortable with the question.

'I told you, I had to work,' he muttered quietly.

'I know, but I'm confused,' I said, sensing that I was pushing some buttons he didn't want me to. 'I'd asked you before what dates you were free, and you checked and said the dates were fine, so I booked the hotel and my flight. It was only when I contacted you a couple of days before that you mentioned work. Otherwise, you probably wouldn't have even told me you couldn't make it.'

'Not true,' he said, edging away from me slightly, causing my hand to fall off his chest. 'I was going to tell you...' He sighed. 'It is complicated. My life then was complicated. It was a difficult time for me.'

'So why didn't you just explain that to me so I could understand?' I asked.

He froze again. Why was I even pushing this? I knew I risked opening a can of worms and ruining what had started to be the perfect day, but it had been niggling at me for months and he'd made me feel so shitty that, before I got in any deeper with him, I just needed to know why he thought it was okay to reject me with just forty-eight hours' notice.

'Sophia,' he said, sighing loudly again. 'I've had a very difficult life. I am very damaged. I have had bad experiences. Especially with women.' He paused. 'It is a long story.'

'That's okay,' I replied, edging closer then wrapping my arms around him again. 'You've got a day off today and I have too, so you can tell me. I'm not going anywhere,' I said defiantly. 'I've got all the time in the world.'

CHAPTER THIRTY-EIGHT

Lorenzo sighed heavily, unlocked himself from our cosy embrace and sat up on the bed.

His eyes bored into me as he tried to gauge whether or not he could avoid divulging the full story, but I had my 'Fran' on and gave him the *I need answers and I won't stop until I get them* look, à la Liam Neeson in *Taken*.

'Okay.' He sighed again like he was mustering up the courage to talk about something painful. 'I try my best to explain in English. So you remember I told you that I broke up with a girlfriend that night before we were together?'

'Yes, I remember,' I said as I also sat up in the bed and faced him.

'Good. So I thought she understood. At first it was okay, because I worked with Taste for another week so I did not see her. You remember, I messaged you on the Friday and was happy? We talked for a long time on WhatsApp, no?' he asked.

'Yes, that's right,' I replied.

'But then, after one week, when I went home, she came round and said we must try again. I told her I did not want to.' His voice began to change. He sounded irritated. 'We argued. I went to the toilet, I came back, I saw she was checking my phone because I left it on the table not locked. She went crazy and asked why I message girls, because she must have seen my messages to you. She hit me, kicked me. She always hit and punched me. All the time in our relationship. Because she knows I am a good man and will not hit a woman. She started to throw things. She went crazy and said I can never leave her.'

'Fuck, that's awful,' I said, trying to picture some crazed woman attacking him.

'So I was confused,' he said. 'I did not know what to do. She stayed there for a few days. She was calm. But I was worried. I tried not to send messages because I was worried she would find a way to check my phone. Eventually, she left. I was happy. You messaged me about dates. I told you the truth. I was not working those dates. I wanted to see you. It was fine. She had gone. She left me alone. I thought, *Good. It is over.* But then she came back. I told her to leave because we had finished,' he said, scowling. 'But she said we are not finished until I give her money.'

'What? She tried to extort—I mean, she wanted you to pay her to leave?' I said, horrified.

'No, no. It is complicated,' he replied, wriggling uncomfortably. 'We were together for two years. When we met, my car broke and I did not have the money to fix it. She said, "Don't worry, I will give you money for a new car," as she knew I cannot work for Taste without a car as it is always far, you know, in the country, and I do not live in the city because it is expensive. So it is very difficult to work without a car. And without work, I have no money.'

'Yeah, I hear that,' I replied. 'All the locations for the holidays seem very remote.'

'Exactly. So I asked her, are you sure? She said yes. I asked her later if she wanted me to pay her back. Perhaps a little every month. She said no. I am her boyfriend. It is a gift. No need to pay. I asked her many times, but always she said no. But then, she told me, before it was time for you to come to Florence, that if I don't give her the money in one month, she will go to the police or take me to court and tell them I stole from her!' The more he explained, the redder his face became.

'But could she do that?' I questioned. 'What proof would she have? Would they really listen to her?'

'I do not know, but she knows people. She is a dangerous woman. She has friends in the police and knows bad people. Anything is possible...' His voice trailed off, as if he was thinking about what she could do. 'Then she say she would also tell people I attacked her. That I went crazy and beat her. That I raped her. She started hitting herself in the face to show me what she could do,' he said, whacking his cheek to demonstrate. 'She told me she will contact Katherine at Taste Holidays and tell her that I am a violent man and should not be left alone with women. She said she would make me lose my job, as most guests are women and they would not want to risk their reputation.'

'That's fucked up!' I said, shocked at his revelations and gently resting my hand on his. 'Women like that make it so much harder for genuine victims to come forward and get taken seriously. What a bitch! So what did you do?'

'I had no choice,' he said, throwing his hands up in the

air, causing mine to fall onto the bed. 'I told her I would get her money. So, I had to call Taste and ask for extra work. I was lucky because another chef was not well and they needed cover, so I took the job. That meant I could not see you. I was sad because I *wanted* to see you. I wanted to explain, but I could not. That woman is crazy, I did not want her to know any more about you. It was not safe. I just had to work to pay her the money.' He hung his head down, staring at the bed.

'What then?' I asked.

'I worked every day. When I was not with Taste, I worked at a restaurant in Florence night and day. For one month. But it was still not enough. I was worried. My mother. She saw I looked tired and sad, so she asked what was wrong. I was not strong. I cried and told her everything. She offered me money. I said no, I cannot take it. But she said I must. So she gave it to me and I gave it to the crazy woman and she left me alone. I was free,' he sighed, clearly relieved.

I sat there, stunned. I didn't know what to say. It was all a bit like some crazy film. Violent ex-girlfriend threatening extortion and crying assault and rape? When I'd asked why he'd stood me up, I was expecting a more simplistic excuse, akin to 'the dog ate my homework' type thing. But not this.

I looked at him and could tell that even recounting the story upset him. He had tears in his eyes. And just like that, he lunged forward to give me a hug. He then rested his head on my shoulder.

'I am sorry,' he said as he lifted his head up to look me in the eyes. 'I did not mean to upset you. I wanted to meet you, but I could not. It was too difficult. Even when I gave her money, I still worked hard for months to pay back my mother. I do not like taking money from people. Especially my mother. She is a wonderful woman. That is why I could not come to London when you asked. I worked, and I had too much in my head. I could not think clearly. I needed to focus on work and not on women.'

'So you didn't go with any women during that time?'

Gosh, Sophia. Is now really the time to be asking questions like that?

'Yes,' he replied honestly. 'One, but it did not mean anything. It was just for—for release. I was stressed, I needed something,' he said, bowing his head.

'With a guest?' I asked. I couldn't help it. I needed to know.

'No, no,' he insisted. 'I told you I do not do that. It only happened a few times,' he said.

'Well, you always look happy in your Facebook pictures huddling up to the guests,' I said, voice tinged with jealousy.

Oops—just let the cat out the bag. If you Facebook stalk someone, you're not supposed to *actually* let them know you're doing it…

'No, no,' he insisted again. 'It's not like that. I told you. My ex-girlfriend was crazy. Once, I posted a photo on Facebook of Erica and me smiling with her hand on my shoulder in the kitchen. She was mad! She contacted Erica and said, "Do not touch my boyfriend or I will kill you". She is crazy.' He shook his head as if reliving the whole sorry incident all over again.

'But maybe she wasn't serious,' I reasoned. 'You know, lots of people say they'll kill people, but they don't really mean it.'

'Sophia. With this woman, anything is possible,' he emphasised again. 'That's why I only post photos with women who are like my mother or grandmother, because she did not feel threatened if I was with someone older.'

Ah, so *that's* why he's always snuggled up with the silver surfers.

'I try to only post with older ladies. Like with your group on Facebook, I only posted a photo with Grace. Not with Fran, who is in her forties, yes? And not with you, because she would think you are pretty and go crazy.'

Everything was starting to make a lot more sense to me now.

'So what is she like?' I asked. 'Your ex. Apart from being a madwoman, is she pretty? Why was she so insecure?'

'Yes, she is a pretty woman. Brown hair and eyes. Good body. She is from the Ukraine. But is a very hard, cold woman,' he said, grimacing. 'Nothing I did was ever right. She did not like my food. When we had sex, she would push me away as soon as we finished. She did not like to hug or kiss. She did not show any feelings. She said I had a fat belly. Just like they did at school. She made me feel ugly and sad.' He leant forward, resting his head on his knees.

'It sounds like it was a very destructive relationship and you're definitely better off out of it. I mean, *you*? A fat belly? Look at this…' I said, pulling his legs down to lie flat on the bed before stroking, then gently kissing his gorgeous stomach. 'Your stomach is beautiful. Perfect, in fact. Which must be difficult to maintain, seeing as you are a chef and spend all day cooking and tasting food.'

We both lay down again, and I continued stroking his stomach.

'Thank you,' he said as he rolled on his side to face me. 'Yes. It is difficult. I am not naturally this way. I have to work hard to stay in shape. When I was younger, I was fat and the children said mean things. I had no friends and the girls called me ugly and said no one will ever like Lorenzo.'

'You!' I shouted with disbelief. 'Ugly? I find that hard to imagine!' He smiled, appreciating the compliment.

'I hated school. But I *loved* food.' He sat up in the bed again, excited to tell the story. 'When I was sixteen, a—how do you say? Hospitality school came to my school to look for students. I went and learnt more about how to cook and respect food. I also started to exercise and I lost weight. I cut my hair. I fitted into better clothes. When I was twenty, the girls began to see me. So I admit, I went a little crazy and had fun with women. *Lots* of women...' he said, smirking a little.

'So you were a bit like a kid in a sweet shop!' I said, laughing as I sat up beside him. He frowned as he tried to process and translate what I was saying.

'Aha,' he said as the penny dropped. 'Yes, yes. I understand. I was like a child who goes to buy caramella, yes. You reason—sorry, I mean you are right.'

'I bet those girls that called you ugly are kicking themselves now,' I said before realising that was another phrase he might not follow. 'Sorry, let me rephrase: I bet those girls are sad that they called you fat.'

'Ha-ha. Yes!' he said, laughing again. 'They try to talk and flirt with me on Facebook now. It is funny!'

That kind of made sense too. Probably why he had so

many pictures of himself on Facebook. It was a kind of *'Fuck you bitches. Look at me now!'* type thing. *That's right. Just call me Ms Freud, master psychologist.*

He rested his head on my shoulder again. I stroked his hair. Now I understood why he'd seemed to crave hugs and affection when we were together in Tuscany.

'Thank you for telling me all of this,' I said, genuinely grateful for the insight it had given me into his life and what was behind his Florence no-show. 'I know it can't have been easy for you.'

'It is okay,' he said, kissing me gently on my forehead. 'I know you are a good woman, and I know I upset you before. But that's why I came to London now. My friend had a job for me in Paris. He said to go there. But I told him I wanted to see you. I did not know if you would speak to me again, as it has been a long time and I did not meet you, but I wanted to try. I felt what we had that night was special. I wanted to explore. See what happens.'

'Well, I'm glad you came to London,' I replied as I stroked his beard. 'I'm really glad you did.'

I knew I shouldn't be, but I was excited. Beyond happy. It seemed like he was hoping that this would be much more than a fling. Like he wanted to stick around. Like he genuinely wanted to be with me. And like he wouldn't hurt me again.

Oh God. Please, please, please let me be right this time...

CHAPTER THIRTY-NINE

T wenty-nine messages!

And that was just on WhatsApp. That included five from Mum, three from Harrison, plus eleven in the Roxy and Bella group chat.

I should really have kept in touch to let them know that I was okay, as it was unlike me to be off the radar for more than a few hours, never mind multiple days. But being in this blissful bubble with Lorenzo was so addictive, and I just wasn't ready to go back to reality yet.

I sat up in bed, took a sip of water from the glass Lorenzo had just bought me and launched my emails on my iPhone.

Oh, Christ—more messages. They must be worried.

I tabbed to contacts and called Harrison.

'Hey. Are you okay?' he asked, sounding concerned.

'I'm fine,' I replied calmly. 'No need to worry. I just won't be coming into the office today. I can see there's about a zillion messages from Mum, Roxy and Bella. Could you do me a favour and just message them and let them know I'm okay and I'll be in touch tomorrow or later in the week to explain?'

'Sure, no problem,' he replied. 'We'll take care of things here. See you tomorrow.'

Did I mention how much I love my brother? So calming. No stress. He'd handle things. That was all I wanted to hear. If I'd called Mum, she would have kept me on the phone for hours, quizzing me. Likewise for the frienmittee. Again, I knew it was because they cared, but I just needed this time. For once, I wanted to disconnect.

I switched my phone off again, put it back in my handbag by the side of the bed, and then lay back down.

Lorenzo was now in the bathroom. He said he'd take a shower and then make me breakfast. I wasn't ready to get up. I was cream-crackered after multiple marathon sessions with him again yesterday.

After our heart-to-heart, we'd slept for most of the afternoon, but then had spent much of the night rolling around the flat. We'd started on the bed, then against the wall, on the sofa, in the kitchen, then back on the bed. I had no idea how many times we had gone at it. All I knew was that generous stash of condoms I'd packed had long gone. The man was insatiable. And to be honest, I'd never thought I had such a large appetite either. I could see now that it was all about compatibility and having that connection.

I couldn't explain it. With him, everything felt so natural. Like breathing. With Charlie, I had to think about what I was doing, how I was feeling, and psych myself up to get in the zone. And everything was so predictable.

With Lorenzo, the only thing that was predictable was that I was going to enjoy every second and scream my head off with ecstasy. Each time was somehow different. *Different* in an amazing way. The attraction was magnetic. I had no idea how he did it, but he sent me so far out of my mind that I couldn't even think straight. It was like, when he touched me, nothing else in the world existed. I just lost myself and all sense and reason evaporated. I went into a trance and lost all my inhibitions. It was like being transported to another world.

As he whipped up another orgasmic feast, Lorenzo swung his hips and danced around the kitchen to the special playlist he'd created for us, with songs from the artists we both loved vibrating through the room. This time I asked for something less Italian. Pancakes and an egg white omelette with spinach, mushrooms and tomato. He explained that Italians weren't big on breakfast. It was all about coffee, but nonetheless, he said he would always be happy to cook whatever I wanted. Gourmet meals on tap (and all served by a hot, naked chef, I might add)? For a foodie like me, this was an absolute dream.

We slept for a few more hours, and we had another nice long talk about more topics than I could remember. We spoke about our childhoods, my fortieth birthday party plans for next year and his hopes to open a small restaurant of his own one day, and debated everything from Brexit to the salaries of footballers and if they could be justified when compared to that of nurses, and even body hair…

After our first intimate encounter together, where I had been paranoid about my overgrown bush, Pubegate with Vincenzo, and my discussions with Roxy and Bella, I was interested in his views on the matter.

'So tell me, Lorenzo…' I'd asked casually. 'What do

you think about women having hair down here?' I'd said as I took his hand and rubbed it slowly between my legs.

'Mmmm,' he'd said as he kissed my neck and continued caressing me. 'It is up to the woman. I would not tell you how to cut the hair on your head, so why should I tell you what you should do with the hair on your body? It is not important. To me, if a woman is comfortable with herself, with her body, then she is confident. And it is confidence that is attractive.'

Couldn't have put it better myself. I adored this man.

I liked that our time together wasn't all about the sex. True, most of the time we couldn't keep our hands off each other, but I genuinely felt like it was much more than that. He stimulated my mind as well as my body.

As well as taking an interest in me, my work and life in general, he'd also told me more about his family. He had one brother. Younger. I think he said thirty-two? He lived in Singapore, which is why Lorenzo had gone to work out there for a while. He adored his mother. The relationship wasn't as strong with his father, but they still got on. He enjoyed his job but sometimes found the hours difficult, particularly as it made it challenging to maintain a relationship with someone outside of the hospitality industry. But there was nothing else he'd rather do. It was his passion, so he did what he had to.

He lived in a two-bedroom house in a small town just outside of Florence. His grandmother used to own it, but when she passed, she left it to him and his brother. And as his brother was living abroad, he stayed there on his own.

He loved dogs but couldn't keep one because he was often away. Like most men, in his spare time, Lorenzo enjoyed watching football and having a drink with his friends.

Lorenzo seemed very relaxed and open to talking. I really felt like I was getting to know him. And the more I learnt, the stronger my feelings began to grow. I was starting to fall for him. Hard.

FINALLY HOME. It was a challenge at work today as I was *so* tired. I should have just packed up and left at lunchtime, but as I'd taken a lot of time off last week to recover from my late-night sessions with Lorenzo, plus been with him all day yesterday, I wanted to at least attempt to get something done. Plus, if I'd stayed at home, I could have had one of those obsessive relapses, where I'd start thinking about him every second. Or staring incessantly at the photos I'd taken of him sleeping (no, it *wasn't* weird—he was always taking candid shots of me, I liked taking pictures, and he looked *beautiful*, so it would have been criminal if I didn't document something that divine on my phone).

I lay back on my bed. I couldn't put it off any longer. I had to read these messages. And start replying.

Roxy's and Bella's chats were concerned 'Where are you?' and 'Are you okay?' texts, which then escalated to *'WTF, Soph? Why are you ignoring us? CALL ME'* (clearly from Roxy rather than Bella). Same sort of messages from Mum (minus the swearing, of course).

I took a deep breath and dialled Roxy's number.

'Finally!' she shouted. 'Where the fuck have you been?'

Exactly why I didn't want to call sooner…

'Hold on, Roxy,' I said, avoiding her questions. 'I need to add Bella to the call. Just dialling her number now.'

'Sophia!' said Bella, answering after three rings and sounding a little bit happier to hear from me. 'We've been so worried! Are you okay? Harrison said you were fine, but it's just we hadn't heard from you and—'

'Bella,' I interrupted calmly, 'I've got Roxy on the call too. Are you both okay to talk?'

'Yes, yes, I'm fine,' replied Bella. 'Paul's asleep.'

'Too right. We're ready to speak Sophia,' barked Roxy. 'We haven't heard from you since, what, the weekend before last? It was before you were going to Charlie's, and then you just disappeared. No text, no call, nothing. Just gone AWOL for over a week. And now you call us like nothing's happened. We were worried, you know. It's just not like you,' she said, voice softening a little.

'Sorry, ladies, I know I've been a bit of a stranger and it's wrong. I should have let you know I was okay,' I said, shuffling up the bed. 'It's a long story, but in a nutshell, after we were messaging on Sunday, I spoke to Charlie and told him I didn't know if I wanted anything serious and that I needed time to figure things out. He was upset, but I had to tell him how I felt. Then, later that day, Lorenzo messaged to say he was in London because he'd come here to work and to see me. We met on the Monday night, and I've pretty much been with him ever since.'

The phone line went silent.

'Hello?' I asked. 'Roxy? Bella? Are you still there?' I checked my phone screen to see whether I'd disconnected the call by mistake.

'Sorry, did you say *Lorenzo*?' said Roxy, clearly

shocked. '*Lorenzo* the lothario chef that stood you up in Florence with five minutes' notice and never bothered to message you back about coming to that food festival? The one that broke your heart and that you were whining on about for months afterwards? The one that showed *zero* interest in you and fucks every guest aged sixty or under? *That* Lorenzo?' she snapped.

'Look,' I said firmly, not rising to the bait, 'I know how it seems, but we've spent a lot of time together and he's not really like that. If you were there and saw how cut up he was about standing me up in Florence and everything, you'd understand.'

'What's there to fucking understand?' shrieked Roxy.

'So you dumped Charlie—no, sorry, you told him you needed "*time*" and then two minutes later, you've jumped in bed with the Italian manwhore?' Roxy yelled.

'Weren't you always telling me to have fun and not get too serious?' I said.

'Yes, but not with him! Look at how he treated you. And from what that Erica girl said, he sleeps with every woman with a pulse. You can't be hanging around or messing about with the likes of Lorenzo. The only thing a man like him is likely to give you is bullshit and STDs!'

'You don't even fucking know him, Roxy!' I retorted.

'And you think you do after a few nights together? Wake up, Soph!' added Roxy. 'I know enough about him from what you've told us to know he just doesn't seem like good news.'

'For fuck's sake! This is precisely why I didn't message you. I knew you wouldn't understand,' I snapped back. 'Why can't you just be happy for me? I'm a grown woman. I'm used to making decisions. Why can't you just trust my judgement?' I barked.

'You might be good at making good *business* decisions, but so far you're looking at this single life through rose-tinted glasses. I'm trying to *help* you, Sophia. I'm trying to save you the pain that I've experienced from dating men like him,' Roxy screamed back at me.

'Ladies, ladies,' said Bella, interjecting calmly. 'Look, this is getting far too heated. Soph, we're glad to hear you're okay, aren't we, Roxy? I understand what you're both saying. Soph, I'm kind of with Roxy on this. Lorenzo does sound like bad news. *But*, you're an adult and usually a good judge of character, so as your friends, we've expressed our concerns, now we just have to leave you to follow the path you feel is right for you. And as your friends, whatever happens, know that we love you and we'll be there for you, no matter what. Won't we, Roxy?' Bella said sternly.

Roxy let out a large sigh. 'Yes, of course.' she said reluctantly, like Bella was holding a gun to her head, 'I love you. I just don't want to see you get hurt.'

'I know, I know,' I said, dialling down my anger and sitting back down on the edge of the bed. Trust me. I don't want to get hurt either. But with Lorenzo, it's just so, so, *magical*,' I gushed.

'Oh good God!' interrupted Roxy. I could feel her rolling her eyes.

'Roxy…' scolded Bella like she was telling off Paul. 'Let Soph finish.'

'I wish I could explain the connection we have,' I said. 'It's *electric*. It's *magnetic*. I want to be with him all the time. I've literally spent a whole week with him. Well, he worked for most of the day, but I'd meet him each night after work and then we spent all of Sunday and yesterday together, and whilst we did have lots of it, it wasn't *just* about the sex. We talked for *hours*. Non-stop. He told me a lot of personal things too, which explains a lot about how he acted towards me and why he couldn't meet me. And he makes me laugh so much my stomach hurts,' I gushed. 'He did so many sweet things, like massage my feet, comb my hair... he really took care of me. And he cooked the most *beautiful* food...'

More silence. I could imagine Roxy's eyes rolling faster than a washing machine completing a spin cycle. Yes. I did sound soppy, but what I said was all true.

'That's really lovely,' said Bella politely. 'You seem happy,' she added.

'I *am*. I really am. It just feels so different. So special with him. I can be myself. Everything is so natural and so easy,' I replied.

'Jesus, woman!' said Roxy. 'He's really done a number on you this time, hasn't he? You sound like some lovesick teenager, not the smart, strong woman I know. So go on, then. Why did the fucker stand you up?' she snapped.

That support didn't last long, did it?

'Well, it's another long story,' I said, ignoring her insults, 'but in short, he had to work because he owed someone money.'

'Oh, great!' Roxy shouted. 'So not only is he an unreliable arsehole, but he has loan sharks after him too?'

'No!' I snapped back. 'Not loan sharks. It was his ex-girlfriend.' Admittedly, saying it out loud did sound a bit pathetic. Perhaps I wasn't explaining it as clearly as I could.

'Oh, that's just brilliant!' Roxy replied sarcastically. 'So he owes money and thinks, "I know, I'll go and see that desperate rich girl from London who was besotted with me. She runs her own business, so she must be loaded".'

'For fuck's sake!' I yelled, slamming my hand on the bed. 'I keep telling you. It's not like that! Lorenzo didn't even know what I did for a living until I met up with him last week. His ex-girlfriend is crazy. She threatened him…'

I heard Roxy tutting down the phone. God, she annoyed me sometimes. This was a pointless exercise.

'Look,' I snapped. 'You've already made up your minds, so it's pointless me wasting time trying to explain it to you. Like Bella said, I'm a grown woman, so I'll make my own fucking decisions. And, yeah. He could break my heart again. But you know what? Life is short. And I can't live it worrying about what may or may not happen. What if he *is* the one for me? What if we *do* end up together? Have you stopped to consider that for a second, instead of always thinking the worst?'

'Well, it's possible, but—' replied Roxy. I wasn't in the mood to let her finish.

'You're my friends and I love you,' I continued. 'But this is something I'm going to pursue, with or without your blessing. So it's up to you if you want to support me. Look, I've got to go. I'm tired and need to sleep, but I just wanted to let you know I'm okay. Goodnight.'

I pressed the end call button abruptly.

I'd never argued with either Bella or Roxy seriously before. Nor had I ever hung up on them. I felt awful, but I just couldn't deal with the negativity. It was toxic.

I hoped I was right about Lorenzo. Otherwise I'd end up friendless—a fate which didn't even bear thinking about. A strong woman could survive without a guy. But surviving without loyal and caring friends? I wasn't so sure.

Shit.

Had I just committed the cardinal sin and thrown away years of friendship, all because of a man?

CHAPTER FORTY

E nd of January already. First month of the new year, and so far, it had been a busy one.

My Christmas and New Year celebrations were fine. Very low-key, which was exactly what I needed. It was great to just sit back and relax with the family, forget about work and eat loads (and boy did I eat—I must have put on about four pounds stuffing my face this past fortnight).

I'd tried to message Charlie to arrange to talk and let him know for sure that there was no future for us, but he didn't reply.

Sadly, I hadn't seen much of Lorenzo. Not because we hadn't wanted to or because anything bad had happened. Far from it.

We'd spent the whole of his day off just before Christmas together and it was magical. I remembered it like it was yesterday.

I'd woken up to the smell of French toast, my absolute favourite, and when I'd opened my eyes, Lorenzo was bringing a plate over to the bed. As always it was presented as if he was serving a customer at the restaurant. I'd told him so many times that it was only for me and it didn't matter, but he always insisted on making it look pretty. He'd sprinkled icing sugar all over, then garnished it with strawberries and a drizzle of maple syrup—yum.

He'd put the plate down on the side table and then leant forward to kiss me.

'I haven't brushed my teeth yet,' I'd said, cringing.

'I don't care,' he'd said, pushing his lips firmly against mine. He'd then reached for his phone.

'Lorenzo!' I'd said, shielding my face behind the pillow, before he'd snatched it away playfully.

'Why do you always want to take photos of me when I wake up?' I'd asked, pulling the covers over my head. 'My hair's fucked, I haven't got any make-up on...I look a mess!'

'You are beautiful,' he'd said, throwing the duvet back. 'You do not need make-up. You are a natural beauty. I just love to take your picture when you are natural. It is sexy.'

'Sexy?' I'd protested. 'You've got to be kidding!' I know you're supposed to accept compliments graciously, but I wasn't feeling at all photogenic.

'Yes!' he'd insisted, planting kisses across my face. 'A woman will not let just anyone see her without make-up, so there is something intimate about it. Like this, I see the real Sophia,' he'd added, stroking my bare cheek. And then he'd said it. The sentence I'd never forget: 'The Sophia that I love. *Ti amo*, Sophia. I love you very much.'

As those words tumbled from his lips, I remember my stomach flipped and then did a million somersaults. He'd said he *loved* me. And I felt it. In his actions, the way he

looked at me and in his touch. My whole body was floating. He loved me and the feeling was most definitely
mutual.

At that moment, I took his face into my hands and
kissed him gently.

'I love you too,' I'd said, pulling back slowly to admire
him. 'With all of my heart. I've never felt this way before.'

I remember laying my head on his chest and inhaling
his woody scent. He always smelt *so* damn good. Then he
wrapped his arms around me and I swear I didn't move for
hours. Everything just felt so perfect, so right…

Since then, he'd been ridiculously busy at the restaurant with all the Christmas parties and had been working
fourteen, sometimes fifteen hours a day, six days a week,
so it was difficult to meet, even after work.

We were desperate to see each other, though, so I
visited the restaurant on Christmas Eve and we managed to
steal ten minutes together during his break. But he was so
tired, he could barely string a sentence together. His eyes
were bloodshot, his skin wasn't its normal glowing, golden
colour, and he was slower on his feet. But to me, he still
looked gorgeous.

Lorenzo was really pushing hard. He wanted to learn
as much as possible, and although I personally thought he
should take some time off to sleep, he didn't want to let the
head chef and the team down (apparently two of his
colleagues had wrapped up their knives and left during
service on Christmas Day, as they couldn't hack the pressure anymore). Long hours, he explained, were part and
parcel of the job he loved, so he was adamant that he must
continue.

I missed Lorenzo so much, but with just one day off a

week, he needed that time to rest. Otherwise he'd make himself ill. Even though he said he'd be fine and asked me to come round, I knew if I did, he'd want to cook for me, we'd spend hours talking and would end up having sex, because we wouldn't be able to resist. So as much as I wanted to see Lorenzo, I wanted him to stay healthy even more.

That's why we reluctantly agreed that even though it would be hard, we'd wait until after the New Year to see each other again. Then all of the festivities would be out of the way, things would be calmer for him at work and we could spend quality time together.

We messaged everyday, spoke on the phone or video-called a few times a week, and exchanged photos, which made it a little more bearable. I still thought about him literally every second, though, especially now that what was supposed to be a two-week break had become almost five…

As he'd worked all over Christmas, after New Year, he had taken a fortnight break to go back to Italy to spend time with his family. Then, when he returned, I was busy getting ready to go to France as the anniversary of Albert's passing was fast approaching.

Marie had told me there was no need for me to come over, but I wanted to be there to support her, Henri and Geraldine, and I'd only got back last night.

I was going to head straight to Lorenzo's, but he was finishing late, and as much as I couldn't wait to see him, after almost six hours of travelling, I was shattered. I was just feeling so tired all the time these days. Even doing the smallest thing felt like moving a mountain. The journey to and from France had clearly had more of an effect on me than I'd thought.

It took all the strength I had to get out of bed, throw on a loose-fitting dress swipe on some concealer, tinted moisturiser, mascara and lip gloss, then jump in the taxi to meet Fran. I felt rough. Nauseous, sore and weird. Just awful.

We met at the Sea Containers restaurant at the Mondrian Hotel on the South Bank, which was still a favourite spot of mine (despite the disappointing date with Charlie upstairs at their Rumpus Room rooftop bar last summer).

I loved the way you could sit at the iron tables and gaze at the views of St Paul's and Big Ben, plus do some people watching.

Fran was already sitting down, sipping what looked like a gin and tonic, when I arrived. She got up and gave me a massive hug.

'Oooh, are you okay?' she asked, sounding concerned. 'You look a bit peeky.'

Clearly even shovelling on a load of Touche Éclat couldn't help me today.

'Hmm, I'm not feeling great, to be honest,' I replied.

'Oh, luv. Why didn't you say?' she said, patting my hand. 'We could have met another time.'

'No way!' I replied. 'I've been wanting to see you for months, and I knew you would have already bought your train ticket and been on your way down to London, so I wouldn't want you to waste your money and time. I'll be fine. Maybe I just need to eat something.'

'Yeah, you're probably right,' she said calmly. 'Well, it's sooooo good to see you! I know we all speak loads on the group chat with Dan, but nothing beats seeing each other face-to-face. So how have you been? Still madly in love with Lorenzo? You lucky cow! He's the most beautiful man I've ever seen. In fact, is he still working in London? We should have gone to his restaurant so we could just gaze at him all afternoon!' she said, giggling. 'Sorry! Is it wrong for me to say that, seeing as I'm a married woman and you two are together? Well, I'm still human, nothing wrong in looking,' she said, chuckling again and answering her own question.

'Ah my lovely Lorenzo…' I gushed. 'Yes, I'm still madly in love! We haven't seen each other since last month, but we spoke this morning and he's well. Just about recovered from working non-stop over Christmas and New Year and has had a lot of stuff to sort out back home too by the sound of it, but I'll be seeing him on his day off next week and I cannot wait!'

As we tucked into our smoked salmon, poached eggs (I had a fried egg white instead) and toasted sourdough, I recapped the full story of what had happened these past couple of months, as I'd kept everything quite short and sweet on WhatsApp. But as I neared the end of the tale, I had to stop. Rather than feeling better, my nausea became worse. In fact, I had to go to the loo *immediately*.

I just about got there in time before I started throwing up. Such beautiful toilets they had here, too. What a shame to sully them…

When I thought it had stopped, another wave of awfulness would return. I was too terrified to go outside in case I needed to be sick again and didn't make it back to the loo in time. So I sat there on the floor, waiting to see if I felt any better.

The room was spinning. I just wanted to lie down. That was the second time I had been ill after eating salmon. I remembered going to a restaurant with Rich about ten years ago and having salmon. It was delicious. But then the next day, I was violently ill. So ill, in fact, that I had to stay at my parents' because Rich went on a business trip that day and I felt like I was dying, so I didn't want to be alone.

From that moment on, I had vowed *never* to eat salmon again. Even the smell set me off. Then slowly, a few years later, I started eating it again. But judging by how ill I was feeling now, my body still wasn't a fan.

'Soph? Are you in here?'

It was Fran. I must have been here awhile, so she'd come to check on me. I quickly flushed the toilet to get rid of the horrendous smell. Should have done that straight away.

'I'm down here,' I cried out, rubbing my sore stomach. 'At the end toilet on the right.'

I heard her heels clink down the black-tiled walkway. 'Are you okay, hon?' she asked, talking to me through the door.

'Not really,' I replied. 'I feel awful. I think it might be the salmon.'

'Oh dear,' she said. 'Do you want me to call you a cab, sweetheart?'

'No!' I protested. 'We haven't finished our catch-up. I want to hear about how everything is going with you. I just need a few more minutes, and I'll be okay.'

'Well, maybe we should move to The Den, then,' she suggested. They've got comfy chairs there, which may be more relaxing. I'll order us a pot of peppermint tea to calm your stomach.'

'That would be great,' I replied, trying to fight another wave of nausea I could feel returning. 'Sorry to ruin our brunch.'

'Don't be silly, hon!' she said. 'I'll go and explain everything to the waiter, and then just come and meet me in The Den when you're ready. If you're not out in fifteen minutes, though, I will come and check on you again.'

What a sweetheart.

After throwing up again, I started to feel a little better. I wasn't sure there was anything left in me to come out. I surveyed the toilet bowl, cleaned it up the best I could and then headed out to the sinks. I stared at myself in the mirror. God, I looked terrible. Tired, washed out, fat and awful. Overindulgence at Christmas and New Year, travelling, grief and eating salmon would do that to you.

After washing my hands, I splashed my face with cold water, rinsed out my mouth and then made my way to The Den.

Sure enough, Fran was seated there with a pot of tea. As she saw me approaching, she poured some out into the pretty china teacup.

I plonked myself down on the cosy green sofa.

'Here you go, my love,' she said, pushing the teacup slowly towards me.

'Sorry again,' I said. 'Maybe the salmon didn't agree with me,' I suggested, desperate for an explanation.

'Hmm. I was thinking, Soph,' she said, leaning forward. 'I don't think it can be the salmon as a) you were ill before you got here and b) I also had the salmon and

I'm fine. This is a top-notch restaurant, and they would have got the fish fresh today, so I doubt it's down to them.'

'Yes, but everyone reacts differently to food,' I reasoned. 'I've had issues with salmon before.'

'Maybe. Or perhaps you're getting your period?' she asked. 'When was your last period, out of interest?'

'Oh no,' I insisted. 'I get stomach cramps and a bit emotional when I have my period, but I never throw up, so it's not that.'

'So *when* was your last period?' Fran asked again.

'Erm…' I paused as I started to do the calculations. 'Well, let's see,' I said as if launching a calculator and a calendar in my head simultaneously. 'It normally comes towards the end of the month. Around the twenty-third or twenty-fifth, I think. Yeah, probably should have had it a few days ago, maybe, so it's a little late as I've been rushing about and upset with it being the anniversary of Albert's passing and everything.'

'So it came as normal between Christmas and New Year, then?' Fran probed again. 'Y'know, seeing as you said it normally comes towards the end of the month. That means you would have been on at Christmas or just after if it was a few days late right?'

I sat there puzzled. Yes, that was right, but had I had my period whilst I was at my parents' over Christmas? I started doing the mental calculations. Christmas Day? No, definitely not. Boxing Day? No, we'd gone to Granddad's for dinner that day. Twenty-seventh? Nope. I was out shopping with Mum all day as she wanted to check out the sales. That was a painful experience.

Twenty-eighth? What did we do again? Oh, yes. Mum's sisters came round. After that, on the twenty-ninth and thirtieth, I was at home making collages of hundreds of photos I'd taken over Christmas, which had taken ages. I would have remembered if I'd had to insert a tampon with all the spray glue I had over my hands.

Then it was New Year's Eve, so I'd gone back to my parents' for a family gathering, and I'd worn a pale pink dress. Something I would have been reluctant to do if I was about to come on or was in the middle of my period. I would have stuck to a darker colour just in case. It would be rare for my period to have started that late in the month, though.

And I certainly hadn't had a period this month.

Shit.

Fran was monitoring my facial expressions, which had gone from confusion, to fear and blind panic in the space of sixty seconds.

'You didn't have a period last month, did you?' asked Fran calmly. 'I can tell by the look on your face…'

'I don't think I did, no,' I admitted. 'I had so much on, I didn't realise.'

'Are you sure you're not pregnant?' she blurted out.

'No! Of course not!' I insisted. 'I haven't had sex for *ages*! Well, ages by my *new* sex life standards, anyway. I've been focusing on work, and then I was off for the holidays and I've just come back from France.'

'How long are we talking exactly?' asked Fran.

I scanned my memory.

'I don't know. Maybe five or six weeks?' I replied, shuffling around in the chair nervously. 'Erm…perhaps not since the third week of December? Okay, let me think: I met up with Lorenzo during the first week of December and we were at it like rabbits the entire week and much of the week after, but then he was working longer hours, so we didn't see each other as much. It's hard to remember exactly. I'd really need to check my diary to be sure, but that's my best guess for now.'

I saw Fran doing some mental calculations of her own.

'Hmm. That would be about right, then. If you're due between the third and fourth week of the month, then the first or second week of December was probably your optimum time for ovulation, as it's normally about fourteen days before your period comes…'

I began to think about what she was saying. On the very rare occasions that my period was late, I would have dismissed this theory immediately as I hadn't been having sex, so it would be a complete impossibility.

But, recently—well, pre-mid-December—I had been. And a bloody lot of it too. Plus I hadn't been using condoms with Lorenzo after the first few times, so that alone would have put our number of unprotected sexual encounters into double figures.

I wouldn't normally have done it without one, but we'd quickly run out, and he'd assured me he'd got tested before he came over to London and got the all-clear. Things felt serious and committed between us. I trusted him, so thought I'd be okay. The pregnancy thing hadn't even crossed my mind. I'd just assumed my ovaries had passed their best-before date.

And if we were talking about early December, then there might also be a second guy in the frame: Charlie. I knew we'd definitely *started* having sex with a condom that last time, but now that I thought about it, I did remember being surprised when I had seen it on the bed beside him straight after we'd finished and remarking that

I hadn't seen him take it off. Had he removed it when I wasn't looking? Perhaps that's why he'd suggested we do it doggy style, so I couldn't see him take it off? You hear about women trapping men to get pregnant. Maybe men did the same. Perhaps he wanted me to have his child so I'd stay with him, and that's why he'd come with so much gusto…

I desperately tried to remember if I could see anything inside the condom to indicate that he had removed it after he ejaculated or if in fact he'd come inside me and the condom was empty? I was drawing a blank. At the time, I think I was too busy worrying about how to break the news of how I was feeling.

Shit. This wasn't looking good.

Then again, like I said, think about my age. It's not easy to get knocked up at almost forty, so I could be worrying over nothing.

'Okay, your calculations might be right and one way or another I *did* have unprotected sex, but although I saw online that there's been an increase, in reality, getting pregnant naturally at thirty-nine is still rare, isn't it?' I asked. 'You said so yourself last year in Tuscany. And the papers are forever banging on about women becoming barren after thirty-five. Yes, I read about celebs getting pregnant even in their mid-forties, but they have the best doctors and resources,' I reasoned.

'It may be *harder*, yes, but actually you'd be surprised. Geriatric pregnancies are one of the commonest groups these days. There's been a sharp increase over the past few years. We're seeing a lot more of them at the hospital.'

'I'm sorry what? *Geriatric*? I know I'm approaching forty, but what's with the ageist terminology?' I retorted, rolling my eyes. 'Anyway, you're only speculating. There could be a million other explanations,' I said.

'Maybe not a *million*, but I get your point. Shall we find out?' Fran questioned.

'What, now?' I asked.

'Yes!' she replied. 'Best to know sooner rather than later. Where's the nearest Boots?' asked Fran. 'We need to get some pregnancy tests.'

I did a mental scan of the area.

'Well, there's not anywhere in walking distance,' I replied. 'There's a massive Boots in Waterloo station, or there's a Boots and Superdrug on The Strand,' I said as I wriggled around the chair again, realising the magnitude of what she was suggesting.

'That's settled, then,' said Fran swiftly. 'I'll jump in a taxi, get some kits and come right back, and we can find out once and for all.'

You could tell she'd been a nurse for years. So cool, calm, collected and caring, despite seeing that I was freaking out.

'Are you sure?' I questioned. 'Do you want me to come with you?'

'Of course I'm sure. You stay here. Best to be close to a bathroom just in case.'

I reached for my bag and fished out my purse. 'Here you go,' I said, taking out three twenty-pound notes.

I knew I'd have to force the cash on her as otherwise she'd try to pay for it all, and God knew how much pregnancy tests even cost. I'd never had to buy one before.

I felt like I'd only closed my eyes for ten minutes before there was a tap on my shoulder.

Fran was back. Large Boots bag in hand. 'Come on,

my love,' she said, tapping me on the shoulder. 'I hope you've been drinking your tea, as we're going to need you to pee on a few sticks.'

'A few?' I asked.

'Of course!' she replied. 'This is your future. We're not going to rely on just one test. A lot of them come with multiple sticks, but I've still bought some different types to be sure. Whatever the outcome, you'll still need to book an appointment with your doctor first thing on Monday.'

As we headed into the largest toilet at the end of the corridor and locked the door, Fran took the boxes out of the bag. There was a digital one and another one with a colour-change tip. She removed the test stick from the foil wrapper, took off the blue cap and handed it to me.

'Now you need to hold the pink tip pointing downwards in your urine stream,' she advised.

I'd never been more apprehensive about weeing. At first it wouldn't even come. Didn't help having an audience either. I wasn't nervous about being in a loo with Fran per se. I was just trying to get my head around the fact that in two minutes' time, my life could change forever.

The tip turned pink. I handed the first stick to Fran, who then popped the cap back on and laid the test flat. Good thing she wasn't worried about touching something with someone else's wee on.

I repeated the process with the next test, then we waited in silence for the results.

One test took two minutes and the other three. It felt like the longest 180 seconds of my life.

Eventually, she looked at them one by one and smiled.

The suspense was killing me…

'Congrats, Sophia,' she said, grinning. 'You're going to be a mum. You're pregnant!'

I looked at the plus symbol in the results window of the first one, then the word 'Pregnant' on the second.

OMFG.

CHAPTER FORTY-ONE

As soon as I saw him walk towards the cab, flashing his big smile, my heart skipped a beat.

'Hello, my beauty,' Lorenzo said as he climbed into the back seat to join me. 'Come here!' he said, pulling me towards him in a tight embrace.

We held each other for ages before Lorenzo released me and began kissing me so forcefully, I thought my mouth was going to fall off. And I enjoyed every single second. God, I'd missed him. I hadn't realised quite how much until I'd felt his lips and body against mine.

Now that my pregnancy had been confirmed, tonight I wanted to tell him about the situation face-to-face. And by the situation, I meant the pregnancy and the fact that there was a slim chance it could be Charlie's baby. It was more likely to be Lorenzo's, though, surely? We'd been at it constantly for weeks. Although, as my doctor had pointed out, it only took the once, so that wasn't entirely relevant.

To find out for sure, I could do a prenatal paternity test, but because it involved inserting a needle through my abdomen or inserting a tube to get a sample of fluid from the womb, it was risky and could lead to miscarriage. Or I could hold on until the baby was born and do a paternity test by doing a cheek swab.

As frustrating as it might be not knowing who the father was, it was a no brainer. I would wait.

Baby.

Me? I'm actually having a baby.

Unbelievable.

Amazing.

Absolutely, bloody terrifying.

How had this happened? Okay, I wasn't stupid, I know how things happened *biologically*, but…

I'd thought it was too late for me, that I didn't have a chance of this happening naturally, so in that respect, I was completely and utterly overjoyed. I had started thinking about whether it will be a boy or a girl, who it would look like, what they'd be called, how they'd sound when they started talking. What it would feel like to hold my baby in my arms for the first time…I had spent hours dreaming about it.

But then, I'd start shitting myself. What if my age caused complications? I'd read about the challenges online, so what if something went wrong?

And what the hell did I know about how to raise a baby to ensure it grew it into a fully functioning adult? Sometimes it was hard enough just looking after myself, never mind a tiny, delicate human.

Then there was the business. How would I even cope with running that too? I knew the team had been great, but I'd still need to keep on top of things.

How would it all work with Lorenzo, anyway?

Would he be okay to move over here? It would mean upping sticks and finding a permanent job to be with us. Things seemed to be going well at the restaurant now, but what if he didn't want to live in London? And what if we did spend months building our lives together, the baby was born and we then discovered he wasn't even the father?

Fuck.

My head was spinning. This was too much to take in. I wanted to tell myself it was going to be okay, but I wasn't convinced that it would be. Especially when I hadn't even figured out how best to tell him.

Every time I tried to think about planning the conversation, another *what if...?* question popped into my head and I would end up stressing even more, so I'd have to abandon my thoughts.

The most important thing right now was to be honest and tell Lorenzo straight away. If I did it immediately, I'd be less likely to chicken out and we could discuss how best to move forward.

Telling Lorenzo straight away might have been my intention. But, as I've mentioned before, I was hopeless around this man. Lorenzo did to me what kryptonite does to Superman. I lost all my powers and was rendered totally and utterly his. All consciousness and logic went out the window.

So, of course, rather than spending the rest of that night and all of his day off talking sensibly about our future, he reacquainted me with his flat. Frolicking on the bed, sofa, floor, kitchen worktops, in the shower and against the walls was all as marvellous as I remembered...

Never mind dancing on the ceiling, Mr Lionel Richie.

If we could've found a way to fuck on it, we would have done that too.

I wondered if I could ever tire of sex with this man. He amazed me every time.

IT WAS NOW WEDNESDAY MORNING. I couldn't leave it any longer to tell him. The timing wasn't perfect, but would it ever be?

'Lorenzo?' I said, unspooning myself from his embrace and facing him. 'Are you awake?'

'Yes, beauty,' he croaked, stirring a little. 'I am tired, but awake. Must get up soon.'

'Before you do, there's something important I need to tell you.' I sat up abruptly in the bed. 'I–I… well, there's no easy way to say this…' I took a deep breath and then blurted out: 'I…I'm pregnant.'

'Huh?' he asked, rubbing his eyes. 'What did you say, Sophia?'

'I said I'm *pregnant*. I'm having a baby,' I clarified, whilst fixating my eyes on him to monitor his reaction.

He bolted upright in the bed. I guess he heard and understood this time…

'What? You are having a baby?' He rubbed his eyes again, opened them rapidly, then began frowning.

Clearly his brain was working hard to juggle trying to wake up, taking in what I'd said in English, translating it into Italian and then attempting to process the enormity of my revelation. 'It is my baby, yes? You stopped seeing that guy, Charlie, before we began our relationship in London?'

'Yes, I'm pretty sure it's yours…' I paused and shifted

in the bed as I considered how best to reply. 'I haven't seen Charlie for ages—like you said. Since we met up again, it has only ever been you. Except—well, the thing is that, having looked at the possible dates of conception, there's a bit of a grey area because a few hours before you messaged and the day before you and I met up again in London, I *had* slept with Charlie. We used a condom, but it *might* have come off during sex—I can't be a hundred percent sure. And then of course I wasn't intending to sleep with you when we went for that drink. I just wanted to hear what you had to say, but the attraction was so strong that I couldn't help myself. So because we were also together and the baby could have been conceived at any point that week, there's some confusion. But don't worry, I'm certain it's yours. I mean, it *must* be…'

Now I was rambling, and it wasn't sounding good at all.

He stared at me blankly, eyes glaring. There was silence for what felt like twenty hours, but in reality was around twenty seconds. That might not seem like very long, but when you've dropped a bombshell like this and are waiting for someone to respond, it might as well be an eternity.

'Aren't you going to say something?' I said, desperate to break the silence.

'I…I am…shocked,' he said. The vein in the centre of his forehead had become enlarged and was throbbing violently. Blood rushed to his cheeks causing them to look inflamed. No doubt with anger. 'Sophia, I am surprised. I…I need time. I must think about everything that you have said.'

He jumped out of the bed and went into the bathroom.

There was silence for a while as if he was in there thinking, but then I heard him switch on the shower.

Shit. I should have thought more carefully about how I said it. This must be a lot for him to take in. If we could talk it through, hopefully I could reassure him. I needed Lorenzo to know what he meant to me. That it *must* be his baby. He was the only father I wanted for my child.

When he came out, he avoided eye contact and got dressed quickly without uttering a word.

'I am going to be late for work,' he said, scooping up his keys and phone from the coffee table. 'I must think. Give me time, please, Sophia.'

Although he avoided looking at me as he fled out the door, I could sense he was shocked. But there was something else, too. Vulnerability, perhaps? Pain? I couldn't quite put my finger on it. I wanted to take him in my arms and somehow reassure him that we'd be okay.

We'd never talked about kids during our conversations. To be honest, I'd steered clear of the subject as I didn't want to highlight the fact that if he *did* want children, I might not be able to provide them. As Monique had said at my birthday dinner last year, men can have children in their seventies and it's accepted. Whereas once women hit thirty-five, we're constantly told that we're over the hill. So if a family *was* on his wish list, bringing it up would only serve to remind him that he needed to pursue a younger model, rather than stay with a woman like me, whose ovaries were fast approaching their expiration date.

In a way, I wished he'd shouted, screamed or just said *something* so I knew what he was thinking. But like he said, he needed time to take it all in, and I had to respect that. I'd known for days and was still coming to terms with it, so I could only imagine how many different emotions were flooding through his mind. If space was what he needed, I had to try and give it to him.

∾

IT WAS NOW SATURDAY, and I still hadn't heard anything from Lorenzo.

It can be annoying to be harassed after telling someone you need space, so I'd initially vowed not to contact Lorenzo until he'd got in touch first. But now it had been three days, and I hadn't even got a 'hello' from him. I was worried. Normally we spoke at least twice a day. I checked WhatsApp. He was last seen when? Wednesday afternoon? That was so unlike him.

I tried calling his phone. Switched off. *Of course. He's working.*

By 7 p.m., after trying to call two more times, I couldn't take it anymore. I booked an Uber and headed to the restaurant.

I knew he'd be busy, but I just needed to know he was okay. Surely he would have had a break at some point in the day and seen my missed calls?

As I entered the restaurant, I saw Gino, one of Lorenzo's waiter friends, in the corner. He caught my eye and when he'd finished taking a customer's order, he headed over to me by the entrance.

'Gino, how are you?' I asked, smiling, but also scanning the busy restaurant on the off-chance that Lorenzo had stepped out of the kitchen.

'*Bene, Sophia*,' he said, returning my smile. 'You looking for Lorenzo?'

'Yes,' I replied. 'Is he in the kitchen? I can't seem to reach him.'

'Sorry, Sophia, but Lorenzo has gone. Back to Italy,' he replied, his face falling.

'What?' I snapped. 'What do you mean he's gone?' I shouted. Some of the guests turned around to see what the commotion was about. Gino touched my shoulder and gently ushered me outside the restaurant.

'This afternoon,' he replied. 'Chef was not happy. Lorenzo said he has personal problems and must go. He called and told me that if you came, to say he is sorry. He said he left a key with his neighbour, Jack, and that if you ring Flat 5, he will let you into his place as there is something there for you. I hope that makes sense?' Seeing how upset I was, he touched my shoulder again. 'I am sorry, Sophia. I must go back inside.'

I was rooted to the spot. I couldn't even speak. Everything was spinning.

Lorenzo's gone back to Italy? Just like that?

He's left me? And our baby? Alone? Without even calling? Without even telling me?

I don't understand. I need to sit down.

No. I needed to speak to him. Maybe he hadn't left. Maybe he was still there. If I hurried, I could catch him at the flat.

I rushed towards the main street, hailed a black cab and headed straight to his place. I buzzed his flat first. No answer. Then again. Still no answer.

What number did Gino say I should buzz? Four. No, no. Five. I pressed down on the buzzer.

'Hello?' said the male voice coming through the intercom.

'Um, is that, is that Jack?' I asked.

'Yep, that's me,' he said suspiciously. 'Why? Who's this?'

'It's Sophia,' I replied quickly. 'I, I had a message from—'

'Oh yes,' he interjected. 'You're after Lorenzo. Come up.' He buzzed me in.

Yes! Maybe I'd just managed to catch him.

By the time I'd climbed the stairs and reached the first floor, Jack was already standing by Lorenzo's front door.

'Here,' he said, pointing to the door. 'I've opened up. I'll come back later to lock up.' He disappeared into his flat across the hall.

I pushed the door and tiptoed inside.

I scanned the flat. It was empty. Cold.

No!

He can't be gone!

Why?

I checked his wardrobe. Nothing inside. Just hangers. I went to the bathroom. The shelf normally filled with his aftershave, toothbrush and toothpaste was bare.

All that was left was some of my stuff, neatly folded on the bed. A black dress, a pair of light blue jeans, an orange jumper, some red underwear and a spare make-up bag.

From the bed, I could see some fruit on the kitchen worktop—a couple of oranges and an overripe banana. The cushions were propped up on the sofa, and there was some post on the coffee table that Jack must have brought in, but apart from that, the flat was empty.

The enormity of everything hit me at once. I didn't do crying. I'd eventually managed to cry a little over losing

Albert, which was understandable. I'd shed a few tears when I'd told Rich we needed to break up but had put a stop to that as soon as I'd realised. That too was justified as I'd been with Rich for a decade and a half. But crying over a man I'd only known for less than a year leaving me? I'd never imagined I would. Even though I knew I loved him, I would have assumed that I could just soldier on. But it wasn't that simple. With Lorenzo, it was as if I didn't have control of my emotions.

This was too much to take in. I crashed down on the bed, sobbing uncontrollably. How could he leave me *now*? I needed him more than ever. *We* needed him.

I must have cried myself to sleep, as when I woke up and fished my phone from my bag, it was 10.30 p.m.

The fact that I'd cried this much meant this was *bad*. It must be the hormones and changes in my body. Or maybe it was the emotions I'd suppressed from Albert's passing, my break-up with Rich and Lorenzo leaving, all rolled into one. Either way, I needed my friends. I had to speak to someone.

Bella. I'll call Bella. It's still too raw with Roxy. No answer. Shit. Maybe she's looking after Paul? Or sleeping?

My eyes were stinging. Everything was so blurry. All this upset couldn't be good for the baby. Thinking about that just made me feel even more emotional.

My phone started ringing. Thank God. Bella had called back. Although I could barely see, I clicked on the green phone icon to answer the call.

'Sophia! I wasn't sure if you'd answer. It's been so long since we've spoken. And, well, I was thinking about you this evening. Well, I think about you all the time, but particularly this evening, and so I thought, what the hell!

Sod this messaging nonsense. Throw caution to the wind. Be adventurous. Call her!'

It was Charlie. This *wasn't* a good time. In fact, it was the worst time possible.

'Hi, Ch-Charlie,' I said, trying to compose myself and not let on that I'd been crying my eyes out for hours.

'Sophia? Are you okay?' he said. 'Are you—are you *crying*?'

I couldn't help it, I just lost it and started bawling like a five-year-old who'd just been told there'd be no presents or birthday cake at her party.

'Oh my goodness,' he said, sounding flustered and unsure how to respond. 'I didn't mean to upset you.'

'It's not—it's not you Charlie. S-sorry,' I said, trying and failing to pull myself together. 'He's left me, Charlie. He's gone?'

'Who's left you?' asked Charlie. 'Where are you? Are you at home?'

'N-no!' I stuttered. 'I'm at his place and he's gone. He's left us.'

'What's the address?' he demanded. 'I'm coming to get you right now!'

Somehow, Charlie had managed to decipher the garbled address I'd given him in between my embarrassing meltdown, as, in what couldn't have been more than forty-five minutes, he was ringing the buzzer, then running up the stairs.

The door was still ajar from when I'd first entered hours ago. He bundled in, saw me on the bed and threw his arms around me. I leant on his shoulder and continued sobbing.

'What *is* this godawful place?' he said, scanning the

room in disgust. 'What are you doing here, Sophia? Who lives in this hovel?'

Shit. I wasn't even thinking. Charlie had just come to 'rescue' me at Lorenzo's place. Lorenzo. The man I had fallen in love with. I shouldn't have let Charlie come here. I should have said I was okay. So stupid! How an earth was I going to explain this?

I sat up straight, then, as gently as I could, gave Charlie a top-line summary of everything that had happened.

I explained that I'd met Lorenzo in Italy, that he'd come to London and I'd agreed to see him, but only when I was on a break from Charlie and I insisted that I didn't mean to hurt him.

When I broke the pregnancy news and asked Charlie about whether he'd taken the condom off early, he simply shrugged his shoulders and mumbled that he 'couldn't remember'. Given the bombshell I'd just dropped, I didn't feel that I was in a position right now to push him on this. I could see his cheeks burning with anger and that he was ready to vent.

'So let me get this straight,' said Charlie, grinding his jaw. 'That Sunday, you told me you needed some time away from me, to be alone to consider the future of our relationship and then, literally days—no, in fact, mere hours later, you jumped into bed with another man?' Charlie began pacing up and down the flat.

'I know how it sounds,' I replied 'but—'

'And now you're pregnant, and the baby *might* be mine, but then again it *might* be that chef's, and now that he knows you're knocked up, he's dumped you and left the country?' he snapped.

'Well…no…well, yes…it's true that I can't be sure

who the father is, and yes, it does seem like he's left, but it doesn't make sense that he's gone when…' I stopped myself mid-sentence. Charlie didn't want to hear my thoughts on Lorenzo and the fact that whilst before, I would have thought it was typical for him to leave, now that I knew him, it was out of character because I truly believed Lorenzo was a good man.

I reconsidered my words. 'Charlie…I don't know what to say. Other than that I'm so sorry,' I added, wiping the tears that were now streaming down my cheeks with my sleeve.

He continued pacing up and down the room, scowling as if he'd just been offered a cockroach sandwich.

'Would you excuse me a moment?' I said as I crept past him. Not an ideal time to break the conversation, but I'd been bursting for the loo for hours, which couldn't be good for my bladder. 'I just need to go to the bathroom.'

I shut the door behind me and glared at myself in the mirror. Puffy, red eyes, smudged mascara and eyeliner, messy hair. My outward appearance was definitely a reflection of the turmoil that was going on inside my brain.

I splashed some cold water on my face and tried to straighten myself up a little. I then sat on the lid of the toilet seat whilst I tried to gather my thoughts.

As tempting as it was to hide away in here and not have to deal with everything, I needed to face Charlie and whatever angry insults he wanted to throw at me.

I took a deep breath and unlocked the bathroom door. Charlie was standing by the coffee table, pushing something into his pocket. Couldn't see what. Couldn't see much of anything, really, as although I'd temporarily stopped the waterworks, my eyes were still a little blurry.

'Sorry I took so long,' I said. I then began to frown. Charlie was acting weird. It wasn't his anger. That was surely still there. It would take longer than the ten minutes I'd spent in the bathroom for him to calm down. He was fidgeting. Flustered. Strange.

'I have to go,' he snapped. 'I…I need to get out of here.' He quickly shuffled towards the door.

'I understand,' I said. 'I know this must have all come as a massive shock…once again I'm sorry,' I added, but before I could even finish my sentence, he was gone.

I plonked myself down on the bed and reached for my phone to order a taxi home. The longer I stayed here, in the place which held so many memories of my time with Lorenzo, the worse I would feel.

I stood up, gathered up my things, then surveyed the bedroom, kitchen and living room areas to check I had everything. Something was different, but I didn't know what. I still wasn't even thinking straight. How could I? Lorenzo had left me. Charlie hated me and my friends were barely speaking to me.

My whole world was spinning out of control and this time, I had no idea how to fix it.

CHAPTER FORTY-TWO

I t was now fast approaching the end of March. Things had been pretty shitty. I was still struggling to get my head around everything. Particularly the pregnancy.

For years I'd longed to have a child, and yet now that it was actually happening, rather than feeling on top of the world, I just wanted to hide under the duvet for the next five months.

It's all a mess.

I had my dating scan last week. Something that I'd hoped would be one of those idyllic moments. Lorenzo would hold my hand as we gazed lovingly at the ultrasound screen whilst the sonographer confirmed that everything was fine. We'd squeal with joy and Lorenzo would wrap his arms around me, tell me how much he loved me and shower me with kisses, as we happily pictured the beginnings of our family.

We'd then walk arm in arm to the taxi and I'd clutch the coveted ultrasound photo firmly in my hand. The photo that I'd seen so many mums-to-be post on social media before me. I'd always wondered if it would ever be me, and now after all the wishing and longing, I was finally about to become a mother.

But that was just a dream. The reality was that I went alone, and as I left, I tucked the scan photo safely away in my bag, which now lay hidden away in my bedroom drawer.

It had been almost six weeks since I'd last heard from Lorenzo. In truth, it felt like six years. I still longed for him every single second of every day.

Rather than being strong and in control Sophia, I'd spent most nights sobbing into my pillow. So much for never being able to cry. Now my eyes were like leaking taps. I couldn't seem to stop the waterworks from flowing.

And even though I had tried to focus on work, the comfort blanket that normally cured all ills, it just wasn't helping. When I managed to crawl out of bed and make my way in, I spent most of the time locked away in my office. Firstly because I was frequently throwing up (why they call it morning sickness when it happens throughout the day, I do not know), but mainly because, as I had realised, even if you give yourself a million 'pull yourself together' pep talks, sometimes deep, raw emotions cannot be controlled.

No matter how hard I tried to fight it, my thoughts would always turn to Lorenzo. I just couldn't understand why he'd left. It didn't make sense for him to disappear like that. Especially when I believed with every fibre of my being that he loved me. How did I get it so wrong?

Every time a notification sounded on my phone, I'd hope it was him, but it never was.

My head was constantly spinning. On the one hand, I

knew Lorenzo was the man I wanted to be with, but how could I rationalise that when he'd deserted me so spectacularly?

Could he not handle the responsibility of being a father? Was it because he didn't want to commit himself to living in London, or to me?

Was it the way I had broken the news to him? Perhaps I should have thought about it more. Chosen my words more carefully. It would have been a lot for him to take in. Particularly as I couldn't be one hundred percent sure that he was the father. How would he feel if the baby wasn't his?

When he'd told me he needed time, should I have contacted him sooner rather than waiting until that Saturday before going to see him? But equally, shouldn't he have called to say he was leaving or explained how he was feeling so that we could discuss any concerns he had? I just didn't get it.

For weeks, I also felt bad because of Charlie. I should have just ended it with him cleanly, instead of wimping out and saying that I needed more time. Although technically, yes, we had been 'on a break', deep down, I had known he wasn't the one for me, so rather than making him think there was some hope, when things had started progressing with Lorenzo, I should have told him outright that there definitely wasn't a future for us.

The way Charlie had looked at me when he'd stormed out of Lorenzo's flat haunted me. The glare of disgust and disappointment as his eyes burned into my skin. He couldn't get out of there and as far away from me as possible quickly enough.

I considered leaving it alone. Letting Charlie just move

on and forget about me. But of course, it was no longer just about me. There was a baby to consider. A baby that still could be his. And if it was, it was important that Charlie is involved. I wanted us to be on good terms. So I called him. After several attempts, he answered and reluctantly agreed to meet face-to-face.

I apologised for any pain that I'd caused and tried to explain that hurting him was the exact opposite of what I'd intended.

Charlie graciously accepted my apology. He said that whilst he did not condone my actions and was still appalled at the speed at which I'd moved on, as we couldn't change the past and Lorenzo was now permanently out of the picture, the important thing was to focus on the future.

If the baby was his, Charlie assured me that it would want for nothing. He or she would have the best. He said we'd need to work closely as a 'unit' to raise it.

I couldn't be sure, but at times, the way he looked at me and spoke about 'us' and 'our baby' did make me wonder whether he had ideas of us reconciling. This, of course, sent my overthinking into overdrive and caused me to consider if I should try again with Charlie.

As my friends with kids have always told me, raising another human being is no walk in the park. So if Charlie was still interested, wouldn't it be stupid to turn down that stability and the opportunity of being with a kind, caring man who was willing to share that enormous responsibility with me? Yes, I'd be unhappy, but isn't making sacrifices what parents do all the time? Even if it means staying in a loveless relationship 'for the sake of the children'?

I'd quickly come to my senses and reminded myself

that I'd already wasted too much of my life when I'd settled with Rich. And I'd also concluded that I was just imagining that Charlie wanted anything more than to do the right thing and be a good father.

Eventually, I had to be honest with myself. I could try to do this alone, which was what I'd planned to do when I'd set the MAP goal of looking into adoption, but I'd prefer not to. I wanted to be with Lorenzo. I wanted to raise this baby with him.

When we were together, everything just felt right. I felt alive. At ease. Deliriously happy. Like being beside him was where I was supposed to be. Just thinking about him made my heart beat faster.

But he was also the man who, on paper, was the illogical option. A troubled man. A man who had seemingly disappeared off the face of the earth.

The last time I looked (which, true to my *obsessively checking WhatsApp* form, had been barely an hour ago), he hadn't been seen online since the day I'd told him I was pregnant.

Lorenzo's non-existent contact was his way of telling me that it's over. That he didn't want to be with me. That he didn't want to be a father.

Somehow I had to face the fact that Lorenzo had gone and I would never see him again.

CHAPTER FORTY-THREE

To help take my mind off things, I'd been busy organising my fortieth birthday party in just over a week's time. Whilst it had been challenging juggling this with work, dealing with my mind muddles, mood swings and ever-changing body (although I must admit, I *did* quite like having these bigger boobs), the party would be one of the last main things to tick off on my MAP plan. And after having to put it off last year, I'm now really looking forward to it.

I'd decided last year to hold it at my aunt Cynthia's Mansion Flat in Victoria. It was actually Lorenzo that had given me the idea during one of our Sunday afternoon conversations. Whilst he was cooking, knowing that they get booked up far in advance, I was on my iPad looking up some of the many amazing venues we'd used to host lots of launches and parties for our biggest clients. But despite being beautiful, none of them felt right for me.

Lorenzo had innocently asked me why my party had to be in a fancy place. He suggested it may be better to keep it simple by just having it at home or somewhere more relaxed, like an intimate dinner party with music and dancing.

'Just because it is a big birthday, it is not necessary to spend big money to make it special,' he'd casually commented whilst chopping up the vegetables. 'What is important is to celebrate with people you love. It is family and friends you are inviting, not clients. No need to impress them. If people are relaxed and have good food, drink and good company, then they will have a good time. If they have a good time, so will you. That is is all that matters,' he'd said like some wise party guru.

And he was right. This past year had shown me that I was much more content when I just did 'me'. Happiness didn't come from being flashy, or having designer clothes. In fact, I'd found that when I relaxed more, things were just better.

I'd thought about having the party at my place, but it would have been a bit more of a trek for Bella, Roxy, Fran and Annabel to get to. Whereas Victoria was more central and my aunt loved entertaining. She threw dinner parties every week, so if I was to have one in a home setting, this was the ideal choice. Thankfully, she was delighted to play host, so it was all settled.

Harrison had created the playlist based on a selection of around two hundred songs I'd sent over, covering everything from classic soul hits to modern dance and pop, plus some sixties and seventies music to keep Dad and the elders happy.

My mum and her sister, Aunt Sheri, were organising the food and I'd ordered plenty of prosecco, wine and spirits, as well as some mixers and sparkling fruit juices for the non-drinkers like me (it was going to be weird not being able to toast my birthday with alcohol this year).

I'd spotted an up-and-coming guitarist at a work event, so I had hired him to sing on the night. My giant birthday cake had been ordered. I'd bought some tasteful individual letter gold balloons which spelt out 'Happy Birthday', along with some other decorations to dress the room, and that was that. With a baby to plan for, I didn't want to stress myself out more than I already was. So even though everyone had offered to help, I kept things simple.

I'd invited fifty of my closest friends and family, including Marie, Henri and Geraldine from France, and so far, everyone bar one person (understandable that Grace couldn't travel from Australia) had confirmed their attendance, which was exciting. Well, everyone bar two people, I should say.

Lorenzo had said he was coming and had made a note of the address when we had last seen each other. But that was *before* I'd dropped the baby bombshell the following day. If he couldn't even be bothered to say goodbye or send a one-line text message, there was no way he was going to fly hundreds of miles to my party. Especially when he'd know how angry I'd be and the fact that my friends and family would be after his blood because he'd left me in the lurch.

I just had to try and push him out of my mind and find a way to move on.

IT WAS the night of my party, and I was feeling calm. The playlist was lined up, a slideshow of old photos of me with family and friends over the last four decades playing on the flat-screen TV in the large open-plan room with sky-high ceilings. Perfect for entertaining, it had large comfy nude-coloured sofas all around one side of the room, a great empty space dividing the living room from the dining area, which was ideal for doubling up as a mini dance floor, and then a large grand solid mahogany dining table where guests could also be seated if they wished to eat more formally.

The prosecco was chilling in the fridge, the cake had been delivered, and Aunt Sheri was in the kitchen putting the finishing touches to the food, so now all we needed were the guests.

Josh had stopped by earlier to style my hair, and make-up artist and good friend Brie was just adding some gloss to my lips to finish my natural look, and then I was done.

I slipped into a long blue dress which was pleated and loose at the front to hide my expanding stomach. Only a handful of people knew about the baby: Harrison, Dad, Mum (who I constantly had to remind to keep it a secret, which was difficult for her, as she was bursting with excitement about becoming a nana again *'at long last'*), plus Bella and Roxy.

On the subject of the frienmittee, things had now kind of got back to normal. We hadn't seen each other much as, since Lorenzo had left, I hadn't really felt up to going out or chatting—especially knowing that they had never really thought much of him.

As always, Bella was more calm and sympathetic, but with Roxy, it had been a rockier path.

Now that 'Loser Lorenzo', as she called him, had in her view shown his true colours, there had been far too many 'I told you so' mentions for my liking. And whilst I didn't entirely agree with her assumptions on what was right for me or her opinion of Lorenzo (although his disappearance had made it harder to defend him), I was looking forward to seeing her tonight.

Two hours in and the party was in full swing. The handsome young guitarist, Valentino, was a huge hit (especially with the female guests). From The Script's 'Man Who Can't Be Moved' to 'Three Little Birds' by Bob Marley and 'Head Over Heels' by the Ecletic Detectives—the band that Lorenzo and I both adored—Valentino's acoustic versions of my favourite songs were performed to perfection and had everyone singing along.

The atmosphere was buzzing, drinks were flowing, food was being consumed with lots of *ooohs* and *yums*, people were chatting, laughing and dancing. The evening was almost flawless.

Every time the doorbell rang, I would secretly hope it was Lorenzo—the missing piece of the puzzle that would make an already magical night, perfect—but sadly it never was.

In an effort to continue to build bridges and stay on good terms with Charlie, I'd invited him along. He'd come alone and seemed to be busy chatting along with Uncle Phillip, who was also an advocate for green causes and passionate about environmental issues.

Time for the speeches. After everyone had said some lovely things about me, it was my turn to stand up and say a few words.

'Good evening,' I said, moving in front of the grand fireplace in the living room, looking ahead at everyone who had gathered around and whose eyes were now transfixed on me. 'I feel so humbled,' I added as I glanced around the room. 'The fact that you've all taken time out to celebrate my fortieth birthday means a lot, so thank you for coming. Now, whilst I organise events for a living, as you know, I don't actually have parties very often myself. But I was inspired to do this by a very special man: my dear friend Albert, who as you know I met in France when I was twenty. I'm delighted his wonderful wife, Marie, and his children, Henri and Geraldine, have joined us tonight.'

I blew a kiss to them in the crowd so that everyone could see where they were standing. I was glad Harrison was filming this. It would be great to send the recording to Marie afterwards.

'For almost two decades, Albert remained an amazing friend. More than a friend, in fact. He was like a second father to me. But sadly, last year he passed away.' I started to feel emotional, but I was determined to carry on. 'He was taken from us far too soon, aged just sixty. But after his funeral, I made a promise to him, and to myself, that I would do my best to honour his memory and everything he taught me by living my life to the fullest. Now, as you all know, before, I was a bit of a workaholic—'

'A bit!' shouted my mother from the sofa. The room erupted with laughter.

'Okay, thanks, Mum!' I said, laughing. 'Yes, more than a *bit*, I'll admit. I was all work, work, work. I was uptight and unhappy. In short, whilst my life appeared to be good from the outside, in reality, I wasn't making the most of it. But despite his passing, Albert has been inspiring me to pursue my dreams and to build a more balanced and positive life for myself. A year on, I've grown so much. I took myself on a cookery holiday with a group of strangers who are now amazing friends.' I smiled at Fran and Dan who were also in the room. 'I learnt to cook Italian dishes, I rarely work at weekends or evenings, and I have experienced so many things, thanks to the extra courage that Albert gave me and the incredible love and support I feel from you all.'

'Aww, bless you, Soph,' said Fran, who was getting all teary.

'Thank you to my parents, not just for having me in the first place, but for always being there for me.' My dad put his arm around my mum's shoulder and pulled her into him as she was also welling up. 'To Harrison, thank you for your calmness and your support both in and outside of work—I couldn't do it without you—and for the killer playlist tonight.' I then turned to Marilyn and Jasmine:

'To the best sister and niece a girl could ask for. To my wonderful friends, old and new: Bella, Roxy, Fran, Monique, I love you. Thanks, Aunt Cynthia, for allowing us into your beautiful home, and Aunt Sheri, for the delicious food. There's too many people to mention—otherwise we'll be here all night and I'll get even more emotional—so I just want to finish by saying a big thank-you to you *all*!'

There was a round of applause. It was strange. I'd presented to audiences of thousands for work and it hadn't fazed me, but in front of close family, it was different. More nerve-racking. Maybe it was the intensity of the emotions rushing through me.

Aunt Sheri and Aunt Cynthia had already begun passing around the glasses of prosecco and were now making their way forward to start lighting the candles on the large gold and cream cake which had 'Happy 40th

Birthday, Sophia' written in icing and mini coconut cupcakes around the edges.

On the count of three, Valentino started strumming his guitar as everyone sang 'Happy Birthday.'

I then took my cue to blow out the candles. It wouldn't take a genius to guess what my wish was. Well, I cheated a little and asked for *three* wishes in one (yes, I was aware that there wasn't a genie in the room to grant them, but as my dad always said, if you don't ask, you don't get), wishing that: 1) I had a healthy baby, 2) that it was Lorenzo's and 3) that he came back to me.

But maybe wishing wasn't enough. If Lorenzo truly was the one, I should fight for him.

Finding someone that you have that strong physical and emotional connection with is hard: particularly post-forty, when there's a smaller pool of men available. So even though I risked looking like a fool, getting rejected, feeling more pain and stressing myself out, which wouldn't be ideal for the baby, I needed to put my pride and emotions on the line and find Lorenzo.

I'll contact the restaurant. See if Gino had heard anything or could get a message to him. I'd fly to Italy if I had to. I couldn't give up on Lorenzo without trying. I needed to know what happened and how he felt. I refused to believe that what we had wasn't real.

As I snapped out of my thoughts, everyone let out a loud cheer and clinked each other's glasses before taking large gulps of the chilled prosecco.

Harrison fired up the music, kicking off with a Rihanna and Calvin Harris hit, which instantly got my cousins dancing, and the rest of the crowd began to disperse as they headed back to their chosen spots in the room.

Then, as I looked straight ahead, I couldn't believe my eyes.

I blinked several times just to be sure I wasn't dreaming.

Stood directly in front of me, glass of prosecco in hand, it was him.

There clearly *was* a genie in the room.

And he'd granted one of my wishes.

I wouldn't have to contact Gino or fly to Italy to start the search.

He was here.

Lorenzo had come back to me.

CHAPTER FORTY-FOUR

As he walked towards me, I was still in a state of shock. A wave of emotions were pulsing through my brain: surprise, elation, confusion, desire and, of course, anger.

He looked *gorgeous*. Tired but just breathtaking. I felt my knees go weak.

He leant over to kiss me gently on the lips.

'I sorry I am late,' he said, taking my hands into his. 'My flight was delayed by hours. I thought I would not make it, but I had to. I promised you I would be here, so I could not break it. You look beautiful, Sophia.'

I was so glad he was there, but also stunned that he'd only apologised for being late and not for disappearing for *two months* without so much as a text message or phone call. I dropped my hands and placed them on my hips. The look of desire and happiness I had shown when I had first seen him had now gone. I was now scowling like a Rottweiler, wondering how he could be so insensitive.

'I should not have come?' he asked, realising that I was livid. 'You are not happy to see me?'

Unbelievable!

I could feel various eyes burning straight through us, notably Charlie's, but I had to find out what had happened.

'Lorenzo,' I said as calmly as I could manage, when really I wanted to scream at him. 'We need to talk. Come with me.'

I led him out of the living room, down the end of the hall, into my aunt's bedroom, through the patio doors and onto her balcony. The minute we stepped outside, he pulled me towards him and started kissing me.

Nooooo! I'm supposed to be angry at you, and I can't if you kiss me…

Oh this man. He did it to me *every* time. How did he always make me feel so *gooooood?*

Stop it, Sophia.

'Lorenzo, no, stop!' I said, echoing Reasanna's concerns and pushing him away. 'You can't just disappear without even bothering to call me, send me a message or anything for *two fucking months* and then just rock up to my birthday party and start kissing me like nothing happened. Why the fuck did you just up and leave me?'

'But I don't understand. Why are you angry?' he said, frowning deeply. 'I wrote you long letter explaining why I had to leave. I told you that my ex-girlfriend tried to find out where I was and threatened to go after my mother and contact Taste Holidays, so I had to rush back to Italy.' He was speaking rapidly, desperate to get the words out.

'What?' I asked, completely confused.

'I explained that I was happy about the baby and, like you, I believed that it must be mine, but I still needed time to think and prepare. To be ready for the big responsibility.' He stroked my stomach gently. 'I said it may take time and I needed to focus, so if you did not hear from me for many weeks, you must not think I had forgotten you. That when I saw you I would explain properly, that I was just not strong enough to talk about it now, but that I love you and even if I took a long time to fix things back home, I promise I would be there at your party. I even left a new email address to contact me if it was urgent.'

'You left me a new email address?' I asked again with no idea what he was talking about.

'Yes!' he replied. I looked into his eyes. He did *seem* sincere. 'The crazy woman tried to track my phone. That's why I wrote a letter. When I called him from my friend's phone in Italy, Gino told me he told you that I left a letter for you at the flat, and Jack told me he left the letter for you on the coffee table, and when he locked up the letter was gone, so I thought you read it and that you understood, no?'

'I've told you, Lorenzo. I have no idea what letter you're going on about!' I scoffed, brushing off his hand as he tried to stroke my shoulder. 'Gino told me you'd left something for me at the flat, but not a letter. All that was on the bed was my clothes and make-up bag.'

'No, I told you!' he said, exasperated. 'Jack left the letter on the coffee table. I rushed to get my plane as I was worried about my mother and the woman. I locked up the flat, went outside, then I remembered the letter was in my pocket and not on the bed with your clothes. I ran back quickly and buzzed Jack. He came down, took the letter, which I told him was important, and the keys so I could go to the airport, and when I called, he told me he left it on the coffee table by the sofa.'

I paused and did a mental scan of what I remembered seeing in the flat.

Yes, I did remember there being a letter on the coffee table when I got there, but I didn't think to look at it. I was in shock. And why would I think he would write me a letter? Who writes bloody letters these days? Especially if English isn't even your first language? I got he had explained why he didn't want to use his phone to me now, but otherwise I'd never have considered that in a million years.

When I thought about it, the coffee table *had* looked emptier when I'd left. I knew something was different, but I couldn't put my finger on it.

Hold on a moment.

When I had come out of the bathroom, Charlie had been pushing something into his pocket was acting suspiciously.

Bastard!

He must have seen the letter, read it and hidden it from me.

All this time! All this time, I'd been hurting, thinking that Lorenzo had just left me without even giving me an explanation. That I must have been wrong and he didn't love me at all. And all along, Charlie had known the truth.

'Wait here!' I shouted.

I stormed back into the bedroom, through the door and down to the living room to find Charlie, who I now spotted chatting to Roxy. I knew I needed to try and stay calm for the baby's sake, but I couldn't help myself. I was livid.

'Charlie!' I screamed. 'Did you take a letter from the

coffee table in Lorenzo's flat that was addressed to me and hide it?'

He looked stunned and immediately turned bright red. His face said it all.

'You *bastard*!' The whole room fell silent and gasped in horror at the unscheduled show that had been added to the party entertainment itinerary. 'You saw how upset I was, and you just left me to think Lorenzo didn't care, when you knew all along that he hadn't just upped and left. You were happy to see me in pain, just to get back at me. I fucking *hate* you!'

I left the room seething, and seconds later I could hear him running after me down the hallway.

'Sophia,' he said, grabbing onto my arm. 'I'm sorry. I didn't mean to…I wasn't thinking clearly. You'd just told me you'd jumped into bed with another man literally five minutes after leaving me, despite knowing what I'd been through with Zara, and I was hurt, so when I saw the letter, I just… I just…he's not good enough for you!'

He followed me into the bedroom, where Lorenzo was now standing, arms folded.

'Sophia, he's just a *chef*, for goodness' sake!' Charlie shouted. 'He can't provide for you and our baby. I can give you both *everything* you'll ever need. What can he offer you? A plate of pasta and some grotty accommodation? I can give you so much more!'

Lorenzo stepped forward and punched Charlie squarely in the face, sending him crashing to the wooden floor.

I gasped in shock. That was one right hook Lorenzo had on him. I could almost see the stars buzzing around Charlie's head, like when the characters got knocked out in the old-school cartoons.

Lorenzo wrapped his arm around my waist and stroked my bump.

'Nobody talks to my wife like that,' he said, looking down at Charlie, who was rubbing his cheek, which was, unsurprisingly, looking very sore. 'You took my letter for Sophia. You made me look like a bad man. You upset her and *our* baby. It is time for you to leave. I will take care of Sophia and *our child*. I am not a rich man, but I know how to respect and love a woman. If you loved Sophia and Sophia loved you, you would not need to hide my letter from her. Go back to your castle, rich man,' Lorenzo said, shooing Charlie away and wrinkling his face with disgust.

My hero!

Wait. Did Lorenzo just call me his wife*?*

Although I wasn't a wedding kind of woman, I had to admit, that was such a sweet thing to say.

Charlie struggled to get back on his feet. 'You two cretins deserve each other,' he barked. 'Sophia, I'm sorely disappointed in you. All I tried to do was to give you a good life, to *elevate* you, and this is how you repay me? You're an ungrateful, common whore!'

Lorenzo lunged forward to punch him again.

'No, Lorenzo,' I said calmly, holding his hand back. 'Leave it.' I turned to Charlie, who was now upright, albeit still a little unsteady on his feet. 'Charlie, I'm very grateful for everything you've done for me, but I was honest with you about how I felt. I tried, but we both know it wasn't working. I want to stay on good terms. That's why I came to you and apologised, and why I invited you here tonight. But what you did hiding that letter from me was just wrong.'

'Oh and sleeping with two guys literally hours apart,

getting pregnant and not knowing who the father is, isn't?' he snapped.

Touché. Although technically, if Charlie would just tell me the truth about what happened with the condom, it would be a lot less confusing…

'Unbelievable,' said Charlie as he turned and left, slamming the door behind him.

I turned to Lorenzo and rested my head on his chest.

'I'm sorry I doubted you.'

'I am sorry I left you,' he said, resting his chin on my head. 'But I have lot of problems. At first when I left, I thought perhaps it is best I did not come back. I looked up Charlie on the internet when I got home. I knew he was a rich man, but not *that* rich. So I thought, perhaps it would be better if you stay with him. He could give you more than I can. Then I worried if I was ready. If I can be a good father…' He paused, and a troubled expression engulfed his face. 'You remember I told you I had difficult life, especially with women?' he asked.

'Yes…' I replied, bracing myself for what was coming next.

We sat down on the sofa opposite the balcony doors.

'When I was twenty-nine, I fell in love with a woman. She told me she was pregnant. We had not known each other a long time. I thought it had happened quickly, but I was happy. I always wanted children. People told me that she was no good. But she was beautiful—looked like the actress Eva Mendes. But I did not listen. I loved her.' He rested his hands on top of mine and his face turned serious.

'Go on,' I said encouragingly.

'I worked two jobs to get enough money to look after the baby and to buy her the nice clothes that she wanted. I loved my son. His name was Stefano. But when he was six months, a man came to the house saying he wants to see *his* son. My girlfriend, she had an affair with a married man, realised she was pregnant with his baby, but because he would not leave his wife and stopped giving her money, she met me and decided to use me to support them instead. Even though she lied, I forgave her. I said I would still look after them. But then the man's wife heard about this and kicked him out, so my girlfriend left to be with him, and she took Stefano with her.'

'Oh God. That's terrible,' I said. Jesus. This man hadn't been joking when he'd said he'd had a tough life.

'I was devastated. I started drinking. I did not go to work. I lost my job. For six months I was a mess.' He paused again as he held his head down—like he was reliving the pain and the shame. 'I slept with lots of women and said I would never trust or stay with one woman again—that way, I cannot get hurt. That is why I got that reputation. But I did not enjoy it. After a while it is boring. It leaves you empty. All I really wanted was a wife and a family and to be loved. It took years before I was strong again. I got a job with Taste and things were better. I tried to trust again. Then I had problems with the crazy woman. So when you told me you were pregnant and you cannot be sure if it is mine or Charlie's, it brought back the pain and memories of Stefano, and I did not know how to deal with that.'

'I'm so sorry. I didn't realise,' I said, wrapping my arms around him.

'Also, when I told you I had important things to take care of when I went back to Italy in January, I had more problems with my ex that I tried to fix, and I did not want to worry you,' he explained. 'I thought it was finished, but then it got worse again, so that is why I had to come back to Italy quickly. You see. My life is complicated. I do not know if it is good for a good woman like you to be with a man like me,' he said, bowing his head again.

He wasn't wrong about the shit he had gone through. And there I was adding to it by telling him about the pregnancy, not considering how it might affect him. Despite all of his issues, it still didn't put me off.

'But, those experiences are in the past. They're behind you now. I'm not perfect, but compared to the women you've been with before, I'm a bloody angel. You won't experience that pain and turmoil with me. And I won't allow anyone to take our baby away from you.'

'You have reason, Sophia. I know you are a good woman. That's why I came back. I love you,' he said as he leant forward and kissed me softly on the lips. 'The time we spent here in London, I have never been so happy. It is not just the sex, which was amazing. We have a connection. We laughed, I felt calm—like I was complete. Especially now with the baby. And I know this baby is mine, Sophia. I *feel* it. So I say, no: *Fuck Charlie!* I am going to show Sophia that I am a man and I am ready to be a good father.'

He reached in his pocket for his phone and unlocked the screen.

'What's up?' I asked, wondering if he had taken it out to call someone.

'While I was away, I started working again with Taste, as it is the new season, and did many extra shifts at a restaurant in town, so I saved up money for us. But on my day off, I worked at my house.' He showed me his phone and started scrolling through photos of a room. In the first pictures, it looked quite messy and disorganised, with a guitar in the corner, a bed in the centre, posters of some rock band I didn't recognise on the flaky walls and bags of clothes everywhere.

In the photos that followed, it showed the room had been cleared out, then the walls had been painted lemon, a new carpet laid and…

Oh my goodness. There was a cot in place of the bed with a cute mobile attached and a little rocking horse and playpen in the corner. Adorable!

'You see?' he said, looking up from the phone and straight at me. 'I cleared out my brother's room and made it into a nursery. For our baby. And I decorated my bedroom too. Before, it looked like a man's room. Now I made it nice for a woman too—for you.'

OMG. All this time he'd been away, not only had he been thinking of me, of *us*, he had been working hard trying to build a life for us too.

'Sophia, I know it is a big decision, but I want spend my life with you.' He put his phone back in his pocket and then took my hands into his. 'I know you have life in London and family and successful business too. But when we talked, I felt like you want a change, no? You are ready maybe for a different type of life. More time to enjoy and less time spent at work? And you said you love me too. So I wondered if you want to come and live with me? In Italy? We can be a family, together.'

What? I couldn't believe it. I tried to compose myself.

'Wow,' I said, picking my jaw up from the floor. 'I don't… I don't actually know what to say.'

'I could only get one day off from work, which was

already difficult because it was a Saturday, so my flight leaves Gatwick tomorrow morning seven forty-five a.m.,' he said. 'I booked a ticket for you to come with me. Not for you to live there straight away. I know that will take many months of planning. But just for you to try. For a few weeks. See if you like it. What you think?'

'I...I...' I replied, still trying to take everything in.

'I know it is a lot to think about, so I will leave you now,' he said, standing up as he still kept hold of my hands. 'If you want to try, meet me at the airport at six a.m. I will wait for you until six fifteen. If you decide you do not want to come, I will understand, but I hope you do.'

He leant over and kissed me on the head and then bent down to kiss my stomach.

'I will go and say hello to your family and then will leave to let you discuss with them. Is better that way, no? Try and enjoy the rest of your party. I hope I see you tomorrow morning, beauty.'

And with that, he was gone.

It was crazy to think that I'd dreamt about this just days after meeting him. And I'd dismissed it because it was ludicrous to let my mind run away with such thoughts after knowing the man all of five minutes. But somehow this *wasn't* some mad fantasy. It was actually real. This was beyond nuts.

I loved Lorenzo with all my heart, but it was such a big decision. Was I really ready to give up my life in London, my family, friends, my home and the business I'd worked so hard to build, in fact almost *everything*, to be with him?

CHAPTER FORTY-FIVE

I leant forward on the sofa, head in hands. *What the fuck am I going to do? It's all so sudden.*

I heard footsteps running down the hallway. Roxy and Bella burst in.

'Soph, are you okay?' said Bella, coming over to me, perching on the edge of the sofa and rubbing my shoulder. 'What's happened?'

'Yeah,' Roxy chipped in. 'First you have a slanging match with Charlie, he runs after you, then minutes later, we see him storm off out the front door with a swollen cheek and black eye, and now we've just seen Lorenzo go over to your folks, Harrison and your granddad, introduce himself and then say he's sorry but he has to leave? What's going on?' she asked, frowning and crossing her arms.

'Well, basically, all this time, Lorenzo *hadn't* just upped and disappeared in the way that I thought. He'd left a long letter explaining everything, but when Charlie came to his flat, he spotted it on the table and decided to hide it from me.'

'You're joking,' said Bella.

'Nope,' I said, shaking my head. 'So I've spent all these weeks, in fact months, upset, thinking Lorenzo didn't care, when all the while he's been back in Italy, working his arse off trying to provide a life for me and the baby, renovating his house with a nursery and doing it all up so I can go and live there and we can be a family, together.'

'Wait, what?' said Roxy. 'What do you mean go and *live* there? In fucking Italy? Is he nuts? Is that why he left, because you told him to piss off?'

'Why would I tell him to piss off, Roxy?' I said, frowning. *She better not be starting her shit...*

'Well, firstly,' she said, crossing her arms again, 'because everyone knows holiday romances, which is essentially what this is, don't last. And secondly, you have a life here, Sophia. A family, a successful business to run, a team who rely on you for their livelihoods, a home and *us*, your friends. You can't just throw everything away and leave it all behind to go running after *a man. Especially* someone like Lorenzo,' she scowled.

'What is *that* supposed to mean?' I snapped. 'And why *wouldn't* I leave to build a life with him? What's wrong with trying to make it work with the man I love and letting him be there for me and our baby?'

'Are you fucking serious?' she barked. 'You don't even know if it is his baby! Look at all the stress he's put you through! Ever since you've met him, it's been nothing but drama, and now you think it'll will somehow be better in a strange country where you don't speak the language, don't have a support network like you have here, or a job for that matter? What will you do for work? It's not like he's Charlie, who can really provide for you. You can't *honestly* be considering give up a multimillion-pound business, your beautiful home and your independence, to go and live with a fucking chef, for God's sake! Where's your feminist backbone gone? Stop being so weak.'

'You know what, Roxy?' I said, jumping up. 'I'm sick and tired of you passing judgement on him when you don't even know him. I'm in love with Lorenzo, and you know what? I am seriously considering getting on that plane with him tomorrow morning! That doesn't make me weak. That makes me strong.'

'How does giving up your career, your success and independence to run after a man like some lovesick schoolgirl with her head in the clouds, just because he's good in bed, make you strong?' she scoffed.

'It makes me strong, because for once, I'm choosing life and happiness instead of what other people define as success. Success isn't about having the biggest agency or the biggest bank balance. It's about having the courage to step away from convention and make the choices that make *me* happy and that are right for *me*. It shows that I believe in myself enough to know that even if I *do* go and live with Lorenzo, I will be okay. I'm not giving up my independence. I'm taking control of my life and what *I* want. And as for my business, I've got options. I can work remotely, get Robyn to run it, or I could just sell it and do something completely different...'

'Now I *know* you're crazy!' shouted Roxy in disbelief. 'Why *on earth* would you sell the company you've worked so hard to build when it's doing so well? That business is your baby. That's what you've always said. Why would you even contemplate just giving it all up?'

'Because, after seeing what happened to Albert and

now having this baby growing inside of me, I realise that there's much more to life than work. Successful people sell their businesses all the time. Look at Jo Malone and Liz Earle. I've had some huge multinational companies hounding me for months if not years to buy me out, and a couple of their offers are *very* attractive. But it's not about the money. After fourteen years of working non-stop, I deserve to take time out. I've achieved more than I ever dreamt I would, so maybe it's time for a new challenge. Fuck it!' I said, getting excited at the prospect of a fresh start and realising that this argument had led me to make my decision. 'To quote one of your acronyms, Roxy: *YOLO*! You only live once. I'm not going to hold out until I'm sixty-five. Look at Albert. He didn't even reach retirement age. I'm not waiting a second longer. I'm going to live my life *now*!'

Roxy's mouth had dropped so far open that you could have fit the *Titanic* in it and still have room.

'Wow, Soph!' said a startled Bella. 'Looks like you've reached a decision. I know you've said you don't want to wait, but tomorrow morning? Isn't that a little hasty? How would you realistically get everything organised by then?'

'Lorenzo's going back tomorrow and has a ticket for me. He's not suggesting I go out and live in Italy permanently straight away. Obviously he understands that would take time. All he's suggesting is that I come out there for a couple of weeks initially to see if I like it, and then we can take it from there.'

Roxy sat down on the sofa. Then Bella came off the edge and sat beside her. They were both silent. They knew me. I was going. And they knew once my mind was made up, there was no point trying to change it.

I glanced at the clock on the wall opposite the bed. It was now rapidly approaching 2.30 a.m. In order to meet him, I'd have to get home (which by the time I'd said my goodbyes and ordered a taxi could take a good half an hour), find my passport, pack and leave by 4.30 a.m. to get to Gatwick by 6 a.m. In fact, I wasn't going to waste another minute discussing or justifying myself to them. I had to leave right now!

'Ladies, I love you,' I said, smiling, 'but I'm going to fucking Italy!' I bent down to hug Bella. 'Bella, love you,' I moved over to Roxy, who was still scowling. I didn't care. 'Roxy,' I said, squeezing her tightly. 'Sometimes you're a giant pain in the arse, but I know your feistiness comes from a good place. I hate when we argue. I still love you. Thank you for caring. But I've got to do this. I've *got* to try. Life is short. I'll regret it if I don't.' I squeezed her again and then let go.

'Wow,' said Bella, whilst Roxy's mouth remained firmly on the floor. 'Well, good luck!'

'I'll message you when I get there,' I said as I rushed out the bedroom door. 'Ciao!'

After running around hugging the remaining guests, apologising for the 'show' earlier and now having to leave my own party early, then kissing a very confused Mum and Dad goodbye, I grabbed my coat and bags and headed out to the main road to hail a taxi.

I BURST into the dressing room, pulled out a medium-sized suitcase from the rack behind the door and began taking clothes off hangers and out of the drawers and frantically throwing them inside. Some casual, loose-fitting dresses (even they were getting tight), leggings, underwear, a couple of long-sleeve tops, a pair of Converse…I tossed a black t-shirt, oversized lightweight yellow jumper and a pair of indigo maternity jeans on the bed, ready to wear.

Shit. It was already 3.15 a.m., the taxi would be here in just over an hour and I still had a million things to do, including packing my passport. *Better find that now.*

3.45 a.m.: *Got it and it's still in date. I need to jump in the shower.*

4.20 a.m.: *Taxi is coming in ten minutes and I can't shut my suitcase. Maybe if I sit on it? There. Done. Must be this extra weight I'm carrying. Nearly busted the zip though. That wouldn't have been funny. Wait. Did I put my toothbrush in there? Nope. Looks like I'm going to have to open it up again…*

4.35 a.m.: *Where's the fucking taxi? It's late. This is stressful! Sorry, little bump. I know Mummy is supposed to be keeping calm, but I'm definitely not used to packing up and heading off to potentially start a new life with just a few hours notice. Breathe, Sophia. Breathe.*

4.45 a.m.: *The driver finally turned up fifteen minutes late. Should still be enough time…*

5 a.m.: *'What do you mean your sat nav isn't working? You do know how to get to Gatwick, though, don't you?' Looks like I might need to direct him using the Google Maps on my phone.*

5.25 a.m.: *We're on the motorway, so I think it's okay to relax now.*

I'm going to Italy—to be with Lorenzo and I couldn't be more excited! So what if I sounded like a loved-up teenager. A teenager I might not be, but I felt like one, I certainly *was* loved up and I didn't care. Being happy was *nothing* to be ashamed of.

Oh, how my life had changed in this past year or so. And like I'd said earlier at my party, it was all down to Albert and the extra strength he had given me.

I reached into my handbag and pulled out my notepad and flicked through to the MAP list I'd made just fifteen months ago.

1) Stop being a workaholic/have a better work-life balance: *Yep. I can check that one off.* I hadn't made a firm decision about whether to sell the company or keep it. I would study the offers more closely, weigh up the pros and cons and decide once I was in Italy. Lorenzo was right, though. I was ready for a new direction. Maybe I'd pursue photography. That's always been another passion of mine. If I sold the business, the payoff I got might allow me to live for a while without working, provided we had a modest lifestyle. Or maybe I could rent out my house?

2) End my relationship: It had been over a year now. I'd heard through the grapevine that Rich was engaged. I was genuinely happy for him. Great guy, but just not the guy for me.

3) Experience passion: Yes, yes, *yes*! Multiple times per night with Lorenzo around.

4) Go on an educational holiday: Check. Who knew one trip would change my life so dramatically? I hadn't even imagined that I'd find love, so that was definitely an MAP bonus. Especially after all the ups and downs I'd experienced with Lorenzo, not to mention my 'interesting' dating experiences. Maybe the cliché about finding 'the one' when you're not looking was true...

5) Throw a party: As of last night, that was another official achievement ticked off the list.

6) Look into adoption: Well, there was an *actual* living, baby, growing inside me right now, so that was an unexpected, but very welcomed check. Who knows? If all went well and we decided to extend our family (did you see how I dropped the 'we' and 'family' in there? Getting carried away again, but it's good to think positively), maybe we could look at adoption then. Never in my wildest dreams would I ever have believed when I wrote this last year that I'd be having a baby naturally. What a gift.

7) Have fun/live life to the full: Hell to the yes! I had thrown caution to the wind and was on my way to Gatwick. I could honestly say that I had continuously tried my best to live by this motto.

So there you have it. A full house. I was proud of myself.

I thought back to Albert's last words to me:

*'Remember, life is short. You only live once. You must enjoy. If you are not happy, you must do something to change it...*rappelle-toi *that it is happiness and* amour *that is the most important.'*

I felt wholeheartedly that not only had I taken his comments on board, but I'd followed through with action too. I hadn't been happy and I'd made changes to address that. And now I was about to follow my heart and be with the man that I loved. The man that made me so very happy.

I hoped that Albert was looking down and feeling proud of me too.

05.58: We pulled up outside Gatwick with just minutes

to spare.

06.04: I looked around frantically for the right terminal. Shit. I had to take the shuttle to the North Terminal. I should have checked that on my phone on my way here…

06.07: Just boarded the shuttle. Just realised I didn't put any make-up on. And my hair? Did I even brush it? *Doesn't matter. Lorenzo loves me just the way I am.*

06.10: *Which way is it now? Fuck. I have five minutes before he leaves…*

06.12*: I went the wrong way!*

06.15: *Where is he? I just made it on time and he's gone already? Shit.*

I looked ahead to the large black-and-yellow 'Departures' sign—*maybe he's just gone through?*

I can't see him.

He wouldn't have stood me up again. *No way.* I was over that neuroticism now. Lorenzo loved me and I trusted him. I'd find him. He was here. I knew it.

Just I was about to go searching for him, I felt someone come up behind me and place their arms behind my waist, pull me backwards towards them and kiss my neck gently.

Ooooh, yes…

I spun round. Thank goodness it was Lorenzo. 'You came!' he said, flashing his giant grin.

'Of course!' I said, mirroring his warm smile.

He kissed me slowly on the lips, and just like the first time, I had major butterflies.

I stared into his eyes, as I reflected on how I was feeling right now, right here in this moment.

I didn't know how this trip to his home in Italy would go, how we'd get on, whether I'd like it there or if it was somewhere I felt I could live happily. I didn't know which direction I'd decide to go in terms of my career or whether I'd continue to work once the baby was born. Hell, I didn't even know if this child was his and whether we would survive the many challenges that lay ahead of us.

But what I *did* know was that I loved Lorenzo. I was filled with positivity, determination and hope and I was willing to take a chance to find out.

Like my dear Albert said, life is short and we must enjoy.

And come what may, I had every intention of living my life with Lorenzo and our baby to the absolute fullest.

THE END

Want to find out what happens next?

Discover what happens when Sophia moves to Italy to be with Lorenzo in the hotly anticipated sequel: *The Middle-Aged Virgin in Italy.*

Order on Amazon now!

GET A FREE BOOK AND EXCLUSIVE BONUS MATERIAL

Building a relationship with my readers is one of the best things about being an author. I occasionally send out fun newsletters to members of my VIP club with details of new releases, special offers, expert dating and relationship tips, interesting news and other exclusive freebies.

If you sign up to join my special VIP club, I'll send you the following, for free:

1) Yellow Book Of Love: a handy little guide, which features essential dating and relationship tips from multiple experts, including the Dating Expert of the Year 2017.

2) A list of *Alex's Top 25 Romcoms*: a definitive guide highlighting 25 top romcoms that are loved by Alex, the protagonist in my novel *Only When It's Love*. Exclusive to my VIP Club – you can't get this anywhere else.

You can get the book and the list of top romcoms, **for free,** by signing up at: www.oliviaspring.com/vip-club/

A MESSAGE FROM OLIVIA

Yay! You made it to the end of my book! I hope you enjoyed reading about Sophia's journey as much as I loved writing it.

If you can, I'd really appreciate it if you could spare a moment to write an honest review on Amazon, Goodreads or anywhere else that readers visit.

When it comes to trying new authors, readers like to see reviews. It makes them more likely to take a chance on me. So, if you'd like to enjoy more of my books in the future (and make my day!), please do share your thoughts.

It doesn't have to be a long review (unless you'd like it to be!). Every review – even if it's just a sentence – would make a *huge* difference.

Thanks again for choosing to buy *The Middle-Aged Virgin*. It really means the world to me.

And if you'd like to say hi, please email me at olivia@oliviaspring.com or connect on social media @ospringauthor. I'd love to hear from you!

Olivia x

ALSO BY OLIVIA SPRING

Only When It's Love: Holding Out For Mr Right

Have you read my second novel *Only When It's Love?* It includes the feisty character Roxy from *The Middle-Aged Virgin*, too! Here's what it's about:

Alex's love life is a disaster. Will accepting a crazy seven-step dating challenge lead to more heartbreak or help her find Mr Right?

Alex is tired of getting ghosted. After years of disastrous hook-ups and relationships that lead to the bedroom but nowhere else, Alex is convinced she's destined to be eternally single. Then her newly married friend Stacey recommends what worked for her: a self-help book that guarantees Alex will find true love in just seven steps. Sounds simple, right?

Except Alex soon discovers that each step is more difficult than the last, and one of the rules involves dating, but not sleeping with a guy for six months. Absolutely no intimate contact whatsoever. *Zero. Nada. Rien.* A big challenge for Alex, who has never been one to hold back from jumping straight into the sack, hoping it will help a man fall for her.

Will any guys be willing to wait? Will Alex find her Mr Right? And if she does, will she be strong enough to resist temptation and hold out for true love?

Join Alex on her roller coaster romantic journey as she tries to cope with the emotional and physical ups and downs of dating whilst following a lengthy list of rigid rules.

Only When It's Love **is a standalone, fun, feel-good, romantic** comedy about self-acceptance, determination, love and the challenge of finding *the one.*

Praise For *Only When It's Love*

'**Totally unique and wonderful.** Olivia's book has a brilliant message about self-worth and brings to life an important modern take on the rom-com. Most definitely a five-star read.' - **Love Books Group**

'I guarantee **you will HOOT with laughter** at Alex's escapades whilst fully cheering her on. If you like romance, humour and a generally fun-filled read then look no further than this **gorgeous, well-written dating adventure**. Five stars.' - **Bookaholic Confessions**

'Such a uniquely told, **laugh-out-loud, dirty and flirty, addictive novel.**' - **The Writing Garnet**

'**An exciting insight into relationships in the 21st century.**' - **Amazon reader**

'With the right mix of romance and comedy, this is **the perfect read**. Five stars.' - **Love Books Actually**

'I've never read a story so quickly to find out who she would choose and if Mr Right would be the one! Five stars.' - **Books Between Friends**

'**Funny, entertaining and clever**. Olivia is an incredibly talented writer, and definitely one to watch. I cannot wait to see what she does next! Five stars.' - **BookMadJo**

'Cool, contemporary, but still wildly romantic! Yet another smasher from Olivia Spring! There's something about the way she writes that really endeared me to the heroine of this story.' - **Amazon reader**

'WOW WOW WOW!!!! *Only When it's Love* is **a dynamite love fest**. I read the entire story with the biggest smile on my face. In case you might have missed the million hints I've dropped, download the book today and jump straight in.' **Stacy is Reading**

Buy *Only When It's Love* on Amazon today!

AN EXTRACT FROM ONLY WHEN IT'S LOVE

Chapter One

Never again.

Why, why, *why* did I keep on doing this?

I felt great for a few minutes, or if I was lucky, hours, but then, when it was all over, I ended up feeling like shit for days. Sometimes weeks.

I must stop torturing myself.

Repeat after me:

I, Alexandra Adams, will *not* answer Connor Matthew's WhatsApp messages, texts or phone calls for the rest of my life.

I firmly declare that even if Connor says his whole world is falling apart, that he's sorry, he's realised I'm *the one* and he's changed, I will positively, absolutely, unequivocally *not* reply.

Nor will I end up going to his flat because I caved in after he sent me five million messages saying he misses me and inviting me round just 'to talk'.

And I *definitely* do solemnly swear that I will *not* end up on my back with my legs wrapped around his neck within minutes of arriving, because I took one look at his body and couldn't resist.

No.

That's it.

No more.

I will be *strong*. I will be like iron. Titanium. Steel. All three welded into one.

I will block Connor once and for all and I will move on with my life.

Yes!

I exhaled.

Finally I'd found my inner strength.

This was the start of a new life for me. A new beginning. Where I wouldn't get screwed over by yet another fuckboy. Where I wouldn't get ghosted or dumped. Where I took control of my life and stuck my middle finger up at the men who treated me like shit. *Here's to the new me.*

My phone chimed.

It was Connor.

I bolted upright in bed and clicked on his message.

He couldn't stop thinking about me. He wanted to see me again.

Tonight.

To talk. About our future.

Together.

This could be it!

Things *had* felt kind of different last time. Like there was a deeper connection.

Maybe he was right. Maybe he *had* changed…

I excitedly typed out a reply.

My fingers hovered over the blue button, ready to send.

Hello?

What the hell was I doing?

It was like the entire contents of my pep talk two seconds ago had just evaporated from my brain.

Remember *being strong like iron, titanium and steel* and resisting the temptations of Connor?

Shit.

This was going to be much harder than I'd thought.

Want to find out what happens next? Buy *Only When It's Love* by Olivia Spring on Amazon now.

ALSO BY OLIVIA SPRING

Losing My Inhibitions

Have you read my third novel ***Losing My Inhibitions?*** It includes Sophia and Roxy from *The Middle-Aged Virgin*, too! Here's what it's about:

Finally free and ready to have fun...

He's hot, single and off limits. She's just got her life together after a messy divorce. Should she risk it all for a forbidden fling?

A year after leaving her controlling ex, Roxy's divorce is finally official. She's got her confidence and career back on track and is ready to start enjoying some no-strings-attached fun.

But just when Roxy thinks she has her dating plan all mapped out, a hot younger single man unexpectedly appears. On paper, he sounds like exactly what Roxy's been looking for, until she's warned that he's strictly off limits. Getting involved with him will put her career, home and everything she's worked for in extreme jeopardy. There's a million reasons why Roxy shouldn't give into his charms. The trouble is, he's just too tempting...

Will Roxy take a chance and risk it all to pursue a forbidden fling? And if she does, can she find a way to let him rock her world, without turning it upside down?

Losing My Inhibitions **is a sexy, laugh-out-loud romantic comedy with a modern twist. This story is about self-love, new beginnings, forging your own path in life and being true**

to yourself. It can be read as a standalone novel or as a prequel to *The Middle-Aged Virgin* and *Only When It's Love*.

Here's what readers are saying about it:

"All hail the new queen of funny, sexy romantic fiction, Olivia Spring. A brilliant read with cringe worthy moments captured perfectly and **genius comedy that had me laughing out loud.** I can't wait to see what Olivia Spring conjures up next but I will snap it up. **All we need now is a movie deal for all three books. Five stars." Love Books Group**

"Oh my word. Ladies **if you haven't already read this, you are missing out. It's steamy, it's sexy and it's very funny.** There is a part in it, of which I can't repeat, that had me doubled up laughing. Totally loved it. **Five stars." Books Between Friends**

"Losing My Inhibitions is **the perfect mix of sexy, romance, drama and comedy which will have you laughing out loud. I would definitely recommend this book! It's perfect for a summer read**, chilled out in the garden with a glass of something lovely. Five stars." **Nicole's Book Corner**

"I really enjoyed reading this - some of the situations Roxy finds herself in **had me laughing out loud!** There's also a few steamier moments in there! Five stars." **Home Full Of Books**

"I read it in two evenings and it was brilliant!! **I couldn't put it down, I just had to know what happened next." Head In A Book 18**

Buy *Losing My Inhibitions* on Amazon now.

AN EXTRACT FROM LOSING MY INHIBITIONS

Chapter One

At last.

I thought it was never going to end.

He'd been pounding away for ten minutes, grunting like a pig, and I'd been listening to the radio playing in the background, trying to figure out what advert the song before last was from. Was it the one advertising car insurance or the one for those panty liners that are supposed to keep you *cotton fresh all day long*? *It'll come to me...*

We should have just called it a night when he'd first struggled to get his machinery working. Based on tonight, it seems like what I'd read about some older men finding it difficult to get it up was true.

It was only about half an hour after he'd popped a little blue pill that he'd been able to get his little soldier to stand to attention, if you catch my drift. Which, unfortunately for me, was around the same time I started to sober up and wonder what the hell I was doing.

But by then, he was really excited, and it had been so long since my last time that I'd got myself worked up and was just as keen as him to give it a go. I mean, when I start something, I like to see it through. *Yep, I'm dedicated like that.*

I'd also read that there are lots of benefits of sleeping with an older guy. Apparently, after years of experience in the sack, they know their way around a woman's body better than a gynaecologist, so I thought I may as well give it a try. *Purely in the name of research, of course.*

But now I was really wishing I hadn't bothered. It was about as exciting as watching a hundred-metre snail race. And this guy wouldn't know his way around my anatomy if I gave him a map.

Still, at least it was over now. I was back in the saddle. First time since I'd left my ex-husband. Frankly, I hoped it got better from here. *Please tell me it does?*

I opened my eyes slowly and glanced up at his crepey skin and flaky bald head, which had tufts of grey at the side. His droopy man boobs hung above my chest, whilst the weight of his large pot belly pressed down on my stomach.

Dear God.

I must have had a lot more to drink than I'd realised.

Don't get me wrong. If I was looking for a relationship and this was a man I'd fallen madly in love with, then I wouldn't be so shallow. It was just that right now, I was looking for fun. To make up for the years I'd wasted with my ex. When I was dreaming of the day that I'd be free from Steve and with another man, this wasn't exactly what I'd had in mind.

I'd pictured a young, hot, sexy guy with abs that would

give a Calvin Klein model a run for his money, with a full head of dark hair I could run my fingers through. A stud who would have me screaming for more, rather than wondering when it would all be over.

It was Colette, my boss, slash landlady, slash house-mate, slash friend, who'd set me up with him at my divorce party earlier this evening. Now that I was officially free, Colette said some male company might be good for me, so she'd invited Donald, her loaded sixty-two-year-old boyfriend, and he'd brought his fifty-five-year-old mate Terrence along.

I knew that I was ready to get back on the horse, and it was already under control. My cousin Alex had been helping me. She'd given me a crash course in online dating two weeks ago, and I wanted to set up my profile ASAP so I could get going on the whole swiping thing, but this big work exhibition kept getting in the way. I'd been burning the midnight oil every night and often over the weekends too, trying to get everything prepared, which didn't leave me with any time for extracurricular activities. And after another long, tiring and stressful day, a hook-up was the last thing I was thinking about. But I guess the booze I'd been drinking all night had made me relax a little too much, so when Terrence had started flirting, my libido had woken up, curiosity had got the better of me, and I'd hastily thought, *Why not just get it out the way now?*

Big Mistake.

Oh well. You live and you learn. We all do things in the heat of the moment that we regret. As long as I didn't do it again, then it was fine. Which meant I better start thinking about how I was going to get this big sweaty oaf of a man off me. *Now.* I'd heard the effects of those pills can last for hours, and I definitely couldn't endure another round.

No way.

Remind me never to drink alcohol again.

Want to find out what happens next? Buy *Losing My Inhibitions* by Olivia Spring on Amazon now.

ALSO BY OLIVIA SPRING

Love Offline

Have you read my fourth novel *Love Offline?* Here's what it's about:

Looking for romance in real life...

Emily's Struggling To Find Romance Online. Will Ditching The Dating Apps Lead To True Love?

Online dating isn't working for introvert Emily. Although she's comfortable swiping right at home in her PJs, the idea of going out to meet a guy in person fills her with dread.

So when her best friend challenges her to ditch the apps, attend a load of awkward singles' events and find love in real life, Emily wants to run for the hills.

Then she meets Josh. He's handsome, kind and funny, but Emily's had her heart crushed before and knows he's hiding something...

Is Josh too good to be true? Can Emily learn to trust again and if she does, will it lead to love or more heartache?

Love Offline is a fun, sexy, entertaining story about friendship, stepping outside of your comfort zone and falling in love the old-fashioned way.

Here's what readers are saying about it:

"**Masterpiece chick lit**. Incredibly funny and through the whole book I was laughing, crying, smiling and I even learned a lot reading this book about social media and self love. I couldn't put it down! Five stars." **Amazon Reader**

"This book just **makes you feel good and all fuzzy inside**, def one to curl up with on the sofa with a cup of tea. Five stars." **Barbs Book Club.**

"**Fun, flirty and fabulous**... I was laughing throughout the whole book. Five stars." **Reading In Lipstick**

"**Hilarious, sexy-romp with heart!** I adored the relationship Emily has with her best friend Chloe." **A Girl With Her Head Stuck In A Book.**

"This book spoke to me on soooo many levels!! **I loved the realness this book shows!!!!** Five stars." **Once Upon A Book Review**

"If you are a fan of Sophie Kinsella and Lindsey Kelk, then this book is for you! *Love Offline* is **a romcom for the modern woman.**" **Girl Well Read**.

"I loved the refreshing take on love and dating in this book....**Definitely recommend!**" **Nic Reads In Heels**

"**A sexy little chick lit read**...A lovely, modern story involving friendship and falling in love." **Mrs L J Gibbs**

"I loved Olivia's last book, but I think this one was even better. Five stars." **Hayley Jayne Reads.**

Buy *Love Offline* on Amazon now.

AN EXTRACT FROM LOVE OFFLINE

Chapter One

Normally, I love social media.

The endless fancy food and envy-inducing holiday pics on Insta, the witty conversations on Twitter, the funny memes on Facebook—I adore it.

When I've got important designs to create for clients and deadlines to meet, I can often be found spending many minutes (truth be told, more like hours) scrolling through strangers' feeds rather than *actually* working. After all, who doesn't like staring at photos of cute kittens?

Like I said. Normally, I *love* social media.

Well, I *did* until precisely 9.29 a.m. today.

The day started off like any other Monday morning. Hitting the snooze button a dozen times before finally crawling out of bed. Having a shower whilst wondering why the weekend flashes by in what seems like five minutes, whereas Monday to Friday lasts for half a century. Throwing on whatever looked clean and didn't need ironing, then dragging myself to my local coffee shop to get the caffeine-and-sugar hit I needed to help me feel remotely human, or at least alert enough to start work.

I'd sat at my desk, taken a generous bite of my blueberry muffin, sipped on my steaming latte and switched on my computer. I had considered going through my emails but, in true procrastination style, decided to check Instagram first instead, because of course that was *much* more important than doing actual work.

And there it was.

That photo.

The picture, which had already amassed thirty-six likes.

The image that instantly made my head spin and my stomach sink.

Captioned with just three words that sent my world crashing down.

She said yes!

My ex-boyfriend Eric, who I always believed would be the man I'd spend the rest of my life with, had proposed to Nicole—the woman he'd been cheating with for the last six months of our relationship—and she'd said yes.

Great.

There they were on what looked like some tropical beach, waves crashing against the golden sand, gazing into each other's eyes, lips locked, her left hand strategically placed on his shoulder, showing off the giant rock adorning her ring finger.

Exactly what I *didn't* need to see on a miserable grey March Monday morning in South London.

After staring at my screen for longer than was healthy, I'd tried to do what any smart, sensible, level-headed, pragmatic woman would if she heard the news that her unfaithful ex was marrying the younger model she'd been traded in for. I'd told myself I couldn't care less, that it was his loss, there were plenty more fish in the sea, karma would catch up with them and to just get on with my day.

Did it work?

Of course it bloody didn't.

So instead I'd dragged myself the ten steps from my home study to my bedroom, put on the 'Life Sucks' Spotify playlist, curled up into a ball and sobbed until my mobile rang.

It was Chloe. She'd heard the news from a friend during the school run and was on her way over. *With cake.*

I'd told her I wasn't sure that even a Victoria sponge the size of the Atlantic Ocean could make me feel better, but she'd insisted. And now she had let herself into my flat using the key I'd given her for emergencies. I suspected that she was probably mentally preparing herself for the sight that was about to greet her.

Chloe knew how much I loved Eric and how I'd struggled to get over him, so she'd realise that this wasn't going to be pretty.

'Emily Robinson!' she shouted, bursting through the bedroom door. 'Up you get!'

I slowly peeled my head from the pillow and tried to gauge whether I really had to force myself off the bed and deal with the situation or if I could get away with lying here for the rest of the afternoon and convince Chloe to give me a bucketload of tea and sympathy.

Who am I kidding? This was my no-nonsense best friend. And she did *not* do self-pity. Especially over an unfaithful man.

'Come on, Em. We're not doing this again. Remember?' She picked up my iPad from the bedside table, frowning as she bashed away haphazardly at the screen before eventually managing to pause the playlist. 'No more listening to sad songs. No more tears over Eric. He's not worth it,' she said, edging closer to the bed. 'You can do *much* better than that tallywag.'

I slowly dragged myself upright, scraped my thick, dark curly hair off my face and tucked my knees under my chin.

'I know he's a loser, but seeing that picture, of *him*, with *her*, proposing after knowing her for all of two minutes, when he *knew* I'd wanted to get married for *years* and constantly fobbed me off, it just—it really hurt,' I said, using the sleeve of my grey jumper to wipe the tears streaming down my cheeks.

'I understand that,' said Chloe as she smoothed down the back of her 1950s-style polka dot dress and sat down on the plain magnolia duvet. 'But you really need to move on, Em. It's been seven months. It's time to start a new life. Unfollow the fool like I told you to ages ago and make new friends.'

'I make new friends all the time,' I scoffed. 'I'm up to almost six hundred on Facebook. Admittedly, Insta is lagging behind a little as I'm low on content, but—'

'For crying out loud!' Chloe crossed her arms. 'I don't mean friends on social media. That's nonsense. I'm talking about *proper* friends. You know, people that you speak to face-to-face in a restaurant, rather than clicking the stupid love heart button on a post of some person from Timbuktu that you've never met.'

Trust Chloe not to understand. She's so old-fashioned, she doesn't even own a smartphone. Can you imagine?

'I know you have an aversion to technology and anything online, Chloe, but social media has been my lifeline. If you think I'm bad now, I would have been *much* worse without the support of my online community.'

'Your *online community*?' Chloe rolled her eyes. 'Good grief! Sounds like some sort of cult!'

'Laugh all you want, but their likes, comments and uplifting posts have kept me going.'

'*If you say so,*' replied Chloe, reaching in her bag and pulling out two forks, serviettes and a container before taking out a large slice of chocolate cake. The rich scent filled the room. *Mmmm.* It smelt delicious. 'Like I've said before, I really think you should venture out of these four walls and try new things. You work from home all day, and apart from coming round to mine, you never seem to go anywhere. If you had a load of hobbies and were out making new friends in real life, you wouldn't have time to think about what that idiot is doing. You'd be too busy having fun.'

Here we go again. It's the *you need to get out of the flat more* lecture. I love Chloe, I really do, but she just doesn't get it.

My whole social circle revolved around my life with Eric. His friends became my friends, and after the breakup, that disappeared overnight. Now it was almost impossible to find anyone to go out with. On the rare occasions that I *did* get invited out, all the people in the group were coupled up and I was the odd one out. I got treated like either a weirdo or a potential husband thief. That's when I wasn't getting pitied or being shown photos of other random single men they were convinced would be ideal for me, purely because we'd both been 'condemned' to a life of solitude. I shuddered just thinking about it. *No, thanks*. I'd rather sit at home and have conversations online than be subjected to that hell.

'It's not that simple,' I huffed as I reached for my own slab of sponge and took a large bite. I wasn't in the mood to use a fork and serviette like Chloe. 'Everyone I know is married and has kids and doesn't have time to go out.'

'I appreciate what you're saying,' said Chloe, stroking her raven bob, which she'd styled into her signature vintage waves. 'But you are not the only thirty-five-year-old singleton in London. There are *loads* of other people out there just like you, so if your old circle of friends doesn't fit your life anymore, make a new circle. Find new friends. Look.' She stood up. 'I hate to leave you like this, but I've been called into work today, so I've got to run. I'll call you later, but please—don't sit here moping. Go for a walk to clear your head and have a think about what I said. There's a whole world out there. So many exciting things you could be doing with your life, but you need to actually step outside of this flat to discover them. Promise you'll give it some thought?'

I looked up at her, fighting the temptation to roll my eyes after hearing her make the same suggestion for the millionth time.

'Yes, yes,' I said. 'I'll think about it.'

'And you'll stop thinking about Eric too?'

'Yes,' I muttered reluctantly. What was I supposed to say? It wasn't like I *wanted* to think about him. Eric was just always there. Right in the front of my thoughts.

'Excellent!' She smiled. 'You'll feel *so* much better

when you do. You don't need his toxic energy around you. Anyway, I'd better go.' She leant forward and hugged me tightly before rushing towards the door. 'Make sure you get stuck into the cake. Love you!'

I stretched over to the container and grabbed another helping of sponge, shamelessly stuffing it into my mouth, then wiped my fingers before wrapping the duvet tightly around me. Getting out of these four walls? Going for a walk? *Not a chance.* That was the last thing I felt like doing. I planned to stay right here in this flat until I ran out of food or was forced to evacuate due to a state of national emergency. Whatever happened first.

Want to find out what happens next? Buy *Love Offline* by Olivia Spring on Amazon now.

ACKNOWLEDGMENTS

Wow: my very own acknowledgements page! Not only do I have a published book, which is a *pinch me is it real* moment in itself, now I also have an opportunity to say thank you to the people that helped make this possible.

Merci beaucoup, A.A. for giving me the inspiration and drive to write this book. You will live forever in my heart.

Mum, thank you for your continued support and enthusiasm at every stage of this process, for reading multiple versions of my manuscript and for feeding me when I was too immersed in my writing to cook (but as you know, I'm *never* too busy to eat!). You're amazing!

To my dear friends Cams and Jas as well as my darling niece, thanks for the constant encouragement, always checking in on me, taking a massive interest in my progress with this novel-writing journey and reading over various drafts. You rock.

Dad, thanks for your love and guidance. You've never

doubted me, and to know that you're always ready to help or offer your words of wisdom means the world.

DWT, you have always believed in me. Thanks for listening and for providing your thoughts and support from the very beginning. I am truly grateful.

Bro, thanks for your positivity, awesomeness, and tech expertise.

Thanks, sis and sis-in-law, for giving feedback.

To my developmental editor, Laura Kingsley: thanks for challenging me. I will be forever grateful for your direct, yet often humorous feedback (...smile). It was invaluable. I'm sorry that you didn't get to see the finished result. I'll miss you.

To my copy-editor, Eliza, proofreader, Donna, cover designer, Rachel, and web designer, Dawn: thanks for your eagle eyes and expertise, which helped me showcase my novel to the world, and make it what it is today.

Grazie, Antonio "Lello" Favuzzi, for giving me a fascinating insight into what life is like for a busy chef.

Nene, thanks for the laughs and chats throughout this new life era of ours. Look how much we've evolved!

My two amigos! So glad I met you both. I treasure our messages and friendship—long may it continue.

Clare—HUGE thanks for your generous advice and for encouraging me to pursue this path—you were *so* right!

Shout out to Mark Dawson, James Blatch, Joanna Penn and Iain Rob Wright for creating such invaluable podcasts, and also to everyone at the London Indie Authors Alliance and ALLi. My journey as a debut author was so much easier thanks to you all.

And last but by no means least, thanks to *you*, dear reader, for spending your hard-earned cash on my book.

As cheesy as it may sound, you have helped to make my childhood dream of becoming a published author come true. Thank you so very, very much.

I'm feeling quite emotional now and could probably go on, but I guess I'd better get back to it. My next book isn't going to write itself!

Olivia x

ABOUT THE AUTHOR

Olivia Spring lives in London, England. When she's not making regular trips to Italy to indulge in pasta, pizza and gelato, she can be found at her desk, writing new sexy romantic comedies.

If you'd like to say hi, email olivia@oliviaspring.com or connect on social media.

facebook.com/ospringauthor
twitter.com/ospringauthor
instagram.com/ospringauthor